Praise for Lorraine Beatty and her novels

"Beatty's story provides a descriptive and poignant
reminder that our careers do not define us."
—*RT Book Reviews* on *Rekindled Romance*

"Beatty's vivid characters remind the reader that
difficult situations help shape us."
—*RT Book Reviews* on *Restoring His Heart*

"It contains a wonderful holiday message."
—*RT Book Reviews* on *Her Christmas Hero*

"The details are beautiful, and the book is well
researched."
—*RT Book Reviews* on *Bachelor to the Rescue*

LORRAINE BEATTY

Rekindled Romance
&
Restoring His Heart

HARLEQUIN® LOVE INSPIRED® CLASSICS

 LOVE INSPIRED BOOKS

Recycling programs for this product may not exist in your area.

ISBN-13: 978-0-373-20874-6

Rekindled Romance & Restoring His Heart

Copyright © 2018 by Harlequin Books S.A.

The publisher acknowledges the copyright holder of the individual works as follows:

Rekindled Romance
Copyright © 2013 by Lorraine Beatty

Restoring His Heart
Copyright © 2013 by Lorraine Beatty

www.Harlequin.com

Printed in U.S.A.

CONTENTS

Lorraine Beatty was raised in Columbus, Ohio, but now calls Mississippi home. She and her husband, Joe, have two sons and five grandchildren. Lorraine started writing in junior high and is a member of RWA and ACFW, and is a charter member and past president of Magnolia State Romance Writers. In her spare time she likes to work in her garden, travel and spend time with her family.

Visit the Author Profile page
at Harlequin.com for more titles.

REKINDLED ROMANCE

A time to tear down and a time to build.
—*Ecclesiastes* 3:3

To my grandchildren: Cameron, Casie, Chey, Andrew, Anna and Addie. You are my treasures.

Chapter One

Shelby Russell steered her gray Malibu onto Highway 34 past the city limits sign of Dover, Mississippi, bracing herself against a sudden rush of painful memories. Coming home was the last thing she wanted to do. She'd turned her back on the small Southern town fifteen years ago and never looked back. Every goal she'd set for herself had been achieved. She'd risen through the ranks of Harmon Publishing to become senior editor of *Tween Scene* magazine, the top-selling publication for preteen girls in the country. It was a high-energy, high-stress job, and she loved every minute of it. But it was also the reason she was coming home.

Shelby eased the car to a halt behind a short line of cars waiting for a train to pass; the blinking red warning lights at the crossing were an unwelcome reminder of why she was back in Dover. A heart attack. She'd laughed in the doctor's face when he'd delivered his diagnosis. Heart attacks were for old people. She was only thirty-four. True, she'd had only a very mild one, but the tests didn't lie, and if she didn't eliminate the stress and change her lifestyle, she wouldn't be around to continue her exciting career. She'd already lost two grandfathers and an aunt to heart disease. She couldn't ignore her medical history.

The crossing gate lifted, and Shelby eased forward with the traffic. So here she was, coming home to stay with her grandmother, her life in chaos, her future in doubt. She was thankful that she had someone here who still cared about her, someone she could turn to when the world didn't make sense anymore. And right now, nothing did.

Her gaze surveyed the changes in the once-familiar surroundings as she followed the two-lane road toward town. The fields and piney woods surrounding the small town had been replaced with new shopping centers and an industrial park. A sprawling attendance center filled what once had been cotton fields. Courtesy of the new auto plant no doubt. Gramma had told her the plant, situated between the towns of Dover and Sawyers Bend, had brought about huge changes to both the once-dying towns.

As the highway gave way to downtown, the changes became more evident. The majestic courthouse still dominated the center of the town, but the surrounding trees were bigger and the elegant wrought-iron fence was a crisp shiny black. The historic gazebo, Dover's iconic symbol, still stood proudly in one corner of the grounds, like a Victorian jewel in the late-afternoon sunshine. The four streets flanking the square, lined with 19th-century brick buildings, all sported freshly painted facades in a variety of colors. Many storefronts had bright awnings providing shade; others had flower-draped balconies. The entire area looked like a watercolor painting of the quintessential small Southern town. The Dover she remembered looked nothing like this.

Shelby pulled to a stop at the red light, willing herself not to look at the store on the corner, but the temptation was too great. Her gaze traveled to Durrant's Hardware. The real reason she'd stayed away so long. Matt Durrant was here. Her heart pounded. Was Matt in the store right now? Had he taken over the family business? Probably. It was the reason she'd left. They had wanted different things out of life. Incompatible things.

The light changed and she focused on the road ahead, trying to push all thoughts of Matt to the back of her mind. She failed. Did he ever think about her? Was he as handsome now as he'd been then? Had he married?

Gritting her teeth, Shelby forced all thoughts of Matt and the past aside and focused on making the turns that would take her to Willow Street. She pulled into Gramma's driveway and stopped, taking a moment to appreciate the two-story redbrick house. Nestled on a tree-lined street on the south edge of town, the foursquare-style home was a mirror image of the house next door. Their expansive lots butted up against the woodlands. Both homes had been built by Gramma's great-great-grandfather and his brother, who helped found the railroad town, then known as Junction City. Her heart warmed as she gazed upon the stately dwelling. The large front porch, the potted chrysanthemums and the massive live oak tree in the yard all welcomed her home.

Home.

Memories of feeling safe, loved and happy flowed through her even as tears burned behind her eyes. She'd left here so full of dreams, determined to conquer the world, but she was returning with her life in turmoil. Mentally she kicked herself for holding a pity party. She might be down, but she wasn't out. She would beat this. She would not let this health issue ruin her future. It was merely a matter of blocking out the fear and taking control of her life. She'd learn to relax. She'd learn to de-stress. She'd learn to be peaceful if it was the last thing she ever did.

Shelby let off the brake, guiding the car to the left of the Y-shaped driveway between the twin houses, and parked beneath the shade of a giant live oak. Her cramped muscles protested angrily as she unfolded herself from the vehicle, and a wave of exhaustion and defeat settled upon her shoulders. The long drive from New York to central Mississippi had been intended to give her time to relax and slow down. Instead, it had allowed too much time for regret and introspection. Neither of which eased her stress.

Gramma Bower burst through the front door and met her as Shelby topped the porch steps. Shelby's mood brightened at the sight of her grandmother's sweet face.

"Oh, my precious baby girl. I didn't think you'd ever get here."

Shelby went willingly into the warm, familiar hug, clinging to the woman who had been her refuge throughout her childhood. The loving embrace siphoned off much of her fatigue and eased her fears. Coming home to Gramma had been the right thing to do. She stepped back, taking a quick inventory. Gramma's hair was grayer, and there were more lines in her dear face. A few more pounds hugged the sturdy frame since she'd last seen her, but Gramma was still the same woman who had always loved her unconditionally.

"Child, let me look at you." She frowned. "You look tired."

Leave it to Gramma to get right to the heart of a matter. "I am. It was a long trip."

"Well, I know you said you needed to rest, but I had no idea. You're pale as a ghost." Gramma shook her head. "Come on inside. I have sugar cookies for you."

The moment Shelby stepped inside the old house, her senses exploded with memories. She inhaled the familiar aroma of furniture polish, potpourri and fresh sugar cookies. The wood floors creaked a welcome beneath her feet as her fingers gently touched the worn spot on the newel post.

Her gaze quickly traveled around the rooms. Nothing had changed. The furnishings were still in the same place, as if time had stood still. Shelby soaked in the comfort of the old surroundings. Her own life might be in turmoil, but Gramma's house would always be her safe haven. "It's good to be home, Gramma. I've missed this place."

"Well, it's right where it's always been."

A lump of shame rose in her throat. "I know." Since leaving town, Shelby had stayed in touch with her grandmother and made the obligatory Christmas visits to her mother and stepfather's home in Pensacola, but she had staunchly avoided a visit to Dover. She couldn't risk running into Matt.

As they walked through the hallway, past the gallery of family photos, Shelby saw the picture of her aunt Teresa on the wall, and her conscience stung. She'd missed her aunt's funeral, her mother's only sister and a woman only ten years older than herself. *Tween Scene* magazine had been putting together their double Christmas issue at the time and that had seemed more important. Now Shelby winced at her callousness. "I'm sorry I didn't make it back for Aunt Teresa's funeral." Shelby followed her grandmother into the kitchen.

"I understood, baby. Really I did." Gramma smiled, handing her a plate of still-warm sugar cookies.

Shelby briefly thought about the dietary rules the doctor had laid out. Her mouth watered at the savory aroma, banishing her guilt. There was no need to start that healthy lifestyle right now. Tomorrow was soon enough. Sinking her teeth into one warm and sweet cookie transported her back in time. She was ten. Her father had deserted her and her mother. Shelby had run to Gramma's, scared, confused and in tears. Ellen had baked a batch of cookies and they'd talked and watched movies well into the night.

Gramma pointed at the plate and raised her eyebrows. "Eat up. Those might be the last ones you get for a while."

Shelby stopped midbite. "Why?"

"I work part-time at the church during the week, and I volunteer at the hospital whenever I'm needed. Besides—" Gramma planted her hands on her ample hips "—you're not supposed to be eating all that sugar."

Shelby pursed her lips. "I don't think a few cookies will do any harm."

Ellen frowned. "I see you haven't lost your habit of avoiding the unpleasant. Is this how you rose to the top of your field? By avoiding things?"

"No, of course not."

"You *are* following the doctors' instructions, aren't you? You're watching what you eat and exercising, taking your medications?"

Shelby reached for another cookie. The sample medications the doctor had given her had nearly run out, and the prescriptions were still in her purse. Filling them would make this whole thing too real. Too final. "I'm going to."

"Going to? When?" Gramma huffed out a puff of irritation. "Shelby Kay, you've got to take your heart disease seriously. This isn't something you can avoid. Baby. I've already lost a husband and a daughter. I don't want to lose you, too."

The pleading in her grandmother's voice punctured her defenses and exposed the gnawing fear in her spirit. Tears welled up in her eyes and clogged her throat. She was a lost and confused child again whose world was crashing in around her. Gramma's love was the only thing that had saved her. And God's grace.

She pressed her fingers to her lips as the fear took hold. "Gramma, I'm scared. How could I have had a heart attack and not even know it? I thought it was indigestion."

Gramma came to her side and pulled her shoulders. "Oh, my baby girl. I know. I'm sure the doctor explained to you that the symptoms are very different in women. But you can get through this if you'll just rely on the Lord."

Shelby shook her head. "It's not only my health, Gramma. The company I work for, Harmon Publishing, was bought by a competitor. I might not even have a job to go back to. The new management assured us everything would continue as before, but it's only a matter of time before the pink slips are handed out."

"I'm so sorry to hear that, but it's only a job, after

all." Gramma squeezed her shoulders again. "It'll all work itself out."

Shelby pulled away, wiping her face with her palms and shaking her head. "It's more than a job. This magazine is my life."

Gramma scowled. "Nonsense."

"My career is who I am." Shelby stood and paced a few steps. "This is what I've worked for my whole life, and now I could lose everything." Shelby buried her head in her hands. Gramma came quickly to her side, patting her back.

"You don't know that. You're facing a lot of obstacles right now, but you have your brains and your experience. You can always find a job. This might be the best thing that ever happened to you."

Shelby gritted her teeth against the idea. "How could losing my career be a good thing?" Her grandmother stiffened, and Shelby realized how belligerent and disrespectful she'd sounded. "I'm sorry, Gramma. But I don't want to lose my job. It's important to me."

"Better your job than your life." Gramma stared down at her. "Seems to me, you've forgotten who to turn to when you're lost."

Shelby sank back down onto the wooden chair and tried to swallow her irritation. She wasn't surprised by her Gramma's comments. Her grandfather had been a minister. "Church talk" had been commonplace here. There had been a time when she had embraced her faith, depended upon it, but after she'd left Dover she'd drifted away. She'd channeled all her energy into school and then her career. Along the way she'd lost her connection to her faith.

Gramma patted her hand and slid the cookie plate

toward her. "Enjoy your cookies. Today is your home-coming celebration. Tomorrow we'll face the changes you have to make."

Shelby nodded, feeling the fear and anger ease a bit. She had resisted coming back to Dover, but now she knew it had been the right decision. A few days here under Gramma's loving care would ease anyone's stress. A new hope blossomed in her heart. She had six weeks in which to accomplish her goals. First, get a handle on her health. Second, avoid Matt Durrant at all costs. That shouldn't be too difficult. She'd have no reason to go to his hardware store, and he lived on the opposite side of town. And maybe, if she could relax quickly enough, she could cut her leave in half and get back to work sooner, and that would decrease her odds of running into Matt.

Matthias Durrant. The only man she'd ever loved. They'd promised to love each other forever, to be to-gether always, but it hadn't worked out that way. Matt had changed the plan, and she'd been terrified of los-ing her dream.

She'd never regretted her decision. So why did she find herself wondering what her life would have been like if she'd stayed here with him? Followed his dream instead of her own? There was no point in thinking about it. The door to the past was closed forever and couldn't be reopened.

Matt Durrant rested his wrists on the steering wheel of the old battered van, smiling as his passenger opened the door and got out. "Thanks for your help today, Carl."

The man nodded and raised a hand. "My pleasure.

That roof should have been repaired months ago. We need more volunteers."

"Amen to that."

"Thanks for dropping me off at the house." Carl smiled. "It saved Nancy a trip to pick me up."

"No problem." Matt watched as his friend walked up the drive toward his house. The front door opened and his wife, Nancy, walked out to meet him, wrapping him in that special kind of hug only a wife could give. Matt looked away, ignoring the sudden ache in the center of his chest, and put the car in gear.

But the image replayed in his mind as he drove the Handy Works van toward his home on the opposite side of town. He'd once had that kind of love. Until three years ago, when cancer had taken his Katie away. He called up a memory, looking for the comfort that normally soothed his wounded soul, but it didn't come. Instead he found a gray void.

For the first time he longed for a real moment, not a vision of what had been. His memories had sustained him, kept him afloat, but lately it had been harder and harder to find solace in the past. Seeing Carl and Nancy just now had cracked the protective wall around his heart, exposing his vulnerability. Loneliness.

He'd been lonely every second since Katie had died, but this was different. This was more like a yearning, a hunger for something more. He wasn't sure what it was exactly. His heart would always be missing the piece that Katie had filled. That first year he'd struggled to manage his grief against that of his children, trying to find a balance between keeping Katie's memory alive and not being crushed under the memory of her illness and death. The decision to leave Atlanta and move home to Dover had been another upheaval in their lives that couldn't be avoided. The pressures of his job had stolen precious time from his children. And they were his primary concern now.

Katie had begged him to not stop living after she was gone. She'd wanted him to find love and happiness again, but the thought had been abhorrent to him. He had no desire to risk his heart or his children's on that kind of loss again. None of them could survive it a second time. It's why he'd made the decision to come home. He wanted to raise his children near their grandparents, in a town where family values were still cherished.

Matt turned the corner onto Willow Street. Envy. That's what had stirred up those old emotions. He was envious of Carl and Nancy's normal life. But he knew he had so much to be thankful for. Two amazing kids, a family that loved and supported him, a job that allowed him to be home a good bit—the van hit a pothole and every bolt rattled and shook. He smiled. And a ministry that helped the community and allowed him to help others. Handy Works had been his sister's brainchild. A mobile neighborhood help program, manned by volunteers who would donate their time and talents to making repairs and cleanup for those in need. He and his friend Carl Young had taken advantage of a rare afternoon free from teaching classes at Wells Community College to devote time to repairing the roof of an elderly man who lived at the edge of town.

Inhaling a deep breath, he reminded himself of his abundant blessings. Too many to count. This sudden feeling of loneliness would pass. Katie was the only woman he'd ever loved. No. There had been one other woman. A long time ago. But she'd abandoned him.

Matt flipped the blinker to turn into his driveway. Funny. Katie abandoned him through death; the other woman had abandoned him by choice. Maybe he was destined to be alone. Losing Katie had shredded his soul. He would never, ever love again. The risk was too great.

Shelby felt like a new person. Almost. Gramma had settled her into her old room on the east side of the house. The wide bay window faced the twin house next door but also afforded a view of the woods out back. This room hadn't changed either. The same white curtains graced the window; the lavender bedspread was more faded but still thick and soft. And at the edge of the window sat her favorite chair, the green-and-white shell back with a tufted ottoman to prop your feet on. For the first time in years, Shelby knew a sense of belonging.

But it was temporary. Only until she could get back on her feet physically. She tried not to think about what effect heart disease might have on her future job search. Would anyone hire her with a preexisting condition? Removing her laptop from its case, she scooped up her smart phone from the nightstand and headed downstairs. She'd worry about that later.

Gramma was looking through cabinets when Shelby stepped into the kitchen. She turned and frowned at the devices in Shelby's hands. "What are you going to do with those?"

"I have a few loose ends to tie up at work. I'm still employed for the moment, and the magazine has to go on. Medical leave or not." Truth was, there was little she could do. Everything was on hold, but it helped to keep busy. It made her feel like she was doing something.

Ellen planted her fists on her hips and pursed her lips. "You're supposed to be relaxing, and if you have any sense at all, you'll follow orders. You'll unplug yourself from those things and you'll rest, eat right and get some exercise."

She acknowledged the necessity of following the doctor's advice, but *Tween Scene* was her baby, and she'd spent every ounce of her time and energy over the years making it successful. To suddenly turn her back and walk away when its future was in doubt seemed irresponsible. Besides, what was she supposed to do with her time? Sit in the rocker and crochet?

"I'm not good at being idle, Gramma."

"Resting and taking care of yourself is not being idle."

"You know what I mean." Shelby placed her computer on the kitchen table. "I need to be busy. You know how Mom felt about being unproductive. If she had any idea how much time I spent looking at your magazines when I was here, she'd have never let me come back."

"Your mother wanted you to have an education and be able to take care of yourself."

"And I can, but now everyone's telling me to stop and stand still."

Gramma exhaled a sympathetic sigh. "I understand. But this is a new chapter in your life, and you'll have to find something different to fill your time. Something quieter, slower paced."

The thought made Shelby's skin crawl. She didn't like being inactive. She like planning and deadlines. "I'm not sure I can do that."

"You don't really have a choice." Gramma patted her shoulder. "I'm sorry to go off and leave you on your first day home, but I'm filling in at the hospital this afternoon for a friend. There's chicken salad in the fridge in case you get hungry. It's made with all low-fat, healthy ingredients. I'll be home in a couple of hours if you want to eat together. In the meantime, relax."

An hour later Shelby tossed her cell phone onto the dining room table and buried her head in her hands. It looked like the other shoe was about to drop at Harmon Publishing. Her boss had called to tell her a meeting had been scheduled for all upper management regarding the sale, but no other information had been given.

The ever-present knot of anxiety in her stomach grew. What would she do if she lost her job? How would she survive? Her mind churned with a frightening list of possible disasters. Her heart rate quickened, and a steady pressure began to build in her chest. She closed her eyes against a wave of fear. Was she having another heart attack or an anxiety attack? The doctor said the symptoms were similar. She'd been oblivious to her first episode, so how did she know if this was serious or not?

"Please, Lord, don't let this be another one." She'd experienced these symptoms before—the light-headedness, then a clammy sensation and a strange sense of foreboding. Her first thought had been a brain tumor. When the symptoms persisted, she'd gone to the clinic, but they'd sent her home with instructions to cut back on caffeine and sugar.

A second episode sent her to the hospital, where extensive tests had been run. That's when Dr. Morgan had delivered his diagnosis and his ultimatum. Time off or face the consequences. She couldn't afford to ignore this any longer. Not when death was the option.

Inhaling a slow, deep breath, she breathed a sigh of relief when her pulse slowed to normal once again and the tension eased. Frustration and anger quickly took its place, driving her outside onto the wooden porch swing. Her favorite refuge. The gentle back-and-forth movement settled her thoughts. It wasn't fair. All she'd ever wanted was to work for a magazine. Her whole life since high school had been geared toward her career. She'd studied hard and sacrificed much to achieve her goal. Now it was all being taken away. Why was God doing this to her? Was this her punishment for ignoring Him all this time?

Tears stung the backs of her eyes. She squeezed them shut, unwilling to give in. She never cried. But since her diagnosis she'd started bursting into tears at the drop of a hat. It was infuriating.

"Chester!"

She looked up at the shout to see a small, scruffy gray dog dart up the steps of the porch and stop at her feet. The little dog growled and barked, inching forward then back as he defended his territory.

Shelby chuckled softly. "Oh, hush. I'm not going to hurt you." Slowly she opened her hand, palm up, and inched it toward the dog. "See, it's okay."

The dog stopped growling and studied her. He retreated, then cocked his head and slowly moved forward. "There. Nothing to be upset about." The dog's tail began to wag furiously and he licked her hand. "Good doggie." She stroked his small head. It was soft and warm.

"Chester! You'd better get yourself back over here before you get in trouble."

Shelby looked up as a young girl came toward the

house from the driveway. She appeared to be about eleven years old.

"Chester!" She hurried up the steps, placing her hands on her waist when she saw the dog. "You are in big trouble, mister." She glanced at Shelby. "I'm sorry he barked at you, ma'am."

"That's okay. I think we worked it out. He's a good watchdog. He knew I was a stranger so he was probably trying to protect you."

The girl shrugged. "I guess." She studied Shelby intently for a long moment. "Does Mrs. Bower know you're here?"

Shelby smiled. "Yes. I'm going to be staying here for a while. I'm her granddaughter."

The girl frowned. "I don't remember you."

"I've been away a long time. I live in New York City." Shelby swallowed the regret that had been nagging at her since coming home. "My name is Shelby. And I take it this is Chester?"

"Yeah," she groaned in disgust and frowned. "I didn't name him. My brother did. My name is Cassidy."

Shelby couldn't help but smile at her grown-up indignation. "Nice to meet you, Cassidy." Footsteps sounded on the steps, and a little boy joined them. He was out of breath.

"Aw, Chester you are in tra-bull. You can't come over here."

Cassidy rolled her eyes. "This is my little brother, Kenny. He's six."

Kenny stared at her.

"I'm Shelby. I'm staying here with my grandmother, Mrs. Bower."

"Oh." He smiled, displaying two deep dimples at the sides of his mouth. "She makes us sugar cookies."

"I know. She made them for me when I was little. In fact, she made some for me today. Would you like one?"

Cassidy took hold of Chester's collar. "Thanks, but we can't take food from strangers."

Shelby was momentarily taken aback. Then common sense kicked in and she smiled at the children. "That's a good rule. You're right. Maybe after we get to know each other, we can share some cookies."

Cassidy smiled. Her thickly lashed, dark blue eyes triggered something familiar in the back of Shelby's mind, but she couldn't place it.

"We have to take Chester home now." Cassidy tugged the dog toward the steps. "Our aunt will be wondering where we are."

"Okay. Nice to have met you. You and Chester are welcome here any time."

"Thanks. I'll tell my dad." Cassidy waved goodbye.

Shelby stood and walked to the edge of the porch, watching the children tugging the little dog back home. She'd wondered who lived next door in the duplicate house. Gramma had told her Mrs. Marshall had passed away several years ago and the house had changed hands a couple of times. Obviously a family lived there now.

As the children neared the porch of their home, an old battered van pulled into the driveway. The sign painted on the side read "Handy Works." Decals of various tools decorated the side panels, proclaiming some sort of handyman business.

Shelby watched as the children hurried toward the van. The door opened, and a man emerged. Tall and well-built with dark brown hair, the deep blue knit shirt he wore emphasized strong, broad shoulders and muscular arms. Faded, well-worn jeans hugged his long legs like an old friend. Dusty, work-scuffed Western boots completed the masculine picture.

He turned, arms open as the children ran to him. He lifted them off the ground in a tight hug, swinging them back and forth playfully. Shelby smiled. Not only was the man ridiculously attractive, he obviously adored his children. A lethal combination. Cassidy and Kenny began chatting away. She could hear their little voices across the wide, shared driveway. Kenny suddenly pointed toward her, and she smiled, raising her hand. The father turned and faced her. Her heart froze. Blood drained from her face.

No. It couldn't be. *Please, Lord, don't do this to me.* The man staring back at her was the last man on earth she wanted to see. Cassidy and Kenny's father was Matthias Durrant, the fiancé she'd jilted for her career fifteen years ago.

Chapter Two

Matt Durrant turned his back and followed his children into the house, his jaw clenched, his gut in knots.

Shelby was back.

He never expected to see her in Dover again. Ever. She'd made her opinion of small-town life abundantly clear the day she gave back his ring. *"I don't want a small-town man with small-town dreams."*

Shelby Russell had broken his heart and abandoned him when he'd needed her most. He'd counted on her love and support to sustain him through a difficult time in his life. But instead she'd cut and run, giving back his ring, accusing him of breaking his promise. But what about her promise to him? Her own future had been more important than their future together. He'd finally come to terms with her rejection, though he'd never understood her sudden change of heart. Never understood how she could claim to love him one minute and walk away the next. It was only several years later, when he'd met Katie, that he'd been able to put Shelby's rejection behind him and move forward.

So why, after all this time, did his heart still sting

from Shelby's rejection? And why had that brief glimpse of her hit him like a lightning bolt, filling his mind with things he thought he'd forgotten? He remembered her brown eyes had small specks of gold in them. He remembered the silken feel of her long brown hair, now worn shoulder-length and soft around her face. He remembered the impish, self-conscious smile that would make his heart skip a beat.

The girlish figure he remembered had given way to soft, womanly curves. Maturity looked good on her. He hated himself for noticing. He hated more that she could still cause a reaction in him after all this time. After what she'd done.

"Daddy, she was really nice." Cassidy's blue eyes were bright with excitement. "And she's from New York."

Matt frowned. He'd been bombarded with his children's disjointed conversation from the moment he'd climbed from the van. Something about a lady and cookies. When he glanced over at the house it had all become clear. He rubbed his forehead in irritation. "How did you meet her?"

"I told you," Cassidy explained, her tone tinged with irritation. "When Chester ran over to her house. She was sitting on the swing, and Chester was barking. I guess he thought she was a stranger so he was trying to warn us. Only she wasn't a stranger. She's Miss Ellen's granddaughter and then—"

Matt placed a hand on his daughter's shoulder. "Okay. I get the picture."

Cassidy smiled. "She's nice."

Matt set his jaw. That's not how he'd describe Shelby

Russell. Self-centered. Insensitive. Career-driven, yes. But nice?

"She was going to give us sugar cookies, but Cassidy said no 'cause she was a stranger," Kenny complained.

"Who's a stranger?"

Matt glanced over at his younger sister, Laura Durrant, who had come to stand at the boy's side. She'd been watching the children after school each day. He had a full schedule of classes this semester, which meant he wouldn't get home until supper time. But she'd informed him two days ago that he'd have to find someone else. "That was the right thing to do, son."

Kenny's shoulders slacked. "Yes, sir, but Mrs. Bower made them. You always let us have her cookies. How come we couldn't have any this time?"

"Because you didn't know Shelby, that's why." Matt struggled to maintain his patience.

Laura frowned. "Shelby Russell?"

Matt jammed his hands into his pockets. "She's back. She's staying with Ellen Bower."

"Oh. I'll bet Miss Ellen is excited. Shelby hasn't been home since you two broke up, has she?"

"I wouldn't know." He could see his little sister's mind digesting the news.

"Hmm. Wonder what brought her back to Dover after all this time?" She glanced at him sideways, an ornery smirk on her face. "Maybe she came to look up old friends and acquaintances."

Matt forced a smile over clenched teeth. "Why don't you ask her?"

Laura raised her eyebrows and tilted her head. "I think I might. You know, I heard she's an editor at some big magazine in New York. Mom ran across her name in an article someplace. Looks like our Shelby has reached the top of the career ladder. Good for her. It's what she always wanted."

"It's *all* she ever wanted," Matt muttered softly.

Laura winced. "Is that the sound of sour grapes being trampled? You know—" she pointed a finger at her brother "—they say you never forget your first love. Well, kids, I'm out of here." She gave Cassidy a hug and Kenny a fist bump.

"You want to stay and eat?" Matt offered the invite as she moved to the door.

She winked. "Not this time. I'm booked for the evening. Oh." Laura turned back to her brother. "Have you found someone to watch the kids yet? I hate that I had to bail on you so suddenly, but I couldn't turn down the restoration job in Mobile. It'll be a huge boost to my company."

"Don't worry about it. But to answer your question, no, I haven't found anyone yet." Matt ran a hand down the back of his neck. "Normally, I'd ask Mom, but since she's running for city council, she doesn't have the time."

"What about Ellen Bower? Doesn't she watch them for you sometimes?"

"Yes, but she's so busy with her volunteer work I rarely see her. Besides, watching the kids for a short time now and again is different from watching them every day. It might be too much for her."

Laura picked up her backpack, fishing out her truck keys. "Well, you could always ask Shelby. She's right next door."

Matt gritted his teeth and followed his sister to the

door. "Yeah, but for how long? She'll probably be gone before you can blink."

Laura turned to face him. "What's bothering you, big brother?"

"Nothing. Forget it." Matt smiled at his baby sister. Looking at her, no one would ever guess the slim, petite woman was a skilled and licensed carpenter and builder. Her company specialized in restoring old homes and buildings. Laura couldn't stand to see anything neglected and ignored.

Outside on the front porch, they both looked over at Ellen Bower's house.

Laura, glanced sideways at her brother. "So. Are you going to go say hello?"

"Why?"

Laura shrugged. "She's right next door. Aren't you the least bit curious why she came back after all this time?"

"No."

"You're going to act like she isn't there?"

He glared in response. It sounded like a good idea to him.

Laura hoisted her backpack onto her shoulder. "You're being childish." She turned and started down the front steps to her truck.

Matt stood on the porch after Laura drove off, staring at the Bower house. Why was Shelby back, and how long was she staying? She'd made it clear long ago that she had no interest in small-town dreams. He'd known Ellen was Shelby's grandmother, but the subject of Shelby had never come up. Besides, the likelihood of her showing up in Dover was not great—or so he'd believed.

"Daddy, can we have mac and cheese for supper?"

Matt glanced down at his son's face, and the eager smile chased away his concerns. "I think your aunt Laura left us some chicken and noodles. How does that sound?"

"With biscuits? Yum." Kenny turned and raced back into the house, shouting the news to his sister. Matt took one last glance at the house next door and followed his son inside. He had more important things to worry about than Shelby Russell's presence in Dover. Like who was he going to get to watch his kids for the next several weeks?

Matt barely heard what his children said as he prepared the evening meal. He was too distracted by the search for a babysitter to pay much attention. He'd made a few calls to women he knew at church and the mothers of a couple of Cassidy's friends, but no one was available long-term. By the time he sat down at the table he was nearing desperation. He glanced down at his empty plate. He had no idea if the meal had been good or not.

"Can Chester sleep with me tonight?"

"No, Kenny, he can't. You know the rules." Matt rose from the table and carried his plate to the sink. He had only one option. Ellen Bower. If she turned him down, he'd be forced to look into a professional childcare service. Not something he felt comfortable doing.

"Okay, you two. Time to clean up the kitchen."

"Daddy, now that we know that lady, can I have cookies if she asks?"

Matt gritted his teeth. He didn't want his kids getting too chummy with Shelby. But then, he probably didn't need to worry. Whatever her reason for coming home, Dover couldn't hold her attention for long. She'd run back to her all-important career after a few days.

"I guess that would be all right. But I'm sure Miss Russell will be very busy. You probably won't see her much."

Kenny frowned. "But I like her. She likes Chester." He bent down and hugged the dog's neck.

Matt exhaled a huff of irritation. His son liked Shelby. It must be some sort of weird gene in the Durrant family that drew them to her. His father and brother had liked her, too. Fifteen years ago, Matt had been engaged to her. For twenty-four hours.

"Okay, kids, finish up your chores and then you can watch television while I run next door for a few minutes."

"Are you going to say hello to Miss Shelby?" Cassidy's smile reflected her delight.

"No. I have to see if Miss Ellen can watch you after school from now on."

Cassidy emptied her glass into the sink. "Why can't Aunt Laura stay with us?"

"She's going to be working out of town." Matt pointed at Kenny. "You make sure you feed Chester and give him fresh water."

Matt made his way to the front door, mentally battling with his emotions. It would be easy to pick up the phone, call Ellen and avoid seeing Shelby. But his little sister was right about one thing. Trying to ignore Shelby, act like she wasn't right next door, was childish.

A small voice inside warned him about being near Shelby. She'd always had a powerful effect on him. She'd made him feel strong and protective. He shoved the thought aside. He was a grown man. Not a lovesick college kid.

He'd speak to Ellen, acknowledge Shelby's presence then come home. Besides, this wasn't about him. He had to protect his kids. His children had spent only a few minutes with her and she'd already cast her spell over them. With Shelby right next door, his kids would likely grow deeply attached, and then what would happen when she skipped town without warning? Broken hearts, that's what. He couldn't let that happen. She needed to understand how emotionally vulnerable Kenny and Cassidy were since their mother's death. All he was asking was that she keep her distance for the few days she was here. It wasn't an unreasonable request. Merely a "good fences make good neighbors" conversation. Setting some boundaries. That's all.

Cassidy stuck her head out the front door. "Will you tell Miss Shelby I said hi?"

Matt nodded and set his jaw. Okay, maybe a wall instead of a fence. "Will do."

Shelby closed her laptop with a firm snap and shoved away from the dining room table. Trying to work was useless. She couldn't get Matt's image out of her mind. She'd stood on the porch earlier immobilized, watching as Matt turned his back and walked away. His message loud and clear. They had nothing to say to one another.

Her insides burned with the rejection. What had she expected? That he'd be glad to see her? She'd run out on him. Told him he wasn't good enough. Her conscience stung when she remembered her cruel words to him that night. She had been so arrogant, so disdainful of what she perceived as his lack of ambition. How could she make him understand that breaking their engagement was the hardest thing she'd ever done? But he was the one who had reneged on all their dreams. She'd had no choice.

She stood and went to the kitchen and searched for something to munch. A bowl of apples sat on the counter. Common sense told her to eat one. A healthy choice. What she wanted was chocolate.

Closing her eyes, she fought the urge to look out the window at Matt's house, hungry for another glimpse of him. He was even more handsome than she'd remembered. Age had broadened his shoulders, deepened his chest and chiseled the planes of his face. There was a masculine confidence in his bearing that couldn't be ignored. And the gentle, tender heart she'd fallen in love with was displayed in the unabashed love of his children.

Matt had been everything she'd ever wanted in a man.

She opened her eyes, staring across the drive. Part of her longed to see him coming toward the house to— what? Say all was forgiven? Let's start over? But another part of her hoped he would stay on his side of the driveway and ignore her for the remainder of her stay. Confronting him would be too painful, no matter the outcome.

Her conscience stung again. Gramma was right. Avoiding conflict was one of her biggest faults. She was avoiding her illness, avoiding making the changes she needed. And now, hoping to avoid Matt.

Forcing herself to move, Shelby picked up an apple and took a bite, her mind bursting with questions. How had he come to live next door, and what had he been doing all these years? Obviously he'd married and had children. What was his wife like? Was it someone she knew from school? What about the Handy Works van? Was that what he did for a living? It would make sense. His father owned the hardware store where they'd met. She had noticed a large pickup in the drive as well, but it was gone now. Apparently he'd followed in his father's footsteps.

Movement outside the window caught her attention. She froze. Matt. He was coming over. "No. Not now. I'm not ready. I can't deal with this right now." She held her breath, watching him come across the drive. She could still see the young man she remembered in his slow, easy gait. The male grace he'd displayed as a young man was still evident. The years had done little to diminish his attractiveness. She turned away, her stomach in knots, flinching when the knock on the door echoed through the house. He was coming to demand an answer for her breaking their engagement. What would she say? *I ran because I was afraid I'd never get out of this place if I didn't?*

Taking a deep breath, she opened the door and lost her breath. He didn't look like the father of two. With his square-jawed good looks and athletic physique, he could have graced the cover of any magazine. His dark brown hair still lay in waves across his head. The cobalt-blue eyes with their thick lashes were still compelling and magnetic. The only thing missing was his smile. She doubted if she'd ever see that again. She cleared her throat, searching desperately for her voice.

"Hello, Shelby."

"Hey." It was all she could squeak out past the lump in her throat.

Shelby motioned him inside. He nodded and stepped over the threshold. She closed the door behind him, struggling to maintain a casual attitude while ignoring the tantalizing smell of his aftershave.

"I had no idea you lived next door." She forced a smile. "It was a surprise seeing you drive up today."

Matt frowned. "Ellen didn't tell you?"

"No, but then she never knew we..." She faltered. "Gramma and Grandpa were on a mission trip the summer we dated."

He nodded, shoving his hands into his pockets.

Her heart pounded so fiercely she wondered if he could hear it. Now that he was here, all she wanted was to get it over with. "Would you like to sit down?"

"No. I need to talk to Ellen. Is she here?"

Shelby's tension deflated like a punctured balloon. Matt wasn't here to see her at all. She should have been relieved, but instead she swallowed a large gulp of disappointment. "She's not here at the moment, but I expect her home anytime. You're welcome to wait."

Matt's jaw worked side to side a moment, as if gauging his next words.

"How long are you staying?"

She blinked. That wasn't the question she'd anticipated. Apparently he was going to get right to the point. Fine. She could take it. Raising her chin, she crossed her arms over her chest and faced him. Matt's blue gaze pierced through her. Blue eyes exactly like Cassidy's. Now she knew why they'd seemed so familiar. "Six weeks or so. My schedule is flexible."

Matt planted his hands on his hips. A smirk curved one corner of his mouth upward. "Six whole weeks. You sure you won't get bored so far from the big city? We pull in the sidewalk around seven, remember?"

"Yes. I remember." Her heart burned. He was throwing her words from long ago back in her face.

"I'm sure you do. So, what brings you back to the small-town life?"

She ignored the flash of pain his sarcasm inflicted. "I had time accrued that I needed to use, and I wanted to spend time with Gramma."

"Can the corporate world survive without you?"

She lifted her chin. He was really getting under her skin with his sour attitude. "It's the wireless age, Matt. I can do my work from anywhere. Have laptop, will travel. Clouds and smart phones are our friends. You do have those things here in your small town, don't you?"

"I know all about working from home."

"Really? So the world of hammers and nails is high tech now?" Her condescending words sent a hot rush of remorse along her nerves. She hadn't meant to handle their meeting this way, as if she were eighteen and scared and confused. She'd wanted to face him as a highly successful, competent woman of the world.

"I don't work at the store anymore, Shelby. That's my father's job."

There was a low, threatening undercurrent to his tone that scraped against her nerves. She ignored it. "So you have your own handyman business now? I saw the van when you drove up."

Matt's eyes darkened, and he shifted his weight slightly as if trying to control himself. "I only do that part-time. You know how we small-town guys are. We work as little as possible so we have more time to hunt and fish. We're not very ambitious."

Shelby cringed at hearing her own words taunting her. So much for putting on a front. Being face-to-face with him hurt more than she'd ever imagined. "Matt, please…"

The sound of a car pulling in the drive meant Gramma was back. Her chance to escape. "I'll let Gramma know you're here." Quickly she moved through the hall and into the kitchen, meeting Ellen as she opened the door. "Why didn't you tell me Matt Durrant lived next door to you?"

Ellen blinked in surprise. "I didn't think you'd care."

"I don't. I mean, it was a surprise, that's all."

Gramma came into the kitchen, a puzzled frown marring her brow. "What difference could that make to you?"

"Because we were—" She hesitated, gauging her words. "We knew each other in school."

Gramma shook her head. "I don't understand. What does that have to do with anything?"

Shelby exhaled an exasperated grunt. There was no way she could make Gramma understand without going into the grim details of her past relationship with Matt, and she wasn't ready to deal with that right now. "Never mind. He's here. He wants to talk to you."

"Well, why didn't you say so?" Gramma set her purse and a small sack of groceries on the counter, then strode toward the living room. Shelby followed slowly behind, stopping at the archway and leaning against the side. The more distance between her and Matt the better.

"Hello, Matt. You wanted to talk to me?"

Shelby listened as Matt quickly outlined the situation. Apparently he was in dire need of a babysitter. Something about all-day classes and needing help after school. What that had to do with a handyman business she didn't know. She had to wonder where the mother was. Out of town perhaps?

"Oh dear, I don't know. I'm so busy with my church work and the hospital. I hate to turn you down but…" Ellen turned to Shelby and smiled. "I have it. Shelby and I can both watch them. We'll be like a tag team. When I'm volunteering she can fill in. It's the perfect solution."

Shelby couldn't believe her ears. It took her a full second to find her voice. "What? No. I can't. I mean—" She glanced over at Matt, who looked as horrified by the idea as she did.

"No. I mean, I wouldn't dream of imposing on your granddaughter while she's visiting. I'm sure I can work something out."

Ellen waved off his concerns. "What are neighbors for? When do we start?"

Matt shifted his weight. "Tomorrow afternoon, but…" Gramma's landline suddenly rang, breaking the tension in the room. "Oh, I'd better get that. That'll be fine, Matt. I'm free in the afternoon. Send the children over here when they get off the bus." Ellen waved at Matt and hurried toward the other room, leaving Shelby alone with Matt again.

Shelby searched for something to say. "Matt, I—"

"You met my kids." His tone was flat and cool.

Shelby nodded, mentally scurrying to regain her footing at his abrupt change of subject. "They're adorable. I like their dog, too." She couldn't help but smile at the thought of them. "They were very well-behaved. Cassidy politely refused my offer of cookies because she didn't know me. You and your wife should be proud. You've done a wonderful job with them."

Matt paled. His eyes turned dark and cold. "My wife died three years ago."

She gasped. "Oh, Matt. I didn't know. I'm so sorry." He pinned her with a cold blue glare.

"My kids have been through a lot. They're emotionally vulnerable and they tend to give their hearts too easily. I don't want those hearts broken by a stranger passing through town."

Stranger? Was that how he thought of her now? Before she could respond, he turned and walked to the door.

He stopped, looking over his shoulder. "Do we understand each other?"

There was a warning in his tone that was impossible to miss—*stay away from my children.* She nodded, stunned and dazed. The door closed behind him with a sharp pop, like a bullet to her heart.

Matt strode across the driveway. He shouldn't have gone to Ellen's. He should have called. He thought he'd been prepared to face Shelby again, but he'd been wrong. From the moment she'd opened the door he'd been rattled. She looked even more amazing up close, as fresh and lovely as he'd remembered. Her nearness had released a kaleidoscope of memories he didn't want to explore. There was so much he'd wanted to say, to ask, but nothing would change the past. Nothing would explain away the wound she'd inflicted.

At the edge of the driveway, he stopped, casting his eyes upward briefly. Ellen's solution to his babysitting problem had blindsided him. He had wanted to turn her down flat, shout that he didn't want Shelby close to his kids. The last thing he needed was for his kids to form an attachment to Shelby, because when she left, and she would leave, the kids would lose another close relationship. He wouldn't let that happen. But he'd been trapped. Ellen was his only option.

If only Katie were here. She'd know how to handle this. But if she were, there would be no need. He'd have his wife back, his kids would have their mom and he wouldn't feel like he was constantly treading water just to survive.

As he walked past the Handy Works van, the words written on the side panel caught his attention. *Showing God's Grace.* He stopped. Remorse surged through him. He hadn't shown any grace to Shelby just now. He'd been curt, rude and unfeeling. Not the way he'd intended it to go. Or was it?

His conscience faulted him for being harsh and judgmental, but his heart told him he had to protect his kids from people like Shelby. People who turned their backs on the things in life that really mattered. He owed her an apology for his bad attitude but not for his position. As far as he was concerned, she was a stranger passing through. Nothing more.

Matt set his jaw and strode past the van toward the house. Shelby had assumed he had a handyman business. He should have expected that. She'd called him "a small-town man with small-town dreams." He'd started to explain, then changed his mind. Let her believe whatever she wanted.

All that mattered was protecting the hearts of his children.

* * *

Shelby stared at the closed door, struggling to breathe through the thickness in her throat. She'd imagined her reunion with Matt in a thousand different ways, but never like that. She knew she'd hurt him when she'd broken their brief engagement, and she'd expected him to be angry. But the man who had walked out of the house wasn't the gentle, tender boy she remembered. He was a fierce, protective guardian warning her to keep her distance from his children.

He'd made his opinion of her crystal clear. He had never forgiven her for what she'd done. She couldn't blame him. She'd turned her back on everything he cared about. Belittled his beliefs and his dreams. She sank into a kitchen chair, fighting tears. "Small-town man with small-town dreams."

How many times had she longed to take back her angry words? She wanted to explain to him how she'd felt that night fifteen years ago. How scared and confused she'd been. They'd had plans to go to college, to escape the backward life of Dover. But the day after he'd given her the ring, he'd changed. Instead of talking about their dreams for the future, he'd talked about settling down, staying in Dover. She'd felt betrayed. He'd said he wanted the same things she did, but apparently a ring on her finger had erased all that. Her mother's dire warning was coming true. She'd said that ring only meant one thing, that Matt would expect her to give up her dreams for his. "You'll be trapped here just like me." She hadn't wanted to believe her mother was right, but at that moment, it had seemed all too true.

It had all been so clear to her then. Either marry Matt and spend the rest of her life in a choked-off life in Mississippi or run like crazy toward college and her dreams of working on a magazine. Only one course of action had made sense. Run. It had been a matter of survival. And she'd achieved her dream. She stood at the top of her field. Though for how much longer, she didn't know.

But at the moment she had a more urgent concern. Gramma was setting the table when she entered the kitchen. "Gramma, I can't babysit Matt's kids."

"You aren't, sweetie. I am. You'll be my backup. It'll be fun. They are darling kids. You'll love them."

"I met them this afternoon while you were gone. Their dog came over."

"Aren't they precious?" Gramma smiled. "Matt and Katie did a great job."

Katie. The wife. Her throat tightened. "How did his wife die?"

"Cancer. That's why he moved back home."

Back home? "He hasn't been here the whole time?"

"No. He owned some kind of big computer business in Atlanta. He sold it and moved back here about a year ago to be closer to his family."

Shelby sorted through this new information. She'd always assumed Matt would never leave Dover. It was the crux of their breakup. It didn't make sense.

Sinking down into the chair, she rested her elbows on the table and cradled her aching head. Could things get any worse? She'd come here to rest, ease the stress in her life, but how was she supposed to do that with Matt right next door? She'd have been better off if she'd stayed in New York. Matt's pointed warning echoed in her mind. "He doesn't want me watching his kids, Gramma."

Ellen set the plates down on the table, a deep frown

creasing her forehead. "Is there something between you two I should know about?"

Shelby inhaled. Great. She couldn't avoid this any longer. "We dated." Might as well tell it all. "We were engaged. Briefly. We broke up." She hoped her grandmother wouldn't press for more details. She couldn't deal with that at the moment.

"I see. When was this?"

"The summer before I went to college. I was working at the Durrant's hardware store. You and Grandpa were in Belize." She shrugged as if it were insignificant, hoping her grandmother would let the subject drop.

"Oh." Gramma lowered herself onto a chair. "I had no idea you were serious about anyone. That does make things awkward, but that was a long time ago. Why should it bother you so much now? Unless..." Gramma eyed her closely. "Ah. I see."

Shelby squirmed. She never could hide her feelings from her grandmother.

"Well, it seems to me you two need to settle this thing between you pretty quick. It's been going on way too long, don't you agree?"

Chapter Three

Matt closed the lid on the Insect Man lunch box and set it beside the matching backpack. A quick glance around the kitchen revealed an escaped homework folder peeking out from under the stack of mail and flyers for his mom's city council campaign. He pulled it out and unzipped Cassidy's pink plaid backpack, sliding the folder inside as he called her name. "Cassidy. It's time to go. Hurry it up, please."

Kenny skidded to a halt beside the kitchen island, holding up his hands and baring his teeth for inspection. Matt turned the little palms over, then tilted his son's face upward. "Looking good, sport."

Kenny smiled and reached for his backpack. "Do we still get to go to Miss Ellen's after school?"

Matt masked his concern with a forced smile. "Yes. And I expect you to behave yourselves."

"Will Miss Shelby be there?" Cassidy slung her backpack over her shoulder and looked at him with expectant eyes. He stared down at her. Something was different. Her hair was sticking out on one side. He'd learned the hard way not to question his daughter's fashion sense too vigorously. Maybe she meant it to look like that. "Uh, I suppose. But I'm sure she'll be busy with her work, so don't bother her. Miss Ellen is your babysitter." And if he could make other arrangements he would. He wanted as much separation between Shelby Russell and his kids as possible.

"Okay, everyone to the van. We're running out of time."

Kenny's eyes widened. "You mean we get to ride to school in the Handy Works van?"

"'Fraid so. I left my car at Grandpa's store yesterday."

Cassidy's shoulders sagged, and she exhaled a disgusted whine. "Can't we go get our car first? The van is ugly."

"Ugly or not, it's your only mode of transportation this morning." Matt touched her shoulder, steering her toward the door.

"At least I'll get to see Miss Shelby when I get home."

Matt groaned inwardly. He had no choice about babysitters for the next couple of days, but he fully intended to beat every bush and look behind every tree until he found someone else to watch his kids.

Pulling the door closed behind him, Matt followed his kids to the van. Confident in his plan.

Shelby stared out the kitchen window at Matt's house. She'd been forced to alter her assumptions about him. Not only had Matt left Dover, but he'd had a successful business and a wonderful marriage. Losing his wife had wounded him deeply. The grief reflected in his eyes still haunted her. As did his very pointed warning.

Did Matt think she would deliberately hurt his kids? Probably. He was assuming that she would walk out on them the way she had him. He wasn't going to forgive her, and she had no one to blame but herself. She was finally reaping what she had sown.

So how was she supposed to babysit and still keep her distance? Hopefully, most of the babysitting duties would fall to Gramma and she'd keep a very low profile for the next few weeks.

The mantel clock in the living room struck the half hour, jerking Shelby rudely from her computer screen. Two thirty. She'd worked through lunch, and now Cassidy and Kenny were due home soon and Gramma wasn't home yet. A rush of anxiety warmed her blood. Where was she? After dialing Ellen's cell number, Shelby waited impatiently. No answer. She tried again a few minutes later with the same result. This was not good.

Shelby paced the living room, her gaze darting through the front window to the end of the driveway. Matt would not be happy if she ended up being the babysitter today. With a nervous sigh Shelby stepped out onto the front porch and stood at the edge of the steps. There was nothing she could do but make sure Matt's kids were safe and sound when he came home. How hard could that be? She really liked his kids. She'd lost her heart to them the moment she'd met them. If it wasn't for his staunch disapproval of her, she'd be looking forward to spending time with them.

The low rumble of a diesel engine sounded in the distance. Shelby moved down the porch steps to the sidewalk, watching as the big yellow bus stopped and opened its doors. Kenny was off first, his little legs breaking into a run that sent his backpack bobbing up and down. He waved, a huge happy smile on his face as he raced toward her.

"Hi. I beat Cass. She walks too slow."

Shelby laughed out loud. She was shocked to realize it had been a very long time since she'd known any true joy. The bus pulled away, and Shelby watched as Cassidy waved to someone then started toward her.

"Hi. I'm glad you're going to watch us."

The child's comment sent a rush of warmth through Shelby's heart. "Me, too. I'm looking forward to spending time with both of you." It was the truth. Whatever problems Matt had, whatever reservations he held, he'd have to handle on his own. She wasn't going to close herself off from these adorable children just because he harbored an old grudge.

"Miss Ellen left you some cookies. Are you hungry?" The responses were unanimous. Shelby followed the energetic kids up the steps and into the house. For the next three hours she was going to enjoy herself. Matt Durrant could just deal with it.

Matt pulled into the driveway, parking his car close to the side door of the house. His tension eased when he saw Ellen's car parked in its normal spot. He'd managed to get off work early. He hadn't been comfortable with the kids being around Shelby. He asked around the campus but found no alternative child care. He'd even called the local nanny service, but the cost was ridiculous. Hopefully he'd be able to make different arrangements over the weekend. His kids were still fragile emotionally. He had to make sure they were protected.

A firm tap on Ellen's front door brought no response. Ellen rarely locked her door, so he tapped again then eased it open. He smiled when he recognized his children's laughter. "Hello, anybody here? It's me."

"Daddy's home!" Kenny's shout echoed through the house. Matt stepped into the foyer in time to catch his son as he propelled himself up into his arms. "Hey, sport. Sounds like you're having a good time."

Kenny nodded and let go. "We're looking at pictures of you. Come see."

"Me?" Matt followed his son into the dining room, trying to find a reason why Ellen would have pictures of him. Cassidy was seated at one end of the table, her chair pulled close to Shelby's. A board game was laid out on the opposite end. His daughter looked over her shoulder and smiled, sending his heart into meltdown. His little princess had him tightly wrapped around her sweet little finger.

"Hey, Daddy. Come see. We found pictures of you in high school. Look, look." She motioned him to look over her shoulder. Matt moved forward, noticing for the first time the smile on Shelby's face. Her brown eyes sparkled, highlighting the gold flecks, and there was a soft rosy glow in her cheeks. She looked contented and happy. Matt stepped to his daughter's right side, away from Shelby, but the faint flowery scent of her fragrance drifted around him.

"Look, Dad, that's you." Cassidy pointed to a picture in a yearbook. He had to smile. Had he ever looked that young? He chuckled softly deep in his throat. "That would be me, all right."

"You have lots of pictures in here."

Matt reached out and folded back the cover to check the date. His senior year. "Yeah, I was pretty active that year. How did this turn up at Ellen's house?" He directed his question to Shelby.

"It's mine. I bought one every year. I was usually on the staff, so." She shrugged. "I kept a lot of my things here at Gramma's. We didn't have much room in our apartment, and my mom liked to throw things out."

"So where's Ellen? I assumed she'd be here." He felt like a heel when Shelby blanched at his question. But he'd arranged for her grandmother to watch the kids. Not her.

"She's next door. Mrs. Horvath is under the weather, and she took her a casserole."

Kenny had climbed back into his chair on the other side of his sister. "Daddy, is Mommy's picture in the book?"

Matt braced against the pain the simple question stirred up. Would it always be this way? "No, son. Your mom didn't grow up in Dover."

"Where did she grow up?"

"In Savannah, Georgia. Remember, we went to the beach there right before she got sick?"

"I remember." Cassidy's happy mood had vanished.

Time to get his kids back into their own safe space. "Come on, kids. We'd better go home. You have homework, and we need to start supper."

"We did our homework first thing." Cassidy pushed back from the table.

"Dad, can we look at pictures of Mom after supper?"

"Sure, son." He turned toward the door, aware of Shelby following behind him and also aware that he had to thank her. The kids gathered up their backpacks, then clustered near him at the front door.

"Matt." He wasn't in the mood to talk to her, but he

couldn't be rude. She had kept his children safe and entertained. He pulled open the door and gestured his kids to leave. "Y'all go on over to the house. I'll be along in a minute." He turned to face Shelby.

"I hope I didn't cause any trouble with the yearbooks. It never occurred to me that they'd expect to see pictures of their mother."

"Not your fault. I never know when the questions will come. They catch me off guard all the time."

"I can't image how difficult this is for you and the children. She was obviously a wonderful mother."

"She was." Sweet recollections drifted through his mind, but this time without the biting sting. "She was funny, always thinking of new ways to entertain them. She knew exactly what to say and do for any situation. Losing her traumatized the kids. Especially Cassidy. I put her in counseling for a while. She was like a lost puppy."

"Is that why you moved back home, to be around your family?"

Her question made him realize that he'd been spilling his guts to Shelby. Absolutely not what he'd intended. But then, she'd always been easy to talk to. She knew things about him no one else did. But she didn't need to know about his pain and loss. Not that she'd care. She was only passing through.

He had to remember his primary goal here. Keep his kids from any more heartbreak. "Yes. I felt they needed some stability. Some security. Atlanta was too full of memories. I sold my business and everything else and came home." He held her gaze, willing her to understand what he was about to say. "My kids have suffered deeply in losing their mother. I want them to be surrounded by people who love them as much as I do. I want them to have people in their lives they can depend on, who won't walk out when they need them most." He stopped, realizing he wasn't talking about his family anymore. He saw Shelby's brown eyes darken.

"People like *me,* Matt?"

He set his jaw. "I didn't say that."

"You didn't have to."

Matt turned to leave. "Tell Ellen thanks. I'm still looking for other babysitting options. I know she misses her volunteer work, and I don't like imposing on you."

Shelby crossed her arms over her chest. "Because I'm not dependable?"

No sense playing games. "No. You're not."

The afternoon light streamed through the windowed walls of the sunroom on the back of Gramma's house, casting a warm glow on the cozy space. Curled up in the old chaise, a magazine in her lap, she reveled in the familiar sense of peace. She glanced around the room at the stacks of magazines and smiled. She'd fallen in love with magazines because of her gramma. She'd hurry over here after school and lose herself in the glossy pages of beautiful rooms, filled with beautiful people doing beautiful things. Life within the pages was always perfect and happy. Magazines allowed her to escape her mother's bitterness and forget for a while that she didn't fit in at school.

She could almost relax completely, if it weren't for Cassidy and Kenny coming over shortly. After a quick hello yesterday, she'd escaped to her room, explaining she had work to do and leaving Gramma to watch over the kids. She'd missed being with them but it allowed her to avoid Matt. She hadn't come out of her room until she'd seen the three Durrants walking across the drive to their house.

Gramma's advice had hovered in the back of her mind. It was time to settle the past. All this huffing and puffing was silly. But how did they do that when it was clear that Matt would never forgive her for walking out?

Today, however, she couldn't use work as an excuse to avoid babysitting. Gramma had called to say she'd been invited to dinner and a movie with friends. She wanted to know if Shelby was okay with keeping the kids. Shelby couldn't refuse. Her grandmother deserved a night out, but that left her to deal with Matt's disapproval.

She set her jaw. She was not going to worry herself into knots over this. Matt needed someone responsible to keep the kids; she was his only option. All she could do was be as conscientious as possible, and hopefully in time he'd come to trust her.

Squealing air brakes sounded outside, and she found herself smiling, even as a trickle of nervousness formed. What did she know about taking care of children? She'd certainly never learned anything from her mother. She'd always made motherhood seem like a burden, the worse choice a woman could make. But Matt's adorable kids were making her take a new look at some of her assumptions.

Shelby met the children halfway down the drive. "Hello there." Seeing their sweet, happy faces warmed her heart in a way she'd never experienced before. Cassidy fell into step with her as they made their way back toward Gramma's house. Kenny raced ahead.

"I'm glad it's Friday. No school for two whole days."

"Don't you like school?"

Cassidy nodded. "But I don't like homework."

"Join the club. No one does." Shelby glanced up at Kenny, who stood on his porch, backpack at his feet. "Kenny, come on. Gramma left some brownies today."

"Can't we stay at our house today? Please? I want to play with Chester. I don't want to wait until Dad gets home."

Cassidy nodded. "Could we? I like being at your house, but I'd really like to go home."

Shelby couldn't think of any reason not to, other than she would feel uncomfortable in Matt's home. But her primary concern was the children. "I suppose. Let me go get the key and a few of my things."

Standing in Matt's house a few minutes later, she couldn't resist the temptation to look around. Unlike her grandmother's house, which retained all its original details, Matt's home had been completely remodeled. Walls had been removed, rooms opened up and windows replaced, giving the home an open, spacious feel. Despite the clean lines and modern style, the furniture was practical and functional. Evidence of the children lay scattered around the room—toys on the floor, a stuffed animal on the ottoman. Matt's work boots stood beside the leather recliner.

She forced herself to ignore her surroundings. Quickly she moved to the kitchen and set her laptop on the table. Cassidy, never far from her side, took the brownies and set them on the island. "Any homework?"

"A little. But I can do it Sunday night."

Shelby laid an arm across the girl's shoulders. "Would you like some advice, woman to woman?" Cassidy nodded, a huge smile on her face. "Do you know what the word *procrastinate* means?"

Cassidy groaned softly. "To put stuff off."

"Yep. I learned after much painful struggle that the best way to enjoy your time off is by getting the unpleasant things out of the way first. It's freeing. I think you should try it."

Cassidy pointed to the treats on the counter.

Shelby shook her head. "Before we have brownies."

With the young girl up in her room and Kenny safely in the backyard with Chester, Shelby took a moment to check emails on her smart phone. There was no more news about the future of the company. Not surprising. Everything was on hold until the upcoming meeting. It was the not knowing that kept her on edge. The cold hard truth was the chances of her being out of work soon were very good. And she couldn't get back to New York to look for another job until she had her health back on track.

"I used to live in Atlanta when I was little," Cassidy stated as they munched on homemade brownies a short while later. Kenny had scooped his up and returned to the yard, mumbling something about finding a lizard on the fence.

Shelby was still picking at her piece, knowing she shouldn't be eating the chocolate treat but unable to completely resist. "So I heard. Atlanta is a very big city."

"There's a lot to do there. Not like here."

Shelby stifled a grin at the girls assumed air of sophistication. "Don't you like Dover?"

"It's okay. I didn't like it much when I first got here. Boring." She rolled her eyes. "But I have friends now so it's not so bad." Cassidy took another bite of brownie. "What do you do in New York?"

"I edit a magazine. You may know it. *Tween Scene.*"

Cassidy eyes widened. "Really? That's the coolest magazine ever."

"Thank you." Shelby couldn't help a swell of pride at the compliment. She'd worked hard to make the magazine a success. It broke her heart to think it might be discontinued under the new management.

"I can't believe that's your magazine. Wait until I tell my friends."

"Well, it's not mine. I don't own it. I only work for it, but I'm glad to hear you like *Tween Scene* so much. What's your favorite section?"

Cassidy thought a moment. "The one where they show you what to wear and what not to wear. And the makeup one, and the part where you talk about TV stars. Only… I'm not allowed to read it."

Shelby stopped midbite. "What? But you're so familiar with it."

"I know, but Dad says it's too grown-up for me. He says the articles aren't good for girls my age."

Tween Scene precisely targeted Cassidy's demographic. Did Matt really disapprove or was he steering her away from the publication because she was the editor? Come to think of it, did he even know she was connected to the magazine? Could his comments be solely objective? Doubtful. *Tween Scene* was perfect. "I'm sorry to hear that. We try very hard to make the magazine appeal to girls your age. If your dad won't let you read it, how do you know so much about it?"

A guilty smile moved her lips. "I read it at Molly's."

"Oh. I see."

"You won't tell Dad, will you?"

"No. But do you think you should be disobeying your father?"

Cassidy shook her head. "But it's such a cool magazine."

Cool in the young girl's eyes. Inappropriate in her parent's. Which one was the truth? As far as Shelby could recall, nothing in *Tween Scene* should cause concern in parents. Apparently, Matt's overprotective streak ran to more than just their hearts.

"I wish I was thin and pretty like you," Cassidy said, her voice soft and wistful.

Shelby made a quick survey of the little girl. She wasn't rail thin, but she wasn't chubby, either. She was nicely filled out and starting to transform into a young lady. "I think you're perfect."

Cassidy smiled. "Thanks, but I want to look like that girl on the cover last time. You know, the one where she was wearing those cool jeans and that striped top with the patches."

She remembered it well. It had been one of the best covers all year. "That was Yasmine."

Shelby thought about the child models and celebrities she worked with regularly. They were nothing like Cassidy. Most were mature beyond their years and bone thin. Nearly all the models were older than the preteen image *Tween Scene* promoted. Something about that bothered her, but she wasn't sure what.

"I wish I could look like that." Cassidy sighed wistfully. "She's so cool."

Shelby could remember when she felt the same way. She'd look at the girls in the magazines and long for a magic wand that could transform her into a glamorous model.

"I have an idea." Shelby moved to the table and pulled out her smart phone and opened her laptop.

"What are we going to do?"

"You'll see." Shelby winked, opening her camera app. "I have a magic wand." She motioned Cassidy to stand against the wall. "Okay, now strike a pose."

Cassidy giggled self-consciously. "I don't know what to do."

Shelby began taking pictures. "Pretend you're a model. Pose like you see the girls on the cover of my magazine."

A few minutes later, Shelby moved to her laptop and pulled up the images. "Come watch." Cassidy came to her side. After selecting her editing program, she scrolled through the shots to find the best image to work with. First she added highlights and fullness to Cassidy's hair. Next she made her eyes larger and deepened the color, adding sparkle for good measure. A click of the mouse slimmed the neck and added hollows to the cheeks. Another whitened the teeth. One more trimmed the body line.

Lastly, she turned her attention to the clothes. She lightened the hue of the jeans and changed the color of the blouse to a jewel tone that better complemented the new deeper shade of her eyes. A few more minor touch-ups, and Shelby leaned back in her chair. "Well, what do you think?"

"Oh, wow. I look like a TV star." She was breathless. "That is so cool."

Shelby gave the girl a quick hug. "You look exactly like the girls on the covers of my magazine. In fact."

She made a few more clicks and added the magazine banner across the top of the page, making the picture resemble the cover of *Tween Scene*.

"It's me, but it's not me. Oh thank you, thank you," Cassidy gushed, bouncing up and down. "This is so awesome. Can I have a copy?"

"Sure. I'm not connected to your printer, though. I can email it to you so you can print it out. What's your address?" Shelby typed in the address, attached the file and hit Send. "There you go. Do you know how to print on your computer?"

"We only have Dad's. He won't let us have our own. He says we're too young."

"I'm sure he'll print it for you when he gets here." She glanced at the wall clock. Matt would be home before long. "What are you doing for supper? Should I be putting something in the oven?"

Cassidy shrugged. "I don't know. Aunt Laura usually made something for us, but she's not here now."

Cassidy's eyes grew wide, and Shelby saw excitement building.

"What?"

"Can I cook supper for Daddy? I could surprise him."

It was a sweet idea. "Do you know how to cook?"

"A little. I help Aunt Laura sometimes. I know how to make lasagna. My gramma showed me how."

Shelby was warming to the idea. She used to love to cook, but like many of her favorite pastimes, she'd given it up for lack of time. "I think that's a great idea. Let's see if we have everything we need." Cassidy jumped into the task with gusto, surprising Shelby with how much she knew. Working with the little girl on the dinner and helping her through the process was a surprisingly satisfying experience.

Shelby watched the clock. Matt should be home any moment and all was ready. "Cassidy, you did a wonderful job." Even Kenny had contributed his table-setting skills. All that remained was for their dad to come home and enjoy their efforts.

Cassidy kept dashing to the front door, looking for Matt's car. "Do you think he'll be surprised? What if he doesn't like it?"

Shelby squeezed her shoulders. "He'll love it because you made if for him."

"He's here!" Kenny dashed out the back door.

Shelby's heart skipped a beat, but she didn't question the cause. This was simple pride. Her heart was bursting. She couldn't wait to see Matt's reaction. Of course then she'd slip out and go home. She had no intentions of intruding on the family meal. The feeling of disappointment over that knowledge was stronger than she'd expected. She found herself wanting to stay and be part of the camaraderie.

Matt strode through the back door, a puzzled look on his chiseled features. Kenny bounced on his feet beside him. "What's going on?" He inhaled deeply. "Something smells good."

"Cassidy did it." Kenny pointed at his sister.

Matt looked first at her then to his daughter. "Did you make dinner?"

Cassidy ran to him and wrapped her arms around his waist. "I baked lasagna. I did it all by myself."

"Miss Shelby helped, and I did, too," Kenny announced.

"I didn't know you could cook." He glanced over at Shelby.

She smiled and nodded. "She did it all by herself. I think you may have a future chef on your hands."

"Well, let's sit down and try it. I'm sure it'll taste as good as it smells." Matt's gaze met hers. "Where's Ellen?"

"She's dining out with friends." He looked like he wanted to say something then changed his mind. Had she overstepped again?

Cassidy scanned the table. "Kenny, you forgot to put a plate for Miss Shelby."

"Oh, no. I'm not staying. This is your family time."

"You have to stay. Please?" Cassidy grabbed her arm and squeezed.

She looked at Matt and cringed. Great. She'd placed Matt in an awkward position once again. Either way he replied would be uncomfortable.

"Of course she has to stay."

She looked over at Matt, gauging his expression. Was he serious or was he merely tolerating her for his daughter's sake? Suddenly she knew what she wanted to do. Lifting her chin, she met Matt's gaze. "Thank you. I'd love to stay. I'm looking forward to having some of Cassidy's wonderful meal." He didn't flinch.

"Kenny, set another plate on the table."

The meal was more pleasant than Shelby had anticipated. Matt was sincerely impressed with his daughter's cooking efforts and Kenny kept them entertained with stories about Chester.

She'd picked at her lasagna, hoping Cassidy wouldn't notice how little she ate. As delicious as it was, the heavy pasta dish wasn't something she could indulge in.

"I'll clean up, Daddy."

Matt raised his eyebrows. "I know when to not argue. We'll be in the living room."

Reluctantly Shelby followed Matt from the room. She'd much rather be helping Cassidy with the dishes. She strived for a topic of conversation. "You have a lovely home, Matt."

"Thanks. Katie, my wife, was a decorator. She always had our home looking like a magazine spread. I have no talent in that department. I go with what I like."

"It's a very comfortable room. Very homey." Her gaze settled on a framed photo on the sofa table. She lifted it, her heart skipping a beat when she realized it was a family picture. A stately blonde smiled out at her. Katie. The wife. "She's a beautiful woman."

"Yes, she was."

The sadness in his voice broke her heart. "Kenny resembles her a good bit."

He nodded "Yes, he does. He has her personality, too. She was always busy, always involved in something. Kenny has only one speed. Fast."

"I've noticed. I wish I had some of his energy." Shelby chuckled and put the frame down. "How did you and your wife meet?"

"At school. She had a project for a design class and she needed someone good with tools to help. A friend mentioned me."

Cassidy poked her head in the room. "Daddy, I just remembered. I need to print something. Can I get on the computer?"

He moved to the desk at the end of the kitchen and tapped the keys. "There you go."

"Look, Daddy." Cassidy came to his side, holding up a picture, a beaming smile on her face. "It's me."

"You? It doesn't look anything like you." He frowned, shooting a quick glance at Shelby.

Cassidy bounced up and down, giggling with delight. "I know. Don't I look awesome?"

Matt sighed and pulled the little girl against his side. "No, princess. You're much prettier than that."

Shelby started to comment, then her gaze fell on Cassidy. The child really was beautiful. Her large, dark blue eyes were rimmed with long lashes, framed in a heart-shaped face. A sweet, happy smile reflected her bubbly personality.

Shelby thought about the photo she'd created on the screen. Matt was right. Cassidy bore no resemblance to the perfect image she'd created. Cassidy was real, blessed with an attractiveness no program could improve upon. She'd never thought about the difference between normal little girls and the airbrushed faces that appeared on *Tween Scene*'s covers. Suddenly turning sweet Cassidy into a too-perfect cover image seemed wrong.

"Cassie, honey, why don't you go on to your room. Miss Shelby and I will finish up in the kitchen."

"Cool. I want to tell Darcy about this picture."

The moment his child was out of earshot, Matt pinned her with a stony glare. "What is this?" He waved the picture in air. "She looks like she's sixteen. I didn't recognize her."

Shelby's defenses kicked in. "I was showing her how we alter images for the covers of the magazine."

"And you thought it would be a good idea to make Cassidy look like some anorexic pop star?"

"No. It wasn't like that. She found out I was the editor of *Tween Scene* and she said she wanted to look like the girls on the covers. So, I took her picture and showed her how we augment the image for the best result."

"Augment? My little girl doesn't need to be augmented."

"Of course not. I only thought that if I—"

Matt held up his hand. "I don't expect you to understand, and I know you probably didn't think you were doing anything wrong, but my daughter is growing up fast enough. She doesn't need to be rushing things. One of the reasons I moved back here was to keep her from the destructive influences of the big city."

"It was a little harmless fun."

"Harmless? Really?" Matt exhaled slowly. "You've basically told her she's not good enough as she is. You've shown her that unless she looks like a movie star or a model, she's not acceptable. Is that really what you were trying to accomplish?"

"No, of course not." How could he even think such a thing? It was insulting. "I do this kind of thing all the time with our models."

"Shelby, Cassidy is a real little girl. Not a seasoned professional like you're used to dealing with. She's very vulnerable at this age. She has enough things assaulting her self-image. She doesn't need any more to confuse her."

Is that what she'd done? Had she confused Cassidy? In making her look perfect, had she done more harm than good? The truth in Matt's words filtered into her heart, filling her with regret. But Matt was overreacting.

"Matt, I'm sorry. I didn't mean any harm. But Cassidy is at an age when she wants to experiment with clothes and makeup and hairstyles. It's natural. I'll talk to her. Make sure she understands the difference between real life and magazine pictures." She'd come to care for her too much. The last thing she wanted was to be a bad influence on Matt's little girl.

Matt ran a hand through his hair and sat down on the arm of the sofa, clasping his fingers together tightly. "This is when I miss Katie the most. Cassidy needs a mother. I'm not sure I can provide her with everything she needs."

Shelby longed to reach out and touch him, give him comfort and reassurance, but she doubted he'd accept it. "But you'll marry again someday and—"

"No."

The steely determination in his dark blue eyes stunned her. He couldn't be serious. "But why? You're still young and there's so much life ahead for you."

The muscle in Matt's jaw flexed rapidly. "I'll never risk losing someone I love again. Watching her slowly waste away, knowing there was nothing I could do to help. I won't put my children through that a second time."

He turned away, but not before she saw the raw sorrow in his eyes. His pain scratched across her heart. "I'm sorry. But the chances of anything happening again…"

"Are too great."

Now she understood his protective attitude toward his children. Matt stared at her a long moment, then stood, slipping his hands into his pockets. "I appreciate what you did today, helping Cassidy with supper and all. Just don't encourage her to look older and more sophisticated. She a little girl. I'd like to keep her that way as long as I can."

Her heart ached for him. He was guarding his family the only way he knew how. By being their protector. "All right."

Picking up her belongings she walked out, grateful that it was the weekend. She needed some distance from Matt and his kids.

Matt scooped up his son's dirty clothes from the bathroom floor and tossed them into the hamper. "Go get in bed. I'll be right in."

"Okay." Kenny dashed off to his room.

Matt headed down the hall, glancing into Cassidy's room. She'd decorated it herself, with his help. The walls were painted in pink, aqua and blue horizontal stripes. Gauzy fabric draped down from above the headboard. A pink fuzzy lamp and a purple futon finished the decor. It was garish and tacky and completely girly. Cassidy loved it.

He doubted Katie would have approved. She had favored elegant, traditional furnishings and decor. Matt had only wanted to make his little girl happy. Stepping inside the room, he smiled at the sight of his daughter stretched out on her bed, ankles crossed in the air as she watched her favorite television program. "As soon as this is over, lights out, young lady. Understood?"

She nodded absently. "Yes, sir."

He moved to the bed and touched the top of her head. "That was a great meal tonight. I'm proud of you." Her dazzling smile melted his heart.

"Thanks, Daddy. I'm going to learn to cook more

things so I can have your supper ready when you get home."

"That's sweet, but concentrate on being a kid first. Worry about my stomach later."

"Love you, Daddy."

"Love you."

Kenny was playing with Chester on the bed when Matt entered his room. His son's room was another matter. The boy was fascinated by reptiles and critters. He loved trees and the woods and would spend every moment there if he could. "What story are we going to read tonight?"

"The slingshot and the giant."

Matt smiled. He was pleased his son enjoyed the Bible stories. In the years after Katie's death they had drifted away from church attendance. It had been one of the things he was determined to change now that they were back home. He wanted his kids to grow up in the faith. He was ashamed that he'd allowed them all to backslide.

Matt finished the story then leaned down to kiss the boy's cheek. "Sleep well, sport."

"Daddy, can I watch *Insect Man* for a while? It's the weekend."

The cartoon superhero who could turn into any bug he wanted was his son's favorite. "I guess so."

Matt stood, signaling to Chester to follow. "See you in the morning." Matt shut the door and started down the stairs. The moment he entered the kitchen he stopped cold, bombarded by images from his unusual homecoming.

Walking into his home this evening had been surreal. The air had been heavy with delicious aromas, the atmosphere warm and welcoming. His children had scurried about the kitchen smiling and laughing. The scene had wrapped around his soul and filled him with such a longing he'd nearly buckled under the weight of it. For the first time since he'd moved back to Dover, this house felt like a home. He'd tried his best to make the place warm, cozy, a safe haven. But tonight it had been real.

And he had Shelby to thank for that. Cassidy and Shelby both had insisted the meal was his daughter's idea. He didn't doubt that, but Shelby had supervised and given all the credit to Cassidy. The pride and joy revealed in Shelby's face had captivated him. She had been genuinely delighted at his little girl's accomplishments. Matt poured a glass of tea, glancing out the window to the house next door.

He'd seen the friendship growing between his children and Shelby. He didn't want her to be friends with his kids. Yet her presence was firmly implanted in the space. Like she'd claimed it. He wasn't sure he liked that.

But he wasn't sure what to do about it.

Chapter Four

Shelby awoke the next morning well rested and feeling like her old self. She and Gramma had settled in on the sofa and talked. Gramma must have sensed her reluctance to discuss Matt and instead had caught her up on all the changes that had taken place in Dover since she'd left.

But memories of the family dinner at Matt's still played in the back of her mind. It had been a roller-coaster evening emotionally. First joy at Cassidy's success, regret over the enhanced picture and sadness as she listened to Matt speak of his wife and vow never to risk his heart and lose another woman he loved. She could only imagine how difficult that had been for him.

She pulled her hair up into a ponytail, then moved to the dresser and reached for her pills. The bottles were nearly empty. What would Matt do if he knew about her heart disease? If she didn't get control of her health, she was flirting with serious consequences, even death. Matt would probably forbid her to be around the kids at all. It would have become his worst nightmare—

allowing his kids to bond with a woman who could die unexpectedly.

She loved being with Cassidy and Kenny. Being denied their company would break her heart and take a large measure of enjoyment out of her life. Better for everyone that she keep her health issues to herself.

Last night had helped her turn a corner. Her future still weighed heavily on her mind, but being home again, around Gramma and the kids, gave her renewed hope and a sense of belonging she'd been lacking. For all her busyness in New York, she'd always felt alone. Her work had consumed all her time, thought and energy, leaving her with few friends and no social life. Not even church. She hadn't realized until now how one-dimensional her existence had become.

But today was a new day. The weekend. She didn't have to worry about Matt or his children until Monday. Today she would focus on her health and start exercising. Shelby groaned. Of all the things she hated to do, exercising was at the top of the list. Right behind giving up regular coffee and sweets. She'd never been very athletic. The only time she'd enjoyed outdoor activities was when she and Matt—better not think about that.

Gathering her sagging determination, Shelby reviewed her plan. She'd start with a five-mile jog around Shiloh Lake outside of town. If she increased it a mile each day, by the end of the week she would be up to ten miles. That should get her back in shape quickly. Encouraged, she finished dressing, grabbing up her iPod and earbuds before hurrying downstairs.

Ellen was at the sink, and she raised her eyebrows as she scanned her from head to toe. "Well, what are you dressed for?"

Shelby poured a cup of coffee, doctored it with skim milk and a packet of artificial sweetener and took a sip. It was still awful. "I'm starting my exercise today."

Gramma nodded slowly. "Good. But don't overdo it. I know you. You'll want to start out with a ten-mile jog."

Shelby nearly choked on her coffee. When would she remember that Gramma could always read her like a book? "I was thinking more like five miles."

Ellen shook her head. "Honestly. I don't know what it is about this family that makes them think everything has to be done quickly. There is nothing wrong with taking life slow." She rinsed out her coffee mug and set it in the drainer. "Start with a leisurely stroll into town or walk the trails in the park. Each day you increase the distance and the pace until you're stronger. Then you can graduate to running like a track star."

Shelby smiled. "That takes too long."

Gramma crossed her arms over her chest. "This isn't a deadline you have to meet. This is your life."

Deadline. That's exactly how she'd been thinking of it. She'd given herself six weeks to learn to relax so she could get back to work. Probably not the best approach for someone in her condition. "Okay, how about a walk, then. Slow and steady, like a turtle."

Gramma smiled. "Better. You could start with the trails out back. There's a shortcut at the tree line. But first, I've fixed you a healthy breakfast. Come and eat."

Shelby stepped onto the front porch, inhaling the heady scent of sweet olive that grew at the side of the house. The slight breeze also carried a hint of fall. Her favorite time of year, when the scorching heat of August was replaced with the balmier temps of September.

She'd always been eager for school to start even though she hadn't fit in with most of the other kids. She'd felt at home in the classroom, studying and learning. Then at the end of each day, she'd hurry to Gramma's to sit in the sunroom or the porch swing and read magazines and eat cookies. It was a beautiful day, and she would try and think only beautiful thoughts. A walk was the perfect solution to her stress.

She started toward the back of the house, past the old garage, trying to remember what Gramma had told her about the shortcut to the trails that would save her the two-block walk to the main entrance. Friendship Park was a new addition to Dover. Once known as the Burton Farm, the city had purchased the land and turned it into a community park, complete with picnic areas, playground and hiking trails. She'd assured Shelby she couldn't miss the shortcut through the trees. She'd obviously forgotten her granddaughter's lack of experience with the outdoors.

"Miss Shelby. Where ya going?"

Shelby turned to see Kenny Durrant running toward her, Chester on his heels.

"I'm going for a walk."

"Are you going to the trails?"

She nodded. "My gramma said it was a good place to walk."

"It's cool. My daddy and I walk there lots of times. I could show you the way." Kenny beamed with excitement.

"That would be nice. But you'd better check with your father first." She glanced back at the garage behind Matt's house. A large SUV was parked in front of it today. Neither the rickety van nor the battered truck were anywhere to be seen.

"Okay, I'll be right back." Kenny darted off, his little legs pumping furiously. Shelby waited, even though she knew there was no way Matt would allow his son to go with her. Especially after the photo incident last night. Kenny returned a few minutes later, his face flushed with excitement.

"What did your daddy say?"

"He said 'kay."

Shelby hesitated for a stunned second, glancing at the house, then back at Kenny. Maybe she'd misjudged Matt's attitude last night. Apparently he wasn't so angry that he would refuse to let Kenny go with her. That had to be a good sign. She shrugged. "Great. Let's get going then. Where's the shortcut?"

"I'll show you. It's way back there at the end of our yard." Chester took off ahead, apparently knowing the way.

Buoyed by the thought of having a companion on her first walk, she started off at a brisk pace.

"Hey! Hey!"

Shelby stopped and turned around. Kenny was several yards behind her, his short legs pumping to keep up.

"You walk too fast."

She hadn't realized she'd been moving so quickly. She'd have to watch that. She was used to doing everything at breakneck speed. Yet another life change she'd have to adjust to. "Sorry, Kenny. I'll slow down."

"Good, 'cause then I can show you the cool stuff."

He was an energetic child, alternately skipping and running, sometimes stopping abruptly. She found it difficult to walk in rhythm with the little boy's stride.

"We're here." Kenny stopped near the tree line, smiling broadly.

Shelby frowned at the wide opening between the trees and shrubs. It looked well traveled, but she didn't relish the idea of walking into the wilderness. "Are you sure?" She turned back to the twin houses positioned at the front of the large lots. They looked far off. Maybe this wasn't such a great idea after all.

Kenny waved her on. "Come on. It's right through here."

Shelby girded herself and followed. If a six-year-old could do it, so could she. Cautiously she stepped past the trees into the cool woods. She remembered these woods from when she was a child, but back then they'd been untamed and she'd braved them only once. Too many unknown sounds and movements had sent her racing back to the house.

"See," Kenny shouted, pointing. "There they are."

A few yards ahead stood a large wooden sign, the name of each trail and a corresponding map clearly engraved into the wood. Shelby quickly assessed the Camellia Trail as the longest. She started forward, but Kenny stopped her.

"This is my favorite one. You can trace the trail with your finger." He stepped to the sign and placed his index finger in the indented line on the map of the Magnolia Trail and traced the path. "First you go here, then you go up here, and then across here and down here, and then up here, and then down here again, and you're home." He smiled at her, pleased with himself.

His bright eyes and dazzling smile were infectious. She could see the resemblance to his mother in his coloring and green eyes and dimples. Cassidy favored Matt with her dark blue eyes and brown hair.

"Let's go. Come on, Chester."

They started down the Magnolia Trail. Kenny skipped ahead, Chester at his side. "Don't get too far ahead, Kenny." The gravity of being responsible for Matt's son suddenly struck her. She'd failed to consider the seriousness of taking the boy along. What had she been thinking? What if she lost him? What if something happened to him? How would she explain it to Matt? She quickly realized there was no need to worry. Kenny stopped every few steps to point out a special tree, to show her a log or to toss a rock into the shallow stream running parallel to the trail. At this rate it would take them all day to walk the half-mile trail. Kenny's preoccupation with nature would keep him close, but it was holding her back.

"Why do you run so fast?"

Shelby stopped and turned to find Kenny several yards behind her again. She hadn't realized she'd passed him. "I wasn't running. I was walking."

"Oh." Kenny frowned.

"We'd better get going. We've barely started our walk."

"Look, it's my favorite spot." He ran toward a bench at the edge of the creek. "Come on."

Kenny sat down. Shelby inhaled slowly, trying to quell her impatience. She sat, then glanced around. Trees. Water. Rocks. More trees. "This is nice, Kenny. Come on, we'd better go."

"No. You have to wait until the frogs come. Chester finds them and makes them ribbett."

Kenny sat patiently. Watching. Shelby tapped her toe.

"Guess no frogs today." She stood. "We need to get to the end of the trail."

"Why?"

His question caught her off guard. "Because we're on a walk and we need to get to the end."

"That's no fun."

"Well, it's not about fun. It's about exercise. That's the whole point. I can think of a lot of things that are more fun than this. I'll bet you can, too."

Kenny shook his head, his expression serious. "No. Walking's not the fun part. The fun part is the looking."

She doubted that. She'd found nothing in these woods worth noting. It was merely a place to start walking, a means to work her way up to a longer, more strenuous level. Maybe she'd get a pedometer, then she could keep track of how much she increased her steps each day. Her little companion continued to stare at the creek. Perhaps a different tack would budge him. "We don't want to take too long or your dad will get worried."

Kenny hung his head and stopped swinging his feet. A sense of unease touched her nerves. He looked over his shoulder at her with a guilty expression. "I didn't tell Daddy."

"What!" This couldn't be happening. She put a hand across her mouth. The possible ramifications settled in her stomach like a stone. "Oh, Kenny. You told me he said it was okay."

"He was working and told me to wait a minute, but I was afraid you'd go without me."

"Kenny, you know that telling fibs is wrong."

"I know." Green eyes welled up with tears. "Is Jesus mad at me?"

"What?" Why did his every question throw her a

curve? And how did she answer that one? "Uh, no. He's not mad. He's disappointed like I am and your dad will be, but none of us are mad." She thought back to a time when what Jesus thought of her mattered. "Jesus loves you."

Kenny came to her side and took her hand. "My mommy is with Jesus."

Shelby bit her lip against the stab of sadness in her heart. "I know, Kenny. Come on. We'd better hurry back." Thankfully, they hadn't traveled too far down the trail before Kenny had dropped his bombshell. They started back at a steady clip. Kenny kept pace, holding her hand the whole way.

She heard Matt calling for Kenny as they stepped through the trees at the property line. She could see him up near the house, jogging in different directions, searching for the boy. His body language told her how worried he was. Matt would be furious. How could she have let this happen? "Kenny, you run ahead and let your daddy see you're all right. I'll come and explain to him what happened."

Kenny nodded and ran ahead across the large lawn. "Here I am, Daddy."

Shelby hung back, walking slowly, watching as Matt jogged toward his son, grabbing him in a tight hug, his relief evident in the way he held him close to his chest for a long moment. His anger quickly became apparent when he set the boy down, his large hands gripping little shoulders, obviously demanding an explanation.

Shelby was glad for the vast yard between them. She didn't want to hear Kenny being scolded even if it was his fault. By the time she crossed the distance from the woods to the house, Kenny was apologizing.

"I'm sorry, Daddy."

"It's my fault, Matt. I thought—"

Matt took a menacing step toward her. "Did you think you could walk off with my son and not tell me?"

Shelby bristled. "That's not how it happened."

Matt planted his hands on his hips. "What were you thinking?"

"Daddy?"

Matt turned to his young son. "Go in the house. I'll be there in a minute."

"But Daddy…"

"Kenny. Do as I say."

Shelby's heart ached for the child. "Matt, don't blame him. He was—"

"I don't blame him. You should have known better. I guess I should be grateful you didn't run off and leave him in the woods alone. That's your usual response, isn't it? Change your mind and walk away?"

Shelby braced herself against his harsh words. He had every right to be angry at her for her actions fifteen years ago, but not where Kenny was concerned. "That's not fair. I would never leave Kenny alone. You have no right to even suggest such a thing."

Matt glared. "I have every right. He's my son."

Shelby tried to control her rising anger. She had to remember Matt was reacting out of fear and a lack of information. She couldn't imagine what he must have gone through when he discovered Kenny missing. "If you'll only calm down and let me explain, you might—"

"Since when do you bother to explain anything, Shelby? That's not your style." Matt set his jaw and turned away.

Shelby grabbed his arm and forced him around to

face her. "And you're as bullheaded as ever. Do you want to hear what happened or not?"

"I know what happened."

Shelby pursed her lips together to keep from saying something hateful. "No. You don't. But when you decide you want to, you know where to find me." She turned on her heel and walked off. The chasm between them was as wide and as deep as ever.

The realization broke her heart.

Matt watched Shelby leave, regretting his harsh words. He hadn't meant to lash out at her that way, but something had come over him. Years of pent-up anger and resentment had erupted from deep inside, blindsiding him with their intensity.

He ran a hand down the back of his neck and turned back to the house. He'd been on the verge of panic, wondering where Kenny had gone. If anything happened to his children— He couldn't allow himself to think of those things. He'd never survive a loss like that.

It wasn't unusual for his son to wander to the edge of their acre lot and not hear when he was called. He was an imaginative boy, and sometimes he didn't pay attention, but he'd never gone to the trails by himself. He knew they were off-limits unless with an adult.

Kenny sat slumped in a chair at the table when Matt entered the kitchen. He looked so little. So vulnerable. His heart swelled with a love so intense it stole his breath. It helped temper his anger and fear at Kenny's disappearance.

He sat down across the table from the boy, clasping his hands together on the surface. "So, you want to explain to me why you broke the rules and went to the trails without asking?"

Kenny looked up, his green eyes, so like his mother's, filled with sadness. "I asked."

Matt frowned. "I don't remember you asking me."

Kenny nodded. "You were at the computer and I asked if I could go with Miss Shelby to the woods."

"I don't remember that, son."

"You were busy. You said to wait."

Memory surfaced. He'd been completely absorbed in bookkeeping for Handy Works when Kenny had dashed into his home office. He should have paid closer attention. "So why didn't you wait?"

Kenny shrugged. "She would have gone without me and I like the woods."

"I know you do, but you were wrong to go without permission. And Miss Shelby shouldn't have taken you with her without making sure I said it was okay."

Tears filled Kenny's eyes and trickled down his cheeks. "I told her you said I could go."

Shock and disappointment lanced through him. Kenny had never behaved like this before. The daddy in him wanted to pull the boy to his heart and hold him, chase away the tears. The parent in him understood that this was an opportunity to teach a lesson. "Kenny. You told her a lie, didn't you?"

He nodded, the tears flowing more now.

"We don't do that in this family. We follow the rules, and we tell the truth. I'm very disappointed. You won't be allowed to go the trails for a week. Is that clear?"

Kenny nodded, his lower lip quivering.

Matt's heart caved. "Come here, sport." He wrapped his arms around the slender boy and lifted him onto his lap. "I love you very much, but I want you to learn to do the right things."

Kenny sniffed and wiped his nose. "Miss Shelby was disappointed, too."

"What do you mean?"

"We were sitting on my favorite bench and I told her you didn't know I was with her. She got upset and we started back. She said you'd be disappointed, but that you'd still love me like Jesus does."

Matt winced with a sudden surge of shame. He shouldn't have jumped to conclusions. Kenny was the culprit in this adventure. Not Shelby. She had tried to explain, but he'd allowed his old hurts to override his common sense. He'd been rude and spiteful. She didn't deserve that.

"She was right. I do love you and I'm not mad. I get worried, Kenny. I don't want anything to happen to you."

"Like it happened to Mommy?"

Matt braced himself against the old pain. "Yes. I want to make sure you're safe every minute. When I can't find you, I get very scared. Do you understand?"

"I don't want you to be scared, Daddy."

"I know." He hugged him close, kissing the top of his head.

Matt watched his son leave the room, painfully aware that he had some serious damage control to handle. He needed to apologize to Shelby, but he wasn't looking forward to it. Ever since he'd seen her standing on Ellen's front porch, his mind had been flooded with memories and his emotions in conflict.

He'd planned a future with her, planned his life around her, and she'd suddenly decided he was too small-town and broken their engagement. She'd left him twisting in the wind and wondering why. Why had she changed her mind? What had he done? His sweet, funny Shelby had become enraged, and he hadn't known why.

Matt stared at his clasped hands on the tabletop. Shelby was here now. He could ask her outright why she'd turned her back on him, but what good would it do? They'd both gone on with their lives and found happiness. Knowing wouldn't change things.

Who was he trying to kid? Even after all these years it was the not knowing that still haunted him. As much as he hated to admit it, he wanted an answer. If he had an explanation, a reason for her behavior that night, then he could put it behind him once and for all.

It shouldn't matter. He'd gotten over her long ago. So why did his heart skip a beat whenever he thought about her? Why did his mind constantly replay sweet moments from their past?

Matt stood, scraping the chair legs across the floor. Because he was a fool with a bruised ego. He was also a man who needed to make an apology. And the sooner the better.

Shelby paced the kitchen, her emotions pulling her in two directions. One minute she was furious at Matt for refusing to listen to any explanation about Kenny. The next she wanted to cry over the lost hope of them ever being civil to one another. After today's incident with Kenny, he would never speak to her again, let alone allow her to help babysit. He was probably on the phone right now hiring a professional. Anxiety and frustration quickened her heart rate. She needed to move, to do something besides replay the ugly scene with Matt. How was she ever going to learn to relax with him next door?

Her gaze came to rest on her grandmother's small collection of pill bottles on the counter. Medications. She still needed to fill her own prescriptions. Now might be a good time to take care of that. A brisk walk into town might be exactly what she needed. She also needed to schedule an appointment with the cardiologist in Jackson her doctor had recommended.

Buoyed by her decision, she quickly changed into a denim skirt and a cool knit top and slid her feet into comfy sandals, grabbing her purse on the way out the door. By the time she reached the center of Dover she was feeling more relaxed than she had in a long time. So many landmarks along the way triggered sweet recollections from her childhood. Odd. She'd worked so hard to get away from this place. She'd been so firm in her resolve to stay away. Yet now that she was here, it felt like home. She felt like she belonged.

The picturesque downtown greeted her like an old friend. She strolled down Main Street past the furniture store and the bank, smiling as she glanced up at the name engraved in the stone lintel. It was the only building in town that spelled the name correctly. Do Over.

Originally a crossroad between the rail line to New Orleans and the wagon traffic from the river, the town had sprung up haphazardly overnight. When a fire destroyed most of the north side, the community saw it as an opportunity to begin fresh, a chance to do over their town more responsibly. The original name Junction City was replaced with Do Over, which was shortened to D'Over and eventually simply Dover. The irony didn't escape her notice. A do-over was exactly what she needed in her life right now.

Adam's Pharmacy was on the other side of the courthouse square, so she crossed the street and walked into the park. The historic gazebo nestled beside a giant magnolia beckoned her like an old friend. Shelby climbed the steps onto the bandstand, taking a slow turn around the perimeter. The gazebo was a landmark, one of the oldest structures in the town, and had become the symbol of Dover. It was as synonymous with Dover as the Dentzel Carousel was for Meridian and the lighthouse for Biloxi.

Everyone in town could trace many of their most important life events to the delicate structure. Her own catalogue was full of happy times with her parents when she was young, then with her friend Pam and lastly with Matt. Those memories didn't need to be visited right now. With an affectionate pat on one of the turned posts, Shelby descended the wooden steps and started toward the drugstore again.

"Shelby. Shelby Russell!"

Turning to see who had called her name, Shelby smiled when she recognized her childhood friend. "Pam Cotter? I was just thinking about you."

The woman smiled happily and approached with arms spread wide. "I'd heard you were back. I couldn't wait to see you."

Shelby hugged her. "How did you know I was here?"

Pam pulled out of the embrace and grinned. "I work at the hospital. Your gramma practically announced it over the public address system."

Shelby nodded. "I should have known. How are you? I see you're still here."

"Yep. And it's Fleming now." Pam glanced at the bandstand. "How many Saturdays did we spend sitting in there eating ice cream and talking about how we would take the world by storm?"

"Too many to count. You look great. Married life agrees with you."

"Fifteen years and three kids." Pam surveyed her for a moment. "I've missed you, Shel. You left so suddenly. One day you were here, and the next you were gone. You didn't call or leave a note. Why? What happened?"

Shelby was beginning to see that she'd left another broken friendship in her wake. "I'm sorry. Something came up and I left for college early." She smiled and changed the subject. "So you've been here in Dover the whole time?"

"Oh, no. Ron and I still went to State and got our degrees."

"I thought you gave that up when you got pregnant?" She remembered her bitter disappointment when Pam had told her they wouldn't be roommates at college because she was pregnant and getting married instead.

"I did until the baby came, but Ron and I knew we couldn't skip our education. He went on and I started a year later, baby and all."

Her trip back to Dover was challenging many of the reasons she'd left and making her wonder if there were options she had never considered. Could she and Matt have had it all? Each other, college and careers? Her life could have turned out differently had she chosen the other path. But she hadn't. She'd chosen college and career and never regretted it a moment. "How did you do it?"

"Believe me, I wouldn't recommend anyone get their

education the way we did. Living in married housing, trying to raise a child and go to school and work. But I'm proud of what we accomplished. What about you? I hear you're some big magazine executive in New York."

"I am, but there's a big shake-up going on in the company and I may be out of work soon." It felt good to share that with her friend. They'd never had secrets from one another.

"Oh, Shel, I'm so sorry. I know you were right there at the top of your field." Pam squeezed her hand. "Are you headed someplace special? I'd love to get a cup of coffee and catch up."

It was on the tip of her tongue to decline, but the opportunity to unburden herself was too appealing. "I have to get some prescriptions filled. Why don't I drop them off and meet you?"

"Great. The coffee shop is right there on the corner. See you in a minute."

A short while later Shelby exhaled a sigh and looked at her friend.

"So, everything in my life right now is in limbo." Shelby took a sip of her iced tea, enjoying the brisk taste and the sense of calm that washed over her. Pam had listened intently as she'd recounted the events that had forced her back home. "The worst part is feeling out of control."

"That's because you're still under the delusion that you have control at all. You don't have the power to change any of your problems right now, Shel, but He does. Let God work this out. But He can't do anything until you let go of it and let Him take over."

"You make it sound so easy."

"It's not easy, but it's necessary. Take things one step

at a time. First off, concentrate on your health. Are you exercising?"

Shelby responded with a feeble shrug of her shoulders, which brought a knowing smile to her friend's face. "Here's my cell number. You can call me anytime. I walk every morning right past your grandmother's house. We can work out together. I'm here for you, Shel. Call me if you need anything."

"Thanks, Pam. I didn't realize how much I needed a friend." A shadow fell across the bistro table.

"Shelby Russell. Well, I'll be."

Shelby glance up into a pair of cobalt-blue eyes and a warm smile. "Mr. Durrant?"

Tom Durrant took her hand and squeezed it affectionately. "I didn't think I'd ever see you back in Dover again. What brings you to town?"

"I'm visiting my grandmother and taking a short sabbatical from work." It was the truth. Just not the whole truth. She swallowed her discomfort and smiled.

"It sure is good to see you." His eyes narrowed slightly. "Are you doing all right? Everything okay with you?"

She smiled with as much reassurance as she could muster and introduced her friend. "I'm great. I see Mrs. Durrant's campaign signs all over town. Wish her luck for me." Mr. Durrant opened his mouth to say something but stopped. She suspected he had started to mention Matt and thought better of it.

"Will do. Oh, and if you're going to be around for the seventeenth we're having a shindig at Shiloh Lake to celebrate our anniversary. The whole town's invited. That includes you."

"Thank you." His sincere invitation cheered her. Mr.

Durrant had always made her feel like one of his own. Shelby watched him go, her heart a tangle of conflicting emotions. She'd loved Matt's dad. One of her biggest regrets when she broke up with Matt was losing him as a father-in-law.

She looked over at Pam, who was studying her intently.

"So, did your sudden departure fifteen years ago have anything to do with Matt Durrant?"

Nodding slowly, she raised her glass to her lips. "Everything."

Chapter Five

Matt strode into the garage and stood at the work-bench. He'd been promising Kenny he'd put up the tire swing for weeks now. But that wasn't why he'd decided to tackle it today. He needed to keep busy so he wouldn't think about the apology he had to make to Shelby. He pulled his tape measure out at the same moment his cell rang. He smiled at the name that appeared on the screen. "Hey, little brother. How's it going?" His brother was a police detective in Dallas. It was a high-stress job, but Tyler thrived on the challenge. "It's good to hear from you. What's going on?"

"The usual stuff. Chasing bad guys."

Matt heard something odd in his younger brother's deep voice. "Everything okay over there in Big D?"

"Yeah. I wanted to let you know I'm going to try and come home for Mom and Dad's anniversary shindig."

"Hey, that's great. They'll love that. It's been a while since you've been home."

"I know. I keep meaning to take a weekend off, but it never seems to work out. You know how it is."

"I do indeed. Hey, the kids will be glad to see you."

"I'm sure they've grown. Look, let's keep this a secret, okay? I'm not a hundred percent sure I can get the time off. I don't want Mom and Dad disappointed if I don't make it."

"No problem, but I'll be praying that it works out. I miss you, bro."

"Same here."

They said their goodbyes, and Matt sent up a quick prayer that Ty would make it to the picnic. Nothing would make his parents happier.

By the time Shelby returned to her grandmother's house later that afternoon, she'd regained her sense of contentment and had managed to keep thoughts of Matt and her career at bay for a few hours. She crossed the front porch and reached for the door handle.

"Shelby."

Matt. Her heart leaped into her throat. She should have known this moment of peace wouldn't last. This whole mess would have been so much easier if he wasn't next door. His boots scraped against the concrete as he mounted the porch steps. Heart pounding, she squared her shoulders and turned to face him. His cobalt eyes bored into her.

"We need to talk."

She shook her head. "No. We don't." She wasn't going to argue over this again. "I tried to explain to you what happened but you didn't want to listen. I'd forgotten how pigheaded you are."

"Shelby."

"Once you get an idea in that thick head of yours, there's no changing it. You charge ahead and won't listen to anyone. It's one of the reasons—" She crossed her arms over her chest and forged ahead. "I know you must have been frantic. I don't blame you, but how could you think for one moment that I would waltz off into the wilderness with your son without making sure he had permission? I know, I probably should have double-checked, but it never occurred to me that Kenny wasn't being truthful."

"Shelby."

"I did ask him, Matt. I really did but—"

"Shelby!"

"What?"

"Kenny told me what happened. All of it. I jumped to conclusions. I shouldn't have."

She blinked. "Oh." His apology was the last thing she'd expected.

"I reacted out of fear and concern for my son."

"I understand. Really."

He held her gaze a moment. "Good."

Shelby grasped the opportunity to bring up another matter she wanted to discuss. "Matt, maybe this is a good time to clear the air between us."

"Meaning?"

"Call a truce. Put the past behind us and move forward. Neither of us can change what happened." She tucked her hair behind her ear, searching for the right words. "I like your children. I like helping Gramma watch them after school, and I think they like me. Isn't that all that matters?"

He met her gaze and set his jaw. "Are you going back to New York?"

"I have a job there." Maybe.

"Right, and what's going to happen to Cassidy and Kenny when you suddenly pull up stakes and leave?

They've already lost their mother. They don't need to grieve over someone else."

Shelby shook her head in disagreement. "Matt, they're smart kids. They'll understand the difference between the death of a parent and a friend moving away." She faced him, holding his gaze. "The problems between us happened a long time ago. We shouldn't let our old resentments spill over onto the children. We're the adults here. Or at least we're supposed to be." Matt ran a hand through his hair and turned away. "Shouldn't we set aside the past and at least try and be friends? For their sake?"

Matt held her gaze a long moment before nodding. "All right. For their sake."

Shelby watched Matt walk away, bittersweet sadness encasing her heart. She'd hoped for a new beginning, a do-over of sorts, but she could see Matt was still unwilling to forgive her completely.

She sympathized with his desire to shield his children from emotional pain, but she wondered if his fierce need to protect was more about him than them. If only she could help him somehow. If only they could be friends again, talk things through the way they used to. Turning, she walked inside the house. There were no do-overs for them. She'd destroyed all hope for any relationship fifteen years ago when she'd given his ring back. She was beginning to think that was the biggest mistake of her life.

Matt picked up the cardboard box and carried it to the far corner of the Handy Works shed. He was helping his dad restock supplies. Setting the box on the workbench, he sliced it open and pulled back the flaps. Friends. She wanted to be friends. Not in a million years. But she was right about calling a truce. He couldn't keep flaring up like a porcupine whenever she was around, and he didn't want his kids caught up in their past.

He stared into the carton of nails. The tension between them still vibrated along his nerves. Something about her bothered him. More than the simple fact that whenever he was near her, his heart did strange things and his blood warmed as if standing next to a fire. He could dismiss that as simple attraction. A leftover reaction from when he'd been in love with her. It meant nothing. What puzzled him was his unshakable feeling that she needed protecting.

Shelby had always been focused and determined. She'd possessed a self-confidence far beyond her years. It was one of the things that had attracted him to her. She was completely different from the silly girls he'd dated in high school, and the coeds he'd met his first two years in college. But he'd sensed much of her bravado was a cover for her insecurities. That realization had always made him feel protective toward her. An assumption he'd learned the hard way was a lie. Shelby Russell didn't need anyone. She was perfectly capable of taking care of herself.

So what was triggering this desire to protect?

"Son, are you going to put those boxes of nails on the shelf, or are you just going to stare into the carton for a while?"

"Sorry, Dad. I've got a lot on my mind."

"Hmm. Shelby Russell?"

"How did you know?"

His dad leaned a hip against the counter and looked

at him. "I saw her in town this afternoon. It was good to see her again."

"Yeah. Great." Apparently no one viewed her return the same way he did.

"Oh. I see. Well, I wanted to find out if you knew why she was back?"

"She says an overdue vacation. Why? What did she tell you?"

"She said she wanted to spend time with her grandmother." Tom shook his head. "But I don't know."

Finally! Someone else who shared his doubts. "You don't believe her?"

"How does she look to you?"

Beautiful. Delicate. Like a balmy spring day. Matt rubbed his forehead. Where had that come from? "I didn't really notice. We've only spoken a few times."

"She doesn't look well to me," Tom observed. "She's too pale, and that sparkle is missing from her eyes. Something's not right there. Your mom grew concerned when I told her, so I thought I'd check with you."

Matt set his jaw. "She's fine as far as I know."

"Your mom mentioned that she and Ellen are watching the kids for you in the afternoons. That's convenient."

"Yeah, but I'm still looking for alternatives."

"Oh. Why? I thought the kids liked Ellen."

"They do. It's Shelby I'm concerned about."

"Why's that?"

Matt pulled out a handful of boxes and shoved them to the back of the shelf. "Because my kids already like her, and knowing her, she's likely to run back to New York without any warning and leave them brokenhearted. I don't want them to lose someone else they've grown close to."

His father nodded, then turned and faced him. "So you think you need to protect them?"

"Yes. They've been through enough."

"Son, you know you can't protect people from caring about others. No one has that power."

"I can try."

Tom came and stood by Matt's side. "Are you sure this is about protecting their hearts or your own?"

The sanctuary of Hope Chapel wrapped around Shelby like one of Gramma's hugs the moment she stepped inside the old church off the square Sunday morning. Her grandfather had been the minister here for decades. It was as familiar as her grandmother's home.

She settled into the pew near the middle, sadness welling up in her heart. How had she strayed so far from her faith? When had she wandered off the path and ignored the beliefs she was raised with?

Gramma smiled over at her, and Shelby clasped her slender hand in hers, taking comfort from the contact. It hadn't been an intentional decision. Nothing had occurred to cause her to reject her faith. She'd simply drifted away until it wasn't even a part of her existence. Being here now made her realize what was lacking in her life—her connection to her Lord.

The organist began to play. Shelby recognized the hymn immediately. "Come Thou Fount of Many Blessings." It had been one of her favorites. One verse came sharply into her mind, the one about being prone to wander from God.

The words and the notes reverberated through her

soul, reminding her of truths she'd too long ignored. She had wandered, and somewhere along the road she'd completely left God behind. Gramma had suggested that her current trials could be the Lord's way of pulling her back to Him. Maybe she was right after all. Maybe what she needed was the strength and comfort only He could give.

Her gaze drifted toward the family sitting a few rows ahead. Matt and his children. Cassidy was whispering to the little girl beside her. Kenny had his head resting against his father's shoulder. The sight warmed her heart but left her with a strange sense of isolation. Shelby turned her attention to the elder as he stepped to the pulpit, only half listening as he reminded the congregation about the youth group outing and family-night supper.

"And now I believe Matt Durrant has an announcement."

Shelby jerked her head up as Matt walked briskly to the pulpit. He smiled. Her heart stopped. In his dark suit, crisp white shirt and patterned tie he looked professional, as comfortable in the boardroom as he'd looked in work clothes.

"Good morning. I want to remind you that we are always in need of volunteers for the Handy Works ministry. We still have a few slots open for the end of the month. Anyone who is handy with a hammer, a rake or a paintbrush, we can use your help. Call the church office or leave a message with our answering service. Thank you."

The lump of shame in Shelby's throat nearly choked her. She bowed her head, afraid to look at Matt. How he must despise her. She'd arrogantly assumed that he was nothing more than a handyman. No wonder he'd been so curt and gruff each time they'd spoken.

Forgive me, Father. Apparently the Lord was trying to get her attention on several levels. Maybe it was time she stopped resisting her situation and followed Gramma's advice. Give it over to the Lord and trust in His wisdom. Do her part and let Him do his.

An hour later, Shelby came downstairs and went into the kitchen. "Anything I can do to help?" Gramma was still in her church clothes as she prepared Sunday dinner.

"Why don't you finish peeling these potatoes while I change?"

Shelby glanced into the pot. "That looks like a lot of potatoes for the two of us."

Ellen smiled and bobbed her eyebrows up and down. "That's because it's not. I want you to run next door and ask Matt and the children to come for dinner."

Shelby whirled to face her grandmother. "You want them to eat with us?"

"Certainly. I often have them over."

Shelby released a nervous sigh as her grandmother disappeared from the room. She and Matt had reached a truce of sorts and they had shared a meal the other night when Cassidy had cooked, but that seemed very different from having them at her gramma's dinner table. A meal here meant family, friends, closeness. At the very least it would have been better if Gramma had invited them herself.

Quickly, she finished preparing the potatoes, then braced herself to deliver the invitation. Well, she'd see just how solid their new truce actually was. Maybe Matt already had other plans. Maybe he'd refuse. Maybe he wasn't even home.

She'd seen him as they were leaving church that morning, but they hadn't spoken. Cassidy and Kenny had waved and smiled. Matt had nodded from across the sanctuary, his expression unreadable.

She knocked on the door, holding her breath. She prayed Cassidy would answer. No such luck. Matt stood there before her, tall, handsome, causing her heart to ache for what could have been. She inhaled a whiff of his aftershave and lost her focus. "Uh. Hi. I, that is, Gramma wanted me to invite you to—you and the children—to dinner. But I'll understand if you have other plans. I know this is short notice, so don't feel obligated." Matt stared at her so long she began to squirm under his scrutiny. Thankfully, Chester scooted out the door and propped his paws on her knees. "Hey, fellow. How are you?" She glanced up at Matt to find his expression had softened somewhat.

"Sure. We'll be right over. The kids love having dinner with Ellen."

"Oh, well, good. It'll be ready in about half an hour."

He nodded. "We know the drill. I'll bring the salad."

"What?"

"That's our usual contribution to the meal."

"Oh. Okay, then. Bye."

Shelby turned and went down the steps, not knowing how to feel about his acceptance. She'd been fully prepared for him to refuse simply because she was asking. It might be an uncomfortable meal. She'd just have to make the best of it. She was the outsider here. She'd cut herself off from this life, run away and never looked back.

No, that wasn't true. She'd looked back several times

and wondered if she'd made the right decision. Doubts had plagued her so relentlessly that the only way she'd been able to deal with them was to block everything out. Dover and Matt simply didn't exist.

A half hour later they were all seated around the large dining room table saying grace. Shelby absently moved her food around on her plate as the conversation swirled around her. Cassidy and Kenny chatted about their friends and their school. Matt and Gramma discussed local issues and his mother's campaign. Shelby might as well have been invisible.

"Shelby Kay, you remember Clara Wilkins, don't you? She had the fabric store next to the card shop."

Shelby shook her head, uncomfortably aware of all eyes on her. "No, I don't remember her."

"Oh, I guess you were off at college about that time."

Shelby groaned inwardly. The one point in time she did not want to bring up with Matt at the table. The conversation continued, leaving her on the outside. Cassidy and Kenny took over the discussion, telling funny stories about Chester. Shelby braved a glance at Matt. He was watching his children with a pride in his eyes that hurt her heart. Every word they spoke, every gesture and smile, brought a light to his eyes. It was obvious to anyone who cared to look that Matt loved his children with his whole being.

She remembered a similar light in his eyes once when he looked at her. But she'd walked away from that love. Odd. She'd left Dover to find everything she'd ever dreamed of. Now she was wondering if what she really wanted had been here all along.

"It's a wonderful ministry, Shelby."

Shelby pulled her attention back to her grandmother. "Ma'am?"

"Handy Works. Matt and his family started it a year or so ago, and it's been such a blessing to this town."

Shelby glanced at Matt. He was staring at her, and she thought she saw a smirk on his face.

"We have a number of elderly and poor in our community who can't afford to hire people to do yard work or repairs on their homes," Matt explained. "We provide that for them. Thankfully we're also blessed with a large number of people who are willing to share their time and skills to help out."

Shelby swallowed her pride. "It's a wonderful thing you're doing."

"Thanks, but it's only a small ambition."

Heat infused her cheeks. Would he never let her forget those cruel words? Gathering her courage, Shelby decided to assert herself. "So what *do* you do for a living, Matt?"

"Daddy's a teacher," Kenny chimed in. "He teaches at a grown-ups' school."

Matt pinned her in place with his navy blue gaze.

"I teach at the local community college during the week and a few online classes at night." One corner of his mouth twitched as he stared at her. "I have a full slate of classes this semester, but normally it's parttime. I want to spend as much time with my kids as I can. They're my only ambition now."

There it was again. That dig at her harsh words from long ago. Shelby decided that silence might be the best course of action for the rest of the meal. She'd been stung enough for one day.

Matt glanced across the table at Shelby, regretting his sarcastic comment. Her gaze was focused on her plate, but he could see the dejected slump to her shoulders. She'd been silent most of the meal, only speaking when spoken to and then responding in clipped tones. She had made few attempts to enter into the conversation.

Their small-town topics obviously bored her. She was too worldly for the likes of Dover. Matt took a sip of his tea, remembering the stunned look on her face when he'd been addressing the congregation about Handy Works. He'd taken a smug satisfaction at the time from putting her in her place. He was ashamed of that now. It was out of character for him to play those games. They'd agreed to a truce, to behaving like adults, and he wasn't holding up his end of the bargain.

"Dad, can Miss Shelby come to Gramma and Grand-pa's special picnic?"

Matt stared at his plate a long moment. How was it that children could always ask the wrong questions at the wrong time? "I'm not sure if Miss Shelby will still be here for the picnic, Cassidy. She has an important job she has to go back to." Shelby shot him a glance filled with fire, her expression dark and challenging.

"I have no immediate plans to leave."

Matt stifled a grin. His gibe had hit a nerve. "Aren't you anxious to get back to the big city?" He still wasn't convinced that she would hang around for the six weeks she had mentioned. He was prepared to wake up one day and find her gone. No explanation, no goodbye.

Shelby raised her chin. "Actually, I'm finding my time here very relaxing."

"That's news to me," Gramma muttered with a frown.

"Well, can she?" Cassidy asked again.

"Can she what?" Matt had forgotten the question.

"Can she come to Gramma and Grandpa's party?"

Matt watched as defiance bloomed in Shelby's eyes and smiled inwardly. She'd want to come to the picnic now simply because he didn't want her to. That was the Shelby he remembered.

Kenny spoke up. "Daddy, can Chester come to Gramma and Grandpa's picnic? He likes to chase the ducks."

Matt stabbed at his food. "I don't know. We'll see."

"Is this the anniversary picnic?" Shelby looked at Matt and smiled. "I saw your dad yesterday. He invited me."

Touché. She'd outmaneuvered him. To refuse an invitation now would be rude. "You're welcome to come. The seventeenth, right after church. Shiloh Lake."

Shelby smiled. "I'll be there." She stood and carried her plate from the room.

Matt followed, stopping beside her at the kitchen sink. "You want to tell me what that was all about?" She didn't look at him.

"I love your parents. I wouldn't miss a celebration in their honor."

"That's not what I meant and you know it."

She turned and smiled. "Oh?"

Matt crossed his arms over his chest. "Suddenly you find our small town relaxing and you might stay on? Ellen seemed surprised by that."

"I don't have a specific date to go back." She shrugged, reaching across him for another plate. "And I am starting to relax. I ran into an old friend yesterday, and I'm looking forward to spending time with her."

He caught a whiff of her perfume and stepped away. "Why are you really here, Shelby?"

She tossed the dishrag into the sink. "I told you. I'm here to rest and visit my grandmother."

"No." Matt shook his head. "There's something more to it."

Ellen breezed into the kitchen clicking her tongue. "I'll handle those dishes. Go outside and enjoy this beautiful day."

Matt turned and placed a kiss on Ellen's cheek. "It was delicious as usual. Thank you."

"I love having you. I also love cleaning up my own kitchen. Now scoot."

"We need to be leaving anyway. My mom is having a birthday party for my uncle Hank this afternoon and we still have to pick up a present."

Ellen glanced over her shoulder. "Tell the judge happy birthday for me."

"Will do. I'll see you tomorrow, Ellen, when I pick up the kids."

Shelby rested her head against the chain supporting the front-porch swing. The gentle swaying motion soothed her troubled thoughts. Once again she was forced to adjust her assumptions about Matt. He wasn't a handyman; he taught college students. The battered van wasn't his job; it was his ministry. What gnawed at her most was his pointed question on why she was really here. Maybe she should tell him she was on medical leave and be done with it. But what if he refused to let him watch the kids? What if he wouldn't even talk to her anymore? The thought saddened her. For all her intent to avoid him, now that they had reunited she didn't want it to end again.

The front door creaked as Ellen stepped out onto the

front porch. "Well, it's good to see you relaxing without all those electronic gadgets in your hands." She eased down into the wicker rocker facing the swing. "What are you going to do the rest of the afternoon?"

"I don't know. I'm feeling lost. I don't know what to do with myself. For the first time in fifteen years, I have no direction. I have nothing to keep me busy."

"Well." Gramma chuckled softly. "If it's keeping busy that you want, there's plenty to do around here. I have a garden out back you could work in. Or you could volunteer to help with Matt's ministry."

Shelby smiled and shook her head. "I'm not handy with tools."

Gramma raised her eyebrows. "Your hand fits a rake, doesn't it? Not all the work they do is repairs." She stood and started back inside. "You can come help me with my scrapbook. All the things you need are right there on my desk in the corner of the living room."

"Thanks, Gramma, but I'll find something to do." Her gaze traveled to Matt's house. She'd better find it fast. She would not spend all her spare time thinking about Matt Durrant.

Chapter Six

Strange how one phone call could change so many people's lives. Gramma had only been gone an hour, but already the house felt sad and empty. Gramma's sister, Aunt Naomi, had fallen and broken her hip and her family had asked Gramma to come and stay with her during her recovery. After a hectic couple hours of packing and rearranging Ellen's various responsibilities, she'd left for Baton Rouge.

Gramma's absence not only left Shelby in charge of babysitting Cassidy and Kenny; it had opened up a new issue. Her health. She had to tell Matt the truth. She couldn't keep this from him now. He was already worried about his kids being hurt by her leaving. If something happened to her while she was watching the children, she'd put them at risk. She wasn't looking forward to breaking all this bad news to Matt when he got home. Once he knew about her heart problems, he would probably end her relationship with his kids. She hated to face that, but better now than when she'd totally lost her heart to them. She couldn't really fault him for wanting to spare his kids further trauma. But her own heart would be wounded in the process.

The afternoon loomed ahead, long and empty. She'd considered texting Matt about the change in babysitting arrangements, but she decided this kind of news was best done in person. The children would be home in a couple hours, so she'd take care of them and explain it to Matt when he got home. In the meantime, she had to do something to keep busy. The thought of telling Matt about Gramma leaving and her heart condition was making her anxious.

Shelby wandered through the hall into the living room. There was no sense trying to work; things at *Tween Scene* were still in limbo. She'd already gone walking with Pam early this morning and discovered that having a friend to talk to made exercising more enjoyable than she'd ever imagined. But what did she do now?

Her gaze fell on the table in the far corner. As she drew closer she saw that it was Gramma's scrapbooking project. The large book was filled with family photos, each page decorated with colorful papers and tiny ornaments. Beside the book was a clear plastic box. Shelby opened the lid to examine the contents. It was filled with all the things she would need. Paper, scissors and tiny decorations. The creative pages reminded her of the yearbook and the amateur magazines she'd made in school. She'd been skeptical when Gramma had suggested working on the scrapbook, but it might be fun. It might help her remember why she wanted to be involved with magazines in the first place.

The afternoon went surprisingly fast. It wasn't until the clock struck the hour that Shelby realized it was time for Cassidy and Kenny to get home from school. Dabbing a bead of glue on a small ribbon, she carefully laid it on the corner of a photo as the bus pulled up at the end of the drive.

Shelby's anxiety about talking to Matt disappeared in the enjoyment of being with the children. They'd had plans to walk the trails today, but a sudden rain shower had squashed that idea. Cassidy had suggested baking cupcakes and Kenny had embraced the idea, digging out all the sprinkles, colored sugar and anything else he could find to put on top of them. The result was a messy kitchen and breakfast table crammed full of goodies. Cassidy was pulling a freshly baked pan of cupcakes from the oven when Matt walked in the door.

"Hey, Dad. We're making cupcakes for dessert."

Matt set his briefcase and other items on the desk, glancing around the room. He was smiling, and Shelby took that as a good sign.

"So are cupcakes the main course tonight?" He glanced over at her.

"No. We pulled out one of the casseroles Laura left. I hope that's okay."

"Fine. How did it go today?"

"Good. I really enjoy watching them, Matt. They make it fun and easy." No sense postponing the news. "But we need to talk." She moved to the far end of the kitchen.

A deep troubled frown appeared on Matt's forehead as he joined her. "Something wrong with the kids?"

She quickly reassured him. "No. nothing like that. It's Ellen. She had to leave town suddenly. My great-aunt broke her hip and Gramma went to Baton Rouge to take care of her."

"I'm sorry to hear that. How long will she be gone?"

"A couple weeks, I'm afraid. Which brings me to the babysitting situation." It was clear from the expression on his face that it had sunk in. She would be the sitter from here on out.

He slipped his hands into his pockets. "I see. So what do we do?"

"Matt, I like being here for the children after school. We get along well together, and I'm perfectly willing to continue watching them. If you're all right with it."

Matt looked over at his children, who were busy decorating the cupcakes. Giggles and teasing conversation filled the air. She watched as his troubled expression slowly changed into affection. "Okay. But I have to be able to depend on you being here every day."

She tried not to be offended by his words. She understood how deeply he loved his children and how much he worried. "You can. But there's one more thing I need to make you aware of. Can we step outside?"

Matt frowned. "Okay. Let's go out to the front porch." He turned and faced her as soon as the door closed. "What's this about?"

"You've asked me why I came back to Dover. I came to stay with my grandmother because I'm on medical leave." She saw Matt tense, his eyes darkening. "I had a very mild heart attack caused by stress. Nothing serious, but it was a wake-up call. I was ordered to change my lifestyle and rest or the next time could be serious."

Matt's jaw flexed rapidly. "So you're saying you could have a fatal heart attack at any time?"

"No. There's nothing wrong with my heart. But I

do have to make changes, take better care of myself. I have a family history of heart disease. I wasn't going to tell you since Gramma was doing the babysitting, but knowing how you feel, and what your children have been through, I thought I should tell you."

The muscle in his jaw flexed rapidly again. "I don't know what to say. This changes everything."

"It doesn't have to. My condition is treatable and stable. I'm on medications, and I'm following the doctor's orders."

"And what happens if you have a heart attack while you're with my kids?"

Shelby clasped her hands together, trying to stay calm. "The likelihood is remote. But that's why I told you. I'll be happy to keep watching the kids until you can find someone else. But I'm perfectly capable of caring for them. And I want to. I really like them, Matt. I wouldn't let anything happen to them."

"What if you can't help it?" Matt paced off, running a hand through his hair. "No. This won't work. I'll find someone else."

Her worst fear had come true. "I'm sorry. But I couldn't continue babysitting and not let you know." She moved to the door. "Let me know how you want to handle this. I'll be here tomorrow unless you've made other arrangements."

Matt crossed his arms over his chest and nodded. The grim set to his jaw told her he was struggling with the news. There was nothing left to say. After a quick goodbye to the kids, Shelby went home, relieved that there'd been no confrontation, no angry words. But her news had shifted their relationship and she could only pray that Matt would let her continue to watch Cassidy and

Kenny until he found someone else. She hadn't realized how much a part of her life they'd become until now.

Matt went through the evening routine in a daze. Shelby was sick. A woman standing at the edge of death. This couldn't be happening again. He'd been concerned about Shelby walking out on his kids, now he had to worry about her dying. His mind flooded with memories of helplessness, pain and wrenching loss. He wouldn't survive it a second time. As soon as the kids were settled he would call his dad. He needed advice.

It was nearly two hours later before Matt had a chance to call his dad. He paced the kitchen, waiting for him to answer.

"Hey, son. What's going on?"

Matt took a deep breath. He was sure his dad would agree with him that he could not let Shelby watch his kids. "Remember when you said you thought Shelby looked tired? Well, turns out she's not back in Dover just to visit Ellen. She's on medical leave. She's had a heart attack and was sent here to rest up."

"What? But she's so young."

Matt paced the room. "She said it was brought on by stress."

"Well, that would make sense, given her line of work. So how serious is this? Has she had surgery or anything like that?"

"No. Nothing like that. She said it was a very mild one and she was told to rest and change her lifestyle. But, Dad, she's watching my children every day. She's alone here with them. What if something happens?"

"Then your mom and I are right here to step in. But

I think you might be worrying for nothing. From what you're telling me, her condition doesn't sound serious."

How could his dad say that? "She's had a heart attack. That sounds serious to me."

"Don't anticipate trouble before it happens. There are all levels of heart disease, and most are manageable. But if you're so concerned, you could get someone else to watch them."

"That's the problem. There isn't anyone at the moment."

"Then why not let things go on for the time being? I know your mom is busy with her campaign and I'm at the store all day, but we're still only a few blocks away. Tell Shelby to call us if she has any problems. Have a little faith, son. Relax and take it one day at a time."

Matt hung up the phone, his thoughts swirling like a hurricane. His father had always given him sound advice, but he wasn't sure he could follow it this time. How did he take things one day at a time when each day held the potential for disaster?

By Thursday afternoon, Shelby had renewed hope that things between her and Matt were going to work out. He'd questioned her about her condition, wanting assurances that she wasn't going to suffer another attack unexpectedly. She promised him she would call one of his parents the moment she experienced any symptoms. He had finally agreed to let the situation stand. In the meantime, he would continue to look for another babysitter.

It was more than she'd hoped for. Apparently he'd come to terms with things because he'd come home in a good mood the last few nights. He'd even asked her to stay for supper again. He'd fired up the grill and the grilled chicken had been too good to resist.

Today the children had opted to stay with her at Gramma's house. After releasing Chester from his cage, they'd gathered on the porch to discuss the day.

"I painted pictures at school and the teacher put them up on the wall."

"That's wonderful, Kenny. What did you draw?"

He stooped down and hugged his furry dog. "Chester. He's my best friend."

"What about you, Cass? Anything exciting at school today?"

The girl shrugged. "Molly got some new nail polish. It was yellow. Way cool. My teacher Miss Jenkins is getting married and she said we could all come to the wedding."

"How nice of her. When is the wedding?"

"Not till next summer. But we had to do collages about things we like, so some of us added wedding dresses to them. Did you ever do a collage?"

"I did. In fact, putting a magazine together is a lot like that. I'm working on my gramma's scrapbook and it's not too different. I'd love to see what you've done. Did you bring it home?"

"No. It's for the open house tonight."

"What open house? At school?"

"Yes. I brought the paper home for Dad to look at."

"Are you sure he saw it? Because I don't recall him saying anything about an open house. What time does it start?"

"Six thirty. But it goes for an hour or so."

"Honey, he doesn't even get home until that time."

Cassidy grew edgy. "I know I told him. Everybody's

parents are going to be there. It's like a huge deal." She
scooted off the swing and darted inside, returning a few
moments later with a wrinkled paper in her hand and a
worried expression on her face. "I forgot to give this to
him. Now he won't be there and I won't have a parent
to show up." Tears welled up in her blue eyes.

Shelby motioned for her to sit beside her, taking the
paper and scanning the information. Unless he could
get off work early, there was no way he could get home
and to the school in time. "Kenny, do you have an open
house tonight, too?"

He nodded. "Did you tell your daddy?"

He shrugged. "I don't know."

Cassidy was weeping now. "I wanted him to see my
collage and talk to my teacher. I'll be the only one there
without a parent."

"Now, don't worry. We'll get it all sorted out. I'll
text your father, and we'll see what we can work out."
A few minutes later her cell rang and she took the call,
walking to the far end of the porch so she could talk pri-
vately. "Matt? I'm sorry to bother you, but I just found
out about this a few minutes ago."

"Why didn't she tell me sooner?"

Frustration was evident in his tone. "Is there any way
you can leave early?"

"No. Not today. In fact I might be a few minutes late.
I have a meeting with a student after classes."

There was an obvious solution, but Shelby was reluctant to suggest it. One glance at Cassidy's sad face
made up her mind. "Matt, why don't I take the children to the school and you can come directly there as
soon as you can? That way they'll feel better knowing
you're on your way and I can stand in as the—" She

didn't want to use the word *parent*. "The adult representative in the meantime."

The long silence on the other end of the phone spiked her anxiety. "All right. But are you sure you want to do this? It's a big imposition."

"No, it's not. I'm curious to see the things the kids talk about every day. It'll be fun. As soon as you get there I'll leave. I don't want to see them disappointed."

"Neither do I. Okay, I'll get there as soon as I can. And, Shelby, thanks. This'll mean a lot to the kids. And I appreciate it, too."

Cassidy and Kenny warmed to the idea and quickly helped get ready. After a quick meal and a change of clothes, they arrived at school with plenty of time. Shelby followed Kenny to his room first, admiring his artwork. She'd have recognized Chester anywhere. The little boy had captured him perfectly, scruffy tail and all.

She met his teacher and explained that his father was coming later and he'd probably want to speak with her. Cassidy was fairly jumping out of her skin to get to her room. Once there she darted off, then came back with two girls in tow.

"Miss Shelby, this is Molly and this is Darcy, my two BFFs." She turned and pointed to Shelby. "And this is my babysitter, Miss Shelby. She's the editor of *Tween Scene* magazine."

Squeals of appreciation and excited comments swirled around her. "I'm glad you enjoy the magazine, girls." She allowed the conversation to continue a few moments, then touched Cassidy's arm gently. "I want to see your collage, and then I'd like to meet your teacher. I want to tell her that your father will be here shortly."

Cassidy's collage was impressive. Shelby found herself swelling with pride at the young girl's ability. She was beginning to understand better Matt's fierce protective instincts. With a heart this full of love, how could you not strive to make your children's life the best they could be? She glanced around the room at the parents, noticing the pride and joy in their expressions as they examined the accomplishments on display. Even Kenny was smiling at the things he saw.

She'd always felt tremendous pride in her work and in the magazine she produced. But none of her achievements had made her feel one-tenth as satisfied as seeing what these two children had done. It was something she was going to have to think about going forward. There might be something more important than *Tween Scene* and her career.

Matt took the steps to the second floor of Dover Elementary School two at a time. He only had a half hour to visit both his children's rooms, admire their projects and meet their teachers. He'd have a nice long talk with Cassidy later about making sure notices from school were given to him.

He stepped inside room 208, his gaze searching for his daughter. He found her standing beside Shelby, talking with a young woman he recognized as Cassidy's teacher, Miss Jenkins. He started forward, noticing how his daughter leaned close to Shelby, glancing up at her with a smile. Shelby smiled back, laying an arm across the girl's shoulders affectionately. His heart tightened in his chest. For the first time since Shelby had started watching his kids, he realized that she genuinely liked them and truly had their best interests at heart.

He also realized what his children were missing without a woman in the home. The sight of his daughter and Shelby brought a warmth into his heart. Kenny sidled up to Shelby and smiled up at her. She ruffled his hair and pulled him close.

Mesmerized, Matt move forward, catching the tail end of the conversation.

"I'm so glad to meet you, Mrs. Durrant."

"Oh, no, I'm Shelby Russell. I watch the children after school. I'm their neighbor. Mr. Durrant—"

"Is sorry to be late."

"Daddy!" Kenny raced toward him, hugging his waist.

Matt spoke with the teacher, then followed Cassidy to her display. Kenny was impatient to get back down to his room. There was barely time to view his pictures before the event was concluded.

Outside in the parking lot, they walked Shelby to her car and said goodbye with hugs and fervent thank-yous.

Matt pointed to his SUV, which was only a few cars down the row. "Go get buckled in. I'll be right there." He turned to Shelby, searching for the right words. "I can't thank you enough for stepping in at the last moment."

"I was glad I could fill in until you got here. It was important to them that you attend."

"But I couldn't have if I'd had to come home and get them first. I appreciate what you did. I'd forgotten how nice it was to know someone has your back. To pick up the slack. It's hard to be everything to them all the time."

"You're doing a great job, Matt. Don't ever question that."

He looked into her beautiful brown eyes and felt something deep inside shift. She'd always had his back, except once. "Thanks again. I'd better go. I'll see you tomorrow evening." Matt strolled over to his car. Shelby was good with his children, and they were happy under her care. But was it wise to let them care for someone who was battling a heart condition?

"Piz-za! Piz-za!" Cassidy and Kenny chanted loudly.

"Please can we have pizza for supper?" Cassidy begged. "I want to go to Angelo's."

Shelby laughed and held up a hand to silence the girl. "I think it's a great idea, but we need to wait for your father to get home and see what he has to say." After the open house, she'd grown even closer to the children. Matt had been more pleasant, too, inviting her to share the evening meal each day. She'd gladly accepted, but she knew she had to back off some. It wasn't a good idea to become too entangled with their lives.

"Daddy will say yes," Kenny announced confidently. "He loves pizza."

"All right. But in the meantime, homework for you, missy. Kenny, you have some chores, remember?"

Shelby watched them scurry off, her heart filled with affection. She grew to love them more each day. But always in the back of her mind lay the knowledge that sooner or later she'd have to leave them, and Dover, behind. She would miss them and she believed they would miss her, too. A shroud of deep sadness settled heavily upon her spirit. "Lord, why have you put me here? Nothing good can come of this. A lot of hearts will be broken. Including mine."

Shelby went to the small table in the corner of Matt's

living room, where she'd set up her scrapbooking supplies. The children were more comfortable in their own home, so she'd started bringing her scrapbooking supplies with her to work on in the afternoons. It helped to keep her mind off the fact that she was spending so much time in Matt's home. It was hard to maintain emotional distance when she was surrounded by his presence at every point. After all, she had to protect her heart, too. She was living a fantasy, seeing how her life might have gone had she made different choices. She'd come to realize the most exhilarating moment of her career was nothing compared to the joy and satisfaction she experienced with these children.

Cassidy appeared beside the table, a smile on her sweet face. But they weren't her children. Never would be. "Hi, sweetie. Homework all done?"

"Almost." She sat down in the chair and rested her elbows on the table. "Is that Miss Ellen's scrapbook?"

"It is." Shelby pivoted the large book so she could see the page better. Cassidy had never shown any interest in the book before. "I'm about finished with this page. This is my aunt and uncle, and that's my mother there."

Cassidy leaned closer for a better look. "Cool. Why did you put a seashell on the page?"

Shelby smiled at the memory. Her last happy one before her father left. "My whole family went to the beach that summer. We stayed in this big hotel for a week and swam every day. In the evenings we'd go out to eat, then play miniature golf or go to the amusement park."

"Could I do a scrapbook?"

What had prompted this sudden interest? "Sure. It's easy."

"Could we do one about my mom?"

Shelby froze, her heart contracting into a tight ball. "I think that would be a great idea. Kenny could help, too."

Cassidy nodded. "My dad's birthday is coming up. We could give it to him then."

Shelby smiled and gave the girl a hug. Cassidy had such a sweet, loving heart. "As soon as you finish your homework, we'll run into town and pick up a book." Cassidy's thoughtfulness brought tears to her eyes. Matt's children were so delightful. What a joy it would be to watch them grow up.

Cassidy pulled the last piece of clear plastic from the new scrapbook as Kenny charged into the room. Shelby had taken the children into town and selected a large scrapbook for them to work on. Each child had picked up a few trinkets and colorful paper to decorate the pages. Cassidy had chosen a sheet filled with hydrangeas because she said it was her mother's favorite flower. Kenny found a piece with books on it because he remembered how his mother would read to him. Shelby had been deeply moved by their sweet memories.

"Daddy's home." Kenny spun on his heel and headed toward the front door.

"He'll see our surprise." Cassidy's eyes filled with worry.

Shelby motioned her away. "You go. I'll hide this with my stuff and take it with me for the weekend. I'll bring it back on Monday." Quickly she gathered up her scrapbooking paraphernalia, meeting Matt in the foyer as he entered. Kenny hugged his daddy's hand. "Can we go get pizza?"

"I guess." Matt smiled, resting a hand on his son's head. "Go get ready."

She looked at Matt. "They've been begging for it all day."

"How did it go?" he asked as the kids drifted off.

"Good. Cassidy's homework is done. Kenny brought home an invitation to Andrew's birthday party tomorrow. I think it might have been in his backpack for a few days. I'll have to do a better job of looking in there."

"I'm not sure that would be safe."

She chuckled and nodded. "Other than that, I think all is well." She shrugged and shifted her cumbersome books and the small plastic box with photos and decorations.

"Can I help you with that?"

She shook her head. "It's not heavy. So, I'll see you on Monday. Unless you've found someone else?" He stared at her a moment, making her feel uneasy.

"No. Not yet." He slipped his hands into his pockets. "Thanks for all you did this week. It means a lot to me that I don't have to worry about the kids while I'm at work. I know they're in good hands."

"I'm glad. I'm enjoying their company. I really care about them, Matt."

"I know you do. I can see that."

"Daddy, we're ready," Cassidy called, hurrying into the room, Kenny on her heels.

"Okay, okay." He smiled and held his hands up in defeat. "Give me a chance to change my clothes." He turned to her. "Thanks, Shelby."

"You're welcome."

Matt opened the door for her, but before she could move, Kenny spoke up. "I want Miss Shelby to come for pizza with us."

Cassidy nodded. "She has to come, Dad." She clasped her hands together dramatically. "Can she, Dad, huh? Please? She doesn't have anything to eat at her house."

Shelby cringed. That would teach her to confide too much in the children. "Oh, no, there's plenty of food. Just nothing I like." A hot flush filled her cheeks. Great. If that wasn't a weak refusal. He'd think she was angling to accept.

Matt met her gaze, a small smile on his lips. "I think that's a good idea. She's worked hard this week and saved the day at the open house. She deserves some Angelo's World Famous Pizza."

Shelby didn't know how to respond. Did he really want her to join them? He had been more pleasant the past few days. He'd even started calling in the afternoons to check on things, listening intently as she told him about the cute and funny things the children would do and say.

The tension between them had eased considerably. Some of their old friendship was starting to return. A result of the truce, no doubt. He'd agreed to the truce for the sake of the children. He would do anything for them, even be nice to her. But inviting her out in public, to a restaurant, was something entirely different. She looked down at the children's hopeful expressions. She would do it for their sake.

"Uh. Sure. I'd like that. I'll be right back."

Cassidy and Kenny cheered and jumped up and down. Matt glanced at his watch. "We'll leave in ten minutes."

She nodded, still questioning the wisdom of spending an evening with Matt and his children in what amounted to a family outing. She was playing with fire. How could she maintain her safe distance if they started behaving like a real family?

sas quoted in a magazine article. "She was growing up." He wished he could maintain a bit of that distance between them once again.

Chapter Seven

Matt quickly changed into jeans and a polo shirt, wondering what demented impulse had prompted him to include Shelby in the pizza trip. The last thing he wanted was to draw her even deeper into his family circle. He had a feeling it was already too late. He felt her presence in his home and in the lives of his children every night, long after she'd crossed the driveway and gone home. He just wasn't sure how he felt about that yet.

Outside on the front porch, Matt locked the door, then glanced up to find the object of his thoughts coming across the driveway. His heart stopped. She was so lovely. Her hair was down from its usual ponytail, swaying against the side of her neck with each step. Her eyes were bright with affection as she smiled at his son and daughter.

Cassidy bounded from the porch and greeted Shelby with a hug. "I'm so glad you're coming, too."

Shelby glanced over at him, and he returned her smile. He was probably worrying about nothing. She was doing a great job with the kids. She was dependable and caring. He'd stopped worrying that she'd disappear. And she'd reassured him repeatedly that she was doing all she could to take care of herself. And he liked the idea of having someone along this evening to talk to. An adult to converse with. A nice change from the chatter of his son and daughter.

Kenny grabbed her hand, claiming her attention. "I like the dessert pizza best."

As they started toward the car, Cassidy proposed a different plan.

"Dad, can we walk to town?"

His daughter's simple request caught him off guard. He looked at Shelby. It was a nice evening. Warm with a slight breeze, the perfect night for a walk into town. But was he ready to spend time walking so closely with Shelby? "I don't know, Cassidy. Maybe Miss Shelby isn't up to the long walk." He cringed inwardly. He'd made it sound like she was an invalid, or worse, that he didn't want her along.

"I'd welcome the walk. It's a lovely evening." Shelby smiled, a twinkle in her eye. "I don't mind if it's all right with you."

He shrugged and placed a hand on his son's shoulder. "Son, never argue when two females have spoken."

"Huh? What does that mean?"

"It means we're walking to town for pizza." He slipped his car keys back into his pocket and started toward the sidewalk. He tried to take a position beside his son as they walked, but the boy skipped ahead to be with his sister. That left him to fall in beside Shelby. He tensed, acutely aware of her at his side. It felt familiar, as natural as breathing. Memories from the past started to bloom, but he plucked them out like weeds. The past was over. It was the present he had to focus on. They'd walked nearly a block before she broke the silence.

"It's a lovely evening."

"Yes. It is."

"Thank you for inviting me. I know you'd rather have the kids to yourself tonight."

He glanced over at her, surprised at her perception. He had been looking forward to some close family time. "I'll have them all weekend. Besides, they like you. They wanted you to come, and you deserve a treat." He thought about Shelby living in that big old house alone. She must miss her grandmother. "Sorry Ellen had to leave town. I know you came home to spend time with her. Instead you're taking care of two ornery kids."

She smiled over at him. "She'll be home soon. My great-aunt is improving rapidly."

"Will you have time with her before you have to go back to New York?"

"We'll have time."

The tone in Shelby's voice made him look at her. She was staring straight ahead, making it hard to interpret her meaning. She never mentioned returning to New York. Odd given her devotion to her career. Was there something else keeping her in Dover besides her health and spending time with Ellen?

They walked in silence again, letting the children chatter up ahead. When they neared the edge of town, they stopped to wait for the traffic signal.

"I can't believe all the changes here since I left." Shelby smiled at him. "In many ways it's exactly as I remember. But in others, it's very different."

His heart skipped a beat. He focused on crossing the street and not the way her smile warmed his whole being. "It's grown a lot in the last ten years. The new auto plant brought in new business and new residents. It's been a good for Dover, and the people have developed a new attitude toward the history of the town. There were a lot of people who hated our old buildings and old houses. But now they've embraced it. The state film commission has really marketed Dover to the movie industry."

"I know. *Magnolia Days*." She bounced slightly in delight. "I saw that movie three times. I was thrilled when I learned it was being shot on location here. It made me proud and a little homesick. I always thought this was one of the most charming towns in the whole state. No one has a town square as lovely as ours."

Matt wasn't sure he'd heard her right. "I thought you hated this place."

Shelby shot him a sheepish grin. "I thought I did, too."

"What changed your mind?"

She made a sweeping gesture with her hand. "I used to look at all those old buildings as walls trapping me in this backward place, preventing me from seeing the world beyond the old crumbling bricks."

"And now?"

She smiled and brushed her hair off her face. "Now I feel like it's a fence, keeping me safe. Like old friends giving me a warm hug each time I look at them."

His heart jumped in his chest. Was it possible she might actually consider staying? That was too outlandish a notion to even consider.

Shelby clasped her hands behind her back as they walked across the square. "I dreaded coming back. I expected to remember all the things I disliked about it.

But since I've been here, it's the good memories that are resurfacing." She smiled over at him, lifting her shoulders in a slight shrug. "It actually feels good, comfortable, to be here again. I was sure I'd feel lost after the pace of the big city, but this feels like home."

Matt forced his gaze forward and ignored the flutter in his chest that seemed to quicken whenever Shelby smiled at him. "I know what you mean. It was a big adjustment moving back after living in Atlanta, but I don't regret it. It's a good town, though we have our share of small minds and busybodies."

Shelby chuckled. "I've run into a few of them. The ones who can't understand why I left, and the ones who don't understand why I came back."

"I guess we never understand the decisions of others." He sensed Shelby stiffen.

"Probably not."

Did they understand each other? Things had been different between them since they'd declared their truce. Their relationship was less tense, more comfortable and friendly. He had to admit his resentment had eased. Even the wound of her rejection was healing over. The concern about her eventual departure and her health issues, however, remained. He was still sorting out his feelings about that.

Matt refilled his drink cup and turned around, catching sight of Shelby and his children huddled at the table, laughing. They looked like a family. He was the only one missing from the picture. When he sat down, anyone who glanced their way would assume they were a family. The idea sent a fist of pain into his gut. But they weren't. Shelby could never be part of the picture. His life was here. Hers was a thousand miles away. Something deep in his chest stirred, leaving him uneasy. He tried to shake off the feeling as he returned to the table, grateful for once that his daughter talked nonstop.

Kenny bit off a large hunk of pizza. "Can we play the games?"

Matt frowned. "Don't talk with your mouth full." He handed each child a few dollars. One of the things that made Angelo's so successful was the area in the back filled with an assortment of video and arcade games. The room was well supervised, and there was only one way in or out of the pizza parlor, so he didn't have to worry about their safety.

Matt watched his son and daughter dash off, only too aware that for the next half hour or so he and Shelby would be forced to converse alone. His earlier comment about understanding another's position had been replaying in his mind. He'd learned long ago to look for the positive in any situation, no matter how bad. He'd also learned that God really did make all things work for good.

He gathered his thoughts. "I owe you a debt of gratitude."

Shelby looked at him, a puzzled expression on her face. "It's not necessary. I enjoy watching the children and it helps fill up my days."

Matt shook his head. "I don't mean that. I mean—" He glanced out the window, gauging his words. "Leaving the way you did taught me a lot."

Shelby stared down at her glass, her fingers tracing lines in the condensation. "I'm sorry."

He was saying this all wrong. "No. You taught me things while we were together." He hesitated again. "I'll admit my attitude when I went back to college was to prove that I wasn't small-town."

"Matt—"

"I came to see that you'd shown me how to think outside the box. I guess your creativity rubbed off on me. It was probably the reason for my success as a businessman." He shrugged. "In an odd way, I owe a lot to you."

"I don't know what to say to that."

Matt wiped his palm across his jaw. "That didn't come out right." He turned to face her. "I guess what I'm trying to tell you is that God took my anger and resentment toward you and used it to make me a better businessman." He sighed. "I'm sorry if that came out as a backhanded compliment."

"No. I understand." A small smile moved her lips. "I was angry and resentful, too. I was determined to excel in school and go to work for a prestigious magazine the minute I graduated. And I did. The difference was, I didn't ask God for any help. I was sure I could do it all on my own. Until recently."

"What changed?"

Shelby looked away. "I hadn't counted on the stress factor."

Matt glanced down at her plate and the barely touched slice of vegetarian pizza. The heart thing. Her job must have been more hectic than he'd suspected. "Do you miss it? Your work?"

She shrugged, toying with her napkin. "Not as much as I'd expected to. To be honest, I don't know if I'll even have a job to go back to. The publisher I work for was bought out. No one knows yet exactly what that will mean for our futures, but probably layoffs and eliminations of most of our publications."

"I'm sorry, Shelby. That's tough." Matt's heart went out to her even as another piece of the puzzle fell into place. Shelby was staying here because she was out of work.

"My whole adult life has been focused on this job. Now it might all be gone."

"I get that. I loved my job, the company I built. But it took all my time and energy and there wasn't a lot left over for my family. I didn't want to sell, but neither did I want to ignore my kids. In the end, I'm much happier here in this new job than I ever would have imagined. Maybe you need to look in a new direction, too."

"That's what Gramma keeps telling me. Actually, I've been thinking about starting an online magazine. Something aimed at girls like Cassidy, only with a Christian focus."

Her idea surprised him. He'd seen a change in her on the outside, perhaps the bigger change was on the inside. Their situation, however, hadn't changed. Whether because of health or career, she would leave Dover sooner or later. "So, you'll be going back?"

"That's where all the publishers are." She stared out the window for a while then looked down at her plate.

Her tone lacked the conviction he'd heard in it previously. Was she changing her mind? Only a short time ago she'd admitted she felt at home here in Dover. Matt wondered if perhaps Shelby wasn't certain herself.

As the silence dragged on, Matt searched for a topic of conversation that didn't involve their past. He realized there wasn't one. She was ingrained with his past the way she was becoming part of his present. He glanced over at her, his gaze locking with hers. Was he crazy or was that affection he glimpsed in her brown eyes? Affection for him. The thought shook him.

Cassidy and Kenny skidded to a stop at Matt's side, forestalling any further small talk. "Can we have more money for the games?"

He shook his head. "Time to go."

Kenny's shoulders sagged, and he tilted his head backward in protest. "Aw. But I don't want to." A stern look from his father abruptly ended the whiny attitude.

"Then could we stop at the Picture Box and get a movie? Please." Kenny clasped his fingers together like a little beggar.

Cassidy chimed in, "Please. It's Friday night. No school tomorrow."

Matt laid a tip on the table, then glanced at Shelby. She was smiling.

"Friday night movie night."

His mind snapped back to when he and Shelby were dating. Friday night was his night off and his brother's night to work in the store. It was the one night when he and Shelby could drive over to Sawyers Bend and catch a movie. They'd sit in the back, share a big bucket of popcorn and snuggle as close as the seat would allow.

"Miss Shelby could watch it with us, too."

The hopeful tone in his daughter's voice brought him back to the present. He started to kill the idea, then remembered she was alone in that big old house of Ellen's. "You're welcome to join us."

"Thank you, but I have some things to do at home. Maybe next time."

Was she telling the truth or was she remembering the past, as well, and not wanting to relive it?

Darkness was closing in quickly as they crossed the

street and strolled through the park toward the far end of town. Matt again questioned his impulse in asking Shelby along tonight. Being around her always left him with a strange longing deep in his gut and wondering if kids and job were enough and if being alone was going to be his future.

He shook off the pointless speculation. Shelby could never be part of his future. She was all about career, not family. Her health issues were an obstacle he could never overcome. He glanced over at her and she smiled, sending a pinprick of guilt into his heart. Okay, that wasn't completely fair. She'd stepped into his life as if she'd always been there. As if she belonged. He'd been worried about her ability to manage two active kids. At times they were more than he could handle. But Shelby had taken charge like she was born to it. What would their lives have been like if things had turned out differently? It didn't matter. There were no do-overs in life. But there were second chances. If a person was willing to brave the dangers.

Was he ready to brave the dangers of loving again? Of risking the loss of someone he loved? Never! Yet he couldn't deny the longing he had to be part of a family again, a complete family. He couldn't ignore the ache inside that cried out for a wife to share his hopes and dreams and those of his children.

Matt turned back to Shelby. His throat thickened at the affection for his children displayed in her soft brown eyes. She'd always had a heart overflowing with love. He'd forgotten that. He'd forgotten many of the good things about their relationship.

As they continued strolling toward the gazebo, the

lights flickered on, bathing the Victorian structure in a gentle light.

"Oh." Shelby exhaled softly. "I'd forgotten how beautiful it was."

Matt looked at the large ornate structure, then turned his gaze to Shelby. Her eyes were bright with happiness. Her brown hair was bathed in the glow from the light on the gazebo. The smile on her face was sweet and lovely and weakened his knees. He remembered a time when they had sat here late at night, talking about their future, holding each other. The memory was too real, too unexpected. Each moment he spent with her further weakened his barriers, and he couldn't afford to let that happen.

He was afraid it was too late.

Shelby let her gaze travel around the framework of the octagonal gazebo, memories resurfacing with each beat of her heart. Many times she'd come here alone to think when she didn't want to go home and face her mother's anger. Other times she'd come simply for the peace and quiet or to be with friends.

Her most cherished memories, however, centered around Matt. They'd often sit in here and talk about the life they would have together. As long as she could remember, she'd been marching toward college. Nothing and no one was going to get in her way. Until Matt. He'd taken her dreams to new levels, given her the courage to dream of things she'd never imagined before. He'd made her believe that together, they could do anything. It had all ended in a flash, leaving their love a pile of tiny shattered remnants.

They started forward again across the park and toward home. The walk home was quiet and thoughtful. Companionable. Shelby allowed herself to enjoy it while it lasted. What a mess. Everything was so complicated. Being near him again, caring for his children and getting involved with his daily life had only created turmoil in her own.

Each day she experienced an odd mixture of joy and despair when she entered Matt's home. The only things keeping her anchored were the comforting task of putting the scrapbook together and the steady resurfacing of her faith.

She had found another ray of sunshine in all of it. Thanks to Cassidy and Kenny, she'd discovered a nurturing side of herself she hadn't been aware of. She loved caring for them, and she liked being back home in Dover. But she relished putting the scrapbook together, as well. It brought back all the reasons she loved working for a magazine. She wasn't ready to give that up. Was it possible to have both? Did she even want both?

Yes. She did.

She glanced over at Matt. He was so close she could easily brush her hand against his arm. The thing that made it all so difficult was that she was still in love with him. She'd never stopped. But it was strictly one-sided, and that was all it would ever be. Even if he had feelings for her, there were too many barriers between them to take down. Her career and her past mistakes, but mostly her health. She couldn't expect him to take on that kind of uncertainty. It would be cruel.

Before she realized it they were home. The kids waved goodbye, and Matt walked with her to the door of Gramma's house. She turned to say good-night. Their eyes locked. For one fleeting moment, Shelby was eighteen again and seeing her future in a pair of navy blue eyes. She forced herself to think clearly. "Thank you for a lovely evening. I had a good time."

"Thank you for taking such good care of my son and daughter."

"You're welcome, but it's my pleasure." She braved another look into his eyes and saw the questions deep within, the lingering doubts. He was still wary of her health and of her return to New York. Two barriers that were too high to scale.

"Good night, Matt." Quickly she stepped back, digging her house key from her purse. Her shaky fingers refused to grasp it tightly, and it fell to the porch floor. She reached to pick it up at the same moment as Matt. The contact knocked her off balance.

"Whoa." Matt grabbed her shoulders to steady her, and she smiled up at him. The look in his eyes froze her breath in her lungs. Her hand rested against the solid wall of his chest. His breath caressed her cheek. Time ceased. It was summer. They were young and in love. Shelby closed her eyes, her senses remembering every detail from long ago. The scent of him. The warmth of him. The tenderness.

"Shelby."

Her name whispered on his lips drew her eyes open. The look she saw reflected in his deep blue eyes was familiar. He lowered his head, lips slightly parted. Shelby trembled and closed her eyes, her heart singing. And then reality reared its ugly head. She couldn't let this happen. If they let old feelings cloud their judgment, both of them would be hurt. She pushed back, struggling to inhale. "It's late."

Matt stiffened. "Yeah." He bent down and picked

up the key, handing it to her. He stared at her a moment, then walked down the steps and across the drive. It was over.

She'd never felt so alone in her whole life.

Chapter Eight

The knock came at the same instant Shelby touched the tip of the glue bottle to the back of the photograph. Letting out a puff of irritation, she quickly and carefully placed it on the page, trying to keep it centered.

Her new hobby had quickly become a passion and given her a special connection to Cassidy and Kenny as they worked on their scrapbook for their dad. The knock came again. Except of course when she was interrupted.

"I'm coming!" She scooted back her chair and trotted toward the front door, pulling it open. A surge of warm affection flowed through her when she recognized her visitor. "Laura Durrant."

"Hi, Shelby." The young woman opened her arms for a hug. "I'm so sorry it took me this long to come see you but I've been working over in Mobile."

Shelby held the hug an extra moment, basking in the warmth of her friendship. One of the joys of loving Matt had been the family that had come with him. Laura had been like the sister she'd never had.

"Come on in. I want to hear all about you." She led Laura to the sunroom, then brought iced tea and fruit to munch on. Once settled in they quickly covered the lost years.

"Okay," Shelby said a while later, after giving Laura a truncated version of her life story. "Enough about me. Tell me about you."

Laura accepted the refill on her glass of tea and picked up another apple slice. "Not much to tell."

"How did you end up running your own construction business? I thought you wanted to be an architect."

Laura stared at her glass a moment. "I did. I went to State, got my degree. Got a job in Houston. Met a guy and got married."

Shelby eyed her closely. From the tone of her voice there was much more to her story. "What happened?"

"He decided being married wasn't for him. He'd rather spend time with his buddies and enjoy a variety of lady friends." She shrugged. "Unlike you, I didn't adjust to big-city life very well. So I came home and bought this business from Mr. Olsen when he retired. We specialize in historic restoration projects."

"I've seen those trucks around town, but I had no idea they were yours. You must be doing really well."

Laura smiled. "So far, so good. LC Construction is never out of work."

"Why the LC?"

She grinned and shrugged. "Laura Claire Constructions sounded too girlie. The initials were more professional."

Shelby couldn't fault her logic. "I see what you mean."

"So, are you coming to Mom and Dad's party tomorrow after church?"

"Oh, I'd like to, but I don't want to intrude."

Laura emitted a short grunt. "Don't be silly. You won't be. Didn't Matt invite you? He was supposed to."

Shelby took a bite of her apple slice, avoiding her friend's gaze. "Not exactly. The kids did. I think he went along with it not to be rude."

"Well, I'm inviting you. I know Mom and Dad would love to have you come. They've asked about you several times."

Her heart warmed. She'd expected them to view her as the villain in her relationship with their son. "I saw your dad the other day. I'm surprised he even remembers me."

Laura peered at her closely. "They loved you, Shelby. They expected you to be their daughter-in-law. We were all shocked and saddened when you two broke up. Don't misunderstand." Laura leaned forward to emphasize her point. "We all loved Katie, but we loved you, too."

"And I loved all of you. Things just didn't work between us. It wasn't meant to be, I guess."

"Well, that's all in the past. So will you come to the picnic? You can hang out with me if you'd like. Ignore that bullheaded brother of mine. Shiloh Lake is a big place."

Laura had a point. "Okay. I'd love to come."

"Good. Well, I have to go." Laura stood and opened her arms for another hug. "Don't be a stranger. We can be friends no matter what your relationship with my brother, you know."

Laura's visit had lifted Shelby's spirits. She'd always assumed that since she'd jilted Matt, the rest of his family hated her. It was wonderful to find she'd been wrong. She'd loved his whole family and had looked forward to being part of it. Laura's history had surprised her.

She'd always assumed that other people's lives were perfect, that hers was the only one filled with trouble. But Matt had lost his wife. Laura had endured a failed marriage. Yet both had found new purpose and new focus in their lives. Even her friend Pam had managed to achieve her goals.

Being back in Dover was opening her eyes to a lot of things and giving her a new perspective about possibilities she'd never considered. What other paths in her life had she missed because she'd been focused on one way with no thought of the alternatives?

Maybe there was something beyond *Tween Scene*. Maybe the door closing on Harmon Publishing would open a new door someplace else. A job with less stress, with more time for a personal life. But she'd never know if she didn't try. A good place to start would be updating her résumé. She was well respected in the business; her reputation was good. Surely there were other companies who would welcome her job skills and experience.

With her determination renewed, she picked up her laptop and headed outside to the patio in the backyard. The weather was beautiful. She'd forgotten how sweet an autumn afternoon in Dover could feel. She'd work awhile then maybe she'd call Pam and see if she'd like to have lunch or go shopping.

After settling into the cushioned lounge chair she started to work, pulling up her résumé and then listing contacts that she could query. She'd been working for some time when she noticed the fan in her laptop was running unusually hard. The computer grew hot on her thighs. She lifted it to allow some airflow underneath. Her fingers brushed the underneath panel. It was hot. Too hot. The fan whined louder.

The heat increased, scalding her skin below her denim shorts. She screamed, shoving the computer to the ground as it burst into flames. Helpless, she watched as the flames crawled over the keyboard and up the screen. "Oh, no. No! Help!"

Someone appeared at her side, pulling her a safe distance from the small fire, which was now burning itself out.

"What happened?"

She shook her head, realizing Matt was at her side. "I don't know. I was working and it got hot. Then it burst into flames." Her laptop was now a blackened, charred mess.

"Are you all right?" He took her hands in his and inspected them. "No burns?"

She pulled them away and touched her thighs. They looked red but not burned. "No. But look at my laptop." She sighed and turned away from the smoking debris. "It's my own fault. I should have taken it back."

"What do you mean?"

"I got a recall notice about the faulty battery over a year ago. I never found time to take it in to be replaced."

"Do you have backup files?"

An inventory of her files scrolled across her mind. The lost information, personal and work related, could never be regained. "I back up all my files on a company system. I can probably access them when I get back." Unless of course there was no reason to go back. The files might be pointless soon.

"What about your personal information?"

She became aware of Matt's hand resting on her lower back, offering steady comfort. She focused on his question only to realize with a sinking heart that there were precious few personal items on her computer to worry about. No pictures to speak of that didn't involve work events, no pets, no real friends. Not even boring travel photos. Tears welled up again. What a sad, lonely life she had. She tried but couldn't stop the sobs that erupted from her chest. Matt held her closer, which didn't help at all.

"Shelby?"

The concern in his voice, the tenderness, was her undoing. She turned into his chest and let the tears fall. His arms enfolded her, chasing away the fear and giving her a safe place to fall.

He made soft soothing sounds, holding her tightly until she ran out of tears. She stepped back, swiping away the tears on her cheeks. "I'll be fine."

"Is there anything I can do?" He reached out and gently brushed her hair off her forehead.

She gestured toward the charred computer. "Can you fix it?"

Matt laughed out loud. "I don't think so. It's pretty much done for."

She frowned and rested her head against his shoulder.

"Come on over to the house. I want to take a look at that burn. You need something on that."

She started to protest, but it had started to sting. In fact it was becoming downright uncomfortable. Meekly she followed him across the drive and into his house. He set her down at the kitchen table, then went to retrieve the first aid supplies.

He stooped down in front of her, steadying her leg with one strong hand and applying the ointment with the other. The contact sent a different kind of quiver up her spine.

"This'll be sore for a few days. Keep the ointment on it and it should heal quickly."

Her gaze drifted to the crown of his head and the thick wavy hair. She could reach out and run her fingers through it with only a slight movement. If only... He stood, smiling down at her.

"I think you'll live. Are you feeling better?"

All she could manage was a nod.

"Sorry about the computer, Shelby, but I'm glad you weren't seriously hurt."

"Me, too. I never expected to be set on fire by my laptop."

Matt smiled, holding up his hand as if he'd just gotten an idea. "I know what will make you feel better."

He moved to the cupboard, pulled something out, then went to the microwave and placed it inside. In a few moments, the aroma of popcorn filled the kitchen. She had to smile. He remembered. It was their preferred snack. Popcorn and movies. When they couldn't go to the theater in Sawyers Bend, they would put in a DVD and watch it in the den at Matt's. She smiled over at him. He looked quite pleased with himself. "You're right. It will make me feel better."

She realized suddenly that the house was very quiet. "Where are Cassidy and Kenny?"

Matt took the bag of popped corn from the microwave and dumped it into a bowl. "Turns out that party Kenny had today was for Molly's little brother. They live up the street, so Cassidy went along to help play hostess. I have a rare day alone in my own house."

"Until you had to play rescuer."

"I'm glad I was here to help."

"Cassidy will make a great hostess."

He snickered and sat down. "You mean because she's so bossy?"

She had to chuckle. "True, but it's good she likes to take charge. She'll be a good leader someday."

"Well, we'll see. She's a challenge at times. I wonder if I'm doing the right things."

"You're a great dad, Matt."

Matt ran a hand down the back of his neck, a doubtful smile on his face. "I don't know about that. I'm afraid I'm getting into dangerous territory."

"What do you mean?"

"Cassidy." He shook his head. "She's changing before my eyes. Physically and emotionally she's becoming a young woman, and I'm finding it harder to connect with her. She really needs her mother now."

Shelby ached for him. "You'll do fine. And you have your mom here, and Laura. They'll help you."

Matt nodded. "They do, but I worry that she doesn't have someone around to guide her, someone she can confide in. I'd like to think she'd talk to me about girl things, but I know that's not realistic."

"I don't know if that's necessarily true." She took a bite of popcorn, reminding herself to go easy on the salty treat. "I had a friend who found it easier to talk to her dad than her mom. Have a little faith. It'll all work out." She reached over and laid her hand on his and felt him tense.

She pulled her hand away and prepared to go. "I've taken enough of your quiet time for today. I appreciate you coming to my aid. I guess I'd better go toss that computer in the trash."

Matt stood and walked her to the door. "Leave it. I'll pick it up after it's cooled down and take it to the recycling station."

"Thanks." His eyes locked on her again, and she wished she could know what he was thinking. Then again, maybe not.

Matt shoved his chair back from the computer desk and stood. He'd been staring at the same screen, the same sentences for ten minutes, unable to concentrate. For the first time in months he had quiet time to catch up on paperwork and he couldn't get thoughts of Shelby out of his mind. Her reaction to the computer fire nagged at him. She'd cried. He couldn't recall a time when he'd seen her break down that way. Granted, it had been a terrifying experience. But the Shelby he remembered would have fussed and fumed, given the offending device a swift kick and gone out and bought a new one. Instead she'd succumbed to tears and, even more surprising, allowed him to comfort her.

He'd never seen her so vulnerable. Was her heart issue the cause? He'd never stopped to consider it from her point of view. Suddenly faced with walking away from her career, forced to change her way of life, with the threat of another, more serious heart attack hanging over her. It couldn't have been easy, not to mention frightening.

Matt rubbed his jaw. Her reaction wasn't the only thing gnawing at his mind. He couldn't shake the very physical memory of holding her in his arms, cradled against his heart. The closeness still vibrated through him like lightning, bringing every molecule in his body to tingling life. He'd wanted to protect her, to shelter her from any harm.

He had to face the fact that he was losing his heart to Shelby all over again. And that was a very unwise thing to do. It wasn't simply his own feelings at stake but those of his children, too. And at the root of it all was the nagging question of why she'd walked out on him fifteen years ago. What had gone wrong? What had changed so suddenly?

One day they were engaged. The next she'd thrown the ring in his face. He'd been over it a thousand times in his head, trying to remember something he'd missed. All he remembered was that from the moment he'd met her, he'd known she was the one he wanted to spend his future with.

Meeting her had changed his life. He'd been filled with resentment and irritation over missing out on his sophomore year of college. His father had been seriously injured in an automobile accident and Matt had been needed to help run the store. Initially he'd been more than willing to do his part for the family. But one semester had stretched into two, and he'd grown more and more dissatisfied. Then his mom had hired Shelby to work for the summer and everything had changed. Until the night she'd walked away and left his heart bleeding. He'd never heard from her again.

Allowing himself to fall for her a second time would be insanity. He had to remember they were only friends and that she was doing him a favor. Reliving the past, allowing those old feelings to be rekindled, would only hurt them both. The past was best forgotten.

Shelby carried her mug out to the front porch the next morning and sat on the swing. For the first time since arriving in Dover, she wasn't obsessing over her future or Matt living next door. She took a sip of her coffee and smiled. It didn't taste so bad today. The house was empty without Gramma, but time alone was a good thing. She had a lot to think about, a lot of soul-searching to do. She and the Lord had come to terms last night. She'd released her stranglehold on her life and given it over to Him. During her reading, she'd been reminded that there was a time for everything, and at this point in her life, everything had been torn down and it was time to build it up again.

The gentle movement of the swing soothed her. She became aware of birds singing in the trees overhead, the breeze stirring the dark leaves on the live oak in the yard. Sunlight filtered through the fading leaves splattered over the ground, and the air held the faintest hint of autumn.

So this is what it meant to be free of stress. To be calm and peaceful. She didn't think she'd ever known this kind of contentment before. She liked it. She'd been running from her past, running from her fears, running from her mistakes so long, she'd forgotten how to stop and rest and it had almost killed her. It might still if she didn't learn to make significant changes in her life.

Glancing down at the red spot on her leg, she gently probed the edge. It felt much better today. It had been tender and sore. Thanks to Matt's gentle ministrations it was going to heal quickly. His thoughtfulness had only made her love him more. Being friends again had given her a sense of peace and joy. But Matt had been deeply wounded by his wife's death and had no intention of risking his heart or those of his children again. She would never ask him to. Even with all her lifestyle changes, her heart disease would be an ongoing concern in her life.

Today, however, she would concentrate on enjoying the time she had left. Time with Matt and the children, time in her hometown and soon time with Gramma. Her great-aunt was recovering quickly, and Gramma would be coming home soon. She'd worry about tomorrow when it got here.

Chapter Nine

For the first time in a long while, Shelby was actually looking forward to something. The anniversary picnic for the Durrants was today. The whole town of Dover was filled with excitement, and she wanted to be a part of it. Not only for Tom and Angie Durrant, but she wanted to reconnect with her hometown and become part of the community again. A notion she was still trying to process.

She was looking forward to seeing Matt and the children, too. She hadn't seen them at church that morning. They probably had gone to the early service so they could help set up the picnic.

Sliding her feet into a pair of comfortable sandals, she walked to the mirror and assessed her clothing choices. She'd opted for a denim skirt and a print blouse. Capri pants and a comfy T-shirt might have been more practical, but she wanted to look feminine today. She didn't want to examine the reasons why. Best just go and not think about it.

Shelby walked toward the Shiloh Lake picnic grounds a short while later, smiling at the number of people already filling the parking lot and milling around the grounds. A large banner was strung between two trees, proclaiming the event. Clusters of colorful balloons bracketed each end of the sign welcoming the guests. The Durrant family was beloved in Dover and she understood, better than most, why.

They were the embodiment of the Dover motto: Faith, Friends, Family. They cared about their community and about each other. They could always be counted on to lend a hand or a prayer. She'd always envied the close relationship she'd observed in Matt's family. They laughed and joked with each other, and genuinely enjoyed each other's company. It was a life she longed for, a life she'd dreamed about. But one she'd never known personally.

Stepping beneath the banner, she glanced around for a familiar face. To her right, a row of grills and cookers had been set up. The delicious aromas wafting toward her made her stomach growl. She knew from experience that the fare would include everything from hot dogs and burgers to chicken, ribs and fish. No one would leave here hungry.

To her left she saw a long table decorated with ribbons. And more balloons. An assortment of gifts covered the top. She walked toward it and added her own present to the mounting pile—the small wheel of flavored pecans. Something she remembered Matt's parents liked.

"Hey, Shel." Pam Fleming touched her shoulder. "Glad to see you made it. I want you to meet my family."

Shelby greeted her husband, whom she remembered from high school, and their three children, the oldest one a strapping teenage boy.

"You're welcome to sit with us."

"I might do that, but first I want to speak to the Durrants."

Pam pointed them out, seated near the edge of the lake. Before Shelby could move, Cassidy waved and ran to meet her. "I didn't think you were ever going to get here."

She smiled, giving her a hug.

"Will you sit with us? Please, please?"

She'd like nothing better. "Sure, but first I want to say hello to your grandparents." Cassidy held her hand as they made their way through the picnic grounds and to the wooden bench where the couple appeared to be holding court. The years had been kind to the couple. Mr. Durrant was a bit thinner, gray around the temples, but still lean and energetic. Matt would no doubt resemble him as he aged. Mrs. Durrant was grayer as well, her hair cut short and her figure a little softer in spots, but her smile was as lovely and warm as ever. A perfect match to her sweet spirit. She was the kind of woman Shelby would like to become.

Angie Durrant rose and greeted her like a long-lost daughter. "Shelby. It is so good to see you again. Not a day has gone by that I haven't thought about you and prayed for you."

Shelby was touched beyond words. She ached for all she'd thrown away. "That is so sweet. I really appreciate that. I need lots of prayers at the moment."

"How are you doing? Tom tells me you are battling some health issues."

"I'm fine. Truly. I just need to take better care of myself. It's nothing serious."

"Good. I hope those grandkids of mine aren't wearing you out. I know I have trouble keeping up with them."

"Not at all. In fact, they were just the remedy I needed. I love watching Cassidy and Kenny. They are delightful."

Angie Durrant touched her arm gently. "Well, I'm so very grateful that you were here to step in and take charge when Matt needed help. I hated that I couldn't come to his rescue, but with this campaign in full swing I just didn't have the time. And remember, if you should need us, for any reason, don't hesitate to call."

"Thank you. I won't."

"Come sit here and tell me all about yourself." Mrs. Durrant patted the bench beside her. Shelby sat down, and Tom and Angie leaned toward her, as if enclosing her into their circle. A lump rose unexpectedly in her throat. If things had turned out differently, these dear people would have been her in-laws.

She'd finished telling the Durrants about the scrapbooking she was doing when Tom Durrant glanced up and smiled.

"Matt, my boy. Why don't you escort Shelby here over to that food table? We've been monopolizing all her time. She must be starving."

She looked up at him, surprised to find a friendly sparkle in his deep blue eyes. "I guess he heard my stomach rumbling."

Matt held out his hand to help her up. "Then follow me. I can get you to the head of the line. I haven't eaten yet myself."

Matt fell in beside her, matching his stride to her shorter one. Shelby tried not to remember how often they had done this, how much she missed it. His hand was so close it would only take a slight movement to slip her fingers into his. "Looks like you had a good turnout. I think everyone in town is here."

"Probably so. My parents know everyone. I think that's why Mom wanted a picnic instead of a formal party. This was a lot easier."

"It suits them, too. Your parents were never the pretentious type."

"No, they're not. They've always been more at home in a park than a country club. How's your leg?"

She slowed and glanced downward. Her skirt ended right above the fading red spot. "Almost all healed up. Maybe you should have been a doctor."

Matt chuckled. "No, I don't think so. Too squeamish. I can't handle being around sick people."

Silence settled over them again, looming like a shadow. Like a woman with heart disease. When they reached the food table, Shelby picked up a plate and started down the line of sumptuous dishes. Matt followed, making conversation with several others as they filed along the food line. When their plates were heaping full, they took them to a table nestled near a large, sprawling magnolia tree. Shelby had tried to remember to make healthy choices, but it was difficult. Hopefully she'd get better as time when on. Matt went back for their drinks then sat down, eyeing her plate.

"You planning on eating all of that?"

Was he worried she wasn't taking care of herself? Out of concern for his children of course. The twinkle in his eyes eased her mind. "Not all of it. But it's been a long time since I've had picnic food. I want to at least taste most of it. But only one bite of each. Then I'll have to double up on the exercise tomorrow."

"Don't they have picnics in New York?"

"Of course. In fact they have a Mississippi Day in Central Park. I just never had the time to attend." Shelby took a bite of potato salad and released an audible moan of satisfaction, all thoughts of Matt and his motives vanishing. "This has to be Mrs. Johnson's."

Matt chuckled. "Oh, yeah. No one makes potato salad like she does."

Shelby swallowed with difficulty. It was nice to hear him laugh again. They'd found so much to laugh at that summer. Merely being together had created joy.

Cassidy and Kenny skidded to a stop at the edge of the table, stalling her train of thought.

"Can we have ice cream now?" Cassidy pleaded. "Darcy's mom brought some triple chocolate chip."

Matt nodded. "Go ahead. But don't blame me if you have a stomachache tonight."

A few moments later the children were back. Cassidy sat beside her father. Kenny climbed in next to her. Her heart ached. With little effort she could envision this as her family. She glanced at Matt, surprised to find him studying her. There was an odd look in his blue eyes. Not angry or disapproving but more assessing. It made her uncomfortable.

"Tell us about you and Shelby and what y'all did in the olden days," Cassidy asked with a huge smile.

Shelby laughed.

Matt frowned. "Olden days?"

"Yeah, back when you were in school. Gramma said Shelby worked at the store. Did you?"

"I did." She pushed her paper plate aside. "I started after graduation and worked until I went to college that fall." The last period in her life she wanted to revisit at the moment.

"What did you do at my grandpa's store?" Kenny wondered. "Did you fix stuff?"

"No." She chuckled. "I was a salesclerk."

"Were you two an item?" Cassidy propped her chin on her fists and smiled in anticipation.

Matt groaned softly. Shelby decided to rescue him. "We were friends."

"Good friends?"

Shelby laughed. "Yes. We'd hang out on weekends. You know, the usual stuff. Movies. Burgers. When the weather was nice, we'd hop on his bike and ride around the countryside."

"What kind of bike?" Kenny asked, resting his elbows on the table and staring at her with interest.

She had to chuckle at the boy's curiosity. He was such an adorable, lovable child, she had to fight to keep from hugging him all the time. "A motorcycle."

"You had a motorcycle?" Cassidy gaped at her father in stunned amazement.

Matt nodded, a serious expression on his face. "That was back in the olden days. The days before time was invented."

"Cool." Kenny's voice was filled with awe and respect. "What happened to it?"

Shelby found herself wondering the same thing. Judging by the kids' reaction, Matt had given up riding long ago.

"Your mother didn't think it was safe, so I sold it." He smiled down at his daughter. "I didn't want to worry her."

Cassidy leaned against Matt's shoulder, a huge smile

on her face. "Were you one of those biker dudes with big boots and a leather jacket and a bandana?"

Matt grimaced. "No. Where do you get these ideas?"

"Where did you go, Daddy? Did you ride all over the mountains and stuff like I see on TV?"

Shelby's heart tightened with a sweet ache. Those days with Matt were some of her most cherished memories. She didn't visit them much; it was too painful. But sharing them here and now with Matt's children made it enjoyable again.

"No," Matt replied with a smile. "We only rode around here. Sometimes we'd go to Jackson, and one time we drove down to the coast."

Cassidy rolled her eyes. "Boring."

"Oh, I don't know." Matt held Shelby's gaze. "I remember a trip to Brookhaven and a certain farmer who might disagree."

Shelby blinked. She couldn't believe he remembered that, let alone brought it up. "We're lucky he didn't have us arrested."

"What did you do?" Cassidy demanded, all ears. Kenny's eyes were wide with fascination.

"I think you'd better ask your father." Far be it from her to be the one to tell tales to his kids.

Matt grinned and shook his head. "Let's say we wandered a little too far off the road and ended up in the wrong place at the wrong time."

"Aw, come on. Tell us."

Two pairs of little eyes stared at her expectantly. Shelby chuckled with the memory. "I'll tell you we were covered in mud. It took me days to get it out of my hair. His leather jacket was ruined."

Cassidy poked her dad with her fingers. "I knew it.

You did have a leather jacket. But I can't see you riding a big old bike. Too weird."

"Well, I did. Guess that was in my wilder days."

Cassidy giggled. "You? Wild? Prove it. You got any pictures?"

"No."

Shelby looked over at Matt. He'd responded too quickly. Did he still have some of those photos? She found that hard to believe. He had never been the type to keep mementos. But oh how she wished he had kept a few. It would mean that somewhere deep inside he still cared.

"Do you have any?" Cassidy asked, looking at Shelby expectantly.

"No. Sorry. I'm sure my mom threw out all my stuff when she got married and moved away." That wasn't completely true. She had a couple photos, but they were packed away and hadn't been seen or even thought about in years.

"Shelby Russell, is that you?" A woman approached the picnic table, a huge smile on her face.

Matt grabbed the opportunity to excuse himself. He wandered off a short distance, tossing his half-empty plate into the trash can. He glanced back at Shelby chatting with her old friend.

His children sat across the picnic table, listening intently. After a few minutes, the friend walked off and Shelby turned her attention back to the kids. They all laughed, talking animatedly. An odd longing tugged at his heart. He turned away from the sight and glanced around the large park. Was it his imagination or was everyone here a couple?

He rarely thought about being single. As a widower, he was too busy with the kids, his job, his ministry. No time to worry about himself. But he'd be lying if he didn't admit he missed having someone at his side. He'd felt the emptiness more strongly over the last few weeks. Since Shelby had come home.

His gaze traveled once again to Shelby. The children were rising from the table, probably going off to the playground. Kenny stopped and gave Shelby a hug before dashing off like a small rocket. A smile lit Shelby's face as his daughter blew her a kiss before hurrying after her brother. Her gaze drifted toward him, stopping as their eyes met. A cold finger of loneliness traced across his senses and into his heart. He longed for companionship again, but the risks were too high. The pain of loss was too great to chance ever again.

He broke eye contact and turned away. He couldn't allow a moment's loneliness to cloud the issues. Cassidy and Kenny were all that mattered. They'd been devastated by Katie's death. Both had suffered serious depression, nightmares and illness. It had taken all he had, and God's grace, to get them through the grieving process.

Still, he worried sometimes about what they were missing by not having a mother. A mother who would hug them, guide them and laugh with them the way Shelby did. He glanced back at the table. Shelby had left. He caught sight of her walking toward the lake. Alone. Maybe he should join her.

"There you are, dear. Laura wants a family picture. You're the only one missing." His mother slipped her arm in his. "Except Tyler, of course. I wish he could get home more."

"Me, too." Ty had called last night to say he wouldn't make it home after all. The case he was working was coming to a head and he needed to see it through. Matt walked with his mom to the arbor, where his father waited. Laura had somehow lured Cassidy and Kenny back from the playground. He had the sudden impression that Shelby should be here, part of the picture.

Once the photograph was taken, his gaze immediately searched out Shelby. He found her standing with her friend Pam and another woman, sharing a laugh. For someone who professed a love of the big city, she fit perfectly into small-town life. For a moment he allowed himself to remember his old dreams. Shelby was supposed to have been part of his life, to have shared all its joys and the triumphs. Instead, she'd chosen her love for her career over her love for him.

He needed to accept the fact that he might never know why. And even if he did, it wouldn't change a thing. Matt turned when he heard his name called, raising his hand in greeting as a friend approached. "Hey, Dave. Glad you could make it." Dave was the local dentist and a good friend of his sister, Laura.

"Me, too. It's a great shindig. We're getting up a game of family volleyball. Get the kids and join us. We're setting up over in the far field."

"Sounds like fun. Thanks."

Matt searched out Shelby again. She had left her friend and was once again with his children. He started forward to recruit them for the volleyball game. Family volleyball. But they weren't really a family. So why did he keep thinking of them that way?

Shelby finished the piece of fruit on her plate and sighed. It had been a wonderful day. She'd been able to set aside all her worries and simply enjoy each moment. She'd played volleyball with Matt and the children. With parents and children all playing together it had been a pretty tame competition, which kept her lack of athletic ability from being exposed. She'd renewed a few old acquaintances and thoroughly enjoyed herself.

The afternoon sun was giving way to twilight, and the picnic was winding down. The grills had been loaded back onto their trucks, the food cleared away and the extra lawn chairs folded and carted off. She was sad to see the day end.

"Bye, Miss Shelby. We'll see you tomorrow." Kenny waved and hurried to her side.

She rested her hand on his waist and smiled. "Yes, you will. Are you leaving?"

Laura Durrant joined them. "I told them we could go watch a movie at my place. I thought it might let them calm down a bit. They're totally wound up."

Cassidy shook her head. "No, we're not."

"Oh, yes, you are," Matt chimed in. "Behave yourselves. I'll pick you up after the movie."

Once they were gone, Shelby stood and smiled at Matt. "I guess I'd better be going, too. I had a good time today."

"Me, too. I hate to see it end. Would you like to take a walk along the lake for a few minutes?"

The idea was tempting. Spending time with him was always on her wish list. "Sure."

They started across the wide grassy area toward the water's edge and the well-worn path along the bank, walking in companionable silence, with only the sound of nature filling the cool, quiet air.

"It's so beautiful here."

"Yes, it is. We used to come here often to walk along this path. Do you remember?"

She stole a quick glance at him. His chiseled features were relaxed, free of the worry she so frequently saw. "I do."

He slowed and stepped off the path, walking toward a large live oak, its branches draped in thick strands of Spanish moss. "Do you remember this?"

She moved closer, her heartbeat racing as she recognized the large heart and the pair of initials carved inside. SR + MD. "Our tree. I'd forgotten about this." She glanced upward to the branches. "It's so much bigger than I remembered."

"It's been fifteen years. Things change."

She traced the heart with her fingers. "Yes, they do. Many things change." A small chuckle rose up from inside. She turned and smiled at him. "I remember the day you did this. You must have planned ahead because you had one of those battery-operated carving tools with you. The kind your dad sold in the store."

Matt chuckled. "I remember."

"You said you wanted it to last forever so everyone could see it when they passed by."

Matt leaned against the trunk and placed his fingers beside the heart. "Looks like it did for the most part. The tree has grown around some of it."

She could see he had something on his mind. "Matt, why did you bring me here?" He was silent a long moment, as if searching for the right words.

"I want to sort things out in my head. About you. About us. I thought maybe we could settle some of them."

Her throat tightened. Was he putting an end to her

babysitting? Asking her to step out of his life? "All right. Maybe it would be for the best."

He faced her, a deep frown creasing his forehead. "What happened that night? Why did you suddenly change your mind about us? One day you're accepting my ring and then the next suddenly I'm too small-town."

Shelby bit her lip, trying to find a good place to start. She ignored the quickening of her heart. They needed to have this out, but it wasn't going to be easy. "Because you changed the plan."

Matt shook his head, puzzled. "What plan? The only plan I had was to marry you."

"Yes, but not until after college." Shelby ran a hand over her arm and turned away, putting distance between them. His confusion hovered between them like the moss dangling overhead.

Matt exhaled in exasperation. "Right. So?"

"I didn't want to give up my education and stay here in Dover. That wasn't the plan we always talked about."

He ran a hand down the back of his neck. "Shelby, I know how important your education was to you. I'd never have asked you to give that up." He paced off a few steps. "None of this is making any sense."

She took a few steps toward him, anxious for him to understand. "When I met you at the gazebo that night you told me you didn't think you were going back to college. You said you'd missed so much already because of your dad's accident that you might as well take over the store. Then you started talking about what a great life your parents had, how owning the store would let us start a family sooner."

"Yeah. I remember, but I was just talking, Shelby. Dad's relapse had thrown everything into chaos. With him back in the hospital, not knowing if he'd survive another surgery, my future was looking pretty bleak. I'd been counting on going to school the next week and then it was all taken away again." He exhaled a heavy sigh. "That night I was angry and confused. I had to face reality. If my dad didn't pull through, I'd be the head of the family. I'd have to take over the store and finishing college would be out of the question." He looked into her eyes, a sad smile on his handsome face. "I guess I was trying to hold on to the one sure thing in my life at the time. You. Us."

Shelby looked over at him, her heart aching. "I didn't know your dad had gone back into the hospital. Why didn't you tell me?"

"I did. I told your mom when I called and left the message for you to meet me."

Shelby quickly sorted through her memories of that day. She'd been troubled about a lot of things. Her mom hadn't been at all happy about the engagement. And she'd just learned her friend Pam, who was supposed to be her roommate at college, was pregnant and getting married instead. "She never mentioned it to me."

"Why would she not tell you? Did she dislike me that much?"

"It wasn't you in particular. It was anything that might tempt me away from school. She was furious when I came home with your ring on my finger. She was determined that I would have a better life than she had, and she didn't think you'd ever be more than the next owner of a small-town hardware store." She stared at the heart carved in the tree trunk. "So when you started talking about taking over the store, I guess I panicked." She braved a look at Matt, but could read only confusion in his eyes. She tried to explain further. "The ring suddenly became a chain and I had to break it."

"So you ran away without a word."

Shelby nodded. "Mom was relieved when I told her I'd broken up with you. She gave me money to leave for school early. I left the next morning."

"That's what your mom told me when I came by the house the next day looking for you. I didn't want to believe you'd do that." He held her gaze. "I called and I wrote to you, but you never answered so I finally got the message. We were through."

"I never got any letters. Or phone calls."

Matt shook his head. "I called your cell phone two or three times a day."

Shelby rubbed the tension between her eyes. "I didn't have a cell phone."

"You must have. Your mom gave me the number and your address at school." He touched his temple as if calling up a memory. "Someplace on Belmont Street."

A sinking sensation formed inside her. "I never lived on a street by that name. Ever."

"Why would your mother deliberately give me bogus information?"

"To ensure I got out of Dover and got the education she never had."

Shelby's gaze locked with Matt's. The realization of what had occurred changed everything. To a point.

His voice was rough, tinged with regret when he spoke. "I should have tried harder."

"I should have reached out to you." Shelby's heart ached with the sadness of it all. She moved to the trunk and touched the carved heart again. "Things could have been so different."

Matt moved toward her. "It's not good to dwell in the past, Shelby. Things happen for a reason. We both moved on. I have my family. You have your career. Those are good things. I guess it was just the wrong time for us."

Shelby looked up into his blue eyes, her heart filled with love for this man. "Is there a right time?"

He reached out and touched a stray hair near her temple. "A do-over?"

She nodded, unable to take her gaze from his. The deep blue darkened as he gazed into her eyes. His hand came up and rested against the side of her face, and she tilted her head into his palm.

"I hope so."

His words were spoken so softly she was certain she'd heard them only in her heart. Matt's strong hands gripped her shoulders, drawing her closer. She thought he was going to kiss her, but instead he pulled her against his chest, wrapping her in his warm embrace. Neither one spoke or moved.

A part of Shelby's heart that had long been scarred began to heal. Nothing could change the past, but now they could finally put it behind them. Slowly, Matt released her, taking her hand in his. They walked from under the old oak and back toward the park.

Shelby curled up in her bedroom chair, flipping through a magazine. It was late and she should be in bed, but she was reluctant to see the day come to an end. She was pleasantly tired and relaxed. A good feeling. Nothing like the exhaustion she normally knew after a busy day at work. She'd come home, showered, had a light meal and called her grandmother.

The Durrants' picnic had been more enjoyable than she'd anticipated. She'd expected to feel uncomfortable, out of sync with the people there. Instead she'd felt very much a part of it all. Like she belonged in Dover.

But mostly her thoughts centered around Matt. It felt good to finally clear away the past. What a mess. The perfect storm of bad circumstances. She could see clearly now how her fear coupled with her mother's meddling had cost her the thing she wanted most. She'd spent the rest of her life trying to replace it with her career.

So what would her relationship with Matt be now? Being held in his arms had torn away the flimsy curtain protecting her emotions. Her love for him was as deep and as strong as the day he'd given her his ring. But no one could go back and redo the past. He'd said he hoped they had a second chance, but he'd probably meant as friends. Anything else was impossible.

The phone rang. She rose and quickly moved to the nightstand. It was nearly eleven. Who would be calling at this hour?

"Hello."

"Shelby, I'm sorry to call so late."

"Matt?" His voice was tense, filled with a frightening urgency.

"I need you to come over here."

"What happened? Are the children all right?" Fear sent a paralyzing jolt through her system. She couldn't bear it if anything happened to Cassidy or Kenny.

"Yes. It's Ty. He's been shot. Mom and Dad are trying to get a flight out to Dallas to be with him. I need to take them to the airport in Jackson. They're both too upset to drive. Can you come over and stay with the kids?"

"Of course. I'll be there in five minutes."

"Thanks."

Shelby hung up, her heart aching for Matt and his family. His brother Ty was her age. They'd graduated from high school the same year. She hadn't known him well. He'd worked at the store the summer she did, but Ty had worked when Matt was off so she'd had little opportunity to get to know him. She sent up a prayer for Ty. She couldn't begin to imagine what Mr. and Mrs. Durrant must be going through.

She dressed quickly and hurried across the driveway. Matt yanked open the door before she could knock. He looked distracted. Lines of worry bracketed his mouth, and his blue eyes were darker than usual.

"Thanks, Shelby." He motioned her inside. "The kids are asleep. I haven't told them anything. I'll do that when I know more. I don't know how long I'll be gone." He rubbed his forehead and glanced around the room. "I need to get to Mom and Dad's. They're frantic."

Shelby's heart ached for him. He was rambling. Trying to think of every detail. She reached out and touched his arm. "Matt. Don't worry about anything here. We'll be fine. Go do what you have to."

"Yeah."

He looked so distraught she wanted to hold him, but that was out of the question. Instead she put a smile on her face and gestured toward the door. "Go. I'll be fine."

Matt pulled out his keys and started for the door. "Oh. In case I'm not back, the kids have to get up around six thirty to get ready for school."

Shelby put her hands on his chest, intending to turn

him toward the door. To her shock Matt laid his hand over hers. "Thank you, Shelby. I don't know what I'd do without you."

She smiled, her heart beating triple time. "That's what friends are for."

His eyes softened, and he touched her cheek with his fingers. "I guess so."

He turned and went out the door. Leaving a fluttering of hope in her heart. Maybe he still cared a little. Slowly she shut the door, knowing that friendship would be a poor substitute for her real feelings. But she would take what she could get and be grateful.

Chapter Ten

It was midmorning the next day before Matt had a chance to slow down and regroup. He poured a second cup of coffee from the pot on his credenza, then sat down at his desk. He was beat. It had been after four in the morning when he'd finally gotten back home from Jackson-Evers Airport. He and Shelby had exchanged only a few words when he'd returned. He'd had nothing new to report on his brother's condition, and he'd sent her home with little more than an appreciative thank-you.

He'd managed a couple hours of sleep before having to get the kids off to school and come to work. It was going to be difficult to focus on his classes today; his thoughts and prayers were all with his brother. A light tap on his open door drew his attention. Carl Young was standing there, a sympathetic expression on his dark face. He must have heard the news.

"Hey, Matt. I'm sorry about your brother. Have you heard anything?"

"Some. I talked to my mom a few minutes ago. He came through the first surgery all right, but there's another one yet to go." His brother had been shot three times and there'd been doubt in the beginning if he'd pull through. Praise God, he was holding his own so far.

"How are your parents holding up?"

"As well as can be expected."

"I'm praying for him."

"Thanks. Never can have too much of that."

"Amen."

"Who's running the store while your dad is gone?"

Matt leaned back in his chair, one hand on the armrest. "He hired an assistant manager earlier this year. Young guy named Troy Ballard."

"Good to hear. I was afraid you'd have to run the place for a while. Then that would leave me to take all your classes." Carl chuckled and winked.

One of the things Matt liked best about his friend was he could count on Carl to lighten any situation. "Get your ugly face out of here."

Carl waved and disappeared.

Shelby's arms pumped in rhythm with her stride as she kept pace with Pam on their daily walk. They'd had to postpone it to the afternoon due to a schedule change at Pam's job. The morning walks had quickly become something Shelby enjoyed. She was feeling stronger every day. Leading a healthy lifestyle was proving to be less of a torment than she'd expected.

"Are you serious?"

Shelby stopped suddenly, turning back to her friend, who stood still in the middle of the sidewalk, hands on hips.

Pam shook her head in disbelief. "I cannot believe your mother did such an underhanded thing to you.

Deliberately giving Matt a phony address and phone number."

"Well, she did." Shelby waved her to catch up and resume their walk. She been telling her friend about the things that had been discovered when she and Matt had compared notes at the picnic yesterday. "I guess she thought she was doing me a favor."

"Some favor. Shel, your life could have been totally different."

"Maybe. But I do love my job, and Matt had a wonderful wife and two amazing kids. It all turned out the way it was supposed to, I guess."

"What now? I mean, do you and Matt have a future? Do you want one? Does he?"

The women walked in place at the street corner while they waited for a car to pass. "I doubt it. We're friends again. But as for anything more—well, he's been through the devastating loss of his wife to cancer. He's not going to get involved with someone who's going to be battling health issues all her life."

"It's not like you're dying or anything, Shel. Your heart condition is very minor. Easily managed with meds and taking good care of yourself."

"I don't think he sees it that way. He sees a woman who might die suddenly and leave him and his children grieving a second time."

"I guess I get it. To a point. Have you heard any more about his brother, Ty? I was just sick to hear about that. So horrible."

"Matt texted me earlier and said Ty came through the first surgery all right but he still has a long way to go." She sent up another prayer for Matt's brother.

They walked in silence for a while before Pam spoke again. "So. Do you love Matt?"

The question brought Shelby to a stop. "What are you talking about?" Pam kept walking, forcing her to catch up.

"You have that same look on your face as you did that summer. You have the same tone of voice when you say his name. Your eyes get all dreamy when you talk about him or his kids. It's a perfectly logical question."

But there was no logical answer. The wall between them now was more like a small curb, easily crossed. The attraction was there on both sides, but as for anything more... "I don't know how to answer that."

"It's simple. Yes or no."

"Yes. I think I always have. I just didn't realize it until I came home and saw him again." He was the reason she'd never found someone to share her life. No one else had measured up.

"Then what are you going to do about it?"

"Nothing. Nothing at all."

Shelby pulled the mail from Matt's box as the school bus rolled to a stop in front of the house. She smiled and waved as Cassidy strolled up the driveway, receiving a halfhearted wave in return. She studied the child closely as she meandered to the sidewalk and plodded up the porch steps. "You all right?"

She shrugged, dropping her backpack on the floor. "I guess."

Resting a hand on the girl's shoulder, Shelby steered her to one of the wicker chairs. "What's wrong, sweetie?"

Cassidy remained silent a long moment, head bowed and shoulders slumped. "I hate the way I look."

Shelby inhaled slowly, her heart aching. She had to resist her impulse to pull Cassidy into her arms and tell her how beautiful she was. Her instincts told her that wasn't what the little girl needed to hear right now. "What don't you like?"

"Everything. My hair is boring and my face is yucky."

"How would you like to look?"

"Like my friend Molly. She wears cool makeup and stuff."

Shelby fought the urge to smile. Was there a female on the planet who hadn't felt the same way at one point in their lives? "Do you wear makeup?"

"No." She huffed, crossing her arms over her chest. "Dad won't let me. He says I'm too young."

Shelby took her small hand in hers. "Maybe if you told your dad how important this is to you, he'd change his mind."

"He won't. He wants to keep me a baby. I'm almost twelve. Besides, even if I could, I don't have anyone to show me how to put it on."

"I can show you." Shelby regretted the words the moment they left her mouth. She shouldn't be going against Matt's wishes.

"Would you?" Cassidy sprang to her feet, her face aglow. "That would be so cool."

Half an hour later, Cassidy and Shelby looked in the mirror of Shelby's bathroom at the final result of the makeover. Cassidy looked years older. Maybe too old. A niggling doubt crept into Shelby's mind. Cassidy was a pretty little girl. She had a fresh, natural beauty of her own. Looking at her now, Shelby wished she hadn't suggested this experiment. "You know, Cassidy, this has been fun, but it's too much makeup for you to wear to school. You know that, don't you?"

"No." Cassidy met her gaze with a pleading look. "It looks good. I look like a teenager." She struck a pose, tilting her head at a coquettish angle.

Sadness settled around Shelby's heart. Cassidy was rushing toward something she wasn't ready for. "Let's wipe this off now."

"But it looks good." She leaned closer to the mirror, staring at her image.

Shelby dampened a rag and handed it to her. "Cassidy, you're a pretty girl. You don't need all this makeup."

A pout pulled down the corners of her mouth. "But I want to look like the girls in your magazine."

For the first time, Shelby experienced a rush of resentment toward the young women featured on *Tween Scene's* covers. "Cassidy, remember when I changed your picture to make you look like a cover model?"

"That was so awesome."

Shelby gently took the girl's face between her hands. "The girls on the covers look exactly like you. We change all the pictures that way. Wait. I'll show you." Shelby moved into her room and retrieved a candid photo from her briefcase.

"Who's that?" Cassidy asked, studying the picture.

"Yasmine."

The girls eyes widened. "No way. I saw the cover of your magazine. She was perfect."

Shelby nodded. "That's what she really looks like before the makeup and hairstylist and the special lighting. And of course the computer enhancements." Shelby watched as the child digested this new information and her shoulders slumped.

"She looks like a regular old girl," Cassidy lamented.

Shelby gently took the little girl's hands in her own. "We all look like regular girls, sweetheart."

Cassidy frowned. "But I want to look beautiful."

"I know. All women do, and makeup helps us look our best, but we have to be careful not to use too much."

Cassidy looked in the mirror at her freshly scrubbed face and frowned. "Now I look like dumb old me."

Shelby rested her hands on the girl's shoulders, peering at their reflections. "Smile for me." Cassidy pouted for a moment then complied. "When you smile, it's like the sun coming out. You have a smile like your daddy's."

Cassidy giggled. "He says I have my mommy's smile."

Shelby ignored the sting in her heart. This could have been her daughter. "Maybe what you really need is a new look. Next time we'll play with your hair and try some new styles. Sometimes a new haircut can change your whole attitude."

"Cool. Thanks, Shelby." Cassidy twisted around and gave her a hug. "You're the best. I'm so glad you moved here. Hey, could I invite some of my friends over and you could show us how to do makeup and hair? For regular girls like us, I mean."

"Sure. I think that's a great idea."

Cassidy's face lit up. "I have a better idea."

Shelby gave her a wary look. "What?"

"We could do it at my slumber party. We could stay

up all night doing hair and makeup and order pizza and stuff."

Shelby liked the idea. She'd enjoy doing girl things with Cassidy, but she'd also welcome an opportunity to teach her and her friends the truth and dispel some misconceptions. "I'd love to help out. You need to okay this with your dad though, and it might be a good idea to check with your friends' mothers. Make sure they know what we're going to do because some moms may not want them trying out makeup yet."

"Cool."

"When is your party?"

"This Friday." Cassidy turned away quickly, walking out into the bedroom.

"Oh?" Odd. Matt hadn't mentioned it to her and he usually kept her apprised of all the children's activities for the week. But then, the party was on Friday and he was off that day, so he probably didn't see any reason to tell her since she wouldn't be involved. Hopefully he wouldn't object to her putting in an appearance at the party.

Matt closed the dishwasher and started the cycle. Kenny was tucked in bed and Cassidy should be on her way. As if sensing his thoughts, she appeared at his side, an impish grin on her face. That usually spelled trouble. He eyed her skeptically. "What?"

"I love you, Daddy."

He grimaced, tossing the dish towel over his shoulder. "Yeah, yeah. Out with it."

"Can I have a slumber party this Friday night? Please? Please?"

Matt sighed in mild irritation. "Sweetheart, we've had this discussion before."

Cassidy set her fists on her hips and frowned. "I know. We have to have another grown-up in the house. But I don't see why."

He hated to deny his daughter a party, but she didn't understand. He looked at Cassidy's disappointed expression and felt himself weakening. "I don't know, kiddo."

Cassidy pounced on the crack in his defenses. "I know. I'll bet Miss Shelby would do it."

"Do what?"

"Chaperone." She smiled gleefully. "We were going to do the makeup thing anyway. I know she'd do it. She's here all the time now anyhow."

He was all too aware of that fact. "What makeup thing?"

Cassidy waved off his question. "It's girl stuff, Dad. You wouldn't get it."

"Why don't we wait until your Gramma gets back from Dallas and she can come stay with us that night."

Cassidy assumed her drooping noodle position. Shoulders sagging, head leaned back, knees bent. It was a pitiful sight. He waited for the whine that always followed.

"No. She won't be back until Sunday. I want someone cool like Shelby to do it."

"Cassidy."

She straightened and tried again. "Please? Can I at least ask her?"

Matt inhaled deeply. "Let me think about it."

It was later that night before Matt could consider how to handle Cassidy's request. He didn't want to refuse his daughter yet again, but asking Shelby to take on such a huge responsibility went beyond the duties they'd agreed to. Besides, this Friday was his day off. He couldn't ask her to work overtime. He was sure she would welcome the break. He thought about his daughter's excitement. He had to at least try. Didn't he?

He picked up the phone and dialed, a smile coming unbidden to his lips when she answered. "Can you meet me outside for a second? I need to talk to you." He hung up, not exactly sure why he'd turned a phone call into a face-to-face other than he wanted to see her again.

She came toward him across the driveway, her hair shimmering in the light from the streetlamps. She smiled into his eyes, and he forgot to breathe.

"Hey. What's going on? It sounded serious."

The sight of her jumbled his thinking and he had to regroup. "Did Cassidy say anything to you about a party this week?"

"You mean her slumber party? Yes. She's really excited."

Matt exhaled a huff of irritation. Apparently his daughter was trying to pull an end run on him. "I haven't given my permission yet."

"Oh. I didn't know. She acted as if it was all settled."

Her calm response confirmed his daughter's scheme. "That's what I was afraid of."

"What's this about?"

Matt rubbed his forehead. "She's been after me for some time to have a slumber party and I keep making excuses. I don't know how to explain to her that a single dad having a bunch of little girls overnight…"

"Oh. I see your problem."

"I don't know what to say to her, and I can't keep making up excuses. Lately when I tell her no she flies into a fit of tears for no reason or turns into a drama queen. She never used to do that. It's like she's an alien creature."

Shelby laughed lightly. "Girls aren't that much of a mystery, Matt. We want to be loved. We want to be taken seriously and respected. We want the men in our lives to listen to us but not always fix everything. But mostly, we want to be cherished and protected."

Matt looked into Shelby's warm brown eyes. Cherished and protected. That's all he'd ever wanted to do for Shelby. But he couldn't protect her from a heart attack and that scared him. He sighed and shook his head. "You make it sound so simple."

"It is. So, are you going to let her have the slumber party?"

"If Mom or Laura were here, maybe. But as it is…"

"What if I acted as chaperone?"

"That was her idea, too." His eyes narrowed. "You sure you didn't cook this up together?"

"Scout's honor. But I certainly wouldn't mind. Now, before you say no, let me explain my idea. You and Kenny could hang around until nine or so then go to your mom's for the night. I'll stay with the girls. In the morning, you can come back and bring breakfast."

Her offer should have surprised him, but it didn't. He was all too aware of how much she cared for his son and daughter. It was part of his ongoing emotional struggle. He liked seeing her with his children. Too much. "I guess that would work. But are you sure you want to spend all night with a bunch of screaming preteen girls?"

Shelby chuckled softly. "I think I can manage Cassidy and a few of her friends. No more than six though."

He couldn't believe he was considering her suggestion. No matter how he looked at her idea, he couldn't find any fault in it. It would satisfy Cassidy's desire to have a party and keep him out of the picture when necessary. "I don't know. I really miss Katie at times like this."

Silence filled the space between them. He realized he'd said that last out loud.

"Matt, I'd be more than happy to chaperone her party if it's all right with you."

"Okay, then. I'll let her know. And thanks, Shelby. You seem to be there whenever I need you."

A small smirk moved one corner of her lips. "That's me. Miss Dependable."

Matt watched her walk back inside her house, not missing the little dig she'd sent his way. He'd said she wasn't dependable, but she'd been there for him every time he had needed her. The one time she hadn't been wasn't her fault completely.

Slowly he turned and walked to the house. A few weeks ago he would never have allowed Shelby to get so close to his kids. Now she was playing mom, chaperoning a slumber party and weaving herself deeper and deeper into their lives.

The old fear in his gut was still there. Not that she'd suddenly run away, but what would happen when she eventually returned to New York? Sooner or later she would. He'd reminded the kids frequently that Shelby would be leaving at some point. So much so that they had started rolling their eyes in disgust. They'd cleared up the past, but it had only increased his longing for companionship. He was becoming more and more aware of the empty places in his heart and his life. Places he was beginning to think only Shelby could fill. But was he willing to risk everything on a woman who was ill?

Shelby pulled the large envelope from her Gramma's mailbox. The latest issue of *Tween Scene*. Her heart contracted when she remembered that this might be the last issue published. Taking a seat on the swing, she idly flipped through the pages, an uneasiness swelling in her mind. The images she used to consider hip and edgy now struck her as a bit exploitive. She kept comparing each too-thin model to Cassidy.

Her gaze drifted across the driveway to Matt's house. All her experience with preteens had been with models, pop stars and child actors. She'd never dealt with a real, normal young girl before. Someone like Cassidy. She thought about the online magazine she'd considered. It wouldn't be hard to do. She had the skills and the experience. Her mind began to fill with ideas. It might be fun. It would be wonderful to have control of the content and not have to compromise her convictions for the sake of sales.

Shelby hurried into the house, grabbed a pen and paper and a piece of fruit and went back to the front porch. Oh, how she missed her laptop. The first chance she got she would buy a new one. She was still scribbling ideas when the bus pulled up and Kenny bounded off. She watched with joy as he raced up the driveway toward her, all thoughts of the new magazine vanishing. What she wouldn't give to experience this feeling every day for the rest of her life.

"I won!" Kenny shouted, grabbing hold of Shelby's arm.

"What did you win?" Shelby asked, smiling. The little boy was bubbling over with excitement.

"I won the drawing contest at school." He dug into his backpack.

"That's wonderful. Congratulations."

"My picture of the woods was better than anybody else's. See what I won? This big thing of drawing paper and special drawing pens and a case and some colored pencils."

Shelby relieved him of the cumbersome assortment of prizes. "I'm so proud of you. Your daddy will be so happy." Kenny smiled and readily accepted the hug she offered. The feel of his sweet little body in her arms brought a lump to her throat.

"They're going to hang my picture in the front hall at school so everyone can see it."

"That's wonderful, Kenny. We'll all come and see it."

"Can we work on our scrapbook?" Kenny asked, stuffing his prizes back into his backpack.

"I think we'd better wait for Cassidy, don't you? She should be home as soon as her club meeting is over. Molly's mom is bringing her home."

"Okay," he agreed reluctantly.

"Why don't we have a quick snack and then take a walk on the trails? By the time we get back she should be almost home and we can work on the scrapbook."

"But she'll have homework to do."

"Well, maybe she won't have very much today." She took his hand and walked across the drive to his house.

The scrapbooking project Cassidy and Kenny had started was progressing nicely. They worked on it each day. Shelby's heart had been touched multiple times by the memories they shared. The fact that the scrapbook was a surprise gift for Matt only added to their joy.

They'd collected a large variety of pictures, trinkets and other memorabilia to include in the book.

They worked diligently each afternoon, talking about happy times with their mother and sometimes shedding a few tears. Since they were determined to keep it a secret from Matt, watching the clock had become Shelby's main responsibility. Everything had to be put away and hidden before he came home. One day he'd come home early and nearly caught them. They'd been extra cautious from then on.

Every day she questioned her wisdom in agreeing to watch Matt's children. She was much too comfortable in his home, and she cared too deeply for his children. Her time with them was like experiencing a tantalizing dream beyond her reach. No matter how hard she tried, or prayed, it would never come true.

Their relationship had vastly improved since their talk at the picnic. Things were more relaxed and comfortable. Much of their old camaraderie had returned. They talked or texted frequently during the day, mostly about the kids or Ty's ongoing recovery. But sometimes Matt would call for no apparent reason. A few times he'd called to ask her a question or remind her about an appointment one of the children had.

Lately, he'd been calling even more. And when he got home, he had been asking for more and more details about the children's day. She had the impression he wanted someone to talk to, and she was more than happy to oblige, even though it was a bittersweet experience. She didn't want to be his sounding board for a few weeks; she wanted to be in his life forever.

She had to constantly remind herself that rekindling an old friendship wasn't the same as rekindling an old love. But Lord forgive her, she counted the moments until she heard his voice.

Matt pulled into his driveway, coming to a stop near the back door. The lights were on in the house, but he was pretty sure Shelby would be asleep. He had to call upon her generosity as babysitter once again. He'd agreed to fill in for his mother at an important campaign event this evening in her absence. Not his cup of tea, but with her still in Dallas with Ty, he was happy to step in.

He climbed out of the car, glancing again at the faint light in the window. He liked knowing there was someone waiting for him. That Shelby was waiting for him.

Somewhere along the way he'd started looking forward to talking to her and hearing her voice. He looked forward to coming home each night and finding her there, helping Cassidy with supper or playing a game with Kenny. The sight of her and his children as he came through the door filled him with a happiness he'd long forgotten. His kids were happy. They adored Shelby. He was grateful to her for that. There was huge comfort in knowing someone else loved them as much as he did. And Shelby did love the kids. It was obvious.

How did she feel about him?

The attraction between them was still there, rekindled no doubt by the closeness required by her babysitting duties. Shelby was a beautiful woman. With her big brown eyes and her deceptively delicate appearance, any normal male would be drawn to her. He was more vulnerable than most, that's all. And, while he no longer feared Shelby would break his children's hearts, he wasn't ready to risk his own.

Matt entered through the back door as quietly as possible. It was after midnight. He'd been cornered with questions about his brother as well as his mother's position on several local issues, but he hadn't expected to be this late. He wouldn't blame her if she was upset. She'd agreed to babysit for a few hours each day, not around the clock. The big house was silent. Too silent.

Frowning he walked through the hall into the living room. The television screen was blue and silent. The small lights on the DVD player and the home theater equipment were on. Odd. Why hadn't Shelby turned it off? And where was she?

He shut off the electronics, then turned around. He froze. Shelby was sound asleep on the sofa, the afghan pulled up near her chin. He opened his mouth to call her name but stopped, captivated by the appealing picture she made. Her dark hair was mussed. Featherlight tendrils fell in wisps across her cheek. One hand lay against her face; bright pink nail polish contrasted against the dark tresses.

His heart ached. They'd had so many dreams, so many plans. But too many things had conspired against them back then. Shelby looked so peaceful. So beautiful. He leaned over, his fingers brushing soft curls from her cheek.

She moaned.

Matt straightened and quickly left the room. In the kitchen he rested his hands against the counter, battling the emotions that were swirled deep inside. Everything he'd ever wanted, every dream he'd had, was lying asleep on his sofa. The first woman he'd ever loved was only a few feet away. And years removed.

Guilt pierced his conscience. Katie had been all he'd ever hoped for. He'd loved her with his whole heart, but she was so different from Shelby that he wondered if he'd deliberately looked for someone as opposite as he could find. Someone who could never remind him of the woman he'd lost.

Seeing her tonight, so vulnerable, made him realize what a slippery slope he was on. He was falling in love with her again, and he couldn't afford to. They could never pick up where they left off. It was too late and there was too much at stake. But he didn't want to be alone anymore.

Katie was still in his heart, but her memory now left a sweetness behind, not the knife-edge of grief it once was. Maybe it was time to move on.

Right now he had to send Shelby home. Fantasizing was a waste of time. He started back into the living room, stubbing his toe against the Bombay chest.

"Matt? Is that you?"

The sleepy voice sent his blood tingling. He swallowed the lump in his throat. "Yeah. It's me."

Shelby sat up and smiled. Matt's heart jumped into his throat. She was the most beautiful woman he'd ever seen. All he wanted at this moment was to take her into his arms and kiss her the way he'd longed to under the oak tree at the picnic.

"How did it go?" She squinted at him from behind drowsy eyelids.

"Good. Sorry I'm so late."

"Don't worry about it." She shook her head. "We had a nice evening. I dug out an old movie and made some popcorn. It's been very relaxing."

She smiled, a silly, sleepy grin, and every bone in his body turned to liquid. "Good. That's good."

"Well. I'd better go." She stood and started to fold

the afghan. "The kids' homework is on the table ready for you to sign. I checked it over. There's a permission slip for Kenny's field trip and a notice about tryouts for chorus for Cassidy. Oh, and you might want to remind your mom that next Tuesday is Grandparents' Day at the school."

She laid the afghan across the back of the couch, then turned and faced him. "Something wrong?"

He knew he could never adequately answer that question. Yes. Everything was wrong. He was in falling in love with her, and he was afraid it was too late to stop it.

"No. Just tired."

"Then I'd better get out of here so you can get some rest. Oh, and remember, tomorrow is the big slumber party."

"Right." He nodded, following her to the door, keeping a safe distance. If he got too close, if he felt the warmth of her, smelled the sweet scent of her, he might do something he'd regret. He reached for the doorknob. Shelby abruptly turned, bringing her up against his chest. His face was only inches from her. He stared at her lips.

"Oh, I'm so sorry. I, uh, forgot my cell phone."

Matt looked down into her brown eyes and forgot to breathe. The warmth of her beneath his hands, her fragrance, set his heart pounding. He'd known if he ever got this close he'd be unable to resist taking her into his arms.

The air in the room stilled, awareness arced between them. His brain told him to let go. Step away. Put some space between them before he gave into his desire to kiss her. He gripped her shoulders and set her away from him. Quickly, he turned and retrieved her cell from the end table. When he stood in front of her again, she was staring at the floor, fidgeting.

She looked up and smiled, reaching for the phone, her fingers wrapping around his own. He saw her lips part. Slowly he released the phone, only to find his hands grasping her shoulders again and pulling her closer.

He knew he should stop, but the attraction between them was a force bigger than he could resist. His hand lightly cupped her cheek. She sighed, resting her head against his palm. Her movement was his undoing. He slid his hand along her neck, pulling her toward him. He couldn't take his eyes off her mouth. He lowered his head, heart pounding in anticipation.

He inhaled her breath, then carefully touched his lips to hers. Her mouth was warm, pliant. He remembered the sweet taste of her and the perfect way she fit against him. She clung to him, returning his kiss. He was sinking in the wonder of her, drowning. He had to surface or be lost forever.

He released her but was unable to take his eyes from hers. He'd known from the moment he'd first seen her he'd lose his heart again. It was why he'd fought so hard. If she'd stayed away, he could have kept his love buried. But now here he was. Lost.

He'd been lonely but comfortable in his grief. Shelby had come home and forced him out of his apathy, forced him to come alive again and confront part of his grief he'd buried. But she'd also brought with her a risk. The risk of losing her, of facing the possibility of loss again. He wasn't strong enough, his kids shouldn't have to face that again.

"Shelly, why did you come back?" It was barely a whisper. He wasn't sure if he'd said the words aloud or not.

Shelby inhaled sharply and stepped back. Without a word, she turned and walked out, the thud of the door the only sound in the empty room.

Chapter Eleven

❧

Shelly. He'd called her Shelly. His pet name for her. Shelby pressed her fingers to her lips, fighting back the tears. The kiss had sealed her fate. She was hopelessly, forever in love with Matt. She should never have let that happen.

But she'd wanted him to kiss her. She'd wanted it so badly. She'd been playing house for weeks, imagining herself as part of his life. Tonight the dream had come true, his kiss had been the fulfillment of all her desires. Then he had shattered the dream with a few words. *Why did you come back?*

Shelby curled up in the chair in her room, staring out the window. What had he meant? You're ruining my life? You're digging up pain? Probably all of that. He'd made it clear all along how he felt. She shouldn't read too much into a kiss, one weak moment on both their parts. To be honest, the attraction was still there, but that's all it was. Attraction alone wasn't enough to build a life on.

She closed her eyes, reliving the kiss once again. Matt cared about her, but did he care enough to accept her as is, flaws and all? A knife-edge of sadness twisted in her heart. Doubtful. And she couldn't blame him. He and the kids had lost so much. How could she expect them to willingly walk into that valley again? Her situation wasn't anything like cancer, but living with the uncertainty, the threat of something happening, would be like walking the edge of a cliff every day. No one could live like that.

Tears stung her eyes and she lifted her gaze upward. "Father, You know how much I love those children." The Lord might never have intended for her to have a life with Matt and his children, but He'd shown her what her future could be. He'd restored her faith and redirected her life. To ask for anything more would be greedy.

The ache in her heart squeezed tighter, choking off her air. She drew her knees up to her chin and gave in to the tears. Her mind might rationalize the pain away, but her heart grieved.

"The number you are calling is unavailable." Matt listened to the monotone voice in his ear, then tossed his cell phone onto the counter. He stared out the kitchen window at Shelby's house and the empty driveway. Where was she? It was Friday. The day of the slumber party. He'd realized he had no idea what to expect or how to prepare. He needed to talk to Shelby, but her car had been gone since early morning and she wasn't answering her cell. He'd tried to reach her all day between Handy Works projects, but she'd not returned his calls.

He pinched the bridge of his nose. He wasn't looking forward to seeing her after last night. He didn't know whether to apologize for kissing her or behave as if nothing had happened. All he knew for certain was that last night had changed everything. He loved her and he could no longer deny it. If her response to the kiss was any indication, she had feelings for him, as well.

So what? It didn't change a thing. All it proved was they were both attracted. That alone didn't spell a future together.

Swallowing his pride, Matt picked up the phone and dialed Shelby's cell again. No answer. Where had she been all day? Had she forgotten her phone? He checked his watch. It was nearing time for Cassidy to get home from school, and she'd have questions and he had no answers.

An hour later he called Shelby's cell again. It went directly to voice mail. A grain of apprehension formed in his gut. If he couldn't locate Shelby in time, he'd have to find a backup chaperone for tonight. His parents weren't due home until Sunday. That left Laura. She was coming home for the weekend.

He paced the kitchen impatiently as he waited for his sister to answer. "You have any idea where Shelby might be?"

"Uh, no. I'm out of town all week. Why would I know that?"

"You two talk don't you?"

"Yes, but only briefly and she doesn't give me her hourly schedule. Why? What's up?"

Matt explained. "I don't understand why she doesn't answer."

"Could be any number of reasons. Don't worry about it. I'm sure she'll show up. She wouldn't miss this slumber party. She's as excited as Cassidy."

"I suppose you're right." He sighed, refusing to think

the worst. His sister was right about one thing. Shelby would never disappoint Cassidy.

He called Shelby's phone several more times but she didn't answer. A knot of anger and anxiety began to form in his gut. No. She wouldn't. She wouldn't leave without saying goodbye. He had to stop thinking the worst.

His cell rang and Laura's name appeared.

"Is she there yet?"

Matt clenched his jaw, trying to quell the knot growing in his gut. "No."

Laura sighed into the phone. "I don't understand. Why doesn't she answer?"

He could find only one explanation for her to be out of touch this long. She was gone and avoiding his calls. He didn't want to believe that, but what other reason could there be?

"No." Laura's voice broke into his dour thoughts. "I know what you're thinking, but you're wrong. Don't jump to conclusions."

"I should have seen this coming."

Laura growled into the phone, "Mathias Durrant, I'd like to wring your neck. There's a perfectly good explanation, and you'll feel like a worm when you hear what it is."

He wanted to believe that. "You're probably right."

"I know I am. In fact, I'll bet she shows up before Cassidy gets off the bus. Have a little faith."

His faith waned, and fear and anger rose as time passed and Shelby failed to appear. He prayed his sister was right, but an hour later when Shelby was still not home, Matt had to face the truth. She'd done it again. She'd grown tired of the small-town life and run back to her career. Only this time, it wasn't his heart she'd left broken in pieces, but his children's.

Matt stood on the front porch waiting with a sick dread in the pit of his stomach. Cassidy had been bouncing off the walls all week with excitement over her slumber party. Now he had to tell her it wasn't going to happen? He watched as his daughter darted off the school bus, her expression filled with joy and excitement. Matt's heart ached. She would be devastated. Not only would she not have her slumber party, but Shelby's departure would crush her.

His cell rang again. Laura. "She's not home."

"Oh, Matt."

He turned away from the sight of his child skipping up the driveway toward him. "How am I going to tell her?"

"Don't. Not yet. The party doesn't start for hours yet. I'll be home around then. I'll fill in if you need me to."

Matt exhaled a tense breath. "She needs to be prepared for the worst."

"*She* does, or *you* do?"

Laura's question was like a thorn in his spirit that he tried to ignore. This wasn't about him.

Matt gave Shelby another half hour before taking his daughter aside. "Cassidy, I think we need to talk." He pulled her onto the sofa beside him, searching frantically for the right words. "We may have to cancel your slumber party."

Dark blue eyes widened with surprise. "Why? What did I do?"

The tremor in her voice broke his heart. "Nothing. It's not you, sweetie. It's Shelby. I think she's gone back home. To New York."

Tears welled up in her eyes, trickling quickly down her cheeks. "No. She wouldn't go without saying good-bye. Besides, she's going to be our chaperone. I've told everyone about her. We're going to do magazine makeup, and she's going to do pictures of my friends like she did me and…" A sob erupted from her throat. She rested her head on his shoulder. "No. She wouldn't do that."

Matt held her close, wishing he could cry himself. He'd believed in Shelby, too. Look what it got him. "She was gone when I got up this morning. She probably missed the big city and decided to go back home."

"You're wrong." Cassidy pushed him away. "You don't like her. I thought you did. You said you were friends, but you're always telling us she'll go away. You're glad she's gone."

Was he glad? There had been a time when he could have answered honestly yes. Now, all he felt was aching sadness and the sting of betrayal again. Right now, what mattered was his daughter's tender heart.

"Everything will be all right. I'll be the chaperone tonight—"

"I don't want you here," Cassidy wailed, sobbing again. "You're a boy! This is a girl night!"

Matt held up his hand. "Only until your aunt Laura gets here. She's on her way home, and she said she'll come and stay so you can have your party."

"That's not the same. I want Miss Shelby. I love her."

Kenny and Chester darted through the room. "Hey. Miss Shelby is home. Can I go see her?"

Cassidy ran to the window, then turned and dashed for the door. "Daddy! She's here. I told you she hadn't left."

Matt walked out onto the front porch. Cassidy ran up to Shelby as she got out of her car and gave her a hug. Matt knew she was spilling her guts and he cringed at the same moment his cell rang again. "She's here."

Laura grunted in his ear. "Imagine that. She showed up in time."

Her sarcasm hit its mark. "Cutting it kind of close."

His sister's tone was icy when she spoke. "If you don't wake up and take that log out of your eye, you're going to lose something special. Is that what you really want?"

Matt watched from the porch as Shelby and Cassidy walked toward him. Shelby looked angry. He braced for the confrontation.

"See, Dad. I told you she hadn't left."

Shelby raised her chin, her brown eyes shooting sparks. "I had a doctor's appointment in Jackson. And then I had some shopping to do. I didn't realize I was supposed to report my comings and goings to you."

"I've been calling you since nine this morning. You couldn't have been at the doctor's all this time." Inwardly, he cringed at his accusatory tone. He shouldn't be attacking her. He should be telling her how relieved and how grateful he was that she hadn't broken Cassidy's heart.

"I turned off my phone and forgot to turn it back on. It happens."

"What was I supposed to think?" She could have at least called and explained her absence.

"That I wouldn't let Cassidy down." She pushed past him and walked into the house with his daughter.

Matt ran a hand through his hair. Why were they always at odds? No. *They* weren't. *He* was. He thought he'd gotten past his fear that Shelby would run off again. She'd proven her reliability over and over since she'd been watching the children. But a part of him was still wary. Laura had warned him he might be losing something special. He knew she was right, but how did he let go and trust Shelby again? How did he let himself love a woman who was sick?

"Molly and Darcy are here!" Cassidy squealed, dashing to the front door.

Shelby gathered her courage. The slumber party had officially begun. Matt had made himself scarce since she'd arrived, for which she was grateful. His sour attitude would have dampened her excitement, not to mention Cassidy's.

Matt's lack of faith hurt. She'd thought they'd gotten beyond the old issues, but she was beginning to think Matt would never completely trust her, or anyone, with his heart ever again. His depth of mistrust and fear of loss could never be overcome. Her main goal now was to make sure Cassidy had the best slumber party possible. Matt would have to deal with his resentment in his own way.

Everything was ready. Food. Movies. Games. She'd bought a new laptop that afternoon, complete with the software she needed for image enhancement. Cassidy was eager to share her new discovery with her friends. It was going to be the highlight of the evening.

Several hours later, Shelby curled up in the chair in Matt's downstairs guest room. It was near enough to the living room to hear the girls if they called, yet private enough that she could get some sleep if possible. Not that she planned on getting much sleep. The girls were giggling and laughing. The music was loud. That meant the evening was a success.

She'd taught the girls all about makeup. They'd taken pictures and tweaked them the way she'd done for Cassidy, only this time it came with a discussion of what was real and what was fake, what was appropriate and what wasn't. She'd been surprised at the girls' wisdom. One girl had brought up the fact that the Lord expected them to behave and dress one way and the world another. It was a topic that went on for some time since a few of the girls apparently didn't attend church.

Their discussion had convinced her that starting a Christian magazine for young girls was a good idea. She had a new desire to publish what was inspiring and supportive, instead of encouraging them to dress and act like celebrities. It wasn't that *Tween Scene* did anything wrong, but she wanted to create something better. Reaching for her drink, she realized the house had gone silent. Not a good thing at a slumber party.

She peeked around the corner at the living room. Sleeping bags filled with little girls covered the floor. Tousled hair peeked out of the covers and little feet protruded from blankets.

Every flat surface in the room was covered with food or makeup. She smiled. She couldn't remember the last time she'd had so much fun, when she'd known such joy and a sense of belonging. Teaching Cassidy's friends about makeup had kept them all in stitches. They'd giggled and laughed until tears rolled down their cheeks.

"Thank you, Father, for this opportunity." She would cherish these memories forever.

A blanket moved, causing Chester to raise his head from his comfy spot beside his mistress. Cassidy sat up and smiled, her eyes drowsy but bright with happiness. Shelby waved.

The girl scooted out from under the covers and hurried toward her, throwing her arms around her neck. "Thank you. Thank you, Miss Shelby. This is the best party ever. I'll love you forever." She kissed Shelby's cheek, then scurried back to bed.

The lump in her throat made it hard to swallow. Fighting tears, she turned and walked back to the guest room and crawled into bed. This is what she wanted. This is what her life should be about. A home. A family. Children.

She loved Matt. She loved his children. She would gladly spend the rest of her life raising them, but the wounds she'd inflicted ran too deep for him to overcome. Her health issues were an obstacle that Matt shouldn't have to confront ever again. She couldn't go on pretending, living a life that could never be hers. It wasn't fair to Matt and his children, and it wasn't fair to her.

Her leave was almost up. Gramma would be home in a few days. Maybe it was time for her to return to New York. Go back to the life she knew and let Matt return to his.

The realization sent a lance of sadness through her heart.

Matt and Kenny stepped through the front door Saturday morning and stopped in their tracks. The room resembled a bedding store after an earthquake. He looked closer and saw little heads sticking out here and there. No one stirred.

He glanced down at his son, putting his finger to

his lips, indicating silence. "Come on, kiddo. Let's go around to the back door so we don't wake anyone." Shelby was perched on a stool at the counter, sipping coffee when they entered. "Good morning."

Her smile was welcoming, though a bit droopy. He doubted if she'd gotten much sleep. "We brought sustenance." He held up a box of fresh doughnuts. "How did it go?"

"Chester." Kenny reached down to hug his dog, who came trotting over. "Can I have a doughnut now?"

Matt nodded and filled a cup with fresh coffee. "Any problems?"

"Not a one. They were perfect little angels. Even Chester behaved. The girls all loved him."

He grinned. It felt natural to have Shelby waiting for him this morning. "Looks like they left a perfect little mess in there."

She shoved the doughnut carton to the far side of the counter. "The bigger the mess, the better the party."

"I'll remember that for next time."

Shelby glanced downward, staring into her cup. Was she thinking the same as he? Next time would happen without her participation.

"How about you bachelors?" She extended her arm, drawing Kenny to her side.

"We lived wild and free, didn't we, sport?" Matt ruffled his son's hair.

"We got pizza at bedtime," Kenny proclaimed. "It was awesome."

The doorbell chimed and shuffling noises commenced in the living room.

"That's probably Anna's mom. She said she'd have to

pick her up early this morning." Shelby rose and moved to the other room.

Matt followed behind, wondering at the ease with which she'd assumed command of his household. Cassidy met him in the hall.

"Good morning, Daddy." She smiled and wrapped her arms around his waist.

He kissed the top of her head. "Good morning, sweetheart. Did you have fun?"

She nodded. "It was the best ever."

He hugged her again. It was all worth it. The worry. The doubt. The second-guessing about leaving Shelby in charge. His little girl was happy. Matt watched his daughter scurry back into the jumble of the living room. Shelby stood in the center of the room, smiling, laughing with the girls as they started to gather their belongings. She slipped an arm around Cassidy and pulled her close.

It was a simple gesture, but it left him breathless. He stared at the tableau before him, blinking as Kenny tore into the scene, skidding to a stop at Shelby's side and taking her hand.

The doorbell sounded again, breaking the spell.

Parents started to arrive in a steady stream to pick up their daughters. Matt pushed through the door with a sleeping bag and a satchel on his fourth trip to a car. Shelby was on the porch saying goodbye to one of the girls and her mother.

"Mrs. Durrant, I can't thank you enough for doing this. I wish I could let Addison have a slumber party, but I don't think I could stand the chaos. You're a brave mother."

Matt stopped cold. His started to correct the woman,

but common courtesy told him to let it pass. His gaze locked with Shelby's, and he saw his own discomfort reflected in her soft brown eyes. Mrs. Durrant. His wife.

Shelby retreated into the house. He deposited the last guest's belongings in their car and waved goodbye. Slowly he started back inside. Cassidy and Shelby were wrapped in a bear hug when he entered the living room. "I love you. Thank you so much." Cassidy tilted her head back and gave Shelby a huge smile.

"You're welcome, sweetie. I had a great time, too."

Cassidy yawned and stepped back. "I'm going to bed. I'm sleepy."

Shelby watched her go, a tender smile on her face. She turned to him and the smile vanished. His heart pounded. Realization hit him like a sledgehammer to his chest. She belonged here, with him, in his home as surely as he did. She started around the room, picking up glasses and half-empty snack bags. He moved toward her, taking her wrist in his hand as she reached for an empty bowl. "Leave all this. I'll do it later. You've done enough. More than enough, and I'm so grateful. Cassidy had a wonderful time."

"Me, too."

He held her wrist, pulling her around to face him. He looked into her eyes and saw her anxiety reflected back at him. Being back together had rekindled embers long damped. He wanted to hold her again, kiss her and never let her go. He was losing his battle, trying to keep her out of his heart. Trying to keep his own heart safe from loss. Touching her face, he said, "How can I ever thank you for what you've done?"

"No thanks are necessary. I love spending time with your children."

"What about their father? Do you like spending time with him?" He hadn't intended to ask that question, but now he found himself bracing for her answer.

"I always have."

She lowered her lashes, but not before he saw the love in her eyes. The same love that had burned so strongly fifteen years ago. Instead of filling him with joy it filled him with fear. This rekindled romance didn't have a happy ending. It couldn't.

She was so loving. So amazing. "Why haven't you ever married? You should have a family of your own." Sadness flashed through her eyes before she looked away.

"I never found anyone who— Anyone I wanted to spend my life with, I guess."

He reached out to her but she stepped away, a stiff smile on her face.

"I've got to go. I'm too old to have this much fun. I need a long nap, too." She slipped past him and walked to the door, closing it behind her. His house and his heart felt empty.

Fatigue and letdown from the slumber party hit Shelby the moment she entered Gramma's house. But after a long nap, a shower and a healthy meal, she was feeling human again.

Pouring another glass of tea, she set her new laptop on the kitchen table and waited for it to power up. She had to work on something. Otherwise her conflicting emotions would tie her in knots. How was she supposed to watch Matt's children and pretend that they hadn't shared that earthquake of a kiss? How could she go along acting as if they were friends when she wanted more? The answer was she couldn't.

In the shower, the water had released the fatigue and tension; it had also washed away her emotional cobwebs and showed her what she needed to do. It was time to go back to New York. Funny thing was, she didn't want to. There was nothing there to go back to but an empty apartment and probably the unemployment line. But she couldn't stay here either. She couldn't stay here in Dover and see Matt and the kids and not be part of their lives. She couldn't be content with being simply a neighbor and friend. She loved them too much. She wanted to be with them forever. But how did she get past the wall between her and Matt?

Gramma was due home in a few days. She'd spend the week with her, then go back up north on the weekend. It was the right thing to do. Shelby pressed her lips together to keep from crying. She opened her email and scanned the long list. One from her boss caught her breath. The decision about the future of Harmon Publishing would be announced at a special meeting Monday morning.

Waves of uncertainly and dread crashed into her mind. Quickly she read through the other emails, trying to find some hint of what was to come. Opinions among her colleagues ranged from minimum layoffs to a complete shutdown of the company. Either way, she, along with many others, were likely looking at unemployment.

Worrying about her health was scary enough. Worrying about her livelihood was paralyzing. Thankfully, she had savings and a few investments, but they were for her retirement, and she didn't want to tap those funds unless it was an emergency.

If she'd learned nothing else from this journey home, she'd learned to let go of things she couldn't control. But that meant keeping her mind on something else. Unfortunately, the something else was that kiss.

What she needed was something fun and creative to do. Like her plan for an online magazine. Ideas had been rolling around in her mind from the moment she'd awakened that afternoon and she couldn't wait to get them organized. Within a few hours she had a rough draft of her magazine all laid out.

The knock on the door was a unwelcome intrusion. "What now?" Growling under her breath, she went to the door, surprised to find Matt on the other side. The sight of him brought the kiss vividly to her mind, weakening her knees. She swallowed and tried to shove it aside. "Oh. Hey." He smiled, which started her memories replaying again.

"Do you have a minute? I'd like to talk to you."

She couldn't imagine why he was here. There wasn't anything to talk about. "Sure." She stepped back, allowing him to enter. "Let's go to the sunroom." She led the way, acutely aware of him behind her. They'd formed a comfortable friendship over the last weeks, but the kiss and his distrust had put them on shaky ground again.

Entering the sunroom, Shelby quickly wished she'd suggested the formal living room instead. This room was too small, too intimate. She motioned for him to sit and took a seat in her favorite chair in the corner, a safe distance from Matt.

She waited. Matt sat on edge of the chair, forearms resting on his thighs. She sensed his tension.

"Shelby, I wanted to thank you again for chaperoning the party. Cassidy hasn't stopped talking about it. She's on the phone now reliving every moment with her friends."

"I'm glad. But you thanked me this morning, Matt."

He nodded. "But I didn't apologize for doubting you. I should have known you'd never do that to Cassidy."

"Apparently not. But this isn't about me. It's about you. You'll never forgive me for leaving you, and I understand." Shelby stared at her hands. "I guess no matter what I do, you'll never trust me fully. So let me apologize to you. I'm sorry for breaking our engagement. I'm sorry I didn't wait and try to understand. I'm sorry I didn't try and contact you again. It just wasn't meant to be."

Matt shook his head. "When you didn't show, when I couldn't get in touch with you, it was like reliving that old hurt. Only this time it was going to hurt my daughter."

"I love that little girl." Tears sprang up in her eyes, and she quickly swiped them away.

Matt stood and came toward her, taking a seat on the ottoman beside the chaise. "I'm sorry. When it comes to my kids, I'm a bit—"

"Overprotective?"

"Now you sound like my dad."

Matt reached out and touched his fingers to the back of her hand. "There's something else I want to sort out." He looked into her eyes. "What happened between us the other night."

Shelby chewed her lip, fighting the mounting anxiety in her stomach. She was afraid to look at him. "There's nothing to sort out. We both got caught up in old feelings. Being together so much complicated things. It didn't mean anything."

"Is that how you really feel?"

She wanted to believe it was disappointment she heard in his voice, but she knew it was relief. He regretted kissing her and wanted to make sure it didn't happen again. "Why do you want to know?"

"I don't know. That's why I'm here, I guess. Having you back in my life, seeing you every day, made me remember what we once had."

"That was a long time ago. Besides, it doesn't matter. I'm going back to New York."

"You're leaving?"

"It's time."

"Just like that?" Matt stood and walked to the window, his hands resting on his hips.

"Not just like that. I'm pretty sure I'm going to be unemployed soon. I need to get back and start looking for another job." What would he do if she told him the real truth, that she loved him and she'd never stopped? What would he say if she explained how much she wanted to be part of his life? His children's lives? Nothing could change the fact that she had health issues. She couldn't guarantee something more serious wouldn't crop up. The risk would always there, hanging over her head, and she would never ask him to endure that with her.

There remained one more painful task. She had to tell the children she was going back home. In some ways that would be the more difficult task because three hearts would be broken, and she knew hers would never, ever heal.

"But what about my kids? They'll be upset. Heartbroken."

"I know. But I've tried to prepare them. I never told anyone I'd stay here permanently. And besides, there's no reason for me to stay. Is there?"

Matt's blue eyes darkened. "No. None that I can think of."

Chapter Twelve

Shelby exited the side door in the Hope Chapel sanctuary and started toward the parking lot. She'd joined Pam and her family at church today. But with Matt and the children seated in her direct line of sight to the pulpit, she'd found it hard to concentrate on the sermon. The moment the benediction was finished, she quickly made her departure and headed for the door. She wanted to avoid Matt. Speaking to him would only shatter what was left of her broken heart. She unlocked her car, only to freeze in her tracks when she heard her name called.

"Miss Shelby."

Cassidy and Kenny ran up to her. Matt followed a short distance behind.

"Gramma and Grandpa are coming home from Dallas today. We're going to pick them up at the airport. You wanna come?"

Kenny nodded, taking Shelby's hand as if to pull her along with him. "Yeah, our uncle Ty is getting better, so they can come home now."

She'd like nothing better. If she had her way, she'd do everything with these precious children. "I'd like to, but I have something to take care of this afternoon. Say hello for me, though."

"Okay."

The children moved off and climbed into their SUV, which she realized was parked only a few spots away from her car. Matt stood in front of her. She forced herself to stay calm despite the knot of nerves in her stomach. "I'd like to take the kids for pizza later if that's all right with you."

Matt frowned. "Why?"

"I want to tell them I'm leaving. I thought it should come from me first."

He held her gaze a moment then nodded. "All right. We'll be back from Jackson around four. Call when you're ready to go."

Shelby watched him walk away. Ready to go? She wasn't ready to go at all.

The house seemed uncomfortably quiet. Usually Sunday afternoons had a sweet peacefulness about them, especially when the kids were gone and he had the place all to himself. But instead of kicking back and watching a ball game, he was pacing like a caged beast, unable to sit still or focus.

Matt massaged his temple, trying to ease the tension building inside his skull. His children were with Shelby, learning she was leaving Dover and going back home. They were going to be heartbroken. Shelby believed his children would understand and accept her departure. He wasn't so sure. His kids adored Shelby. Every word out of their mouths was prefaced with her name. She would leave a big hole in their lives when she left. One he had no idea how to fill.

Walking out onto the porch, his gaze went immediately to the house next door. A few weeks ago his life had been calm, orderly and safe. Now his children's hearts were in danger and his own was shredded. He'd known from the start Shelby would go back to her career. So why did it hurt so much now that she was? Because he loved her, that's why. No matter how hard he tried to deny it, Shelby held his heart.

A heart that could fail and take her away without warning. The very idea plunged a razor-sharp knife into his gut. He might love Shelby, but he couldn't afford to love her. The risk was too great. It was best she was leaving. Once Shelby was gone, they could go back to their normal life and everyone would be better off in the long run.

He turned on his heel and went back inside and headed upstairs. As he passed Cassidy's room, he glanced in and frowned. The room was a mess. Clothes and shoes were strewn all over the floor. Nail polish bottles lay on top of scraps of homework papers. Schoolbooks, pencils and backpack were tossed carelessly on her desk. Her bed was unmade. A small table in the corner was bulging with junk, haphazardly covered with a sheet.

Matt grimaced. It was time for his little princess to clean her room. He pulled off the sheet and small pieces of paper fluttered onto the floor. A large book shifted to the edge of the card table. A photograph caught his eye. Katie. He looked closer. It was a picture of his wife and children taken at an Easter-egg hunt several years ago. What was it doing here? Matt sorted through the items on the table. Large pages held photos of Katie that the kids had decorated with tiny trinkets and ribbons. A scrapbook.

He'd seen Shelby working on her grandmother's scrapbook during the weeks she'd been here. She'd told him it was her therapy since being displaced from her job. He could easily imagine Cassidy wanting to do one, too. She wanted to do everything Shelby did. She was wonderful with his kids. For all his concerns about her, she'd never once disappointed him.

He sat down on the edge of Cassidy's bed and looked through the book. He could detect Kenny's hand in several of the pages. Shelby's creativity was clearly visible, as well. He'd always envied her that ability. She found beauty in even ordinary things. It was as if she saw the world with different eyes than most people.

The doorbell echoed through the house. Quickly he replaced the items on the table and drew the sheet over them. Hurrying downstairs, he found his father waiting at the back door. "Hey, Dad. Is something wrong? News about Ty?"

Tom Durrant smiled. "Nope. I just left my best pair of sunglasses in your car." Matt retrieved the glasses and invited his dad inside. He didn't have to tell his father something was on his mind.

"So what's troubling you? Care to talk about it?"

Maybe a different point of view would help him sort things out. "Shelby's decided to go back to New York. She's leaving in a few days."

"Well, that's not much of a surprise, is it?" Tom took a can of soda from the fridge and opened it.

"No. It's probably for the best anyway. She took the kids for pizza to tell them. They'll be heartbroken. They really like her."

"Yes, they do. What about you? Will your heart be broken, too?"

"No." The look on his dad's face said he didn't believe him for a second. "Maybe. Some. But it can't work."

"Why? Because she has a medical condition?"

"It complicates things, yes."

"How so?"

"Because she is sick. She's had a heart attack. How can I ask my kids to accept a mother who could die? I can't put them through that again."

"So you do love her, then. I mean, if you're thinking about her being a mother to your kids."

Matt stood and walked to the sink. "No. I'm not. I mean, if it were just me, then maybe, but it's not."

"Let me get this straight. You love Shelby, but she has a minor medical condition and might die at some point, so you can't marry her because she's not perfectly healthy."

It sounded so callous and selfish when his dad said it.

"Tell me, do you regret marrying Katie? Do you regret having those two precious kids with her?"

"Of course not. I loved every minute of our life together."

"So if she'd never been a part of your life, what would you have missed?"

"Everything wonderful and—"

Tom rose and came to his side, resting a comforting hand on his shoulder. "Let go of the fear, son. It's time to move forward. Even Job received a new family out of God's grace. Give the Lord your broken heart. Let Him put the pieces back together."

How was it possible to love someone so much yet be

so afraid of that love? And how did he let go of the fear of being hurt again? His dad was right about one thing. The Lord couldn't fix a broken heart if you didn't give Him all the pieces.

Shelby watched the stunned expressions on Cassidy and Kenny's faces, bracing for their response. She'd broken the news that she would be leaving Dover at the end of the week. Their sad little faces mirrored her own.

Cassidy tugged her straw up and down through the plastic lid. "Are you going back to New York?"

"Yes." Cassidy looked at her with wide blue eyes, eyes like her father's.

"Daddy kept telling us you'd leave one day. But I don't want you to."

A lump of sadness settled in her chest. She should have expected him to do that.

"Can't you stay here?" Kenny's voice was filled with pleading.

Shelby hugged him to her side. "I don't have a job here, sweetheart."

"You could do scrapbooks for people." Cassidy's sweet face lit up with hope.

"That's a good idea." Shelby chuckled. "Gramma has complained she has to go all the way to Jackson to find a good assortment of material." A local scrapbooking store might do well here. Dover was certainly big enough now to support such an endeavor. There were several available storefronts around the square, and she'd always wanted to start a business of her own. Except she couldn't stay here now. She turned her focus back to the children and their crestfallen expressions.

"I know I didn't give you very good news, but I wanted tell you myself because that's what friends do."

Kenny's bottom lip stuck out. "Who's going to watch us after school?"

Cassidy nodded. "And what about our scrapbook? I can't do it without you, Miss Shelby."

"I'm sure my gramma will be happy to babysit. She was supposed to from the beginning, remember? I was only her helper. And I'll bet she'd love to help you finish the scrapbook, Cass."

"Don't you love us anymore?"

"Of course I do." She reached across the table and took Cassidy's hand. "I want you to know that no matter where I am, I will always love you and we'll always be friends. You can call me whenever you want to talk, and maybe you can come and visit me in New York. There's all kinds of cool things to do and see."

"Daddy won't bring us." Cassidy shook her head slowly.

She was probably right about that. "Then maybe your aunt Laura will bring you. She's my friend, too. Or I can come and visit you. Remember, my gramma still lives next door, and I don't think she's planning on moving away."

Kenny looked over at her with wide eyes. "Are you going to die?"

"What?"

Cassidy and Kenny exchanged glances. "We heard Gramma talking about you on the way home from the airport. She said you were sick. That you had a heart attack."

Shelby sighed. She should have anticipated this, but she wanted to spare them any unnecessary worry. "Yes.

I did, but it wasn't a bad one. Just a very little one. Kind of a warning attack." She squeezed Kenny's little hand.

"So, it's not a sure thing. I mean, it's not like when Mom had cancer?" Cassidy asked, her eyes moist.

"No, it's not like that," Shelby reassured her quickly. "There's a lot I can do to stay healthy. I'll take medicine, I'll exercise and eat right and I'll be fine. There's a lot of heart disease in my family, so I have to be extra careful. Plus, I had a checkup and the doctor told me I'm much better." The doctor had adjusted her meds. And, while he was pleased with her improvement, he'd admonished her to continue watching her diet and exercise regularly. He'd also strongly recommended she avoid stress. He probably wouldn't approve of her decision to return to the hectic pace of her life in New York. But she had no other option.

"Well, we'd better get back home. It's a school night, remember."

"Will you still watch us tomorrow after school?"

She swallowed the lump of sadness in her throat. How could she face that final moment of goodbye? "Sure. I wouldn't miss that." Shelby gathered up the children and started toward the door, painfully aware of the dejected slope of their small shoulders. Seeing the fear in their eyes when they had asked about her health made her fully realize the depth of their grief in losing their mother. Maybe Matt was right. Having her in their lives wasn't a good thing. But how was she going to face leaving them?

The sun had barely topped the trees when Shelby gave up hope of sleeping. She'd spent the night wrestling between her heart and her common sense. Her heart longed to stay in Dover, be near Matt and the children, but her common sense told her that would cause pain for everyone. Today's meeting at Harmon Publishing had only added to her worries. Not since breaking up with Matt had she wanted so desperately to run and never look back. But she'd learned the hard way that running and avoiding only made things worse.

Tossing aside the covers, she rose and went to the window, pulling back the lace curtain to look at Matt's house. One afternoon was all she had left with Cassidy and Kenny. Gramma would be home tomorrow and she would take over the babysitting duties. A sob formed in the center of her chest. How she dreaded this day and that moment when she'd have to say goodbye. She'd decided to take the children to a movie that afternoon or to the park. Anything to keep her busy and out of Matt's house. Sitting there waiting for the end to come would be torture.

Sadness rose up without warning, swamping her like a tidal wave. The smallest thought of Cassidy and Kenny brought her to tears. Her heart burned like it was being slowly pulled from her chest. She couldn't allow herself to even think about Matt.

Turning away from the window, she prayed for courage and strength to face the challenges of the day. She had to stay busy today. Keep her mind occupied. After a quick shower and breakfast, she devoted herself to finishing the scrapbook as a welcome home for Gramma. She ached for her comforting hug. Being alone made all of this worse.

When her cell rang later in the morning she jumped. She'd been so absorbed in her task she'd forgotten about the meeting. One glance at the screen told her it was the call she'd been dreading. She answered, listening as her boss relayed the bad news, her heart sinking into the pit of her stomach.

Stunned, Shelby dropped her phone on the table and buried her face in her hands. Her worst fears had come true. No one at Harmon had been spared. *Tween Scene,* along with most other publications, was being discontinued. The new company was restructuring everything, moving in a different direction. Severance packages were generous but wouldn't last long. She'd have to find a different place to live, a new job. Her head throbbed with the enormity of the prospect.

She thought she'd been prepared for this moment, but now that it was here, it was more frightening than she'd expected. Her heart raced. Pressure began to build in her chest. A sob rose up from deep inside, doubling her over with its force. It was too much. Matt. The children. Her job. How was she supposed to go on when her life was in ruins?

Her throat tightened, making it hard to swallow. Closing her eyes, she shook her head, fighting the sense of impending doom crawling across her mind. She straightened and started across the room for a glass of water to calm her nerves. A wave of dizziness brought her up short. She couldn't catch her breath. A vice grip squeezed around her chest. Fear closed her throat. Her palms grew damp, broke out in a cold sweat.

Black fear rose up from her core, coiling along her nerves like a deadly serpent. "No. Oh, please, God. Not again." She couldn't be having a heart attack. She forced herself to remain calm and think. She'd been following orders, eating right, exercising, taking her meds. Why was this happening again?

What should she do now? Call the paramedics? The cardiologist she'd seen was an hour away in Jackson. Shelby closed her eyes, struggling to calm herself. Dr. Morgan had given her reams of information to read to educate herself on her medical condition. Why hadn't she read it?

One thought screamed loud and clear in her mind. She didn't want to die. This wasn't about Matt or a job. This was about life and death.

Hurrying to the phone, she dialed 911, praying she hadn't waited too late.

Matt strode down the hall toward his office, eager to lock himself inside and grab a bite to eat. He was having a hard time concentrating on lessons today. He kept thinking about Shelby and her decision to leave Dover. It was for the best, but the thought of her being gone left a hollow feeling in his chest.

His cell phone rang the moment he grasped his office doorknob. The name displayed on the screen brought him up short. Pam Fleming. Why would she be calling him at work? A finger of concern touched his mind. "Hello."

"Matt, this is Pam Fleming, Shelby's friend."

"Yes, I know. What can I do for you?" There was a pause that sent Matt's concern spiking.

"I just found out that Shelby was brought in by ambulance earlier. They think she's had a heart attack."

Icy fear froze the blood in his veins. "Is she—"

"I don't know any more right now. I'm headed down to the ER to check on her. I thought you should know."

"Yes. Thanks. I'll come right over." His mind struggled to grasp what had happened. He had to get to the hospital. He had to see her, to know she was all right. Within minutes he was in his car heading for the hospital on the other side of town. He'd arranged for a replacement for his classes and called his mom to come stay with the kids after school.

Pulsing urgency coursed through him as he navigated traffic. Why was everyone driving so slowly today? He turned onto a side street, hoping to make better time on the lesser-traveled streets.

He'd feared this moment since Shelby had first told him of her heart problems and he'd tried to steel himself against this very thing. Yet here he was, living his worst nightmare. His heart pounded violently in his chest. If she died… He couldn't go through this again.

Flashing blue lights appeared up ahead and Matt slowed his speed, passing the group of vehicles on the side of the road. An ambulance was parked in front of a wrecked sedan. He sent up a prayer for the victims and another one for Shelby. It hit him then that it could have been her in that car. In fact, it could have been him. No one knew the number of days the Lord had assigned to them.

How many days had the Lord given to Shelby? What if this were the day He called her home? The thought rocked him to his core.

He loved Shelby. He'd admitted that, but not enough to risk committing his life to her. But if he lost her, his life from here on would be empty. He didn't want to live in fear any longer. He wanted to be happy again, and having her in his life would be worth the risk.

He knew the exact moment when he'd lost his heart to her again. Friday night in the middle of the pizza place. He'd turned to see Shelby at the table with his kids, relaxed, comfortable, as if she belonged there. He'd tried to deny it, but he'd known in that instant she belonged in his family, in his home and in his life.

He'd loved Katie; they'd been happy together. But she was gone. What kind of happiness would he miss out on if he kept Shelby out of his life? He didn't want to find out. He prayed for her life and for time to set things right between them.

The Lord had given them each a number of days. Wanted them to live in the present, allowing their faith to light the next step, not the next mile. He'd been relying on his own to protect his heart and those of his children. Dad was right. He couldn't prevent people from loving and caring about each other. It was time to trust in the Lord and make the most of this day.

Matt battled a gnawing fear as he followed the nurse through the emergency room corridors. No one would tell him anything, instructing him to talk to her physician. He tried to prepare himself for the worst, praying every second for the chance to tell her how he felt. The nurse stopped and pointed to a curtained-off cubicle. He stopped outside room 219, suddenly afraid of what he would find on the other side.

"Miss Russell, there's someone here to see you." She pulled back the curtain and walked away. Shelby was standing beside the bed, dressed and sorting through her purse. She turned, her beautiful brown eyes wide with surprise when she saw him.

"Matt?"

"I came as soon as I heard." He'd expected to find her in bed, pale and weak. Instead she looked as healthy as a fall rose. "What are you doing out of bed?"

"How did you know?"

"Pam called. Are you all right? They said you'd been brought in by ambulance. That you'd had a heart attack."

She smiled, further confusing him. "No. Well, they thought so at first. The tests confirmed that it was only an anxiety attack. Nothing to do with my heart at all. Just stress."

"Stress?"

She nodded, focusing on her purse again. "Yes. It's official. I'm out of a job. Guess I wasn't as prepared for the news as I'd thought."

"I'm sorry to hear that. So you're all right?"

"Fine. Sorry, I didn't mean to upset you."

"Upset?" He walked toward her, searching her eyes for confirmation that she was telling him the truth. He reached out and took her arms in his hands. "I was frantic. I thought you might be—" Relief surged through like a dam bursting. He pulled her into his arms, one hand cradling the back of her head. "I thought I'd lost you. Thank God you're all right." He held her face in his hands, his thumbs gently caressing her cheeks. For the first time in a long time, he felt whole. "Shelly—"

"Oops. So sorry, didn't mean to intrude."

Matt turned to see Pam Fleming in the doorway, a knowing smirk on her face.

"I was just coming to get our patient. Admissions has cleared you to leave, girlfriend."

"You're going home? Now?"

Shelby nodded. "No reason to keep me. Pam is going to drive me home."

Matt glanced over his shoulder. "No need. I can take her. She lives right next door, you know."

"Fine with me. I'll go get the wheelchair. And, yes,

Shelby, you have to ride in it. It's hospital policy, so don't argue."

He looked at Shelby. Her eyes were filled with questions. He wanted to answer them all, but not here. Not now. He'd been a coward. So deeply wounded by Shelby's leaving and Katie's dying to risk his heart again. God had given them a second chance and he vowed to make the most of it.

The moment Matt parked his SUV beside the house, Shelby opened the door and climbed out. They hadn't spoken the entire way home. If she didn't get away from him soon she'd be in the throes of another anxiety attack. "Thank you for bringing me home." She tore her gaze from his handsome face and started toward Gramma's house.

"Shelby."

She turned reluctantly to face him. She raised her chin and met his gaze.

"Where are you going?"

There was a strange tone in his voice she'd never heard before. The truth pierced her heart. "I'm going home."

He moved closer, his blue eyes holding her gaze. "Why?"

"It's where I belong."

He stopped in front of her, so close she had to tilt back her head to see him. His nearness made her want to cry. Only a short time ago she was safe in his embrace. Now she had to walk away.

"I agree."

Her heart shriveled inside her chest. Nothing had changed. He still wanted her gone, out of his life. Tears filled her eyes and she turned away. Matt gently pulled her around to face him.

"What do you want from me, Matt?" She tried to pull away, but he held her tightly.

"That's not your home." He tightened his grip.

She tried to pull away again, but he held firm. "I'll be leaving in a few days. You were right, after all. It wasn't a heart attack, but it could have been."

"No. You're wrong."

Shelby shivered as he slid his hands slowly down her arms.

"Because if it hadn't happened, I would never have realized what a coward I was and I would have lost you a second time."

Shelby wasn't sure she'd heard him right. "I don't understand." She searched his eyes for some explanation.

"I love you, Shelly. I always have."

"No." She struggled to grasp what she was hearing. "You can't. What if—"

Matt pressed his fingers against her lips. "What if a plane falls on the house tomorrow? What if a storm blows everything away? We had no warning Katie was going to get sick. Ty didn't see those bullets coming. It happened. The same could happen to any of us any time. None of that matters. I love you. My children adore you. Whatever the future holds, we'll face it together. Your home is with us. Nowhere else."

Shelby wanted to believe what she saw in Matt's eyes, what he was saying, but she'd given up hope.

Matt brushed a strand of hair off her forehead. "All I could think of as I drove to town was how much we would have missed because of my stupid fear. How much joy my children would never know because I tried to protect them in the wrong way."

"Matt, are you sure?"

He grinned and pulled her into his embrace. "Yes. I know you love me, too. Don't you?"

She nodded against the warmth of his chest. "How did you guess?"

He chuckled softly. "Only a woman who loved me would help my children make a scrapbook about their mother."

"I do love you. I never stopped. I was such a fool to—"

Matt silenced her with a soft kiss. "That's in the past. I want to look to the future. Marry me?"

"I want to, but can you deal with my problem?" Maybe he didn't understand what she'd told him. Maybe he wasn't thinking clearly.

"Can you deal with mine?" He leaned close and whispered in her ear, "I snore."

She stared at him a moment, then giggled. "That could be a deal breaker."

"Come home, Shelly. You belong with me. With us."

She looked into his eyes and saw her future. "I know."

* * * * *

Dear Reader,

I hope you enjoyed meeting Shelby and Matt and their small Mississippi town of Dover. It's always fun when old loves reunite and the sparks fly. And that's just what happens with these two. But old resentments and misconceptions can distort even the best relationships if we're not careful.

Trust and communication were key factors in Matt and Shelby's breakup and their reunion. Trusting God with our lives and communicating daily with Him through His word are vital to our faith journey.

I enjoyed writing Matt and Shelby's story because like many of us, they believed they were in control of their lives. We all have plans for our lives, visions of how things will unfold. But oftentimes we forget to ask God what His plans are for our lives, and I've learned we can never think up, create or envision a plan that is better than the one Our Father has laid out for us.

I enjoy hearing from readers. You can write me at LorraineBeatty.blogspot.com or through Love Inspired Books.

Lorraine Beatty

RESTORING HIS HEART

Give, and it will be given to you. A good measure, pressed down, shaken together and running over, will be poured into your lap. For with the same measure you use, it will be measured to you.

—*Luke* 6:38

To my sweet hubby, Joe, who is always there cheering me on and offering hugs. I love you. And to Melissa for her help, her guidance and mostly her patience. I couldn't have done it without you.

Chapter One

Adam Holbrook stood and faced the bench of the Honorable Judge Hankins A. Wallace. The man seated there didn't look anything like what he'd expected. He'd envisioned the judge in a small rural town like Dover, Mississippi, to be a balding, overweight, quirky character with horn-rimmed glasses perched on the end of his nose. One look at this magistrate had given Adam his first moment of concern.

Judge Wallace was stern-faced and imposing, and it had nothing to do with his being elevated behind the bench. Broad shoulders, steely brown eyes and a set to his jaw that made it clear he was in charge. Adam's throat went dry. He glanced over at his court-appointed attorney. He'd considered calling his own attorney yesterday after he'd been arrested for reckless endangerment and destroying public property, a result of his accidently running his car into the town's park and damaging a small building. But his attorney was also his most recent girlfriend and the relationship had ended badly, so he'd chosen to go with a court-appointed lawyer. Now he questioned that decision.

"Adam Holbrook?"

"Yes, Your Honor." He put as much respect and sincerity into his tone as possible.

"Were you driving drunk in my town, Mr. Holbrook?"

"No, sir."

The judge's dark gaze pierced him from across the room. "So, then what were you doing when you decided to destroy our beloved landmark?"

He opened his mouth to protest, then changed his mind. Better to eat crow and be on his way. In twenty-eight days he had to be seated at the board of directors meeting of his father's company, Holbrook Electronics, or lose the yearly allowance from his trust fund forever. There were no excuses acceptable. Either be in Atlanta on time or face financial ruin. "I was trying to use the GPS on my phone."

The judge nodded knowingly and glanced at the papers on his desk. "Uh-huh. Well then, let's get straight to it. I'm sure you're anxious to get this over with."

Adam allowed a small grin. "As a matter of fact I am. I have interests in Atlanta that require my immediate attention." He was pleased with his calm, respectful tone. Hope rose. All he had to do now was meet the bail, pay any fines and he could be on his way.

"Do you now?" Judge Wallace took the folder in front of him in his hands and scanned the contents. "It says here you're some kind of minor celebrity. That you like to indulge in all manner of extreme sporting adventures." His tone was thick with disapproval.

Hope took a nosedive. He might have grossly underestimated this small town's justice system. He waited, a heightened sense of anticipation sparking his nerves, similar to the sensation he experienced right before he jumped out of a plane or dived off a cliff.

The judge leaned back in his chair, frowning. "We do things a bit differently here in Dover, Mr. Holbrook. We believe in the punishment fitting the crime."

"I'll be more than happy to have the structure repaired, Your Honor." That should score a few points.

"That's good to hear. That's what I had in mind, as well. You see, that wasn't any old structure you crashed your flashy silver car into. That was an historic landmark. It's the symbol of this town. It's one hundred and thirty years old and we're rather fond of that gazebo."

A small bead of sweat trickled down his back. "Yes, sir."

"So, here's what you're going to do." The judge straightened in his chair and banged his gavel on the bench. "You're hereby sentenced to thirty days under house arrest. And you will spend those days rebuilding the gazebo you damaged. Any spare hours will be spent doing community service."

Adam struggled to grasp what the judge had just said. He couldn't be serious. "Your Honor, I have urgent personal matters in Atlanta that require my presence."

The judge shook his head. "That's unfortunate. Thirty days."

No. Thirty days would mean he'd miss the deadline. There were no contingencies with the rules of his trust fund. No leeway. He either showed up for the meeting or he was cut off. Permanently. Once Arthur Holbrook made a decree it was carved in stone. Especially something like this. "Your Honor, what about bail? I'm able to meet any amount you deem equitable."

"Yes, I'm sure you're more than able. That's the

point, Mr. Holbrook. I suspect buying your way out of things is a bad habit with you. No bail."

"Your Honor…"

The judge held up his hand. "I figure that gazebo damage is well within the felony limits. You're fortunate that no one was injured in your little stunt or you could be facing manslaughter charges."

Dryness in his throat made it hard to swallow. He had been greatly relieved that no one had been injured, but he couldn't afford to be stuck in rural Mississippi for a month. He searched frantically for a way out of this mess. He looked to his attorney, who shrugged and shook his head. He was on his own. A surge of anger rushed through his veins. What else was new? Adam faced the bench again. He flashed his most engaging smile. "With all due respect, sir, I don't know how to repair that building."

"I suspect not. That's why I'm assigning an expert to help you out. And because you're such an unusual case, you'll be housed with a local family instead of the jail, and you'll be wearing an ankle monitor at all times until you've completed your sentence."

The tone of the judge's voice and the look in his eyes told Adam there was no point in trying to press his case. He'd have to find some other way to get home in time. Missing the yearly meeting with his father was out of the question. He had to be in Atlanta on time or lose everything.

Laura Durrant shut the tailgate on her truck and walked to the cab, pulling herself up into the driver's seat. She'd stopped by her workshop to pick up the tools she would need to get everything secured at the gazebo.

Her heart ached when she thought about the damage the accident had caused. Some daredevil rich guy had lost control of his sports car and driven through the fence surrounding the courthouse square and rammed into their historic gazebo. Now it was up to her to fix it.

As a licensed contractor and builder, her company, LC Construction, specialized in restoring old homes and buildings. Her job was physically and mentally stressful, but she loved every second of it. At least she usually did. At the moment she had more work than she could handle and more problems, too.

She was still kicking herself for agreeing to this project. Her uncle, Judge Wallace, was fond of sentencing those who passed through his court to unusual punishments. Normally she applauded the idea, but this was the first time the punishment had included her. When her uncle had requested her help, she'd been eager to repair the gazebo. No one would do it more lovingly or more accurately than she would.

What she disliked was having to work with Adam Holbrook for the next thirty days. She didn't have time to rehabilitate some spoiled rich guy who had nothing better to do than tool around the country in his vintage sports car. He would only get in the way and slow things down. Unfortunately, she had no choice. But she would make sure he pulled his weight.

One thing she knew for certain. The gazebo would be restored in time for the Founder's Day Festival, Dover's most important event of the year. She'd do whatever it took to make sure that happened.

Adam followed Officer Don Barnes down the hallway, the weight of his newly attached ankle tracking device a grim reminder of his fate. He'd been processed for his house arrest. Now he was being taken to meet his jailers.

Once seated in the back of the patrol car, Adam tried to think of some way out of his predicament. He touched the bandage on his jaw where it had hit the steering wheel when he crashed. He'd been lucky. No major injuries. A scraped jaw, a bruised shoulder and a seriously wounded ego were all he'd suffered. He'd gotten off better than the little gazebo had. He glanced down at his once-elegant silk shirt and the dirt marring his tuxedo pants. He probably should have changed when he left the party in Dallas yesterday morning, but he'd been anxious to get his newly purchased '63 Porsche 356 out on the open highway. He sighed, letting his gaze drift to his feet. He tugged up his pant leg and looked at the ugly black monitor. He was trapped. In a prison without bars.

Turning his attention to the scenery outside the vehicle, he shook his head with bewilderment. The streets along the town square were lined with what most people would see as charming old buildings and an even more charming old courthouse. To him they were just old, out-of-date and dull.

He liked things big and wide open. Dangerous. Risky. For fifty-one weeks a year he was his own man. He went where he wanted and did what he wanted. He'd surfed the big waves in Waimea, heli-skiied in British Columbia and raced a car at Daytona. He lived a life of danger and excitement other men only dreamed of.

At least he used to. Lately, he'd been finding it harder and harder to catch that high. The adrenaline rush wasn't coming as quickly, and the satisfaction from each thrill was missing. He'd been restless and irritable for over a year now and he could find no explanation for the sudden change.

The cruiser pulled to a stop in front of a large two-story white house on the corner that resembled something from a Norman Rockwell painting. Tall columns braced the wide porch. Broad front steps were decorated with pumpkins and fall flowers. Maybe this was a bed and breakfast. He could handle that.

The officer got out of the car at the same moment a man emerged from the house. He stopped at the edge of the porch steps and waited. When the officer opened the rear door, Adam got out, making a quick scan of the neighborhood. The street was lined with giant trees, the stately homes positioned in manicured lawns. Maybe staying with this family wouldn't be so bad after all. Still, he didn't like the idea of being watched over by strangers like some errant teenager.

He glanced up at the man on the porch. His stern expression said it all. He'd tolerate no nonsense in his home. Adam hid the smirk that fought to emerge. Just like his dad. My way or the highway. It was beginning to look like a very long thirty days ahead.

"Don, how's it going today?"

The officer kept a firm hold on Adam's upper arm as he led him to the foot of the steps. At least he'd been spared the handcuffs. "Doing good. I brought your houseguest." He turned to Adam, a disapproving scowl on his narrow face. "Mr. Holbrook, meet your jailer, Mr. Durrant. This here is Adam Holbrook." Without waiting for either man to speak, the officer released Adam and placed his hands on his hips. "His ankle monitor is set for one mile. If LC needs more range, just have her call and we'll adjust it. You need me to go over anything before I go?"

"No, Don. Hank and I worked it all out. Thanks. I have it from here."

The officer offered a small salute and walked off. Adam squared his shoulders and faced the man. Whatever it was, he would endure. He'd jumped out of helicopters. Surviving a month in a small town should be a piece of cake.

The man came closer toward him, a warm smile on his face. Adam's guard went up. What kind of people would welcome a prisoner into their home?

"I guess Don was in a hurry to get back to work. I'm Tom Durrant. Welcome to our home, Mr. Holbrook." He held out his hand.

Adam grasped it, surprised to find the hand strong and calloused. It didn't fit with the stately old home. Adam had always been good at knowing when someone was conning him. Something was going on here.

Durrant turned and went back up the steps, motioning for Adam to follow. Mr. Durrant looked to be late fifties, early sixties. Tall, broad-shouldered, with silver-gray hair, his quick movements spoke of a man in good shape physically. So what was the catch?

Inside the house, Mr. Durrant stopped in the foyer and waited for him to enter, that same pleasant smile on his face. "I know you're anxious to get settled, but I think we need to have a little talk first. Are you hungry? Did you get breakfast this morning?"

"No, sir." Adam followed him into a bright sunny kitchen at the back of the house. The room was large with a round table positioned in a cozy corner filled with windows.

"I thought not. Have a seat and I'll get you fixed up. Coffee?"

He nodded, growing more confused by the moment. Was this where he'd stay? What was going on? Were they trying to kill him with kindness for damaging the little gazebo in the square? Cruel and unusual punishment for sure.

Adam sat down, realizing how out of place he looked in his bedraggled tuxedo. This kitchen was more suited to the jeans and polo shirt his jailer was wearing. Mr. Durrant returned to the table with a plate of cinnamon rolls and a steaming cup of coffee, which made Adam's stomach growl. He'd barely touched his food since being arrested yesterday.

"Here ya go. Eat up. Those rolls were homemade this morning by my wife. She's a great cook."

Adam eyed the man suspiciously. "Thanks." Mr. Durrant waited while Adam doctored his coffee with a little cream and sugar and took a roll from the plate.

"I imagine you have some questions. Let me go over the high points and then I'll show you to your room. Number one, this will be your home for the duration of your sentence. You will be allowed to wander anywhere on our property, but nowhere else. Check-in is whenever you stop work for the day, and you're required to call the police station within five minutes of your arrival here. You'll be picked up for work each day and brought home each night. Oh, and only one phone call per day."

He pulled a cell from his shirt pocket that Adam instantly recognized as his own. He started to reach for it. Mr. Durrant shook his head.

"Sorry. I know how you young people live and die by these things, but we'll keep it down here on that table over there. You can make your calls in here." He smiled. "Don't worry, we'll give you all the privacy you need."

Adam swallowed a bite of cinnamon roll. It was the best he'd ever tasted, but he wasn't in the mood to truly enjoy it. "Is that all?"

Clasping his hands on the table, Mr. Durrant leaned toward him. "Treat my wife and me with respect, behave yourself and everything should be fine. Any other questions?"

Adam set his coffee cup down with a firm thud. "Why are you doing this? It doesn't make sense."

Tom Durrant smiled again. "You'll understand soon enough. But I will tell you that the judge is my brother-in-law. Apparently you're something of a celebrity and he thought you'd be better off here with us than being locked up in the county jail. Because you'll be working on the gazebo, this was a logical place to put you. And—" Mr. Durrant inhaled a deep breath "—I have a personal stake in the matter."

Adam was beginning to wish they'd locked him up in a nice safe cell with ordinary criminals. He was used to dealing with people who wanted something from him. But this was different. He didn't like being off balance, and this situation had him teetering like a tightrope walker over a canyon.

"Well, you'll be going to work soon, so we'd better get you settled in."

Adam followed Tom Durrant through the large home. And it was a home. A place where people lived. Signs of life were on display everywhere. Magnets held scribbled drawings on the refrigerator door. An open book lay upside down on an end table. A sweater draped over a chair. The furniture was traditional and tasteful, but comfortably used. A pile of magazines lay on the stairs as if waiting to be taken up. Family photos covered the wall along the stairway. Too many for him to process as they passed by. He'd never seen pictures displayed like this. The only picture in his home growing up was the portrait of his mother in her favorite ball gown which hung over the fireplace in the main salon.

Upstairs, Tom Durrant led him to a room at the far end of the hall. Adam stepped inside, his attention falling on the items on the bed. "My bags." He walked to the bed, quickly sliding open the zipper on the small case. The sight of his personal items filled him with a rush of comfort.

"They sent your things over this morning. I knew you'd need some different clothes to work in. Carpentry is dirty work." He walked across the room and opened another door, flipping on the switch to reveal a private bathroom. "I think you'll find everything you need. If not, just ask and we'll see what we can do." He smiled again. "Within reason of course."

A sudden lump of gratitude rose in Adam's chest. While he still harbored serious doubts about this arrangement, at least he'd have a place to retreat to each night, a place to be alone. And alone was where he was most comfortable. "Thanks. This will be fine."

"Daddy!"

Adam turned at the sound of the female voice.

"Up here, Boo."

Adam waited as the sound of pounding footsteps rumbled on the steps and along the hall. From the noise being made, he expected someone large and sturdy to appear in the doorway. He wasn't prepared for the woman who stepped into the room.

"Hey, Daddy."

She was short, five foot four tops. At first glance he thought she was a teenager, but on closer inspection he realized she was probably not much younger than himself. Perhaps thirty-one or thirty-two.

"You're putting him in Matt's room? I thought you'd put him in the spare room over the garage."

Tom Durrant shook his head. "Too isolated up there. I thought it would be better if he was close by."

Adam didn't like the sound of that. Was Mr. Durrant going to monitor him every moment?

"Mr. Holbrook, this is my daughter, Laura Durrant."

She made no move to shake his hand, so he merely nodded. From the scowl on her face, he had a feeling she was not going to be one of his fans. She turned to look at her father and Adam felt a small skip in his heartbeat when her features suddenly changed from disapproving to near worshipful. The love in her eyes for her father gave her a glow.

"We need to get going. How soon will he be ready?"

"Ask him."

She turned and glared, the loveliness on her face gone. "I assume you have something else to wear other than a tuxedo? We'll be doing real work today, Mr. Holbrook. This won't be a party."

Her attitude irked him. He started to say something smart, but remembered Mr. Durrant's request for respect. Something she'd said suddenly clicked into place. "We?"

Laura Durrant placed her hands on her hips and took a step toward him. "We. You'll be under my supervision for the duration of your sentence. I'll be showing you how to rebuild what you destroyed, and I want to get started today if that's all right with you."

Adam looked over her head to her father. There was a knowing and sympathetic smile on his face. He shrugged.

"My daughter is a skilled carpenter and contractor. Trust me, she knows her stuff." He took his daughter's arm and tugged her along with him out of the room. "We'll leave you alone to get ready. Don't take too long. She gets cranky when she has to wait."

"Dad."

The door shut behind them, but not before Adam heard Tom Durrant gently scold "Boo" for her attitude.

Adam dragged a hand across his face. Surely this had to be some kind of bizarre parallel universe. No way could he take orders from that little slip of a thing. He had to find a way out of this mess. And fast.

Laura followed her father downstairs to the kitchen. "He'd better not take all day primping. I want to get started on that gazebo today. I've got too many other things I need to take care of." Her dad pointed to a kitchen chair.

"Sit. I'm sure he'll be down directly. How's the Mobile situation?"

Laura sat down, resting her head dejectedly on one palm. Her last restoration project had been in Mobile, Alabama, on a historic downtown building. Unfortunately, the owner had suddenly declared bankruptcy and everything was on hold. Including her pay. "Awful. The lawyers are going to draw this thing out as long as possible so they don't have to pay up."

"What does your attorney say?"

"He's doing all he can, but you know the court system works like molasses." She exhaled and leaned back in her chair. "I never would have taken that job if I'd known the company would go belly-up a week after I completed the work."

Her dad chuckled. "We all wish we had a crystal ball to see into the future, but that's not how the good Lord set things up. We're supposed to rely on Him, not ourselves. You upheld your part of the deal. That's all you can do."

"I know, but in the meantime, I have payroll to meet. That job was going to give me enough financial security to breathe easy for the next year. And then there's the Keller building." She looked over at her father, wishing he could make it all better the way he had when she was small. But at thirty-two, her troubles were her own to battle.

Her dad laid his hand on top of hers. "I wish I could help you somehow. Your mom and I have been talking to everyone we know looking for people who would be interested in stepping up to save the old place, but no luck."

"I know. Money is tight everywhere. I don't blame anyone, but it's so frustrating. If I could only have convinced Mr. Keller to sell me the building or get it listed on the Historic Registry before he died. Now it's going up for auction in a few weeks and I've run out of options. Buying it myself was the only one left and now that's off the table, too. Without the profits from the Mobile job I can't afford to even bid on it."

The old three-story building at the corner of Main and Peace streets downtown would make a perfect senior center once it was restored. Something she'd

wanted to do for a long time. The center would provide a safe place for seniors to meet and do their crafts.
It would also be a place where they could teach others
the numerous skills they possessed. Crocheting. Knit-
ting. Tole painting. Sewing. Quilting. She hated seeing
the old building falling apart when it could be brought
to life again and made useful. It was structurally sound
and perfectly located. All it needed was some work.
Okay, a lot of work, but work she was more than willing to do.

Laura stood and walked to the door leading to the
hallway. "What's taking him so long?"

"Give him time, Boo. He'll be down soon enough."

"And that's another thing. I've got the Conrad job
going on. My foreman keeps running into problems
every time we open a wall or rip up a floorboard. I
don't have time to spend repairing what this poor little
rich boy did. And there's only a few weeks to restore
the gazebo in time for the Founder's Day Festival. That
doesn't give me much leeway for finding materials.
Dealing with him will double the time needed to make
repairs. Not to mention the mistakes that will have to
be undone and the wasted lumber from incorrect measurements."

"I can speak to your uncle Hank. He could find
someone else to restore the gazebo," her father said.

Laura whirled around. "No, I want to do it. I just
wish I had someone competent to help me. Not an amateur." She puffed out her irritation and paced the room.

"Maybe he'll surprise you and be a quick study, or
maybe he already has a few skills that will be helpful."
Her dad came and gave her a hug. "It'll all work out,
Boo. Have a little faith."

Laura smiled at her dad. She hoped he was right this time. "So, what do you think of him?"

"Hard to say. I've only spoken to him briefly. I think he's unhappy with his situation, but that's understandable. He reminds me of your brother Ty. As I recall, you had no trouble keeping him in line."

She smiled. "So you're saying I can take him?"

"No doubt, but don't get carried away. Something tells me this man has a thick wall of protection around him. With Ty you always knew where he stood. He didn't keep his feelings hidden. I suspect Adam has kept his feelings buried most of his life. Don't be too hard on him." He turned and picked up his cell phone and slipped it in his pocket. "Time to get to the store. Your mother will be wondering where I am."

"You're leaving me here alone with this stranger?"

"I don't think you're in any danger. That's one of the reasons your mom and I agreed to let him stay here. I wanted to make sure he understood that you're my baby girl and he'd better watch his p's and q's." He chuckled and started for the door. "Maybe I should have warned him about you. You're tougher than both your brothers put together."

Laura waved goodbye to her dad, then checked her watch again. She'd lost nearly half an hour waiting for Mr. Rich Adventurer. If he wasn't down in ten minutes, she'd go in and drag his spoiled self out by the scruff of his neck.

She had to admit, she'd been surprised at her first glimpse of him. She tried to ignore the way his startling green eyes had made a swift but thorough assessment of her. Doubtful she could compare with the kind of women he was used to. And she felt sure he was used to taking his pick of leggy beauties.

She couldn't blame her fellow females for falling for this guy. He had all the right stuff on the outside. His six-foot frame and thick light brown hair made him boyishly handsome.

But she preferred a man of faith. A man with character in his face and compassion in his heart.

Heavy footsteps on the stairs let her know Holbrook was finally ready. He stepped through the kitchen door and stopped, his green gaze slamming into hers. Her throat closed up and her heart skipped a couple beats. A short while ago he'd resembled James Bond fresh from saving the world. Now, he stood in the kitchen looking ready for a photo shoot for a Rugged Men of the South calendar. The gray knit Henley shirt hugged his chest and broad shoulders like an old friend and brought out the vibrant green of his eyes. The jeans called attention to his narrow waist and long powerful legs. A pair of well-worn dark boots anchored him to the floor. Apparently, adventurers needed sturdy footwear in their wardrobes.

She shook her head, trying to regain her composure. "If you're ready, we need to get going."

There was a half smile on his face. "Ready as I'll ever be."

Laura pushed through the back door and headed for her red truck. "I hope you're ready to work because we have a lot to do and very little time to get it done."

Chapter Two

Adam followed Laura Durrant to her truck and climbed in, wondering how so small a woman could command such authority. Her no-nonsense attitude was intriguing and a bit intimidating. He'd decided to be a good scout, do what he was told and get the lay of the land. Eventually he'd find a loophole, some way to get out of Dover and back to Atlanta on time. Of course there was always his last resort—calling one of his dad's lawyers. He didn't want to think about the repercussions of that.

He glanced over at Laura Durrant. Her slender figure was obscured by stained and faded jeans, ending in heavy brown work boots. That explained the loud thumping on the stairs. Her purple T-shirt was worn and faded, with a quarter-sized hole in one sleeve. Her head was covered with a ball cap and spikes of hair stuck out from the adjustment opening in the back and the edges over her ears. He guessed at its color. Dishwater blond? What stood out the most were her violet blue eyes. Eyes that were staring at him with disdain. She looked small behind the wheel of the big truck but absolutely in control. Which raised a lot of questions. "So, you're in charge of the work detail, huh?"

"That's right. You answer to me."

"What do I call you?"

"You can call me Boss or LC."

"I thought your name was Boo." He saw her scowl at the name.

"My dad is the only one who calls me that. And my brother Ty sometimes. LC is the name of the company. LC Construction and Restoration."

Adam wanted to ask what the initials stood for, but decided it might be safer to wait on that. "So how long do you think this repair job will take? How much damage did I do?"

She glanced at him briefly, eyes narrowed. "It's not a repair job, Mr. Holbrook. It's a restoration and that takes a lot more time."

"Restoration. Repair. Same difference, isn't it?"

"Not even close. The building you drove your little car into is a National Historic Landmark. Which is why I'm doing the job. If all it needed was repairing, any competent carpenter could do the work in a few days."

"And what makes you different?"

"I'm a certified restorationist."

"Meaning?"

"I'm qualified to restore old homes and buildings to their original state when possible. That's what I do."

"I didn't know there was such a thing. How did you get to be one?" She exhaled an exasperated sigh as if reluctant to explain.

"I studied architecture in college, but I found I didn't like the designing as much as I liked the hands-on ground-level work. When I moved home, I bought this construction company from a local man who was retiring. He did a lot of restoration work, so all I had to do was expand on that customer base."

"Still, a girl in construction. Where did that come from?"

Laura turned and smiled, her expression softening the way it had when she'd looked at her father earlier. Something inside Adam shifted.

"Oh. My dad owns the hardware store in town. I grew up around nuts and bolts."

She turned back to the road ahead. "So how did you come to lose control of your car and ram it into our historic gazebo?"

For a moment Adam considered avoiding the question, but then he remembered her uncle was the judge and her father his jailer. No point in trying to hide the truth. "I left a friend's house in Dallas early yesterday morning and planned on spending a few days in New Orleans. You know, eating fine food, listening to good music, maybe do a little deep-sea fishing. I got hungry, saw a billboard for some mom-and-pop diner in Sawyers Bend—"

"Jingles."

"What?"

"The name of the diner is Jingles."

"Right. Well, somehow I missed the turnoff and ended up in your fair community. I was trying to find a way back to the interstate on my smartphone and the rest you know."

"You didn't have GPS in that fancy car of yours?"

"No, it's a vintage machine. I was going to have it installed after my meeting in Atlanta."

Laura Durrant pulled the truck to a stop along the

fence line near the gazebo. "Too bad you didn't have that done before you left Dallas. Might have saved everyone a lot of trouble."

Adam scanned the area. Yellow police tape marked the site. His car had been removed and he could clearly see the gaping hole in the side of the little building. He climbed out of the cab and joined the boss lady at the back of her truck. "Where do you suppose my car is?"

"I have no idea. Impound probably. You won't be needing it for a while."

"No, but I'd like to see about having it repaired. I'll have to leave here eventually." He took the hard hat and work gloves she handed him. He tucked the gloves in the back pocket of his jeans and tried the hat on for size, pulling it off again and adjusting the band inside.

LC broke the caution tape and walked toward the damaged section of the gazebo.

"Should you be crossing that police line?"

"We'll put up our own safety fencing."

Up close, Adam was surprised to find the gazebo larger than he'd expected. He figured it was about twenty-four feet across. He also had a clearer picture of the damage he'd caused and he wondered if anything could be salvaged. He saw tire tracks in the dirt where he'd tried to stop, and pieces of glass were scattered around the ground from his broken windshield. A gaping hole in the brick foundation of the gazebo marked the spot where his car had come to rest. He looked upward at the roof which sagged from the loss of several broken support beams. The cupola on top tilted at a precarious angle and the decorative spindles were little more than kindling.

He glanced over at Laura, stunned to see a deep sadness in her eyes. For a moment he thought she might burst into tears. Did the old gazebo mean that much to her? He didn't understand. It was just a small building in the center of the town.

But the sadness in her eyes made him so uncomfortable that he looked away, scanning the area. Surely the workers would show up anytime now. He was anxious to meet the real carpenters. She may own the construction company, but a woman her size couldn't lift a can of paint by herself, let alone a two-by-four. He could, however, see her as the boss. With her hardline attitude and biting comments, he doubted any man would dare to cross her. "So when do the others arrive?"

"What others?"

"The carpenters and guys with the muscle."

"Sorry, Holbrook, no others. Just you and me. My guys are all busy on other jobs. I can't afford to pull them off to do this restoration."

Adam frowned. "I wasn't expecting it would be just the two of us."

"I'm sure there's going to be a lot of things you aren't expecting."

He stared at the small structure, rubbing his jaw. "You sure we can't use more help?"

"It's not that big a deal. We'll do the woodworking and I'll sub out the other trades." He drew his eyebrows together. "I employ four full-time carpenters, one fabricator and a cabinet maker. The rest of the work is hired out to subcontractors. Like the brick work, electrical and drywall and tile. The mill will build the post and spindles. Any other craftsmen I need I'll hire to do the work."

Adam nodded in understanding and followed her

to the damaged corner, watching as she stooped down and inspected the gaping hole in the brick foundation. She pulled out one crumbling brick and examined it, a look of disgust on her face. She stood and held up the partially destroyed pale red brick.

"Do you have any idea how hard it's going to be to find more of these?"

He grinned. "Can't we run over to the local brick-yard?"

She tossed the brick on the ground and glared. "That gazebo is over one hundred and thirty years old. Those bricks are handmade. I can't walk into a store and buy more like you can replace that little car of yours."

"That car was built in the 1960s. It's worth ten times your little house."

"House?" Laura set her jaw, eyes blazing.

"It's a gazebo. It's old. I'll give you the money to build one twice that size with all the bells and whistles."

She crossed her arms over her chest. "First, we don't want a bigger, better gazebo. We want this one. It's a historic landmark. Second, I know you have no idea what you've done to this town or the history that you've destroyed, but believe me, it's significant. Third, I'm sure paying for everything is your usual method of getting out of trouble. Well, not this time. You're going to help me rebuild this and I can't wait to see you sweat and break your back doing it." She stomped off. Adam watched her go, tempted to walk out of this small insignificant town. Then he remembered the ankle bracelet.

He wouldn't get far.

Laura worked off her irritation by pulling out the orange plastic safety fencing and the stakes to anchor it from the truck bed. She had to regain her sense of control or she'd end up with a helper who might go AWOL on her. As much as she hated to face it, she would need his upper-body strength to wield some of the beams and timbers she'd need to rebuild things. She started back toward the gazebo, her heart tightening at the sight of the wounded structure. Adam came toward her, arms extended.

"I'll get those." He took the cumbersome material from her grasp. "Where do you want them?"

"I want you to set up a perimeter about twelve to sixteen feet from the gazebo to give us room to work and set up the equipment we'll need. Be sure to leave an opening so we can come and go. You'll find a special fencepost driver tool in the back of the truck. It's red and looks like a pipe with handles. Use that to set the posts about eight feet apart." Adam started to move off, then turned back.

"You want exact spacing or approximate?"

"Approximate will do. I just don't want people getting too close while we work." Laura stapled the building permit encased in protective plastic to one post, leaving Adam to figure the mechanics of the fencing. Retrieving her electronic tablet from the truck, she started her detailed list of the materials she'd need and the specifications for the gazebo to start tracking down the lumber from the correct era.

She glanced at Adam smiling as he tugged the flimsy orange fencing between the posts. She let him struggle for a while, intending to give him some pointers, but the next time she looked, he'd gotten the hang of it. He finished his task at the same time she completed her list.

"How did I do, boss?"

The grin on his face made his eyes sparkle. "Fine. You'll have to check it each day. It tends to sag over time."

"What's next? Power tools?"

"No. We have to stabilize the roof, then take all this damaged section apart." She picked up a pair of protective goggles. "But first we need to go over a few safety rules. You will wear these when using power tools, and earplugs when running the saw. Use a waist support when we do heavy lifting and never, I repeat, never treat a power tool with anything less than the utmost respect. They aren't toys."

Adam nodded. "I might not understand the tools, but I do know a thing or two about safety and being cautious. I make sure my sports equipment is thoroughly checked out before I use it. I don't take unnecessary risks."

Laura huffed under her breath. "Yet you still risk your life for nothing more than a temporary thrill." She turned and motioned for him to follow. "We need to support the roof before we do anything else. I'll get the jack, you bring that four-by-six post over here."

Laura positioned the jack in the center of the gazebo and instructed Adam how to position the heavy post to take the weight of the roof. She'd anticipated his resistance today, but so far he'd followed her every command without question. She held the post in place while Adam put his strength behind the jack, pumping the handle. She glanced down at him, surprised to see him watching the upward movement of the beam closely as he worked. She also was suddenly aware of the muscles in his arms and the way the fabric of his shirt strained across his shoulders as he moved.

"Is that enough?"

Laura jerked her attention back to the beam. It was touching under the center of the roof but not firmly enough. "Another inch should do it." Satisfied, she stepped back, watching as Adam rose to his full height and placed his hand on the beam.

"Will this one piece of wood hold up this whole building?"

She swallowed and took a step back. "It's only a temporary fix until we can assess the damage to the rafters and make the repairs."

"Okay." He smiled. "What's next?"

Laura searched her mind for the next task she wanted him to do, but her thoughts were muddled with things she rarely thought about. Like how strong Adam was, and how small she felt beside him. He made her aware that she was very female and he was so male. She forced herself to focus on the work. "We need to start stacking the loose bricks over there out of the way. We'll reuse the ones that aren't too damaged. Make a pallet out of scrap lumber and stack them on that. It'll keep them from sinking into the ground. I need to make some phone calls."

Without waiting for his response, she walked to her truck and climbed inside. She needed time to think and space away from Adam Holbrook. He reminded her a little too much of her ex-husband, Ted—concerned with his own life with never a thought to anyone else and no appreciation for anything of value. She closed her eyes and offered up a prayer for tolerance and forgiveness. It didn't matter what Holbrook was like. All she needed was for him to help her get the gazebo restored in time for the festival and then he could go on about his merry way.

* * *

Adam pried the last loose brick from the foundation and stacked it with the others. He was hot, sweaty and his back ached. He had no idea dismantling the little building would be such hard work. He wasn't quite sure what to make of his new boss. It was obvious she loved what she did. To him, the debris looked like so much broken wood. To her, each piece was a special hand-crafted treasure.

Adam leaned against the side of the gazebo, wiping his forehead with his sleeve. Reaching down, he took a bottle of water from the small cooler she kept nearby. His gaze traveled around the square inventorying the rows of businesses. The usual stuff. Couple of banks. A diner. Pizza place. Antique shop. Drug store. Hardware store. Her daddy's store? He smiled. Daddy could keep an eye on his little girl all day long from his store. Interesting. The damaged gazebo. A daughter in construction. A father willing to help out to keep her safe. Normally he would scoff at such behavior, but having met her father, and her, he could hardly blame Tom Durrant for wanting to keep watch. He found it a bit old-fashioned but sweet.

Laura had made it clear she thought he was incapable of doing anything without assistance. He was looking forward to proving her wrong. How hard could swinging a hammer be? He finished his water and tossed it into the trash can just outside the orange fence.

Laura came toward him from the truck, slipping her cell phone into the small holster on her hip. "Okay, I found brick down in Long Beach, left over from a Katrina salvage. They're shipping it up. Should be here by Tuesday."

She stared at him expectantly, as if he should grasp the significance of her words. The excitement in her expression lit up her violet-blue eyes. He'd never seen a color like that before. Nor had he realized how the hard hat made her features appear delicate and fragile. But Adam knew better. There was nothing fragile about this lady. He blinked. She was waiting for some reaction from him. "Is that good?"

"More than good. But replacing that foundation will take time."

"Is time a big deal?"

"Yes, it is. We're having our annual Founder's Day Festival at the end of the month and this 'little house' is the centerpiece. If this gazebo is unusable for the festival it'll be like Christmas without a tree. It's *that* important." She sighed and pulled on her gloves. "I don't expect you to understand."

He watched her out of the corner of his eye, captivated by her passion for the little structure. Her eyes flashed like a summer storm, her cheeks flushed, turning her violet eyes to deep purple. He forced his mind back to the job at hand. "What now, boss?"

She pointed to the broken railing. "Start pulling that apart and stack it over there. Keep all the like pieces together. We'll have to use them as templates later. Don't throw anything away unless I okay it."

"So you're going to recycle all this? Saving the planet and all that?"

"In a way. All this lumber is original. I want to keep as much of it as possible not only for the historic value, but to keep the historic designation, too. The structure has to be comprised of a certain percentage of original materials to be on the registry."

Adam worked a spindle loose from the splintered floor board. His gaze drifted toward Laura again. She moved like a little dynamo, never still. Even when she was on the phone, which was frequently, she paced. He'd seen her sitting on the tailgate of the truck once when she was studying her tablet, but she hadn't sat there long. It was easy to see why her business was a success. She worked hard and with passion.

"Good morning."

Adam turned and looked over his shoulder. A man a few years older than he was standing near the orange fencing, a warm, friendly smile on his face. He studied the gazebo intently, while slipping his hands into the pockets of his jeans. Adam braced himself for some nasty comments. Several locals had drifted past this morning, but all they'd done was scowl. Sooner or later he'd known the words would start to fly.

The man nodded toward him. "You the man responsible for this damage?"

Adam stood and faced the man. "I am."

The man's smile widened. "It's nice to meet an honest and forthright man." He stepped forward and extended his hand. "Jim Barrett. You must be Adam Holbrook."

The man's handshake was firm and steady, his smile and friendly tone took any condemnation out of the words. "I seem to have acquired a reputation overnight. Literally."

"So you have. But because you're working to make things right, the good folks of Dover will forgive you soon enough. Provided it's finished in time for the big festival."

"Jim, what are you up to today?" Laura walked past

Adam to the fence, opening her arms to the man for a quick hug. Apparently they were close friends.

"I just got back from rounds at the hospital and thought I'd come by and see how things are going here." He glanced over at Adam. "Mr. Holbrook looks like he will be a competent assistant for you."

Laura looked askance at Adam. "He might make a good saw boy eventually. We'll see." She turned to Adam. "Jim is the associate pastor at our church."

Adam took another look at the man. He guessed him to be in his late thirties. He had kind eyes and a gentle manner. He could easily see this man leading a flock of believers, but then, his exposure to men of the cloth was very limited. Barrett noticed his assessment and chuckled softly.

"My church is the big red one just past the corner over there." He pointed northward. "If you ever need to talk, or if you need a friend, just call."

"I appreciate the offer." Adam grinned and glanced down at his ankle. "But I'm limited in my social interaction at the moment."

"No problem. I'll come to you." He handed Adam his business card before turning to Laura. "You'll let me know if I'm needed, won't you?"

"Of course."

He started to leave, then turned back. "Oh, I meant to ask you, how's it going with the Keller building? Any luck? I understand the auction is coming up soon."

Laura sighed. "I'm still working on a solution, but at the moment it's not looking good. I'm praying something will turn up because I'm nearly out of ideas."

"Don't give up. I'm sure the Lord is working it out. We just can't see it yet. Well, I'll let you get back to work. I don't want to be the cause of this gazebo not being ready for the festival."

Adam watched the pastor walk away, then looked at his boss. The expression on her face was one of sadness and disappointment. Apparently the little gazebo wasn't the only thing she was concerned with. He started to ask, then thought better of it. "Hey, what's a saw boy?"

She glanced at him and smiled, tugging her hat more firmly onto her head. "You are. You're going to get to cut all the wood on this project."

Adam grinned in anticipation. "We're talking power saws, whirring blades, danger, stuff like that?" Laura grimaced and shook her head, motioning him back to work.

"I was just wondering, how long do you think this job will take?" Adam asked.

"If all goes well and everything arrives on time, two to three weeks. What's the matter, Holbrook? You bored already?"

"No, but I have someplace I need to be at the end of the month. I don't suppose you could put in a good word for me with your uncle? Convince him that the quickest way to get this job done on time would be to hire another professional?"

Laura frowned. "I don't suppose I could. What's so important that you have to be there? Some sort of big celebrity party?"

He should have expected her to react that way. He doubted she'd be sympathetic to his dilemma anyhow. "Never mind. Forget it."

Adam watched Laura return to the table saw. She was a hardworking, hands-on kind of woman. People were expecting her to restore what had been damaged.

She'd find it hard to identify with a guy who never had to question where his next paycheck was coming from. But then, no one had ever expected anything from him. Until now.

Adam rubbed his protesting shoulders and stretched his back to ease the kink in his spine. He'd been working nonstop since the pastor's visit and his body screamed for relief. Almost as much as his stomach craved food. Apparently, Laura stayed small because she never ate. He was beginning to wonder if he'd ever taste food again when he heard a familiar voice call out.

"Hey, y'all. I thought I'd treat you to lunch today." Tom Durrant walked toward them across the courthouse park, a large pizza box in his hand. Laura went to meet him.

"Thanks, Dad. I hadn't even thought about eating. Too much to do."

"Hello, Adam. Is she working you too hard?"

"Nothing I can't handle so far." Adam brushed off his hands and joined them.

"How's it going, Boo?"

"Fine. We should have the damaged section cleared away by tomorrow, then we can get a better idea of what we're looking at." She handed Adam the hot pizza box and turned to give her dad a warm hug. "Thank you, Daddy. You're the best."

Adam watched with interest as the two embraced. A moment ago Laura Durrant had been all business—determined, focused and self-assured. But she'd turned into a happy little girl when her father showed up. He found himself wondering what other sides there were to his boss.

"Well, I won't keep you. Enjoy your lunch and I'll see you both later at the house."

Laura smiled over at Adam, her eyes bright. "Isn't he just the sweetest? Someday I'm going to find a man just like him to marry."

Adam saw the love and admiration in her expression, feeling sorry for the man who tried to live up to the image Laura had created. Even in the short time he'd known Tom Durrant, he knew he was a man worthy of admiration. But few men on the planet could measure up. Adam held out the pizza. "Where do you want to eat this?"

"Over here." She walked to the truck, lowered the tailgate and hopped up on it, feet dangling. She held out her hands for the box.

Adam joined her, wiping his hands on his jeans. "I thought tailgating was for football games."

"And construction sites. I have some hand sanitizer if you need it."

There was a teasing glint in her eyes. "I'm good, thanks." He took a slice and bit into it with gusto. He couldn't remember when he'd last worked up an appetite like this. He glanced over at Laura. "So, I take it your family is close?"

"We are. My older brother, Matt, lives here in town with his two children. He teaches at the community college. He's getting married next month to his high school sweetheart. His first wife died of cancer."

"That's tough."

"It was, but then Shelby came back to Dover. She'd had some serious health issues and came here to stay with her grandmother while she recuperated. She had no idea Matt lived next door, but once they saw each other again, all the old feelings came back."

"Just like that?"

"No, but they worked things out and now they're getting married. My other brother, Ty, is a cop in Dallas. He's single. He was shot recently and he's still recuperating. We're hoping he'll be able to come home for Thanksgiving."

"What about you? No one special? Like the pastor, maybe?"

"What? No!" Her cheeks turned pink. "He's married. Besides, I don't have time for a relationship. I've got too much work to do. Especially now."

"So what's this Keller building the pastor mentioned? Another restoration project?"

"In a way. See that old building on the corner opposite my dad's store? That's the Keller building. It used to be a pharmacy way back when. When I was a kid, it was a candy store. I've been trying to save it for three years, but nothing has worked out. It's going up for auction in a few weeks and I've run out of options."

"Is there something special about that building, like this gazebo?"

"If you mean is it part of the history of this town, then yes. Is it a landmark? Officially, no. Mr. Keller would never cooperate with getting it designated. He owned that whole block at one time. I've been unable to find funding or grants, anything that will keep it from being sold to some developer who will either tear it down and use it as a parking lot, or put up some kind of modern building that would destroy the charm of Dover."

Adam tried to imagine the corner with a parking

lot or a sleek office building. He might not like small towns, but he could fully understand her concern. And he admired her devotion. "What do you plan to do with it?"

"A senior center. A place for them to gather, share their experiences and their life skills with others."

"Interesting."

She shrugged, a small smile on her lips. "I like older people. They are so wise and knowledgeable about life. They have so much to teach us. But most people today are too busy to listen, let alone pay attention." She took another piece of pizza from the box. "As long as we're sharing, it's my turn to ask a question. Why do you do the crazy, risky stunts you do? I don't understand."

"For the thrill. You never feel more alive than in that moment when you plunge down a hillside." He looked into her eyes and the skepticism and disapproval in them pierced his spirit. She'd just told him about wanting to save an old building for senior citizens and he talked about jumping off a cliff. Suddenly his lifestyle felt petty and insignificant.

"Is that the only time you feel alive?"

He didn't know how to answer that, so he fell silent, and took another bite of his pizza, hoping she would move on to another topic.

"Is that all you do? Drift from one adventure to another? You don't have a real job of any kind?"

Adam grew uncomfortable with the direction this conversation was going. He didn't like talking about his personal life and Laura Durrant had a way of making his love of extreme sports seem trivial. "I have a few endorsement deals."

"So, people pay you to wear their clothes or use their gear?"

"That's the general idea behind endorsements."

Laura wiped her hands and took the last swig of her drink. "I thought so. I recognized your type right off."

"Oh, really? What type would that be?"

She counted them off on her fingers. "Never done an honest day's work in your life. Only concerned with your own life. No thought of anyone else. No idea how to love anyone but yourself."

The fierce tightness in his chest made it difficult to breathe. She'd seen through his shield with the precision of a surgeon. When had he become so transparent? He'd have to be more careful. Keep his guard up. He couldn't give her a chance to see any more. "You don't pull your punches, do you?"

"Let me ask you, do you have one close friend? Someone who would stick by you no matter what?"

Adam ran down the list of people he knew, the guys who followed him around. Could he count any of them as a true friend? The truth hit him like a shard of ice in his heart. "No."

"I rest my case." Laura slid off the tailgate and closed the box of pizza. "Time to get back to work. We can't rebuild until we take it all apart."

Sucking in a breath, Adam tried to ignore the sting of his new realization. He had no real friends because he'd never wanted any. Casual friendships were easy to walk away from. Anything more was messy and complicated. But now he wondered what his lack of relationships had really cost him.

Chapter Three

Laura Durrant pulled the truck to a stop in her parents driveway, keeping her eyes straight ahead. Adam reached for the door handle at the same time she started to talk. "We got a lot done today. I couldn't have gotten this far without your help. Thanks, Holbrook, for being so cooperative."

She braved a look in his direction. One corner of his mouth was hooked up into a grin.

"That wasn't cooperation. That was fear. You scare me."

A chuckle escaped her throat. "I doubt anything scares a man who can swim with sharks and run with the bulls."

He leaned forward slightly to look at her. "How did you know about that?"

Warmth infused her cheeks and she shrugged to hide her discomfort. "I looked you up on the internet." Now he would think she was interested in him. No way.

Adam sighed and shook his head. "Ah. A man can't have any secrets anymore." He started to get out of the truck, but when she didn't move he glanced back at her. "Aren't you coming in?"

"No. I need to check on my other jobs." Gripping the steering wheel, she gathered courage. "Holbrook, I want to apologize to you."

"For what?"

"I shouldn't have said those things to you—about you being selfish. That was unkind and judgmental. You worked hard today and you didn't deserve my nasty comments. I'm sorry."

It was clear from his expression her apology had caught him by surprise. He held her gaze a long moment then rubbed his forehead. "It's all right. You weren't wrong. You hit the nail square on the head."

Remorse flooded her conscience. "I'm so sorry."

He shook his head. "It's okay. As a matter of fact, it's nice to hear the truth for a change."

It's not what she'd expected him to say. "What do you mean?"

"Most people I know tell me what they think I want to hear. They don't want to offend the hand that drives the adventure train."

She'd never thought about that side of things. It must have cost him to admit that. What would it be like to know people didn't really care about you, only what you could do for them? "I'm sorry, Adam. I have a bad habit of speaking my mind. It was one of the things my…some people don't like about me." He smiled over at her, causing a small skip in her heartbeat.

"Really? I think it's one of your more interesting qualities." He climbed out of the truck, offering a little salute before shutting the door. She waited while he took the steps to the back porch before backing out of the driveway. Every time she thought she had the guy figured out, he threw her a curve. No one liked her forthright attitude. Why did he?

Adam knew Laura was watching him as he climbed the back steps to her parents' home. She probably wanted to make sure he didn't bolt. Or else she was feeling sorry for him. He hadn't intended to speak the truth but something about Laura made him want to. He was glad to be away from her penetrating assessment.

He reached for the door knob and hesitated.

But he wasn't sure he wanted to be back at the Durrants' either.

Adam grew uneasy at having to walk back into the Durrants' home. Since coming to Dover, nothing he'd experienced was familiar. He didn't like that. He pushed open the back door, stepped into the kitchen and froze.

The air was warm with rich delectable aromas. A woman he'd never seen before stood at the stove. For a second he wondered if he'd returned to the wrong house.

"Oh, hello, Adam. I'm Angie Durrant. Sorry I wasn't here this morning to greet you, but Tom thought it might be more comfortable for you with only him. Sort of a man-to-man thing."

Adam stared at the scene in front of him, trying to process it all. Mrs. Durrant was an older version of her daughter. Slender with short dark blond hair turning gray. Her smile was like her daughter's, as well. It lit up her eyes.

"Oh, don't forget to call the station. Use that phone over there. The number is beside it."

Her thoughtfulness caught him off guard. She'd actually tried to make things easy for him, acting as if she cared about what happened to him. He moved across the kitchen to the desk, noticing the table was set with colorful dishes and bright placemats. This wasn't normal. He placed his call, then turned back to Mrs. Durrant.

"I hope you're hungry."

His stomach answered for him. "Yes, ma'am, I am."

"Good. You have time to clean up if you'd like. Tom will be here in about twenty minutes. Come on down when you're ready."

Fifteen minutes later Adam returned downstairs certain he'd been mistaken about the warm welcome to find only one thing had changed. Tom Durrant was home. They sat down at the table, and after Mr. Durrant had offered the blessing Mrs. Durrant passed the food. He'd never tasted anything so good. Tuna casserole, she'd said. Nothing fancy. But it was definitely on par with some of the haute cuisine he'd tasted in his travels. The conversation revolved around various events in Dover. He answered questions put to him, but offered nothing more. He made his escape as soon as he could without appearing rude, explaining he was tired from the day's work.

In his room he stretched out on the bed, every muscle in his body protesting the abuse he'd given them today. He tried to watch television, but couldn't concentrate. He wanted to sleep, but he was too tired. If only he could get this situation sorted out, find some solid ground to stand on and get through the month. Trouble was, he had no frame of reference. No experience with family and home-cooked meals. How was he supposed to behave here? What did they expect from him? He didn't know how to talk to these people. He'd never talked to his parents. They were never around.

A knock on the door brought him to his feet. He opened it to a smiling Tom Durrant holding a book in his hand. "I forgot to mention that we'll all be going to church in the morning. It's important that you attend." He handed the book to Adam. It was the Holy Bible. "Thought you might need one. This belonged to my younger son, Ty."

"Mr. Durrant, I appreciate what you're doing here— letting me stay with you instead of in the jail—but you don't have to go to any trouble on my account."

"Call me Tom. And I'm not sure what you mean."

"Eating together, fixing big meals, all that. I can take my meals up here. It's not a problem."

Tom frowned. "We're not doing anything differently, Adam. We always have our meals together. Always have. That's what families do. Service is at ten thirty. Good night."

Adam shut the door, thinking of all the places he'd rather be than with the Durrants in Dover. Bible stuff. He fingered the worn leather cover, an odd tension swirling deep in his gut. It had been a long time since he'd looked at the words inside. A friend in college had led him to the Lord and for the first time in his life he'd felt as if he belonged someplace. He was loved and accepted for who he was. Someone—God—cared what happened to him and had a plan for his life.

Then he'd gone back home. His parents dismissed his newfound faith as a fad that he would hopefully get over. And he had in a way. He'd tried to find a church to attend, but the arguments with his father had escalated. When Adam had declared his intention to live his life in his own way, and refused to go to work at Holbrook Electronics, his father had retaliated by disowning him and placing a restrictive condition on his trust fund that demanded his appearance each year to collect. His father's way of keeping him in line and making him see the error of his ways.

His faith had taken a backseat to his troubles and he'd drifted. But lately he'd sensed the Lord tapping his shoulder, trying to get his attention. Maybe that's why he'd ended up here in Dover.

Laura ended the call to her foreman, Shaw McKinney, and smiled. So far everything was on track with her other jobs. She hoped she would be as blessed with the gazebo project. The last thing she needed was another job. Her schedule was full and teetering on a wobbly budget. She should be helping on the Conrad place or pushing her attorney to settle the Mobile mess. Instead, she'd be spending the next four weeks tracking down two-hundred-year-old timber to replace the damaged wood. The Dover gazebo was one of the few historic buildings in town that was absolutely pristine. The only changes made over the years had been the addition of electricity, which had been upgraded for safety reasons a decade ago. Only the most minor repairs had been necessary. Until Adam Holbrook had come to town.

Pouring a glass of sweet tea, she called for her little dog, Drywall, to follow her out onto the front porch of her house. She settled into the old glider, inhaling the pungent fall air and letting her gaze drift to the small buds that were starting to form on the winter camellia bush at the edge of her porch.

Adam Holbrook hadn't behaved like she'd expected him to. She'd been prepared to prod, threaten and argue about everything she asked him to do. Instead he'd been cooperative and helpful. His reaction to her apology had thrown her a curve, as well. She'd expected him to say something smart, to defend his lifestyle. Instead he coolly acknowledged her comments as truth.

She couldn't figure him out. But it was only the first day. Sooner or later he'd show his true colors and balk at the work. It was all new and exciting to him now, like one of his wild adventures. She doubted he had the staying power or the attention span. He'd grow bored and then she'd be working alone. She felt sure he was incapable of any kind of commitment.

She scratched behind Wally's ears. And yet, there was something about him that hinted at another man beneath his polished exterior. Someone nice. No. She was simply tired and irritated, building castles in the sky, and it was time to go to bed. There was nothing worthwhile about Adam Holbrook.

The knot of tension in Adam's gut tightened as he followed Tom Durrant down the aisle and into a pew midway in the sanctuary the next morning. It had been years since he'd been to church, other than a wedding or a funeral. The Bible in his hand felt heavy and awkward. He could sense the eyes of the congregation on his back, and he was thankful when they finally took their seats.

Adam glanced down at his khaki pants, relieved to see most of the congregation dressed casually. But it was more than his outward appearance that made him edgy. Inwardly he wasn't prepared to sit in God's house. He allowed his gaze to travel around the old church, struck by the eerie familiarity of the place. With its stained-glass windows, carved wood moldings and massive pipe organ, it reminded him of the church he'd attended in college. Strange that he'd find one so similar here in Dover.

Mrs. Durrant stopped at the pew, Adam stood and stepped into the aisle to let her in to sit beside her husband. He took his seat again only to feel a tap on his shoulder a few moments later. He looked up to find a lovely young woman smiling at him. With a shock he realized it was Laura Durrant. She gestured for him to scoot over to allow her to join them. He'd lost his voice. He realized it was the first time he'd seen her without either her baseball cap or hard hat. The hair he'd guessed to be dishwater blond was in reality a rich honey brown with amber highlights. It hung in soft waves, caressing her neck and shoulders like fine silk. The flowing black-and-white skirt flirted around her calves. The white top gently skimmed her curves, something the loose-fitting T-shirts never did. Her violet eyes were wide with thick lashes. The graceful line of her jaw was the perfect frame for soft lips and a tilted nose.

Until now, he'd only seen the stern, no-nonsense contractor. There'd been glimpses of her softer side, but it had been hidden behind her tool belt and power tools. He looked at her again, unable to take his eyes off her.

She frowned at him in disapproval. "What?"

"You look nice."

She blushed and faced forward.

He groaned inwardly. Brilliant. What a dumb thing to tell a woman. When the music started, he sent up a grateful prayer. He needed a distraction. More important, he needed to hear what was said here today. He'd been away from his faith too long. The liturgy unfolded in a welcome and familiar way, creating a deep ache in his chest. Pastor Jim's words hit their mark in his spirit as he spoke of the rich young man who asked how to gain eternal life, but when told he had to give up his possessions and follow the Lord, had turned away.

The story could have been his own. He'd found his faith, but once away from the campus and out in the real world, he'd drifted away. Now, he felt an overpowering need to reconnect and restore the faith he'd been ignoring.

Laura stood when the pastor called for prayer, uncomfortably aware of Adam Holbrook beside her. Dressed in a white long-sleeved shirt and khaki pants he didn't look much different from the other men in the church. And yet, he did. The white shirt highlighted his deep tan, reminding her that he spent a lot of time outdoors. There was a crisp, clean look to him today that was ridiculously attractive and appealing. Each time she inhaled she drew in the tangy scent of his aftershave. She was grateful when the music started. She was in church to worship. Not admire a man. Her voice faltered, however, when she heard Adam join in the praise song. He didn't sing loudly, but he knew the words and he had a nice singing voice. A rich baritone that flowed over her senses like warm honey.

Her mind churned with questions. She hadn't expected him to know anything about church, but he focused intently on the service, never taking his eyes from the pastor. She breathed a sigh of relief when the service ended. She needed to put some distance between herself and her new saw boy.

As the congregation started to file out, her father reached over and touched her arm.

"Will you take Adam to the house? Your mom and I need to meet with the worship committee chairman for a few minutes. We won't be long."

Laura nodded, hiding her reluctance behind a smile. She glanced up at Adam to find him smiling down at her. She searched for something to say. "You have a nice singing voice."

He chuckled softly. "You didn't think I'd know how to behave in a church, did you?"

"No, that's not true."

Adam leaned down and spoke softly into her ear. "It's not nice to lie in church, Boo."

Her cheeks flamed. She opened her mouth to deny it, but remembered his comment about people telling him what he wanted to hear. "No, I didn't."

Adam chuckled deep in his throat. "I'm a believer, Laura, just not a very faithful one." They stepped into the aisle, Adam placed his hand lightly on her back and they made their way to the door. "I had a friend in college who brought me to the Lord. I was pretty active for several years."

"What happened?"

"I graduated."

She started to ask more questions, but they'd reached the door and the waiting pastor. She shook Jim's hand and moved through the doorway, waiting for Adam. He stood in front of the pastor a long moment. Jim nodded a couple of times, then smiled. Adam joined her, a thoughtful look on his face. He looked down at her, his gaze probing and slightly amused. Her heart quickened. Suddenly, being this close to Adam Holbrook was not a good idea. She turned and hurried to the truck.

* * *

Adam eased back out of the Durrants' crowded kitchen and found a spot in the adjoining family room where he'd be out of the way. The aroma of roast beef and steaming vegetables sent his taste buds into overdrive. All his other senses were being bombarded, as well. From the moment he'd stepped into the Durrant home after church, the house had been buzzing with activity. Laura had stopped by the gazebo to check on things before going on to her parents' house. He'd found it distracting, trying to reconcile the woman he'd worked with yesterday with the lovely woman who'd sat beside him in church. Being in the close confines of the truck cab had only highlighted the difference. A difference that made him curious about this new side of Laura Durrant.

Angie Durrant caught his eyes and smiled. "Adam, could you come and give us a hand?" He swallowed the knot of unease in his throat but obeyed. Laura handed him a potato peeler and a spud when he joined her at the large center island. He stared down at the items in his hands. He'd peeled a potato. Once. He heard Laura chuckle and glanced over at her. Her violet eyes were sparkling with amusement.

"Like this." She demonstrated the technique quickly and handed the items back to him. "Then cut them into pieces and drop them into the pot on the stove."

He did as he was told, but when he put his pieces of potato in the pot, they didn't look the same. He turned to Laura to inquire, but she was hurrying from the room.

"Matt and Shelby are here, Mom."

He searched his memory. Matt. The oldest brother who was getting married to his former sweetheart.

Angie Durrant wiped her hands on a towel and hurried to the hallway. Adam sought out his little corner in the family room. No need to intrude on family time.

Before he could take a few steps, the women were back, forcing him to stop and get caught up in the moment.

Mrs. Durrant touched his arm gently and smiled at the tall man who came into the kitchen. "Adam, this is our oldest son, Matt. Matt, our houseguest, Adam Holbrook."

Houseguest? He appreciated her not spelling out his situation. Matt extended his hand and shook Adam's hand. "Nice to meet you."

He resembled a younger version of Tom.

"And this is his soon-to-be wife, Shelby Russell."

The elegant brunette smiled, but didn't shake his hand because her hands were full of a pie and a basket.

"Hello. Could I get you to take one of these, please?"

Adam relieved her of the pie, setting it down on the only clear spot in the kitchen.

He turned around to find a little boy staring up at him. He had green eyes, sandy hair and a nose full of freckles. "Hello."

"My name is Kenny. What's your name?"

"Adam."

"Like in the Bible." Kenny frowned and wrinkled his nose. "There aren't any Kennys in the Bible."

"I don't think I've ever heard of any," Adam admitted.

"Are you the man who broke the gazebo?"

Adam's felt a rush of embarrassment warm his face. "Kenny."

Adam glanced over at the boy's father, who looked

as embarrassed as he felt. No sense in trying to hide his guilt. "Yes, I am. I wasn't paying attention and I wrecked it with my car."

Kenny looked up at him with sympathetic eyes. "Sometimes I don't pay attention. I get in trouble a lot. But it's okay because my daddy loves me anyway. That's what daddies do."

A large knot formed in the center of Adam's chest. It was hard to find his voice. Not all daddies. "That's good."

A young girl joined the boy. "Hi, I'm Cassidy. Aunt Laura is helping you fix the gazebo, right?"

"She is."

"Good, because we like to hang out there a lot and now we can't."

Shelby Russell came and steered the children to the other room with instructions to set the table.

Adam glanced around the kitchen. Everyone was going about their business, not paying any attention to him at all. Suddenly, he wanted out. Away from all the warm and cozy nonsense. He tried to battle his impulse to flee. He wanted to go to his room to sort things out, but to do so would be rude. He took a step backward, seeking distance. Everyone seemed happy, even joyful. It couldn't be real. Did every happy family act this way?

Angie Durrant caught his attention, motioning him to the kitchen. She handed him the bowl of rice and smiled. "Go put that on the table then tell the boys we're ready to eat."

He nodded, wondering for the tenth time how he ended up here. He'd never felt so out of place, so awkward, in his whole life.

Were they trying to rehabilitate him? Were they

trying to make him feel the burden of his damaging their landmark? Or was it money? Did they think he would compensate them later for their kindness? The thought immediately filled him with shame. These people weren't like the ones he normally associated with. The Durrants were people he had little exposure to.

Adam placed the bowl, then moved slowly into the family room. The guys were focused on the Saints football game. "Food's ready."

Matt turned and smiled. "'Bout time. I'm starving." He punched his dad playfully in the arm. "Chow."

Tom stood and tapped his grandson, Kenny, on the head. "Come on, kiddo."

Adam followed them into the dining room, a strange tightness in the center of his chest as he watched the family come together. Laura smiled and motioned him to the seat beside her.

He asked himself again if what he was seeing was real. Probably not. They were all on their best behavior for his sake. Trying to put on a show. The way his parents did whenever they came home. Once a year his mother would parade out her best china and invite the crowd. They'd all smile, put on a display of family happiness, then the next morning, they'd all go their separate ways.

Something told him this family wouldn't change with each day. How did they do that?

Tom Durrant bowed his head and stretched out his hands. Before Adam could register what was happening, Laura took his hand in hers, completing the circle around the family table. The room was suddenly hot. His hands began to sweat and he wished he could let go of Laura's hand, but to do so would be rude. He inhaled a slow breath and tried to focus on the grace being said.

"…for family. For your sacrifice and redemption and for never-ending love. Bless our guest. We ask that you make his time here a benchmark for his life. Amen."

Adam wanted to ask Mr. Durrant what he meant by benchmark, but he didn't feel comfortable doing so. He'd only been here a day and a half and he'd never been so unbalanced in his entire life. He could face any danger, risk his life on the flimsiest of whims, but spending an afternoon with a real family left him tense and edgy.

The moment the prayer was over, Adam released Laura's hand, surprised to find his fingers missing the contact. Her hand was small and deceptively delicate, but he was well aware of the strength, as well. He'd seen her in action. She could handle power tools with the best of them. This was the first time he'd seen her in a more domestic setting. She looked at home here, too.

"So, Adam," Matt said, once dinner was under way, "Laura tells me you're some kind of daredevil?"

Adam spared a quick glance at Laura. "I wouldn't say daredevil. I participate in various extreme sports. I like adventure. I want to experience life to the fullest."

"How does your family feel about your dangerous pursuits?"

Mrs. Durrant's question blindsided him. He'd never considered their feelings before. Adam looked at the expectant stares. *They don't care.* Swallowing his hurt, he forced a smile. "It's not a problem."

"I've read about you," Matt said, gesturing with his fork. "There was an article in an issue of *Sports Lookout* a few months back. You were in Nepal, rafting."

Adam nodded, remembering the roar of the white

water and the ache in his arms from fighting the force of the river. Then there had been the rush when he'd thought they were going to crash into the rocks. "That was a wild ride."

Matt chuckled. "I'll say. I'm afraid I don't have that kind of courage." He reached over and took Shelby's hand. "I've got too much to lose."

The smile on Adam's face froze. What did he have to lose? Nothing. If he'd died in that river, not a soul would have shed a tear. His death would have made headlines. His funeral would have been well-attended, but not a person on earth would have cared.

"It's a unique lifestyle," he muttered, trying to wipe the picture of Matt and Shelby's loving glance from his mind.

Conversation drifted to other topics, for which Adam was grateful. Normally he loved entertaining folks with his adventures, but his exploits seemed out of place here. Everything he said felt contrived against the simple, honest lives of this family. He was more determined than ever to get out of here. He didn't belong here. He didn't belong anywhere.

"Old family tradition," Tom announced when the meal ended. "The women cook, the men clean up."

Adam followed the men's lead, stacking plates and silverware and taking it to the kitchen. Even little Kenny carried his own plate from the dining room.

It wasn't like he'd never cleaned up after himself. His adventures often took place in locales with few amenities. It was the sense of inclusion that made him uncomfortable. The Durrants all behaved in a way that assumed he would participate. No formal invitations. No awkward suggestions. Merely the understanding that since he'd shared a meal he would, of course, share the work.

The gesture made him uneasy. He could chitchat with the rich and famous, but he had no idea how to talk to a pair of regular guys.

Tom pulled down the dishwasher door and slid out the rack. Matt began scraping the dishes. Kenny and Adam finished clearing off the table.

"Didn't I read that you jump out of helicopters?" Matt asked.

"That's right."

"Cool," Kenny gushed.

Adam shared the finer points of heli-skiing with the guys. To his surprise he found a new kind of delight in telling the stories and seeing their reactions.

Once the dishes were done, Kenny urged them outside for a football game. Kenny wanted to be on Adam's team which made him nervous. He didn't want anything to happen to the boy. It didn't take long for him to get the gist of football Durrant-style. All the roughhousing was done with great enthusiasm and flourish, but with care and restraint. The result was fun for all and Kenny felt like he'd played with the big boys.

Adam had played plenty of pickup games with his buddies, but never had he enjoyed a game as much as this one. Tom came up and placed a hand on his shoulder.

"Good game."

"Thanks. I think Kenny had fun."

Tom chuckled. "Yeah. We play a bit differently when he's in the game. You should see us when my younger son is here. He's over-the-top competitive."

Adam did a quick search of his memory. The brother who was a cop. "I hear he's doing better."

Tom turned serious. "He is, but there's still a long way to go."

"Sorry to hear that."

"The Lord will work it out. We have to leave it to Him."

"What if He doesn't work it out the way you want?" He regretted the question the moment it was out of his mouth. These people had been generous and hospitable to him today and he was questioning their beliefs. "I'm sorry. I shouldn't have said that."

"It's all right. It's a valid question and you're right. The Lord may not work it out the way we hope, but He'll work it out. Maybe better. Maybe different. Either way, we have to trust that He had the best plan for my son. God sees the whole of Ty's life. We see only a small part."

"So you're saying, no matter what the future holds for your son, you're okay with it?"

Tom shook his head. "Not okay, but at peace. The Lord may be teaching Ty life lessons for some future purpose that I know nothing about."

He'd wanted to ask more, but the family was congregating in the kitchen again, talking and laughing. The kids were squealing for dessert. Angie was cutting the pie and giggling with Shelby and Laura. Suddenly the commotion was overwhelming. He had to get away and think. Find someplace quiet to regroup. Going to his room was out of the question. He'd have to walk past them all and explain why he was leaving. He caught sight of the back door and he remembered the patio.

Slowly he moved away until he was just inside the small mudroom leading to the back porch.

Quickly he ducked out and hurried down the steps, making a beeline for the far end of the patio and the bench that circled the large oak tree. He sat down, taking a few deep breaths, placing one foot on the bench seat and closing his eyes. Never in his wildest dreams would he have thought that being around a family would be more stressful than jumping out of a helicopter or skiing down a mountain.

He took a few deep breaths, letting his heart rate slow and the tension ebb away. The cool evening air helped settle his muddled thoughts.

"Are you all right?"

He jerked his eyes open to find Laura standing in front of him. Even in the fading light he could read the concern in her violet eyes. "Yeah. Just tired, I guess. This is all new to me."

"You mean the carpentry work? You'll get the hang of it. You did great yesterday." She sat down beside him and he felt his heart speed up again.

"No, not that. It's all the family stuff. It's different."

Laura looked at him curiously. "We're just an ordinary family. Nothing different about us."

Adam shook his head. "No, not like any family I ever knew."

"What was your family like?"

"Nonexistent." He laughed to make light of it, but he knew she wouldn't let it pass.

A frown creased her forehead. "Are you an orphan?"

He shook his head. "Just an only child." She waited and he knew he had no choice but to satisfy her curiosity. "My parents don't really live together. I don't think they ever did. My mother has her life, my father has his. Once or twice a year we'd meet at the old family mansion and throw a big dinner party. Everyone would make nice, brag about their latest exploits, and then in the morning, go their separate ways."

"Well, who did you live with? Your dad?"

The laugh escaped before he could stop it. "No. He was working 24/7. And Mom was traveling most of the time." He set his jaw. He didn't like talking about his family or his past. "I went to boarding school or sleepaway camp." He lowered his leg and turned to look at her. Her lovely eyes were filled with compassion. For him.

"I'm sorry. I guess I forget that not all families are like ours. It's all I've ever known. For what it's worth, sometimes I need to get away from them, too. That's why I have my own home."

"Adam, Laura. Dessert is on the table," Angie yelled from the house.

He was grateful for the interruption, but he wanted to talk about her, to learn more. They started back inside.

"Don't let them get to you. Take them in small doses. Mom with smother you with food and kindness if you let her. She'll be all up in your business. And Dad watches everyone like a hawk. You're under his roof, so you're one of his for the time being."

"And I'm working closely with his baby girl."

"Yeah. You figured that out, huh?"

Her smile turned a light on behind her violet eyes. She was so lovely. So easy to talk to. He'd have to be careful. She had a way of seeing through him. He had to remember his only goal was getting home in time. He *had* to find a way to make that happen.

Chapter Four

Laura curled up on the sofa, patting the cushion to signal for Wally to join her. The little buff-colored dog buried his nose in her hand, begging for love. She couldn't help but smile. He always put her in a good mood. "You're such a sweet boy, aren't you?" She stroked the soft fur, her eyes on the television, but her mind on Adam Holbrook.

She was more confused than ever about him. He'd been full of contradictions today at her parents' house, one minute helping as if he belonged and then other times tense and withdrawn. Several times she noticed him pull back, watching the activity from a safe distance. At first she'd thought he didn't like her family. But then she'd glimpsed something in his dark eyes, a shadow of longing, a flash of puzzlement. His comment about his family and childhood haunted her. Nonexistent. Was he serious? If so, her heart ached for him.

She couldn't fathom such a life. She was so close to her parents and brothers. They got together as much as possible, helped each other, comforted each other. Of course, it wasn't all roses. Mom could be a meddler at times and Dad tended to be overprotective where his kids were concerned. She and her brothers got along most of the time, but there were petty issues that caused differences of opinion now and again. Matt was way too uptight and serious. Tyler was hotheaded and easily angered. She'd been the fixer, the one who wanted to save things and make things better. But they were family. First and foremost.

Her cell phone rang and she scooped it off the end table, smiling at the name on the screen. "How did you know that I needed to talk to someone?"

Shelby, her soon-to-be sister-in-law, chuckled. "Just a feeling. Actually I wanted to see if you wanted to go with me to look at wedding flowers next week. I need to decide what I'll carry down the aisle."

"Of course. Just let me know when." There was a slight pause.

"I also wanted to ask you about your new hired hand. I know he nearly destroyed the gazebo, but he's seriously good-looking. You might have trouble concentrating on your work."

"Aren't you about to marry my brother? You shouldn't be noticing other guys."

"I'm engaged, but not dead. He might be handsome, but he can't hold a candle to my Matt. No one could. Seriously, though, what do you think of him?"

"He's an entitled rich guy who only thinks about himself. Been there. Done that."

"You mean Ted, your ex? Is he really that bad?"

Laura sighed. "Okay, he's not that bad. He's actually been easier to deal with than I'd expected."

"Well, Kenny and Cassidy thought he was way cool. Kenny hasn't stopped talking about him."

She had a point. The kids had followed him around like little groupies and he'd treated them with kindness at every turn. She'd seen his joy in participating in the family football game, and her brother and dad had both treated him like one of their own.

"Matt and I liked him right off. And from what I saw, your parents like him, too."

That left her as the only one with doubts. Maybe Shelby could help her sort things out. "He told me our family wasn't like anything he'd ever known."

"What did he mean?"

"I think we made him uncomfortable. He said he was raised in boarding schools and rarely saw his parents because they were too busy with their own lives."

"How sad. Though, I have to tell you, the first time Matt brought me to your house on a Sunday I was totally intimidated. I can sympathize with Adam."

"I guess we do take a little getting used to," Laura said.

"You know, I think he's attracted to you, Laura. I saw him watching you a couple times today."

"No way. I'm his boss. Besides, I'm not his type. I'm sure his taste in women runs toward sophisticated and wealthy. Maybe even a supermodel or two."

"Laura, don't put yourself down. You're beautiful and sweet, and somewhere out there is the perfect man to appreciate you. Maybe he's right there in your father's house. Oh, sorry, I've got to go. Cassidy is picking on Kenny again. Time to play referee. I'll talk to you tomorrow."

Laura hung up the phone, shaking her head at the nonsense Shelby had spouted. Adam was *not* attracted to her. Sure, he'd actually opened up to her and told her a bit about his life. But that didn't mean he was interested in her.

She stood and headed to bed. Adam Holbrook was not attracted to her. Besides, the only men she wanted in her life were skilled workmen, not some self-centered adventurer. Right?

The room was closing in on him. He'd been here with the Durrants for three nights now and he still felt awkward and on edge. It was a nice room. Spacious and comfortable, but it wasn't his room. It belonged to a stranger. Everything in this house was strange to him. He was used to hotel rooms, or tents and huts on the way to his latest adventure. He even felt at home in the most luxurious of homes, but he didn't feel any more comfortable in this happy family homestead.

His gaze landed on the trophies lovingly and proudly displayed on the dresser. Matt was a grown man with a family, but his parents still cherished his accomplishments. Adam had no idea where his trophies were. Tossed in a closet? Thrown in the trash? He couldn't remember either parent looking at one.

He stretched out on his side, surfing through TV channels as a distraction. He was dog-tired and sore all over. The hot shower had helped, but now he couldn't relax. He needed to sleep if he was going to keep up with Laura tomorrow. For such a little thing she had more energy than five men. Though she treated him like he was incapable of doing anything without her detailed instructions. She'd been telling him for two days she'd teach him to use the saw, but so far he hadn't touched anything more than a crowbar and a hammer.

He was anxious to show her he had some aptitude. All he needed was a chance to prove it to her.

He looked at Laura differently since Sunday. She'd been relaxed and happy, moving with a grace and femininity that mesmerized him. She'd laughed with her mom as they prepared dinner. Teased her brother mercilessly and played with her niece and nephew. During the football game, the women had cheered the men on and he'd found himself looking in her direction to see if she was watching him.

Over the past couple of days on the job, she'd stopped and spoken a kind word or shared a hug with nearly everyone who had passed by the gazebo. There appeared to be no end to her caring nature. Love came naturally to her.

Which only made him more aware that he didn't belong in Dover or with the Durrants. He needed to get home. Maybe it was time to eat crow and call his ex-girlfriend/lawyer, Gail. The thought didn't sit well. But he didn't belong here, and if he didn't get home in time, he wouldn't belong anywhere.

Laura parked the Handy Works van in her dad's driveway and honked the horn. She hoped Adam was ready because they had a lot to do today. The old bricks had arrived on time and her brickmason, Tony Donato, would be hard at work for the next couple of days bringing the foundation back to its former glory. The damaged section of the gazebo had been dismantled, stabilized and all the pieces catalogued.

Adam hopped into the passenger seat, glancing around the large vehicle. "What's this? Aren't we working today?"

She shook her head. "Tony is starting the foundation repairs. That will take a couple days." She looked over at him and raised her eyebrows. "Today you start the community-service phase of your sentence."

He frowned. "Let me guess, serving up soup in a kitchen or picking up trash along the highway?"

"Neither. Something much more fun and educational."

"Now I'm scared. Like what?"

"Have you ever done any plumbing?" She glanced over at him, choking back a giggle at the look on his face.

"You're kidding."

"Nope. And we have a long list of good deeds to do today."

"Good deeds?"

"That's right. We'll be doing a few Handy Works projects for the next few days."

"Handy what?"

"Handy Works is a ministry my brother and I started. We do repairs, chores and anything else people need who can't afford to hire the work done or are unable to do it themselves."

"And you do this because?"

"We're called upon to help those less fortunate. Didn't your mother ever teach you it's better to give than to receive?"

"No." He looked away. "Like I said, she wasn't around to teach me anything."

Her cheeks burned with remorse. She realized that Adam always used the past tense when speaking of his mother. "I'm sorry. When you talked about her the other day, I didn't realize she was dead."

"She's not. She's in Thailand lounging on the beach. No, that was last month. This month I think it's Australia."

Laura stared over at him. He was completely cool and indifferent when he spoke about his mother. She'd found his comments about his parents so hard to believe that she'd convinced herself he had been exaggerating. Now she had to consider he might be telling the truth. "Surely she was home when you were little."

"Nope."

"Then who raised you?"

Adam exhaled a bitter laugh. "Nannies. Seven, if I remember correctly. What's our first stop?"

How sad. His parents absent from his life, never experiencing the closeness and love of a family all added up to a picture of neglect that made her heart ache. She was a soft touch for anything or anyone who'd been neglected. She'd have to watch herself. Adam wasn't an old building or house she could restore. He was only a man passing through her life. She wasn't God. She couldn't restore people. In a few weeks he'd be gone.

Later that morning Laura backed the van out of the narrow potholed driveway of the Randall home, bracing herself for what she knew was coming. The repairs on the bathroom had been hampered by a drunken and belligerent Mr. Randall. It had gotten so bad that at one point Adam had been ready to plant a fist in the man's face. It was her reminder that punching Mr. Randall would only lengthen his stay in Dover that had stopped him.

She knew he had a mind full of opinions to spew. It was easier to let him get it out than try to restrain him. She'd barely cleared the drive when he cut loose.

"Why are you helping a man like that? He's a lazy bum. He doesn't deserve any charity. All you're doing is making it easy on him."

"I didn't do it for him. I did it for his wife and children. They deserve running water. They deserve to live in a house that has a working toilet. Or would you have me let them suffer because he's a jerk?"

Adam stared out the window a long moment before answering. "It doesn't seem right."

Laura understood his outrage. It was hard for her, too. "Yes, Will Randall is a mean drunk. No, he doesn't provide properly for his family, but that's not the issue. Our ministry is to help, not judge or rehabilitate or condemn."

Adam sighed and propped his foot on the dash. "Who's next on our charity list?"

"Edith Johnson's house." She pointed ahead a few houses. "She needs a wheelchair ramp built from her front porch to the driveway."

"Doesn't she have family who could do that?"

Laura nodded. "But one son lives in Vicksburg and the other is in New Orleans. They've been trying to co-ordinate their schedules, but they have teenaged kids. It's hard. She finally called and asked us for help."

"So you step in like a fairy godmother."

"No, as a friend wanting to help. Sometimes people are too proud to ask. As Christians, we're called upon to help those less fortunate."

"Handy Works, you mean?"

Laura glanced over at him, gauging his expression. He seemed sincere enough. "Yes, I wanted to do something to help."

She parked the van and got out, walking up to the

house. Adam followed at a distance. She knocked. The door opened slowly, a face peered out through the narrow opening. "Miss Edith? I'm Laura Durrant from Handy Works. We're here to build your ramp."

"Oh, bless you." The little woman cooed happily. "I'm so glad you're here." She opened the door wider, making way for her walker. "I'm so ready to get out of this house and I can't until I have a ramp."

Laura entered the house, stopping just inside the door. "Are you doing better? I thought you were confined to the wheelchair?"

"Oh, no, not all the time. I'm supposed to use this contraption as much as possible while I'm home." She jiggled her walker slightly. "But if I leave the house I need the chair. The senior shuttle won't pick me up unless I have a ramp. All my friends are going to all sorts of exciting places and I'm stuck here."

Laura patted her arm. "Not for long you aren't. We'll have that ramp done this afternoon. You'll be ready to run the roads with all the other girls."

Edith giggled. She glanced at Adam. "Who's your handsome friend?"

She'd almost forgotten about her shadow. "This is Adam Holbrook. He's going to help me build your ramp."

Edith nodded, studying him closely. "You're the one. I heard what you did." She shook her head, making a clicking sound with her tongue. "It's good that you have to fix what you've broken, young man."

"Yes, ma'am."

Laura appreciated Adam's respectful tone.

Edith smiled then and reached over and patted Adam's

arm. "You're a good boy. I can see it in your eyes. You just need some attention."

Adam didn't respond and Laura seized the moment. "Well, we'd better get started. You go on about your business and we'll check in with you on our progress."

Back at the van, Laura opened the double doors and stepped inside. "You grab the worktable, and I'll get the circular saw." Adam followed directions without comment. Within minutes they had the work area set up. Portable workbench. Table and miter saw. Lumber.

She instructed Adam on how to measure for the ramp and how to figure the correct grade to prevent the wheelchair from rolling too quickly. "First rule. Measure twice. Cut once."

"Sounds redundant."

She couldn't tell if he was being sarcastic or not. "You miscut a piece of lumber, you waste money, material and time."

"Got it. So when do I get to cut?"

She had to let him do it eventually, but she hated turning her tools over to someone else, especially a novice like him. But she needed his help and for that he had to learn to handle the equipment. Resigned, she picked up a couple pieces of scrap she'd brought along for just such a purpose. She placed a section of two-by-four against the fence of the miter saw and stepped back. "Okay, hold it firmly in place, grip the handle, pull the trigger first, then lower the blade."

Adam looked uncomfortable, but he did as he was told. Laura watched carefully.

"There." He held up the severed board. "How's that?"

"Okay. Do it a few more times until you get the feel of it."

Adam smiled after cutting his fourth piece. "I like this."

Laura frowned. "It's the easiest one to use. Next up, circular saw."

"I'm ready." He rubbed his hands together eagerly. "Bring it on."

Twenty minutes later Adam made his first real cut. He surprised her by doing it quickly and correctly. With his help, the base for the ramp was completed in short order. He'd measured wrong only once. Laura tugged on her cap and wiped her forehead. "All we need now is to cut the plywood to fit and Miss Edith will be set free from her home. Go get a piece of three-quarter-inch plywood out of the van and bring it over here while I set up the saw."

Laura adjusted the blade angle, then glanced at the van. Adam was walking toward her, the four-by-eight sheet of plywood balanced against his shoulder. The muscles in his arms strained against the weight. His long, sure stride accentuated the powerful legs.

She told herself to look away, but she couldn't. He was the very image of masculine power. Of course he was in good condition. He'd have to be to pull off some of the fool stunts he did. Laura gritted her teeth and forced herself to look away. She couldn't deny Adam Holbrook was an attractive man. Too attractive. Which had nothing to do with anything.

Adam held the edge of the plywood as she guided it through the table saw, taking its weight as the blade did its work. He set it aside and followed Laura to the ramp base. Pulling a handful of screws from her apron, she handed them to Adam. She'd have preferred to use her nail gun, but the nail gun required a compressor and the van they were in today didn't have one.

Adam set the last screw, then stood and stretched. "Is that it? We done?"

Laura slipped her hammer into her holster. "We just need to get Miss Edith's approval." Laura knocked on the door, eager to see the smile on her face. She wasn't disappointed. The older woman touched the rail tenderly and shook her head in disbelief.

"You did it so quickly. Thank you so much. Oh, I have something for you both." She disappeared inside briefly, then emerged with two small bags. "Please accept these in appreciation for all your hard work. I know you won't take any money, but what you've done for me is such a blessing that I can't let you go without saying thank you in some way."

Laura took the two small bags with pleasure. The chocolate-chip cookies were still warm from the oven. She wrapped her arms around the slight woman in a warm hug. "It's our pleasure, Miss Edith. And thank you for the cookies."

Once in the van she handed Adam one of the bags. "If you want a thrill, then you need to bite into one of those. No one makes cookies like Miss Edith."

He examined the bag of cookies. "Do the people being helped contribute anything to this arrangement?"

"Like what?"

"Money. To help with the costs."

Laura shook her head and started the engine. "Handy Works is a volunteer organization. We rely on donations to keep operating so we don't have to ask for funds from those needing help."

"That doesn't sound like a good business plan."

"We're not in it to make money. We're in it to help others."

"But you get nothing in return."

"Oh, I get a great deal in return. You just can't put a price on it. We're a charity, not a business."

"I understand that, but who pays for the supplies, the gas for the van? What if no one volunteers one day? What then?"

"It's worked so far."

"I'm just saying there might be a better way to do things and still keep it voluntary, but provide you a little financial security, as well."

"You sound like my dad."

"From what little I've seen he appears to be a good businessman."

"He is." Her father had always told her if she got the same advice from two different sources, she should pay attention. But why did one of those sources have to be Adam Holbrook?

Adam leaned back in the large chair in his room and bit into one of the homemade cookies Edith Johnson had given him, slowly savoring the taste. He loved chocolate-chip cookies. He'd tried every brand on the market. At one time he'd even had the nation's undisputed best cookie, Jamison's Premier, shipped to him wherever he was in the world.

But he'd never tasted anything like the ones made by the little old lady he'd met today. They weren't the biggest or the most visually appealing. They were small and misshapen. But the melt-in-your-mouth, deep chocolate taste was amazing. All that was lacking to make it perfect was a big glass of milk.

In the time he'd been living with the Durrants he'd never left his room once he'd retired for the night. He didn't want to intrude into their private time and he didn't want to call attention to the fact that he was technically a prisoner in their home. Angie had repeatedly told him to make himself at home, but he'd never taken her up on the offer. Until tonight.

Moving to the door, he cracked it open, listening for sounds of activity. Quiet as a church. He eased out and went down to the kitchen. Taking a glass from the cupboard, he poured some milk and sat down at the table. He'd eaten two cookies when Tom entered the room. He glanced up, prepared to apologize, but Tom held up his hand and took a seat at the table. Adam offered him a cookie.

"Oh, Edith Johnson's, right?" He pulled one from the sack and took a big bite. "Wonderful. Was this your reward for doing community service? Homemade cookies?"

Adam grinned. "Unusual but effective."

"I'm guessing this is a new kind of charity work for you."

"You could say that. I usually write a check or make a pledge. Sometimes I attend a gala charity party."

"Those are all good ways to help others, but using your own two hands, actually doing the work that's needed, that's a different thing entirely."

Adam understood the concept. He'd learned long ago that watching someone do extreme sports bore little resemblance to experiencing it firsthand. "I'm starting to understand. Can I ask you about Handy Works? How can it keep going if you rely only on donations and volunteers? Even the best of charities require some form of financial base to operate. Laura's ministry wakes up each morning not knowing whether they'll be able to do business that day or not. I just think there might be a better way to structure Handy Works and keep it volunteer-based."

Tom studied him a moment. "I agree, but I have to let Laura do it her way for now. In case you haven't noticed, my Boo is a very loving and giving young woman. She's also very passionate about anything she takes on."

"Oh, I've noticed." She'd worked on the ramp with her usual energy and dedication, wielding power tools and a hammer with gusto. Then she treated the elderly Miss Edith with the gentle love and care of a nurse.

When she smiled, it was as if a light came on inside her. She glowed with happiness. The woman's joy over her new ramp was reflected in Laura's violet eyes. Laura had said her payment had nothing to do with money. He was beginning to understand. The satisfaction she received from the project was larger than the ramp she'd built for the older woman.

"I understand you have a conflict with the length of your sentence."

Adam shifted uncomfortably. He was learning quickly that nothing was secret in a small town. "I do. My father and I haven't been on good terms for a long time. When I refused to go to work in the family business, he cut me off. Left me a trust fund, but I have to show up in person each year to get my paycheck or I lose it all. This sentence won't be over until two days after the deadline."

"So you come from a family-owned-business background like Laura does."

The comment caught him off guard. He'd never

thought about it. "Yes, I suppose so." Holbrook Electronics had been started by his grandfather. He was the third generation, but he wanted no part of the business. Was that why his father had put the conditions on his inheritance? Had he been hoping that his son would eventually see the value of his legacy and join the team?

"Parents have expectations for their children. Some men work to build a business with the goal of creating it to pass on to their son. If the son doesn't want it, then it can feel like a slap in the face. All their sacrifice and hard work was for nothing." Tom stood and pushed his chair under the table. "I'm sorry to hear about your conflict, Adam. I wish there was something I could do to help."

"Thanks, Tom, but it's my fault, my situation to deal with. I'll figure something out." He *had* to. There was no alternative.

Laura poured water into her coffeemaker, set the timer and turned off the kitchen light. Tomorrow couldn't happen unless the coffee was ready and waiting when she got up. Today had been a good day. The brickwork was coming along and both Handy Works projects had gone well. Adam had been more help than she'd anticipated. He'd never complained. Never refused any task she'd assigned. Though he was totally puzzled by the Handy Works ministry.

She'd been blessed to be able to make a living doing work she loved and to be surrounded by people who cared about her. Her ministry allowed her to help others and give back.

She let Wally out the back door, waiting on the stoop while he attended to his business.

But was that enough? She'd been content with her life until Matt and Shelby had gotten engaged. Lately she'd been wishing for someone to come home to. Someone other than a dog.

An image of Adam Holbrook came to mind—his make-your-knees weak smile, the broad shoulders that had come in handy today. Good grief, what was she thinking? "Wally, come on."

The moment the dog returned, she closed the door. The wedding, that's what was causing all these crazy thoughts in her head. Seeing her brother and Shelby so in love and planning their wedding was making her all dreamy.

The phone rang and she ran to get it. "Hello?"

"Hey, Boo. You have time to talk to your old dad?"

"Of course. What is it?"

"I learned something today that I think you should know about. It concerns Adam."

Laura listened as her father explained, her mind trying to absorb what she was hearing. When she finally said goodbye she knew she'd spend several sleepless hours tonight considering his suggestion.

Chapter Five

Laura watched Adam as he came down the back porch steps and walked toward the truck. His usual enthusiasm was missing today. They'd worked together nearly a week now and she'd come to recognize his moods. Normally he jogged down the steps and hurried to join her. Today he was dragging his feet and the relaxed grin he usually wore was missing, as well.

He climbed in and shut the door with barely a mumbled hello. She allowed him some space. She'd been working him pretty hard. He wasn't used to the physical demands of construction work. Maybe it was catching up with him. But her concern mounted when he kept silent for more than a block. "Is everything all right?"

He glanced over at her and nodded. "Yeah. I think the confinement is getting to me, that's all."

"I'd hardly call staying at my parents' home confinement."

"It is when you aren't free to go anyplace but there. Don't get me wrong, I'm grateful to them for taking me in. I'd rather be there than in jail. But I'm used to being on my own, not sharing a house with someone else. I could use a good run. I normally get in five miles a day, but that's out of the question for now."

"I know this must be hard for you, but it can't be helped."

His mouth moved in a small grin. "Time to pay the piper, huh?"

"In a way. If it makes you feel any better, I think you're doing a great job at the gazebo. In fact, if you wanted to put your mind to it, you could be a decent carpenter."

"Thank you. I'll keep that in mind. I might be looking for work soon." He turned back toward the side window, ending the conversation.

Laura thought about what her father had told her last night on the phone. That Adam would lose everything if he wasn't in Atlanta on time. Unfortunately, his deadline was two days before his sentence was over. Her father had offered a suggestion, but she wasn't sure she liked it.

Slowly, Laura drove the truck up over the curb and parked beside the gazebo. The city had removed a portion of the iron fence so she could park closer and keep tools and materials handy. She went immediately to the newly restored foundation and made her inspection. Tony had done his usual outstanding job. The was no sign of the damage.

Now she could start the woodwork. She was looking forward to it. It was what she loved. She hoped Adam wouldn't be a hindrance. If he caught on to everything as quickly as he had during the construction of the ramp yesterday, she might have to revise her opinion of him.

"What do we do today?" He lifted the nail gun from

the truck bed and examined it closely. "This should be a blast to use."

Laura grinned. Typical man. They reverted to ten-year-olds when they had a power tool in their hand. "It doesn't work that way. You can't fire a nail gun like a pistol."

"No? Then how does it work?"

"You have to compress the tip before the trigger will engage."

Together, they worked on rebuilding the floor of the gazebo. A few hours later, Laura decided they needed a break. She brought Adam a cold drink, hoisting herself up onto the edge of the nearly completed deck.

Adam had been very helpful. His strength had made replacing the joists and sistering in supports for the less-damaged ones quick and easy. "I got a call from Edith." She took a sip of her drink. "She loves her ramp."

"Good." He came and sat down beside her. "Have you known her long?"

Laura shook her head. "Not well. I've met her once or twice."

Adam frowned. "I thought you knew everyone in Dover."

"We're not that small a town. Not anymore. I was born and raised here, but I don't know everyone."

"But you like the slower pace, the quiet?"

Laura raised her eyebrows. "That's a misconception about the South. We work just as hard and long as anyplace else. My days fly by faster than I can handle sometimes, and I never feel like I'm going at a slower pace."

"No insult intended. I guess I like the big city because there's always something happening. I like the unexpected."

"I like predictable."

"And that's why I'd go crazy living in a place like Dover."

A small twinge of disappointment settled in Laura's mind. She should have expected him to feel that way, but she'd hoped he was at least coming to appreciate her hometown.

"How did you like Miss Edith's cookies?"

"Fantastic, but they're all gone."

Laura laughed. "They never last long. But don't worry. Miss Edith sells her cookies over at Cynthia's gift shop. We can pick some up next time we're in the area."

"Good, because Miss Edith needs to patent that recipe. She could make a fortune."

"Can't." Laura shook her head. "It's not hers. She uses the same recipe everyone else does, the one on the package."

"Nah, I don't believe it. There has to be some kind of secret ingredient."

Laura chuckled softly. "Oh, there is. It's called love."

"Right."

"Honestly. She loves making the cookies. She loves giving them away. She loves selling them. It's the same way your mother's cooking always tastes better than anyone else's—the love she puts into it for her family."

"I wouldn't know about that." He stood and tossed his empty bottle into the trash.

Too late she remembered his comments about his mother. She bit her lip. She'd have to watch what she said from now on, but it was hard to monitor her words when her life was so full of family.

"I don't suppose there's any way I could get my car fixed before I'm released?" Adam glanced back over his shoulder.

"I wouldn't know."

"Do you have someone around here who knows about vintage cars? That baby's a classic."

"If it was so valuable, why were you driving it in the first place?" She tossed her hammer onto the workbench and picked up her notes.

"I'd just broken up with someone and I was soothing my bruised ego with a new car." Adam set his hands on his hips. "So, what do we tackle next?"

Laura dared a look into his green eyes, darkened now by some emotion. Sadness? Loneliness? He walked back to the workbench, leaving her with questions. It was hard for her to grasp that Adam had never known even the most basic of family experiences. Things she took for granted, like her mother's love and attention, her close relationship with her brothers and being brought up to care for others. Maybe her father's idea had merit after all. It would be a win-win situation for both her and Adam.

As they worked together on securing the final screws into the floorboards, Laura waited for a good time to start a conversation. "When are you supposed to be in Atlanta?"

Adam turned and studied her, his green eyes narrowed. "The twenty-eighth. How did you know about that? Oh, wait. Your dad."

She nodded. "It's important that you get home in time for this meeting?"

"Crucial."

She took a deep breath and crossed her arms over her chest. "I want to propose a deal."

"Meaning what?"

She heard the skepticism in his deep voice and she couldn't blame him. "Maybe there's a way we can both get what we want." She braved a glance at him. His expression was expectant but wary. "Dad talked with my uncle last night and he's agreed to let you out in time for your meeting, but the gazebo has to be done or no deal."

"Is that possible? To finish early, I mean?"

She nodded. "I've got the materials and the subcontractors lined up. If all goes well, we could actually be finished a week ahead of schedule. Plenty of time for you to get home and meet your obligation."

Relief was clearly visible on his face. He dragged a hand along the back of his neck.

"All right, it's a deal." He caught her gaze. "Thanks. This means a lot to me."

His probing gaze made her uneasy and she glanced away.

"Good. Okay." She went back to work aware of his eyes still on her. It hit her then. If they got the gazebo done as quickly as she'd hoped, she'd have one less week to deal with Adam Holbrook. The idea wasn't as welcome as she'd expected.

It had taken them until noon to finish placing the screws to firmly secure the floor. Adam was a big help, even though he still worked slower than her regular guys. She placed her drill bit on the final screw, driving it in with gusto before letting out a triumphant shout. "Done!"

She climbed down and stepped back to admire the work, unable to keep from smiling.

"So what are we celebrating?" Adam came to her side, watching her curiously.

"The floor. We are ahead of schedule. You don't know what a blessing it was to have those oak planks in my shop. Trying to find more would have taken days." She smiled up at him, almost giddy with delight.

He chuckled and smiled. "Okay. If you're happy, I'm happy."

She wanted to dance around the park, but that would be undignified. Her joy evaporated when her cell phone rang and she read the name on the screen. "Oh, no." She answered the call, her mood plunging with every word spoken in her ear. She hung up and sagged against a sawhorse.

"What's wrong?"

"That was the supplier at Ashley Salvage calling to tell me I can't get the cypress I need for the roof. I'll have to find a new source."

"Won't some other wood do?"

"No. I'm required to restore with original materials when possible."

"And when it's not possible?"

"It's always possible. It'll just take longer to find and have it shipped here. I may have to go get it."

"So will this mess up the schedule?"

Laura shrugged. "Not necessarily. I just hope we can keep up this pace. People will be so disappointed if it's not done for the festival."

"Well, then, we'll just have to work harder. What do we tackle next?"

"I have to check on my other jobs. I'm not sure what I'm going to do with you, though."

"Couldn't I tag along?" He straightened, slipping his hands into his pockets. "Wouldn't helping you on other jobs qualify as community service?"

"I suppose so. Okay, I'll get you extra leeway on your ankle monitor, then we'll get something to eat first." Laura crossed her arms and studied him a moment. "Burgers or chicken?"

"What?"

The bemused look on his face made her chuckle. "Well, we have to eat. Might as well do that first. I'm starving." She started gathering up her tools, then climbed into the cab and slammed the door. Adam hurried to join her. She turned to face him, fingers paused on the keys. "What will it be? Burgers or chicken?" The smile Adam gave her sent her heart tripping. It really was a great smile.

"Burgers."

"I know the perfect place. Best burgers in central Mississippi."

"Don't forget to call about my monitor. I don't need to get on the wrong side of your uncle again."

She cranked the engine. "Don't worry about it."

"Easy for you to say."

They rode in silence until they pulled up at a refurbished gas station. The sign read Fill 'er Up Burgers. Adam had to smile at the owner's sense of humor. The old filling station had a lot of charm, from the old gas pumps outside to the vintage car parked as if waiting to be serviced. It was right out of a 1950s postcard.

"Interesting." He smiled as they walked through the

door. The decor inside continued the theme. Hub caps and old license plates adorned the walls. Refurbished motor oil stands and vintage road maps completed the effect. The tables were made of stamped steel. An antique cola chest-type container served as the payment counter.

Adam felt all eyes focus on him the moment they stepped through the door. A hush fell over the diner. He was suddenly more aware of his ankle monitor than he'd been before, even though it was well-hidden beneath his jeans and boots. These people saw him as the bad guy. A destroyer of their beloved landmark.

Laura walked toward a table in a far corner and sat down against the wall, allowing him to sit with his back to the other customers. He relaxed a bit. At least over here he was protected from the accusing stares. "Do they stare at everyone who comes in or just me?"

"It's a small-town thing. They look at anyone who comes in. You just warrant a longer look. Don't let it get to you. They did the same to me when I moved back home. They'll get over it."

He picked up the menu. "I thought you might be trying to put me in my place."

"No. I just thought you might like a good burger. I never meant for this to make you uncomfortable."

Before he could answer, the waitress arrived. "Good afternoon Laura, Mr. Holbrook. What can I get for you today?"

Adam looked from Laura to the waitress. Her tag said Sally. "You know who I am, Sally?"

"Oh, sure." She smiled while popping her chewing gum. "We all know who you are. You gonna have that gazebo done for the festival?"

He glanced around the diner, swallowing the lump in his throat. No way was he going to fail. "Count on it."

Sally pointed her pencil at him, her eyes narrowed ominously. "I'll hold you to that."

They placed their order, and Adam felt himself relax a bit. Apparently the fascination over his arrival had waned. "Clever decor in here."

"Thanks."

"Did you do this?"

"I had a hand in it." She smiled. "Mostly I restored the building."

"Really?"

His simple question opened a floodgate. For the next ten minutes Laura explained with enthusiasm how she saved the old gas station from decay and gave it new life. Adam saw a side to her he'd never suspected. Her eyes sparkled and her face glowed as she described how they'd searched the entire South for the authentic period details. How she'd traveled to Florida to find period tiles to line the walls and how they'd refinished the old metal displays to use as serving stations.

Her passion was overwhelming, born of a deep love of her work. He was envious. He'd never experienced that kind of enthusiasm for anything and now he wondered why.

The food arrived and Adam bit into his burger with gusto, emitting a low groan of appreciation. It had to be the best burger he'd ever eaten. Laura glanced up, her violet eyes sparkling. A flicker of a smile touched her lips and Adam froze. She was lovely.

"I told you they were fantastic."

"Nothing like a good old American hamburger."

"So I guess you've traveled all over the world, chasing your thrills?"

"Pretty much."

She shook her head. "That's not for me. I'm a hometown girl. I like it right here. Surrounded by people I love and a place that's familiar."

"No wanderlust, huh?"

"Nope."

He rested his forearms on the table edge, leaning toward her. "Come on now. You can't tell me you wouldn't like to see other parts of the world, or maybe even do a few of the things I do. Everyone longs for some kind of adventure, even small ones."

Laura toyed with her napkin. "Not really. I'd be too nervous trying to find my way around foreign countries and learn new languages."

"Name one place you'd like to go. I promise not to tell anyone."

"That's easy. Great Britain. I'd love to see all those beautiful old castles."

"I should have figured that. And what about that adventure? What would you do if you had the chance? If you knew there was no way you could get hurt?"

Laura stared off in the distance awhile. "Well, I think I'd like to try the zip line. It must be amazing to fly among the trees, sailing in the air. But I don't think I'm brave enough."

Adam laughed out loud. "Are you kidding me? You manage a successful construction business, climb up on roofs and handle power tools that would make most women faint, and you say you're not brave? That sounds plenty brave to me."

"Maybe, but sometimes I think I took the easy way out."

"How so?"

"I told you I studied architecture in college. I married a man whose father owned a prestigious firm in Houston. We were going to be this great team, designing wonderful buildings. I thought I wanted to live in the big city, away from Dover. But it didn't work out that way."

"What happened?"

"My husband didn't want to actually work in the family business, he only wanted to enjoy the financial benefits. He also decided I was a bit too unsophisticated for his taste. I tried to fit into city life, but I was pretty much a fish out of water. When the marriage ended, I ran home. The rest you know. I haven't been very adventuresome since."

He reached over and touched her hand lightly, staring into her lovely violet eyes. "You're wrong. You are adventurous every time you start a new project."

She held his gaze a moment, then slipped her hand away. "Those are adventures I understand. The surprises are things I'm pretty sure I can deal with."

"Maybe you'd feel differently if you could travel with someone who knew how to speak the language and navigate the unknowns. Someone who could hold your hand each time you encountered a new surprise."

"That might make things easier. I might be braver if I wasn't alone."

"Since when do you have time to sit down and eat?"

Adam looked up at the man who had stopped at their table. He smiled down at Laura, nudging his glasses up on his nose.

"Greg, it's so good to see you."

Adam glanced from the bright smile on Laura's face to the matching one on the stranger's. The man was medium build, medium height, medium all around as far as he could see. Nothing worth causing such a warm reaction.

Laura scooted over, indicating for the man to join them. Adam frowned. He wasn't sure he wanted to share his lunchtime with anyone.

"Sorry, I can't." The man waved off the invitation. "I'm running late as it is. I just wanted to say hello."

Laura stood and hugged him. Adam listened as they discussed Handy Works and something called Martha's House. When she finally thought to introduce him, he was unable to even fake a warm greeting, despite the man's sincere handshake and the obvious way he chose to not comment on Adam's status as the town villain. He didn't like Greg.

He watched the man leave, noting with irritation the warm smile that lingered on Laura's face. He stabbed a French fry. "So who's the boyfriend?"

"He's not a boyfriend. Only a good friend, but he's a remarkable man. He started Martha's House to help battered women. What he's been able to accomplish in the past few years is amazing. I really admire him."

Adam grunted. "What's so admirable about him? He seems pretty ordinary to me."

"He has a heart for others. He gives of himself one hundred and fifty percent. You don't find many people with that kind of dedication and commitment. I doubt you'd understand."

He killed another fry. "I understand more than you think." Is that the kind of guy she liked? Nerdy. Altruistic. He stared at her a moment. Did she think he wasn't giving his all to his sentence? For some reason he didn't want to examine, he wanted her to praise him the way she had this Greg guy. It was time to show Little Miss Contractor what he could really do.

Adam looked out the window as Laura slowed the truck and pulled between two brick pillars holding an intricate iron gate. The Conrad place was an impressive old plantation on the outskirts of Dover. Most of the architecture he'd seen in the small town consisted of Victorian styles and early-twentieth-century homes. Laura had assured him there were newer parts of Dover, but with his electronic leash he'd probably never see those parts of town.

Laura pulled around to the rear of the house and parked. He'd seen a lot of magnificent homes in his life, but this one was impressive with its massive columns on three sides and the intricate iron railing on the balcony.

He followed Laura across the wide brick sidewalk to a smaller house nestled under the trees. Construction noise filled the air. He glanced back at the plantation. "You're not working in the mansion?"

"No. The owners have brought in special craftsmen from overseas to handle most of the restoration. This is Catalpa Grove Plantation. It was the largest in the area at one time. Our job is this smaller building. Originally it was the dowager's house, where the grandmother would live. But the owners want this to be their actual dwelling. They plan on opening the mansion as a bed and breakfast."

From the moment Adam stepped into the work zone, he felt the tension spike. Three men halted their work as if by command and turned to stare at him. All of them looked to be six feet tall and close to two hundred pounds. It felt a little like facing a hungry shark without a cage.

"Don't stop on my account, guys." Laura smiled and motioned them all back to work. "We're behind schedule, remember?"

The men returned to their work. Adam smiled. One word from Laura and grown men toed the line. One man stepped away from his work and came toward them. He stood an inch or so taller than Adam, with a stern expression and sharp features. He was built like a navy SEAL he'd once gone diving with. Not someone you wanted to rub the wrong way. From the daggers shooting from the man's dark eyes, Adam figured it was already too late. The man stopped in front of them, placing himself slightly in front of Laura.

"Shaw, this is Adam Holbrook. Adam, my foreman, Shaw McKinney. Those two over there are Jay Barton and Chris Storm."

The men barely glanced his way. So much for Southern hospitality. Adam offered his hand to McKinney, somewhat surprised when he shook it. Their gazes locked as they sized each other up. Adam had the feeling he'd come out on the short end of the stare-down. The foreman clearly saw himself as guardian to his employer.

He kept out of the way as Laura and Shaw moved about the room. Laura asked questions, for which it appeared Shaw had a ready answer. Adam watched her with fascination. As he'd suspected, she knew how to handle the workmen, somewhere between firm and respectful, but still displaying a no-nonsense attitude that reminded them who was in charge.

Laura moved off with the foreman into another room, leaving Adam to explore on his own. He was careful to keep a safe distance from the burly men working around the room. His carpenter skills were insufficient to tell if the men were doing a good job or not. But he doubted if they'd do less than their best with Laura as their boss. The work he saw here was more detailed and refined than what he was doing on the gazebo. He doubted he'd ever have that kind of ability.

Laura's laughter preceded her into the room and Adam spun around to see her and the foreman return. Something about the guy set this teeth on edge. He was too tall. Too rugged. And he didn't like the way the man held Laura's full attention.

Normally he didn't care a hoot what women thought of him. So why did he suddenly care what Laura thought? This small town was doing strange things to his head. Being on a short leash didn't help either.

Adam turned and went outside to wait near the truck. He'd seen enough for today. One thing had impressed him and he wanted to ask her about it. He brought it up as soon as they pulled out onto the street "So how do you do it?"

"Do what?"

"Keep those big guys in line? They have a lot of respect for you."

"I'm good at what I do. That's the main thing."

"Is that all?"

"I mastered the mommy stare."

She grinned over at him, the pretty smile causing him to lose his train of thought. "What?"

"You know that look your mom always gave you when you'd messed up? That stern 'You're standing on my last nerve' glare that said you'd better shape up or face the consequences? My mom could get us kids to behave with one quick look."

"I don't know what you're talking about."

"Didn't your mom ever—" She paled and looked away. "I, uh, just glare at them and they tremble in their boots."

Adam remained quiet for the rest of the afternoon, content to ride with Laura as she did a few errands. He got a quick peek into her workshop when she went to check on the progress of some custom cabinets, followed by a stop at the drive-through at the bank. Finally a stop at McCarver's Millwork to see about the gazebo spindles.

He had no idea how complicated woodworking could be and he wanted to learn more. He wanted to learn more about Laura, too. He'd never met anyone like her. And he was growing more and more fascinated with her each day that passed.

"How are the repairs going?" Angie Durrant finished wrapping colorful paper around a small container, placing it with the others on the kitchen table.

Laura had invited her mother over to work on decorations for Shelby's shower. She'd also wanted to talk to her alone. With Adam in her parents' home she never had the opportunity.

"Good, but not as fast as I would like. Tony rebuilt the foundation, and I already had the oak planks, so we were able to repair the floor joists and the decking. If things go as planned we might actually finish early.

But I still need cypress shingles for the roof, and I need some large pieces of oak so new posts can be turned. I'm not having any luck finding that so far."

"How's Adam working out?"

"He's a big help and he's a quick study. I think if he put his mind to it, he could be an excellent carpenter. Though I don't see that happening. Woodworking doesn't have the same thrill as surfing a fifty-foot wave in Waimea."

"You don't like him?"

"I do." She shrugged. "I guess. He's been polite, helpful."

"But he reminds you of Ted and that makes you nervous."

Her defenses went up. "No. Okay, maybe, a little. Every time I think he might be a decent guy, he'll do or say something that reminds me he's from a different way of life." Laura frowned and pushed the colored paper away. "I mean, when I ended a bad relationship, I bought a business. When he does, he goes out and buys an expensive toy car. Who does that?"

"You know, your dad and I never liked Ted. We didn't think he was right for you or that he treated you with respect. But we didn't know him as well as you did, so we trusted your judgment."

"And I was wrong. Believe me, I won't make that mistake again."

"Aren't you? You're putting Adam into a cubbyhole before you really know him."

"Mom, he's a big-city guy, a man who travels the world. He told me in no uncertain terms he could never live in a place like Dover."

"My point is, don't let one mistake push you too far

in the opposite direction. Your father and I like Adam.
I think he's a good man deep down. But I think he's
been hurt somewhere along the way."

Laura told her mother what Adam had shared with
her about his parents.

"Oh, that breaks my heart. Maybe his time with us,
working with his hands, getting to know you, will turn
him in a new direction. We'll pray for him."

She shrugged off her mother's concern. Her mom
saw only the good in people. Laura had learned to be
a little less gullible. While her mother was praying for
Adam, she needed to pray for herself. Because she was
attracted to Adam Holbrook and she couldn't be. He was
all wrong for her. In a myriad of ways. But letting that
attraction for a handsome man go any further was not
only stupid, but also dangerous. She had to be careful
and guard her heart. Because she didn't want to get it
broken a second time.

Chapter Six

Daylight had faded into deep twilight, leaving a hazy glow over the neighborhood. Adam stood on the back porch of the Durrants' home watching Laura and Shelby back out of the driveway. They were going to Laura's to work on wedding details. Matt and the kids had left earlier. This Sunday had been different from the first one he'd experienced with the Durrants. There had still been a hearty meal, but only he and Mr. and Mrs. Durrant had shared it. Laura, Matt, Shelby and the kids had dropped by later in the afternoon and they'd all visited over a rich apple dessert Mrs. Durrant had made. It had been a more quiet and relaxed time today.

A small part of him was disappointed there'd been no big family gathering, no football game. Which made no sense at all because he'd felt so awkward and out of place last week. Still, he'd found himself looking forward to the commotion. There had been a moment today, as he'd watched the Durrants sitting on the back porch talking, when he'd been overcome by an odd sensation. As if someone had pulled back a curtain and revealed his deepest dreams, his secret longing. Needs so hidden and long denied even he hadn't realized what they were. But in that instant, he'd known what he'd wanted—a home. A woman to love him. Children.

For the first time in his life he'd found something he couldn't buy. Something he wanted more than anything he'd ever known. He wanted what Laura had. He wanted a home and a family.

He made a fist and thumped it against the porch post. He had to get control of his emotions. He had to stop thinking about Laura. Because the hard truth was he had nothing whatsoever to offer her. He rubbed his forehead, battling the strange churning in his gut. He needed to get out of this small town. He wasn't cut out for family dinners and ball games with little kids.

"Adam, I brought you some tea."

He turned and took the glass from Angie. "Thanks." She sat down in one of the cushioned patio chairs, motioning for him to join her.

"This is always a bittersweet time on Sunday for me. I love having my family around, but I'm always tired at the end of the visits. Getting older, I guess. But then once they're gone, I feel the quiet of the house, and the silence is sometimes as loud as the clamor when they're here."

Adam studied her a moment. She'd read his mind. Put into words what he'd been feeling.

"How are you and my daughter getting along?"

"You want the honest truth?"

Angie laughed. "Please. I'm her mother. I'm well aware of all her flaws."

"Things are better between us now. I had my doubts in the beginning. She was pretty irritated with me."

"Furious might be more accurate."

"Has she always wanted to be a carpenter? I know it's not all that unusual these days, but she seems too—"

"Feminine? I know. She wanted to be a ballerina when she was little. But she also followed her daddy around from the time she could walk. She wanted to dress like him, talk like him. She mimicked everything he did."

He remembered the look of adoration he'd seen on her face when she looked at her father. "He's a shining knight in her eyes. I feel sorry for any man who tries to take his place."

"I worry about that myself. But I think when she finds the right one, she'll have a new knight to love."

Adam stared into his glass. "I can't quite figure her out. She's a contradiction. One minute she's this tough, determined builder, wrangling the burly men of her crew, the next she's pouring out love and kindness to an elderly stranger."

"My Laura has a heart for others. She wants to take care of them, fix things for them. When she gives her love to someone, she gives it completely. And when her heart is broken, it takes a long time for it to heal."

Adam looked at Angie. Was she warning him to stay away from her daughter?

"Did she tell you she'd been married?"

He nodded. "She mentioned that it didn't work out well."

"It shook her self-confidence, damaged her image of herself. Starting her business did wonders, but I worry that she uses her business to keep from finding love again. She needs someone to remind her how beautiful and special she is."

Was she suggesting he should be the one or warn-

ing him to steer clear for someone else? Like Greg or
the foreman?

"Well, I'm going to pull my husband out of his office
and force him to watch a DVD with me tonight." She
stood and placed a hand on his shoulder as she passed.
"Good night, Adam."

The conversation with Angie Durrant replayed in his
mind as he tried to sleep. She'd said Laura loved completely. He didn't doubt that. He'd seen her with dozens
of people over the past few days—she loved everyone
and everyone was drawn to her. The only people drawn
to him were those who wanted something—to bask in
his fame or siphon off his money. They hung around
as long the fun lasted then went off in search of more
stimulating companions. And he hadn't cared.

Until now. He was drawn to Laura Durrant, but at
the same time she intimidated him. He didn't understand his conflicting emotions. She wasn't his type on
so many levels. But something about Laura made him
want to be a better person. She made him believe he
could be different, that he could change.

But people didn't change like that. Did they?

Adam secured the last plank on the scaffold, then
leaned his arms on the metal railing and looked down
at Laura, who was assembling the smaller scaffold inside the gazebo. Time was moving quickly. He was
well into his sentence now. And while he still went to
bed each night physically tired, his muscles no longer
protested. In fact, he felt more fit than he had in years.

From his vantage point near the top of the gazebo, he
had a new perspective on the town of Dover. His gaze
drifted to the name carved in stone above the door of

the bank. He'd have to ask Laura about that name some-time. Everyone pronounced it Dover, as in the White Cliffs of. But the name over the bank read Do Over.

He scanned the area, taking in the now-familiar quaint brick buildings that encircled the town square. His gaze fell on the Keller building. He'd heard Laura on the phone today discussing it with someone. From her expression it hadn't been good news. He didn't un-derstand why she wanted it, but it was important to her, so that was all that mattered. He could understand why she liked it here. There were more than enough old buildings and houses to keep her happy. But was that all she wanted? To save the next run-down store or abandoned church? She was meant to have a family, yet he'd never heard her speak of that kind of future.

"Adam? Would you run over to Dad's store and get a package of blades for the saw?"

He climbed down from the scaffold and joined her at the workbench. "Alone?"

She turned and nodded. "It'll be fine."

"If you say so." He'd come to accept that things were done differently here in Dover. "What kind of blades? Is there a particular one?"

Laura removed the broken blade from the recipro-cating saw and handed it to him. "Show him this. He'll know what I need."

Adam shrugged and started across the park toward Durrant's Hardware on the far corner. He knew finding the right materials for the restoration wasn't going as well as expected. He'd seen a deep sadness in her violet eyes today that had touched off that unfamiliar surge of protectiveness in him. She loved the old gazebo and took a deep pride in repairing it. If it wasn't completed in time for the big town party, she'd take it personally. That knowledge made him want to work harder to ensure her success.

At the corner, Adam waited for the light to change, suddenly overcome with an almost-intoxicating sense of freedom. If it weren't for the weight of the ankle monitor, he could almost forget he was on a legal leash. He had to admit, though, he was starting to get the hang of this carpentry thing. He'd never tell Laura, but he was looking forward to seeing the little gazebo completed.

He stepped into the entrance of the hardware store, glancing down at the tiny black-and-white mosaic tile on the ground. Pushing open the door, he stepped back in time. Durrant's Hardware was a museum.

Wooden floors, warped and creaking, moved gently under his feet. Bins with glass tops lined the center aisle. To one side were long counters in front of wall shelves filled with boxes. On the other a wide staircase with a giant arrow on the wall directed customers looking for paint and tile to go to the second floor. He continued on toward the back where a more modern sign announced the checkout counter. Laura had told him her father would either be there or in his office at the very back of the building.

As he strolled through the antique surroundings he began to realize that the old stuff was merely window dressing. The merchandise itself was up-to-date. Tom Durrant had managed to keep the historic feel of the hardware store yet incorporate all the modern elements needed to run a successful business. He wondered if Laura had been responsible for the decor the way she had made the old gas station into a hamburger place.

"Adam, what can I do for you?" Tom Durrant extended his hand across the counter. "Let me guess, Laura sent you for supplies."

Adam nodded, handing over the broken blade. "New blades for the reciprocating saw."

Tom strolled off a few feet to fill the order.

"Nice place. I feel like I'm in a time capsule."

"Guess who we have to thank for that?" Tom smiled.

Looking around, Adam asked, "So was this a family business, before you, I mean?"

"My dad started the store after World War Two. He died when I graduated from college, so I took it over."

Adam thought back to Tom's comments about fathers leaving their businesses to their children. "I guess your kids will take over after you retire?"

"No, none of them want it. Matt's pretty well-set since he sold his business in Atlanta and started teaching. Laura is content with her career and my son Ty is a policeman to the core."

A heavy sadness settled on Adam's shoulders. He hated to think of this unique place being sold away from the family.

"There you go. Tell my daughter I put it on her tab and that it's getting bigger by the day."

"I'll do that." He took the bag and decided to brave a question.

"Are you disappointed that your kids don't want your business?"

Tom exhaled audibly. "Well, I'd be lying if I said no. I didn't have any huge career aspirations when my dad died. I was content with running the store. I'd like to see one of the kids keep the store going, but as their father, I want them to do what they feel called to do. The

Lord's given them each a talent and they should use it. I don't want to derail that out of petty pride."

Adam sorted through Tom's comments as he started back to the job site. He'd mentioned petty pride. Was that at work in his father? Wounded pride and shattered expectations because his son hadn't followed in his footsteps, or had there been something else in his mind? Had he merely been, like Tom Durrant, disappointed that his only child didn't want the business his family had labored to build? Hadn't he wanted what was best for his son?

"Oh, good, you're back. I need your help with the trim."

Adam handed her the bag, reaching for his tool belt. "So why don't you want the store?"

She turned and frowned. "What?"

"I asked—"

"I heard you. Why are you asking?"

"Your dad and I were talking about it."

"I don't want to be a merchant. I don't want to own a store. I have my own business to run and I love what I do."

"What will happen to the store when he retires?"

"I don't know. He'll sell it, I guess." She glanced across the green. "I thought about it. But…" She turned back to the workbench. "He understands."

"Probably. But does he like it?"

Adam reached for the right angle and a carpenter's pencil. His conversation with Tom had given him a new viewpoint on things. Like God-given talents for one. What were his? Did he have any? It never occurred to him to look. Laura had hers. Her siblings had found theirs. What did he want more than anything? What did he want to do? He turned and looked at Tom Durrant's store. Could he be happy here, owning a little store?

It was nearly noon when Adam felt the scaffold shift. He'd been working on removing the damaged shingles. He looked over to see Laura climbing up, one hand holding a large paper bag. He recognized it as the lunch her mother had packed for them this morning.

"Lunch break. Mom's meatloaf."

He helped her get settled, dangling her feet over the edge of the scaffold, then joined her. "I figured out pretty quickly that if I compliment your mother's cooking in the evening, then I get to have it again for lunch the next day. Not a bad deal."

"You found her weak spot."

"Can you tell me what that is about?" He pointed toward the east side of the square. "The Do Over on the bank?"

"Oh, that's the real name of our town. Its original name was Junction City. It was a crossroad between the railroad and the wagon trails to the river. It burned down and the residents decided that because they had a chance to do it over they'd make it worthwhile. So they named it Do Over. Over time the name was shortened to D'Over, then eventually just Dover. The bank's the only building that still has the original name on it."

Adam took another bite of meatloaf. Do Over. He had a funny feeling that God was trying to steer his life, give him a do-over. But how could he be sure?

The foot traffic on Peace Street and the now familiar groaning school buses told Adam the day was winding down. He turned off the table saw and inspected the end of the board, smiling when he felt the smooth even cut. He was definitely getting the hang of this saw-boy thing. He started toward the gazebo to brag a little, but Laura's shout sliced into him. He dropped the wood and hoisted himself up into the gazebo.

Laura was staring at her hand. The sight of blood flowing down her fingers turned his stomach. "Laura, what happened?" He moved toward her, taking her wrist in his hand to assess the damage.

"I went to pick up this piece of lumber and caught my arm on something." She brushed tears from her cheek. "I can't believe I was so careless."

He held her hand, inspecting the cut. "It doesn't look too deep, but that's going to hurt for a while. You have a first-aid kit in the truck?" She nodded and started to move. He wrapped his arm around her shoulders and led her to one of the benches on the undamaged side of the gazebo. "Sit still. I'll get it." Quickly he ran to the truck and returned with the small medical kit.

Adam sat beside her, taking her arm in his hands and carefully cleaning the wound. He applied a disinfecting ointment, then added a bandage to keep it clean. He looked at her, suddenly finding it hard to breathe. Her violet eyes were bright with unshed tears, her mouth was in an adorable pout. He cleared his throat. "I think you'll live."

She smiled at him, her voice husky. "Thanks."

Adam held her forearm, unwilling to let go. Her skin was warm and soft and he could feel her pulse under his fingertips. He'd worked side by side with her for over two weeks yet he'd never been this close to her—their faces only inches apart. She was smaller than he'd realized. "You might want to have that looked at."

She shook her head, her gaze locked with his. "I

get cuts and scrapes all the time. Just part of the job. I should have paid better attention."

"Please be more careful. I don't like seeing you hurt." He couldn't resist the impulse to touch her tear-streaked cheek. He saw her catch her breath as his fingertips met her skin. "Promise?"

She nodded and pulled her arm from his grasp, quickly moving to the edge of the gazebo. She jumped down to the ground and picked up her tablet.

He took a deep breath, attempting to slow his racing heart. She may be all right, but he wasn't sure he'd be. Laura was getting under his skin.

He found it hard to concentrate now and was eager for the day to end. Adam cut a section of trim and turned off the saw. He started toward the scaffold to hand the piece up to Laura.

"Hey, up there."

Adam turned at the sound of a female voice and saw Shelby Russell and Kenny Durrant coming toward the gazebo. Laura leaned over the top of the scaffold and shouted back. "Hi. I'll be right down."

Shelby stopped at the orange fencing. Kenny waved, bouncing up and down on his feet in excitement. "Hi, Mr. Adam."

"Hey, Kenny." He joined the visitors at the safety fence, keeping one eye on Laura as she climbed down the scaffold.

Shelby waved up at him. "Hello, Adam. How's it going?"

"Slow. I've got a lot to learn."

"Lucky for me he's a fast learner." Laura leaned over the fencing and gave Kenny a hug.

"Can I help do something, Aunt Laura? I learn fast, too."

"I know you do, but there are a lot dangerous things around here, and I don't want you to get hurt. That's why we have the fence up, so people won't get hurt."

Kenny pouted, looking longingly toward the tools and materials just outside his reach. Adam inclined his head toward the truck. "Didn't you say you needed a small door for the crawl space under the foundation? I could use some help picking out the best pieces." Laura looked at him with a puzzled frown before she caught on.

"Oh. Right. There are some scraps in the truck. Maybe you can piece it together from those. Kenny, why don't you help him?"

"Cool."

Adam motioned the boy to join him at the makeshift gate on the other side. He heard Laura mention something to Shelby about invitations as he walked away. Kenny skipped happily along beside him as they went to the truck.

"Can I use the 'ciprocating saw?"

Adam stopped in his tracks. "How do you know about those?"

Kenny shrugged. "My grandpa sells them at the store."

"Right, I forgot. No, we won't be using any tools right now. But I will need some strong muscles to help me carry this wood."

"I got muscles. See?" He held up his arms to show off his six-year-old biceps.

"Impressive." Kenny kept up a steady chatter as Adam selected the pieces of wood. He'd hand them to the boy, who would run them over to the fence and pile them up one by one. Adam had more than enough to build the small door, but he was getting a kick out of watching the boy have so much fun. "I think we have all we need. Let's see what we can do about making a door." They started back toward the fence.

"See that pond over there?" Kenny pointed to the opposite corner of the park. "Sometimes my daddy brings us here to feed the fish. You scared the fish when you broke the gazebo."

"What do you mean?"

"Cassidy and me were feeding the fish and then there was a big boom and your car crashed and stuff flew up in the air and scared the fish. Scared me, too."

Cold shock seized his heart. "You were here the day of the accident?"

The boy nodded. "It made a big noise."

"Kenny, let's go." Shelby called to him and waved.

"Bye, Mr. Adam. Can I come help you again?"

He struggled to find his voice. "Sure. You're a good helper."

Kenny dashed off to join Shelby. Adam fought to pull air into his lungs. His heart pounded violently in his chest. Shame and horror filled his head. Quickly, he strode to the other side of the truck, seeking privacy. He laid his palms on the fender, bowing his head, willing his stomach to stop churning.

For the first time since the crash, he truly saw the magnitude of his carelessness. Suddenly there was a flesh-and-blood consequence to his actions. How could he have been so stupid? Unfortunately he knew the answer. Because up until now he'd never had to face his mistakes. He'd paid his way out and gone on to the next thrill.

"Oh, God. Forgive me."

Laura was right. He was self-absorbed. A man with no thought for anyone but himself. He wanted to walk away, leave Dover and never come back, but he was stuck here. Maybe if he talked to Pastor Jim. Maybe he could help him sort it all out…

Laura waved goodbye to Kenny and Shelby. She'd lost track of time. Nora Gibson, the woman who was doing Shelby and Matt's wedding cake, had stopped by to talk and Laura had lost sight of the fact that she should be working. She turned back to the gazebo but didn't see Adam anywhere.

She started back toward the work area, catching sight of him on the other side of the truck. She rounded the tailgate and stopped. Adam had his forearms on the front fender, his head bowed. Slowing, she moved toward him trying to decide whether to speak or wait for him to acknowledge her presence.

She stopped at his side, resisting the urge to touch him. "Adam, are you all right?" He looked over at her and the torment in his eyes pierced her heart. "What's wrong?"

He straightened. "Why didn't you tell me your niece and nephew were in the park the day I crashed my car?"

Laura took a moment to gather her thoughts and calm her racing heart. "At first I didn't think you'd care. Then later, you and Kenny had hit it off and, well, I didn't want to upset you."

Adam shook his head and turned away, running a hand through his hair.

"I'm sorry, Adam. I guess I should have said something, but..."

He whirled around and came toward her. "I'm the one who's sorry, Laura."

He took her shoulders in his hands, staring at her with dark, troubled eyes. "I would never hurt anyone, especially your family. And I would never hurt you."

Laura felt tears form behind her eyes. She could feel his hands trembling against her shoulders. She'd never imagined he'd be this upset. It broke her heart to see him this way. "I know that, Adam. I do."

Suddenly he pulled her close, holding her tightly against his chest, his chin resting on the top of her head. "Forgive me?"

She nodded, unable to speak. She allowed her arms to move around his waist. The sense of comfort and belonging she felt wrapped in his arms had cracked open a wall deep inside she'd long ignored. She breathed him in, letting herself imagine sharing his embrace every day.

He pulled back, his gaze drifting downward to her lips, and lingering. She held her breath. Waiting. Part of her brain warned her to stop him, but another part longed to know his kiss. He bent his head, his breath caressing her mouth. Then he pulled back, his hands gently squeezing her shoulders.

"I've already made one mistake today. I don't want to make another." He stepped back and walked away.

It took her several seconds to gather her composure and join him at the table saw. "We could knock off early today if you'd like." She fully expected him to refuse. He never wanted to stop working.

"Yeah, maybe we should call it a day. I won't be

much use to you." He started to unplug the tools and dismantle the portable table saw.

Laura worked beside him in silence. Something had happened between them today and she needed time to sort it all out. Seeing Adam so vulnerable and emotional had demolished all her perceptions about him. And the man she'd glimpsed just now was more unsettling than the cocky daredevil had ever been...

Chapter Seven

Laura pulled on her work jeans, inhaling the sweet autumn breeze that drifted in through the window. The day had dawned clear, cool and with a gentle breeze from the Gulf to make it a perfect day. She'd not slept well, her mind filled with dreams of brides and flowers and a gazebo draped for a celebration. Obviously the result of spending so much time helping Shelby with her wedding plans.

She ruffled Wally's fur, then moved to the dresser for an LC Construction T-shirt. She stopped, the shirt halfway out. On impulse she shoved it back in and opened the next drawer. The pale green scooped-neck T-shirt fit her better, yet was still loose enough not to be suggestive.

For some reason she felt like dressing more feminine than usual. She moved into the bathroom and ran a brush through her hair. Maybe she'd leave it down today instead of knotting it up on the top of her head so it would fit under her cap. Her hand was on her makeup bag when she realized what she was doing. Idiot. There was no point in letting herself be attracted to Adam Holbrook. He was a temporary presence in her life. A man who craved excitement and adventure, who by his own admission could never survive in a small town like Dover.

But from the moment she'd seen Adam standing in her brother's old room, his easy charm and his self-assured attitude had left her feeling edgy and uncomfortable. She hadn't been able to ignore the way he looked at her and the way that look made her feel.

Adam saw her as a woman first and a contractor second. Her crew never saw her as a woman and she liked it that way. She was their boss, doing a man's job in a man's world and she dressed the part. Jeans, boots, tees, flannel in winter. Hard hat and baseball cap. She couldn't do her job effectively if she dressed girly all the time.

Except Adam had made her remember how it felt to wear feminine blouses and skirts. She didn't want to feel that way. She didn't want to remember how it felt to be held in a man's arms, to love someone completely. Yesterday had changed all that. Starting with Adam's tender concern over her cut. She glanced down at the bandage he'd applied with such gentleness. She could still remember the feel of his hand holding her arm.

But what had kept her tossing and turning all night had been the moments behind the truck. When he'd pulled her into his arms and held her to his chest. She knew he was expressing his apology, his deep regret for his actions, but that had taken a backseat to the feelings he'd unleashed in her. She'd thought for a moment he was going to kiss her, but then something stopped him. What had he meant when he said he didn't want to make another mistake? Would he have regretted kissing her? Or had he meant that kissing his boss would have been out of line?

Either way, the end result was the same. Adam wouldn't want to get involved with a small-town girl. They were too different, miles apart in what they wanted from life. Unexpected versus predictable. She should be thanking him for keeping things in perspective.

Snatching up a stretchy band, she pulled her hair into a ponytail and changed out of the green top for a comfy large T-shirt. She had only one focus right now and that was getting the gazebo done. She had to stop thinking about what she didn't have. It was a waste of time and energy.

"Nice work." Laura smiled at Adam and gave him a firm pat on his shoulder. The contact sent a quick current along her nerves and she quickly withdrew her hand.

Adam glanced over his shoulder, holding her with his gaze. "Thanks. I'm starting to like the idea of rebuilding the little house. It all started to make sense to me today, you know. I could see how the pieces fit." He straightened and placed the jigsaw on the floor of the gazebo. "It's like folding a parachute. Each section has to be folded in an exact pattern, a precise order. This construction deal is like that."

Laura slipped her hands into the back pockets of her jeans. "Good."

"You ever going to let me tackle something on my own? I think I'm ready."

"Adam, you're an amateur. A talented one, I'll admit, but all you've done so far is to follow my instructions.

Cut here. Nail there. You don't really know the basics of construction. It's more than knowing how to measure and use a circular saw. There's a progression to the work that takes place and you have to understand it from the ground up."

"I know, but I know enough that I could have built that little door for the foundation yesterday if you would have let me. I'm not saying I want to build a deck or house, just something small, one of the Handy Works projects maybe."

Laura shook her head. "I don't think so, but I appreciate your enthusiasm. Let's start packing up. We're at a temporary standstill until I can find the wood for the posts. I want to squeeze in a Handy Works project before lunch and I need to stop by the church at some point and pick up the list of Handy Works volunteers."

"No problem. I'd like to say hello to Pastor Jim."

"Sure." She tried to curtail her curiosity about Adam's relationship with Jim. The pastor had come by the gazebo a couple of times during lunch and the men had sat on the bench beneath the old magnolia tree and talked for the entire hour. Her dad had mentioned Jim coming by the house once or twice to see Adam, but he hadn't elaborated. Were the two men simply friends or were they discussing spiritual issues? She knew it was none of her concern, but that didn't stop her from wondering.

Laura took another bite of her club sandwich, keeping one eye on her saw boy. Adam sat silently across the table, staring out the window of Magnolia Café. She wasn't sure what was eating at him. The Handy Works job had gone extremely well. The family was happy, friendly and very grateful for the help. For some reason Adam had been quiet and somber the entire time, and his mood had carried over into lunch.

"Tomorrow we'll remove the cupola. I have a crane scheduled to lift it off the roof. Jeb Bryant will make the repairs at his shop, then we'll have it put back when the shingles are done."

Adam stared out the window. "How can they do that?"

"Do what?"

"Those people we helped today, the Watkins. They had nothing. A shack. Barely a roof over their head, but they were happy. How can they be happy when they have nothing?"

"How can you be so unhappy when you have everything?"

Adam met her gaze, shaking his head. "I don't have everything."

The hollow tone in his voice pierced her heart. "You have a lot. Two hands. A brain. Abilities you haven't realized."

A sardonic grin moved his lips. "Maybe. But if I don't show up in the hallowed halls of Holbrook Electronics on time, I'll be just like these people you help. Out of work. No money. No roof over my head."

"Don't give up. We can still finish in time for your deadline. We're only a little behind schedule."

He shook his head. "Maybe it's time to be realistic. I need to be prepared for the worst."

Something in the set of his jaw and the odd tone in his voice worried her. "I don't understand why your father would do this. It's so harsh." She couldn't imagine her dad forcing any of his children into anything.

Adam grunted softly and turned to the window. "I

think he figured sooner or later I'd come around to his way of thinking and take my place behind the nice little desk he had for me."

"What will you do if you don't get back in time?"

Adam smiled tightly. "You looking for a new saw boy?"

Laura watched Adam position the last stringer for the gazebo steps and secured it in place. As much as she hated to admit it, Adam had cut them perfectly. He was becoming a competent assistant. He had the potential to be a good carpenter, or anything else he wanted.

"Adam, when you're finished, come over here. I want to show you how to use the router." She glanced over at him. He was staring off into the park, an odd expression on his face. "Adam?" When he didn't respond she looked to see what had captured his attention. A woman about her age was approaching the orange fencing, slowly, deliberately, like a model on a runway.

The woman stopped at the fence, her gaze never leaving Adam. "I need to talk to you."

The words were issued as a command but with a definite intimate undertone. Adam put down the drill and stepped over the fence to join her. Laura heard him mutter something before he took her arm and steered her toward the large magnolia tree a few yards away.

Laura tried to focus on her work, but her curiosity was raging. Unable to resist, she gave up and watched the pair. The woman was sleek, polished and reeked of sophistication. Her tailored suit accentuated her feminine figure while still announcing to the world that she was all business. Her three-inch heels made her already-long legs appear endless and her black, expertly styled chin-length hair wouldn't dare move in the breeze. She was the kind of elegant women Ted had favored.

The woman and Adam stood face-to-face. They were too far away for Laura to hear what they were saying, but the body language wasn't hard to decipher. When the woman reached up and touched Adam's chest in an intimate gesture, a surge of jealousy burned in her veins. When Adam wrapped his fingers around the woman's wrist, she had to turn away. She had more important things to do than watch Adam making goo-goo eyes at some high-maintenance city woman.

Picking up the router again, she placed it on the board, unable to remember what she was supposed to do. All she could think of was the vast difference between herself and the woman. Jeans, T-shirts and a faded cap weren't exactly the kind of clothes designed to elicit appreciative glances from men. As an architect she'd worn stylish suits and heels, but construction didn't lend itself to designer shoes and suits.

"Don't worry about it, Gail. I'll handle it."

Adam's voice broke into her thoughts and she turned to find him and the woman approaching the fencing. Adam stepped over it, his eyes locking with hers. He stopped and looked back at the woman.

"Gail, this is Laura Durrant, the contractor."

Laura opened her mouth to speak only to find herself looking at the side of the woman's face.

"You'll call, Adam, when you've had enough of this backward kind of life. You'll be aching for a real adventure and the excitement of the city." With a condescending glance at Laura, the woman walked off, sashaying across the park as if she owned it.

Adam placed his fists on his hips, staring at the

ground a moment. "I'm sorry. I shouldn't have called her, but I never expected her to show up here."

"Who is she?"

"My attorney, Gail Breckenridge. She's also the ex-girlfriend I told you about."

Laura's heart lurched. "Why is she here?"

"To get me out. But your uncle refused. Besides, I told her I didn't need her help. Not anymore."

Laura wasn't sure what that meant and she was in no mood to find out. Her ego had been trampled enough for one day. "We need to finish these steps. Unless you're expecting more visitors."

Adam shook his head and went back to work.

Adam stole another glance at Laura as she pulled into the driveway of an old carriage house later that day. She'd been aloof, downright chilly, all afternoon. Only answering his questions with short replies and not initiating any conversation. He debated whether to approach her or wait until her mood shifted. He'd decided to wait, but now he feared her mood might never change. He climbed out of the truck, following in her wake as she entered the house. "What are we doing here again?"

Laura didn't look at him. "Making sure the taping and floating are done."

Adam stopped at her side. "Care to translate?"

"Ready to paint."

Once inside Laura made her inspection in silence. When they stepped into a large room at the back of the house, Adam couldn't contain his curiosity. "So what's this going to be?"

"A music studio. The owner is a pianist."

"I wouldn't think this would be a good studio. The acoustics are lousy."

"It will be fine when we get the sound panels installed."

"I thought you had to follow strict guidelines on these old places."

"This property isn't on the National Register. The owner can do as she pleases."

"I can put you in touch with someone at Holbrook Electronics. That's our specialty. Sound systems."

She stopped and face him. "Really? What kind?"

"Everything. If there's a concert someplace, our equipment is there. In music studios large or small, they probably have our systems in place." He could see her weighing his offer.

"It would help keep my budget on track."

"Say the word. Give me the specifics on what you need and I'll make a call."

"I thought you hated your family business."

Adam shook his head. "I said I didn't want to work there. I never said I didn't understand the business."

Laura stared at him a moment, then went back to her inspection. Her cold-shoulder act was growing old. He had to know what was behind it. He stepped in front of her when she headed for the door. "Care to tell me what's wrong? You seem irritated."

"Irritated?" She set her hands on her hips and glared. "Yes, I am. I'm behind on the gazebo, I've been pulled away from other projects and saddled with an assistant who needs to be told step-by-step what to do. Then to top it off, you walk off the job to go talk to Business Barbie, leaving me to do all the work."

Adam rubbed his forehead. He'd had no idea she'd

been so upset by Gail's appearance. "She means nothing to me."

"Oh, I wish I had a dollar for every time I've heard
that."

He remembered what she had told him about her ex-
husband. Maybe Gail's visit had dredged up some old
pains. But why was she so upset with him? Unless...
"Laura, there's no reason to feel jealous. Compared to
you, Gail's a one-dimensional cardboard cutout."

"Which makes me what?"

Adam searched for the perfect word, but the purple
sparks shooting from Laura's eyes unsettled him. "Unexpected." He watched her eyes widen, her arms sag to
her sides. She held his gaze a moment, then walked off.

"Let's go."

He followed behind, kicking himself three ways from
Sunday for his stupidity. There were dozens of words
he could have said. Beautiful. Exciting. Fascinating.
And he picked *unexpected?* It was going to be a long
ride home.

The heavy guilt riding his shoulders was a new sensation. One he didn't like. He'd lied to the Durrants this
evening. He'd told them he wasn't feeling well and had
gone to his room without eating. Truth was, he was too
disturbed by Gail's appearance and Laura's reaction to
eat. But now that he was in his room, the walls were
starting to close in. He paced a few steps, then noticed
the door to the small balcony off his room. He stepped
outside, the cool evening breeze filling his lungs. The
air here in Dover was clean and fresh, tinged with pine
and a sweet fragrance Laura had told him was from the
sweet olive shrub.

His gaze drifted from the house next door to the street out front and toward a hazy light of downtown in the distance. He wished he could forget Gail and the way she'd dismissed Laura as unworthy of her acknowledgment. He'd wanted to say something, but it would only have made things worse. Looking back, he wondered what he ever saw in Gail. She was hard, grasping and insensitive. Much like he had been. Seeing her next to Laura, with her warmth and compassion, her vibrant personality, had been like looking at darkness and light. In the past all he'd wanted was fun and the next big thrill. Now he wanted something different, but he wasn't sure how to go about getting it.

Adam was savoring his second cup of coffee in the Durrants' cozy kitchen when he heard the back door open. He saw Laura walking in. She was dressed in a dark blue business suit; the narrow skirt ended at her knees revealing her shapely legs. The jacket skimmed her curves and highlighted the golden color of her hair. He'd seen her dressed up for church, but she'd worn casual things then. This was a different picture. She looked tiny and delicate. He stood and walked over to her. "What's this? I don't think we'll get much work done with you dressed like that. I'll be distracted all day."

She blushed and tucked her long hair behind her ear. "I'm sorry to spring this on you at the last minute, but Mom and I have a meeting with the Mississippi Heritage Trust committee first thing this morning."

"Sounds important." Adam smiled, his gaze traveling upward to her hair again, wondering if it felt as silky as it looked.

"It is. This is my last chance to save the Keller building from auction, so I have to take advantage of it."

"So we'll work this afternoon, then?"

She shook her head, a look of regret clouding her features. "No. In fact we won't be working for a couple of days."

"Days?" A wave of disappointment sent his mood plummeting.

"I'm leaving for Arkansas right after the meeting. I finally tracked down the wood I need for the gazebo posts at a reclamation company in Mountain Home. It's exactly the right age and they have more than I need. I think I'll take it all. I can always use it other places. I'd given up hope on finding oak that old. I couldn't believe it when my contact called last night."

She tugged at her hair again. Was she uncomfortable around him now? Was she thinking of him with Gail? Had his lapse in judgment ruined their relationship? "So what will I be doing in the meantime?"

"Oh, you'll be working with Dad. He has a big Handy Works project he's been needing help with."

"Good morning, Adam. Boo." Tom entered the kitchen, making a beeline for his daughter. He gave her a hug and turned to Adam. "Did she tell you the news? You and I are going to tackle a big project together."

"She did. I'm looking forward to it. No more taking orders from a girl." He smiled and winked, relieved to see Laura respond to his teasing with a small grin.

"Oh, good, you're here." Angie breezed into the kitchen dressed for business, as well. Adam noticed again how much the women resembled one another. He couldn't blame Tom for being protective.

The women gathered up their things and headed for

the door. Adam stepped forward and touched Laura's arm to draw her attention. "Be careful today. I want you back safely. I really don't mind taking orders from a girl." Her violet eyes widened, then she nodded, holding his gaze a moment before following her mother outside.

Adam followed Tom Durrant up the back steps to the house. He'd worked harder today with Tom than he had with his daughter. Now he knew where she got her energy. They'd replaced the roof on a small house from plywood to shingles. Adam had a whole new level of respect for men who did that type of job for a living.

Tom slapped him on the shoulder as they walked into the kitchen. "A few more days like this and you can apply for a contractor's license."

"A few more days like this and I won't be able to move."

Angie Durrant met them with a warm smile and a kiss for her husband. "How did it go today?"

"Thanks to Adam we got the roof done on the Taylor house today."

"Good." She looked around the room. "What's that I smell?"

Tom grinned and placed the small box he'd been carrying on the table. "In grateful appreciation for our hard work, Ida Taylor sent us home with one of her meat pies."

"Oh, wonderful, because I've been gone all day and you were looking at leftovers." Angie took the pie out of the box, the aroma filling the room. "Y'all can take this for lunch tomorrow, too."

"How did the heritage committee meeting go?"

Angie's expression turned regretful. "Not so good.

We tried everything we could to find a way to save the Keller building. Now the auction is in a few days. I just feel so bad for Laura." Angie sighed deeply. "I'll fix a salad with the meat pie and we'll eat as soon as you boys clean up."

Tom turned and left the room, and Adam moved into the family room where his cell phone was plugged in. He'd only made one personal call since he'd arrived here. One he'd come to regret. This call was different. The idea had been forming in his mind for a while now, but he'd been uncertain how to proceed. Now he knew exactly what he wanted to do.

The bell on the microwave in the small break room of Durrant's Hardware signaled the cooking time was complete. Adam pulled his reheated meat pie out and sat down at the table. Tom walked in and smiled, pointing to the plate.

"It'll taste just as good this morning as it did last night." He moved to the fridge and removed his piece, sliding it into the oven.

Adam swallowed his first bite, nodding agreement. He'd spent his second day apart from Laura helping out at the store, unpacking shipments and stocking shelves. He liked the work, and he enjoyed learning about the different kinds of merchandise Tom offered his customers.

"No customers at the moment?" The store had seen a steady stream most of the morning.

"No, but just wait until I take the first bite of my lunch and that door will buzz." Tom opened his can of soda and took a sip. "Truth is, it's getting harder to keep up with the competition. A big-box home-improvement store opened over near Sawyers Bend last year and I've seen a steady drop in business. I might move up my retirement if things keep going the way they are."

Adam didn't like to think of Tom's giving up the store. It hadn't taken long to realize that the hardware store and all the small businesses in Dover were woven into the fabric of the town. Losing Durrant's would be a blow. "Isn't there anything you can do to keep business coming in?"

"I'm going to start looking into some things. I'm a bit out of my element in that regard. I've never had to attract customers. But times are changing."

"Would you mind if I used your computer? I could do a bit of online research in the evenings, maybe come up with some ideas."

"I'd appreciate the help."

The buzzer on the front door of the store sounded, announcing a customer had walked in. Tom smiled and took one last bite of his lunch. "See? Never fails."

Adam liked the idea of helping Tom find a solution to his problem. Perhaps he could repay him in a small way for his kindness. The internet might help him with another matter he was working on, as well. A surge of excitement raced through him when he thought about what he hoped to accomplish. The thrill was familiar, but it had nothing to do with danger and everything to do with helping someone else.

Adam propped his feet up on the dashboard of Laura's truck, enjoying the familiar routine. She'd been home for a few days now and they'd settled back into their usual pattern. Up early, a quick breakfast with the Durrants, then ride with Laura to the job. They'd work until five, either on the gazebo or Handy Works projects. Then it was home, shower and supper with the Durrants. He found the predictability strangely comforting. Tom and Angie Durrant were always there, always together and always including him.

Somewhere along the way his skepticism had died, his edginess had disappeared and he'd come to look forward to the peaceful, welcoming tone of the Durrants' home. He started to feel comfortable around the couple. Almost like a member of the family. He didn't want to think about the end of his sentence. Once he left, he'd never see them again. He was simply a person passing through their lives. That thought bothered him. He wanted to be more important to them than that. He wanted to be important to Laura, as well.

The streets flying by the truck were unfamiliar to him as he rode with Laura later that morning. New directions usually meant new adventures, or more Handy Works projects. "Road trip?"

"I need to pick up some supplies from my house first. I forgot to load them this morning."

Her house? The idea made him smile. This might prove interesting. He'd wondered about her personal life. He'd almost come to the conclusion that Laura Durrant was all work and no play. All tool belt and chalk line. With her take-charge attitude, she probably lived in one of those renovated loft-type places in an old factory. Clean, sleek and no-nonsense. Everything practical and useful. No fluff for her.

He glanced out the window, surprised to see an idyllic tree-lined street. This was a part of the town he'd never seen. A quick flash of apprehension raced down his spine. "We aren't going outside of my monitor range, are we?"

"I don't think so."

Adam swallowed. "Well, I'm going to let you explain that to the cops when the alarm is triggered and they swarm the truck."

Laura slowed the truck and pulled into the driveway. Adam studied the one-story pale blue Victorian. Intricate gingerbread dripped from every angle of the porch and the gable. The broad wraparound front porch held planters filled with ferns and colorful flowers. The entire place was picture-postcard perfection.

"This is your place?"

"Yes."

He followed her toward the detached garage at the end of the drive, puzzled by this new glimpse of Laura's life. It took a few minutes to load up the boards and tie them down securely. Laura locked the garage and started back to the truck. Adam followed along, enjoying the way her chin tilted upward aggressively as she moved. He had to admit she was extremely good at her job. And extremely cute while doing it.

"Oh, no." Laura stopped in her tracks.

"What?"

"I forgot my tablet."

Adam held up his hands and leaned against the truck. "Go ahead. I'll wait right here."

She chewed her lip thoughtfully for a moment. "No. We don't know how close to the limit we are with your monitor. You'd better come inside with me."

"You have my word I won't go anywhere."

"But if something should happen and the police show up and you're not in my sight." She shook her head. "No, come in."

Laura led the way up the curved walk and across the

porch to the front door. Adam took a quick inventory of the cozy decor. Wicker chairs with flowered cushions and old metal glider painted bright aqua formed an inviting seating area at one end. Lush plants and a swing lured you to the other. It was cozy, but at odds with his impression of her.

A small bundle of fur greeted them at the door, tail wagging like a flag. "Who's this?"

"That's Drywall. Wally for short."

"Friendly little guy." Adam gently scratched the animal's neck.

Laura sifted through the stack of items on a desk across the room, mumbling under her breath before turning her search to a pile of paper on the coffee table.

Adam glanced around the room, his ideas about Laura Durrant taking another hit. No sleek loft style here. Her home was a charming mix of traditional furniture and antiques, muted colors and lush fabrics, but all of it was very definitely feminine.

"I'll be right back."

He nodded, hooking his thumbs into the ridge of his pockets. Laura disappeared down a hallway and he took the opportunity to take a closer look at her home. A part of him knew a moment of guilt for prying into her private world, but a bigger part of him needed to satisfy his curiosity about his lovely boss.

Her home was warm and welcoming. That fit. He'd seen her display that side of herself to others. He moved farther into the room. A flat-screen television took up one wall. He wondered if she liked sports, given she had two older brothers. Dog toys were scattered around the floor, a rose-colored throw lay over one arm of the sofa. He took a step forward to see what was peeking out from under the edge. A romance novel. He smiled. So, she wasn't all drill bits and tape measures after all.

The phone rang and Adam peered around the corner into the kitchen. It rang again. "You want me to get that?"

"No."

He shrugged and moved into the kitchen. It was bright and cheery with top-of-the-line stainless steel appliances, but with a decidedly cozy, feminine appeal. A glimpse outside revealed a sunroom and just beyond a well-kept yard. Laura definitely had a domestic side.

Footsteps sounded in the hall. He turned and walked back to the foyer, arriving in time to see Laura emerge from the back of the house. She looked relieved. "Good news?"

She glanced over at him as if she'd forgotten he was there. "Yes. That was my mother on the phone. She just talked with my brother Ty in Dallas."

"How's he doing?"

"Better physically, but emotionally he's struggling. But he might be coming home in a few weeks."

"That's good to hear. I know your parents will be happy."

She nodded, wiping tears from her cheeks. "We were so scared. At first we thought he might…" She turned away.

He started toward her, eager to offer her comfort or let her cry out her worries on his shoulder. But after the other day's near kiss, she might not welcome such an intimate gesture from him. "If he's anything like the rest of the Durrants, he'll come through in good shape."

"That's what I'm praying for."

He searched for something to say to give her time to

regroup. "I like what you've done with the place. Did you restore this house?"

Laura nodded. "It didn't need much. The previous owners took good care of it." She turned and faced him, her composure once again in place. "We'd better go. We need to get those rafters replaced so we can get the roof under way."

She walked toward him and he reached over to open the door. He misjudged her movement, however, and she bumped into him. Every nerve in his body went on high alert. He remembered holding her the other day, the way she'd felt in his arms. He shoved the memory aside and stared into her warm, welcoming violet eyes. "I didn't expect you to have a home like this."

"Why?" She stood still as a statue, shifting her gaze downward, refusing to look him in the eyes again.

"I pictured you in some ultrachic loft. I hadn't taken into account your feminine side." He lifted his hand to touch the soft tendril of honey-colored hair that had escaped from her cap, but thought better of it and lowered his arm. Instead he leaned a fraction closer, inhaling her sweet tangy scent. "Don't you know what a lovely woman you are?"

She stepped back and moved past him out onto the porch.

Adam followed close behind, his mind kicking himself for getting too close again. But he couldn't seem to help himself when she was near. In fact, the only time he felt truly alive was when they were working side by side. The feeling was nothing like the adrenaline rush from one of his extreme sports. This was deeper, richer and he didn't understand it at all.

* * *

Laura snapped her cell phone closed and slipped it into her pocket. There were problems at the Conrad site. The last thing she needed was another crisis. They were popping up like weeds. This was the fourth phone call this afternoon. She was beginning to wonder if there was a conspiracy afoot to keep her from having a relaxing evening at home.

Thankfully, Shaw had everything under control, but she was the boss and the buck stopped with her. While her trip to Arkansas had been successful, it had put a strain on her budget. She didn't want to lay off any of her crew. There were a couple of prospective jobs in the works, but nothing definite yet.

Walking out into the kitchen, she glanced at Wally's empty dish. "Aw, poor little guy. You must be starved." She filled his dish and scratched lovingly behind his ears. She'd been so distracted lately, she had to resort to a daily to-do list to make sure she didn't forget anything.

Pouring a glass of tea, she carried it into the living room. Her heartbeat quickened when she looked at her front door. The memory of Adam standing there filled her mind. She'd made a huge mistake in allowing him to come into the house today. Unfortunately, she hadn't anticipated the repercussions his presence might cause. Her home had always been her sanctuary, her cozy retreat from the pressures of her job. Within these rooms she was safe to be herself, a woman instead of one of the guys. Her little Victorian house was her insulation from the world. But now, Adam had breached her private walls and seen into her heart.

She closed her eyes, rubbing them with her fingertips, attempting to erase the sight of him filling her doorway. He'd dominated the room. All that male strength in the middle of her frilly decor had been a startling and compelling contrast. She hated even more the sense of security she'd felt at his presence. He'd stood like a protector between her soft private world and the hard, real world outside. Adam's presence in her house had pointed out the one gaping hole in her life. One she wanted filled but was afraid to pursue. A husband and family.

Wally barked, jarring her from her thoughts. "It's okay, boy." She bent down and stroked his soft fur. "I'm tired and behaving like a fool."

Picking up her tablet, she managed a whole five minutes of work before she thought about Adam again. Like a video projection, his tall frame appeared in her mind's eyes. The broad shoulders, the nonchalant way he'd leaned against the door frame. The keen interest in his green eyes as he'd scanned her living room. The way he'd smiled and reached down to pet Wally with great gentleness had both surprised and touched her. She tugged Wally into her lap for a warm hug. "The way to a woman's heart is through her pet."

Thanks to his help, the gazebo should be completed in plenty of time and he could get home for his meeting with his father. Then her life could go back to normal. The prospect didn't sound as appealing as she'd thought it would. Probably because she was in serious danger of falling in love with Adam.

Her gaze drifted to the doorway again. She was afraid it was already too late. Because now, every time she walked into her living room, he'd be there. She'd slipped up and let him into her home. She couldn't afford to let him into her heart. But there might be a way to show him her gratitude. Reaching for the phone again, she dialed, hoping her dad could come through for her one more time.

The Durrant house was quiet. Peaceful. But he'd never felt so out of sorts before. He'd come to appreciate the hustle and bustle that marked the Durrants' Sunday gatherings. After that first one, he'd relaxed, convinced that the family really did get together each Sunday after church and truly enjoyed being together.

But this Sunday was different. Laura and her mother had gone to the early service, leaving him and Tom to attend the late one. Adam had enjoyed the sermon and had grown more comfortable with the citizens of Dover, who no longer stared at him like a stranger but greeted him as one of their own.

Coming home to the empty house had left him out of sorts and a bit lonely, though. Tom had jokingly encouraged him to enjoy his "free" time, explaining he had long-neglected yard work that would keep him busy most of the day. Adam tried to watch the ball game on television, but found himself restless and unable to concentrate.

Laura and her mother were giving a bridal shower for Shelby today and wouldn't be back until early evening. He missed seeing Laura flitting around the house. In fact he was beginning to miss her anytime she was out of his sight. He'd lost his heart to her from the moment she'd appeared in the doorway to his room that first day. Now he was completely lost in her beauty, her determination and her heart, and he had no idea what to do about it.

Adam made his way through the Durrants' kitchen on his way to the back porch. It had become his favorite place to relax. His gaze fell on the calendar on the wall near the door. The last day of the month mocked him. How was he going to make it to Atlanta in time for his meeting? And the way things were going, the gazebo wouldn't be finished in time for Founder's Day. Work had slowed, the materials Laura needed kept getting held up or wrong shipments delivered. They were working hard, but everything took longer than expected.

He tried to envision life without a bottomless bank account. He couldn't. For most of his adult life he'd had only one thing that he could count on—his yearly allowance. Adventures came and went. Friends drifted with the wind. But the money was constant. It gave him an identity. An anchor. When that was gone what would he have? Who would he be?

Who did he *want* to be?

Laura let herself into the front door of her parents' home. The welcoming silence and familiar smells wrapped around her like an old sweater. She walked softly through the front hall, stopping at the office door where her father was working away. "Hey, Daddy."

"Hello, Boo. How was the shower?"

"Fun. Noisy. Mom will be along in a little while. She wanted to stop by Matt's and see the kids. Where's Adam?"

"I'm not sure. He was on the back porch a while ago."

Laura made her way to the kitchen, her heartbeat quickening a little. She'd missed him today. She'd gotten used to having him nearby, ready to help or talk to.

His time was winding down and she had a feeling she'd miss him even more after he left.

He was seated on the large cushioned love seat facing the backyard. He looked comfortable and relaxed. Like he belonged there. He turned and smiled when she stepped out the door.

"Welcome back. How did the big event go?"

She joined him on the love seat, drawing her feet up under her and angling her body toward him. "It was a huge success. Everyone had a great time. Shelby was overwhelmed with all the gifts. She got a lot of pretty things. Vases, candles, decorative items. Because she and Matt both had household items already, they didn't need much."

"It sure was quiet around here. I missed you."

She looked over at him, seeing the truth reflected in his eyes. "I thought you'd enjoy some alone time."

He reached out and touched her hand. "I thought so, too, but I like it better when you're around."

She looked away, searching for something say. He touched her arm. His fingers were warm and gentle. His hands were broad, strong and tanned.

"I was looking at the photos along the stairs earlier and there's a wedding picture with the name Laura Frasier underneath it. Was that your married name?"

"I took back my maiden name when he…when the divorce was final."

"What happened?"

She sighed, trying to decide how much to tell him. "I thought he was the man of my dreams. He was handsome, smart, rich and the life of the party. To a small-town girl, he was everything exciting and glamorous. But after we were married, he didn't want to settle down. He wanted to keep having a good time with his friends. A wife was a hindrance, especially when he enjoyed the company of other women more."

Adam squeezed her hand. "He was a fool."

Laura stroked her fingers over the back of his hand, enjoying the connection. It made it easier to talk. "His philandering got worse. The last straw came when I opened the newspaper and saw Ted and a woman photographed at some big social event and the caption read Mr. and Mrs. Ted Frasier." She heard Adam groan softly. "I filed for divorce the next day. We reached a settlement and I came home and bought Mr. Shuler's construction company and never looked back."

"It hurts when someone you care about betrays your trust. When you've opened your heart to them and they trample it like it's a worthless trinket."

She looked at him, but he was staring off into the distance. "You and Gail?"

"Pretty much. We'd been dating six months. I thought it was serious. Until I found out she'd been having an affair with my friend for weeks, right under my nose."

Now she understood his attitude toward the woman. He really did understand. "I'm sorry. The betrayal leaves you feeling so confused. I kept wondering what was wrong with me. Wasn't I smart enough, pretty enough? I couldn't compete with all his glamorous women." Adam suddenly placed his finger against her lips to silence her, leaning forward to gaze steadily into her eyes.

"Stop. Don't say those things. The man was an idiot. You're smart, vibrant and strong, and the most fascinating and beautiful woman I've ever met." He trailed his finger to the side of her jaw and along her chin.

Laura held her breath, gazing into his eyes, filled with anticipation. She wanted him to kiss her. She wanted to know that sense of comfort and belonging she'd felt before.

The kitchen light came on, shattering their shadowed cocoon. Adam laughed and stood, pulling her to her feet. "It's been a long time since I've had the old porch light 'time to come inside' warning. Your father's got impeccable timing."

Adam stood at a distance the next afternoon as an elderly couple greeted Laura like a long-lost daughter. He watched her, warm affection filling his heart. He'd gotten used to her receiving this kind of reception. Everyone, friend or stranger, adored her. Laura embodied compassion and love. The sight of her never failed to steal his breath. She was capable of love so deep, so intense it would overpower a man with the sheer force of it. What would it be like to be loved like that? To be buried in love and trust so profound you'd never feel lost or alone again?

She'd stirred his conscience, his sense of right and wrong. Another part of his soul he'd long ignored. When he looked at the man in the mirror now, he didn't like what he saw. Being around Laura made him want to be a better man. A man worthy of her love. Forcing himself to inhale, he turned away, running a hand down the back of his neck. But could he ever be that kind of man? And where did he start? All he knew was that somehow, Laura Durrant had slipped behind his barriers and penetrated deep into his soul. The knowledge thrilled him and scared him at the same time.

"Adam."

He jerked his attention to her as she came toward him. "Yes?"

"We're going to replace the front steps."

"Great. That's right up my alley. Why don't you let me handle this one?"

Laura hesitated a moment, then smiled. "All right. We need to replace the screens in the back door, too. I'll take care of the work needed inside."

"Sure thing." It took him a moment to register that she was actually trusting him to work alone.

For the entire time he'd been here she had watched over him like a hawk, never allowing him more than a flicker of unsupervised time. He'd been itching for the chance to show her he wasn't a complete idiot and that he could handle a job from beginning to end. He wanted her to trust him to follow her orders, to show her that he'd learned more about carpentry than she knew.

For some strange reason, proving himself to Laura meant more to him than anything had in his entire life, and that scared him. Why was the approval of this one small-town woman so important?

He suspected he knew the answer, but he didn't want to examine that right now. At the moment, all he knew was that he wasn't about to let this opportunity get away from him.

Adam turned and smiled at the elderly man who had introduced himself as Mr. Norwood. "Well, I guess I'd better get busy."

The man harrumphed, his thick brows nearly touching as he scowled. "We don't need you, you know."

"Oh? I thought Ms. Durrant said you needed the screens fixed and the back steps replaced."

"I could do that. She didn't need to call you."

Adam nodded, wondering about the man's attitude. "You lived here long?"

"I built this house."

He stared at the slightly bent old man. "You did?"

"That's right. From the ground up. Did all the wiring and plumbing myself, too."

Adam made a quick survey of the house. With a little imagination he could see how it might have looked in its heyday. "Amazing job, Mr. Norwood."

"Call me Frank. Yeah. It took a whole year."

He moved forward and Adam was shocked at how slowly the man moved. It was obvious he was in a great deal of physical pain. He must be experiencing emotional pain, as well. Seeing the home he built with his own hands being repaired by a stranger.

"Well, maybe you could give me a hand. You're more familiar with how things work than I am."

Mr. Norwood held up his arthritis-twisted hand. "I don't have the dexterity I used to."

"No problem." Adam stepped a bit closer and lowered his voice. "See, the truth is, I'm new at this stuff. I'm surprised Ms. Durrant let me tackle this on my own. I could use your help."

Frank huffed under his breath. "Nothing to it."

An hour later, Adam stretched out his hand to Frank. "I couldn't have done it without you."

"You're a fast learner."

"Thanks. You're a good teacher." Frank stared at the front of his home.

"Been in this place forty years next week."

"Really? Is that how long you've been married?"

"Nope. Fifty-three on that end."

A few days ago he couldn't begin to imagine being

with one person that long. Now all he wanted to do was to have the chance to try. "How did you do it?"

"Do what?"

"Put up with another person that long?"

Frank looked puzzled. "You've never been in love, have you, son?"

"No, guess not."

"When you do, you'll understand."

Adam shook his head. "I don't know. How can you make a woman happy for all that time?"

"You keep one hand in hers and the other in the Lord's."

The front door opened and Laura and Mrs. Norwood emerged onto the porch.

Adam and Frank joined them. "Mission accomplished." Adam smiled at Laura.

She nodded, making a quick inspection of the steps and screens. "Good work."

Adam opened his mouth to crow about his accomplishment, eagerly anticipating her praise. Finally, she'd have to admit that he wasn't as useless as she'd wanted to believe.

He caught sight of Frank Norwood out of the corner of his eye. His wife was at his side. The old man's words reverberated inside him. His pride at what he'd built, and his anger and humiliation at not being able to take care of his home, had touched something deep inside Adam. He made his choice. "Well—" he laid a hand on Frank's shoulder "—I can't take the credit. I thought I knew how to do these repairs, but I guess I'm not as smart as I thought I was. Frank had to take over and guide me every step of the way."

The old man shrugged, uncomfortable with the attention. "Oh, I don't know 'bout that. The boy's got the ability. He just needs practice, that's all."

"Did you fix all this?" Marion Norwood asked.

Adam's heart skipped a beat at the love and admiration that flooded the woman's eyes.

Frank shrugged again. "Oh, you know."

"Sweetheart, I should have listened when you said you could make the repairs." She wrapped her husband in a warm embrace.

Frank's eyes sent a message of appreciation that brought a lump to Adam's throat. Truth be told, Frank had kibitzed the entire time. While his guidance had proved valuable, he'd not actually done the work himself. It would have been easy and honest to tell everyone that he, Adam, had accomplished these small feats. Finally, he would have looked good in Laura's eyes. She would have been forced to admit that he was doing a good job at picking up carpentry and home repairs. In the past it's exactly what he would have done.

But allowing this man a chance to look like a hero in his wife's eyes one more time was worth the small sacrifice. The feeling inside his heart was like nothing he'd ever experienced before. Stepping out of the spotlight and sharing with another was foreign to him. But he liked the feeling. He liked helping. This was such a small thing. All he'd done was emphasize what Frank had done and ignore his own part in the project. Why should that make him feel almost giddy with joy? It didn't make sense.

Is this what Laura meant when she talked about giving instead of receiving? Is this what drove her desire to help others?

It confused him. Why should being less make him feel like more? He had a lot to discuss with Pastor Jim at their next meeting.

Laura stole a glance at Adam. He was staring out the truck window. She had a dozen questions she wanted to ask him, but she doubted he'd give her a straight answer. He was reluctant to talk about his personal life. But she had to know what made him behave so generously to Mr. Norwood. It went against every perception she had of him. What had changed?

She pulled the van to a stop in the Handy Works lot and Adam moved to leave. "Why did you do it?" He looked at her, puzzled. "Why did you pretend Mr. Norwood had done all the work himself?"

Adam shrugged. "He did."

"No, he didn't. I happen to know the Norwoods. They attend our church and I know Frank is incapable of doing that kind of work." She waited for him to respond, but he continued to stare out the side window.

"I know you've been anxious for me to let you work alone. So what changed?"

Adam sighed, obviously irritated with her questioning. "He was a nice old man. I wanted to help him, that's all." He turned and pinned her with his green eyes. "Isn't that what you've been preaching to me since I got here? Helping others?"

"Yes, but…"

Adam chuckled harshly. "You didn't think I had it in me."

Laura looked away. He was right and she was ashamed about that. She'd been working overtime to keep him in the nice little cubbyhole she'd assigned him to, only he refused to stay there.

"Don't worry about it. You're not completely wrong. My family wasn't big on altruism. We had more of a 'me first' kind of philosophy."

"I'm sorry." She didn't know what else to say.

"It's not your fault. Those are the cards I was dealt."

"So what changed?"

Adam smiled at her, his eyes warm. "Guess you're starting to rub off me, boss lady."

Laura replayed the conversation in her mind a dozen times that night. Something was different about Adam. Something had changed him and she wasn't arrogant enough to believe it had anything to do with her.

His kindness today had broken through her biggest concern that Adam and her ex were cut from the same cloth. Deep in her heart she'd known that wasn't true early in their relationship, but it was easier and safer to keep believing it.

Now she was forced to look at Adam Holbrook with new eyes, not ones clouded with old mistakes. In doing so, however, she had to acknowledge the fact that her attraction to Adam was much more than simple physical appreciation. There was something sweet and tender about Adam that she couldn't ignore.

She'd labeled him selfish, incapable of thinking of others. She'd been proved wrong, not only today, but every moment she'd been with him. Adam had the capacity for great compassion. He was as attracted to her as she was him, but she still couldn't forget that he was a man who craved adventure, the thrill of extreme sports. There were few thrills in Dover. They were too different. Unexpected versus predictable. Those things could never mix.

But the truth couldn't be ignored. Adam Holbrook had stolen her heart and she knew there was no hope of getting it back.

Laura rubbed her eyes and shoved aside the papers she'd been studying. She'd gone over the guidelines for restoring the gazebo, wondering how she could meet the requirements, locate the approved shingles and have them shipped to Dover all in time to complete the job by Founder's Day. None of that mattered if the forecast didn't change. Rain was predicted off and on for the next ten days. A late-season hurricane in the Gulf had skimmed the coast of Mississippi and bands of rain were spreading over the whole state.

As if that weren't bad enough, the Conrad project was behind schedule. The owner had requested last-minute changes that meant ripping out what had been done and starting over. Which in turn upped the cost and time for everyone and put her budget deeper into the hole. The situation with the Mobile job was still in limbo and her bank account was in a serious bind.

A while back, she'd considered taking a second mortgage on her house to bid on the Keller building. Her dad would have been furious, especially because there was no guarantee she'd win the auction. Now she was thinking about a loan to save her business.

She swiveled in her desk chair and looked out the window in her small office to the workshop beyond. Adam had spent the past few days doing whatever work was needed in Laura's shop. Sweeping, inventory, ordering supplies. Surprisingly, she could almost believe he enjoyed the work. Yesterday they'd spent the rainy day at the Handy Works warehouse stocking the van and inventorying materials. He'd even manned the phone one day, taking requests for assistance. Another long rainy day had sent him to her dad's store to work when she couldn't find anything else for him to do.

They were back at her shop today, Adam hovering around her cabinet maker, Jeb, as he worked. If she didn't find something for him to do they'd all go nuts.

"Adam, stop bothering Jeb and go sweep or something." She hadn't meant to sound so curt, but she was in a horrible mood. He glanced over at her and she could tell by the expression on his face that he would want an explanation.

She turned her back, but she knew the moment he came near. Her nerves always tingled in a strange way when he was close. She turned and faced him. "I'm sorry. I shouldn't have snapped at you."

"Something on your mind? I know the weather isn't doing either of us any good, but there's not much we can do about it." He looked past her to the calendar on the wall, his expression filled with understanding. "Oh. Today's the auction, isn't it?"

She didn't want to think about that, although she was touched that he'd remembered. "It's going on right now and there's nothing I can do to stop it or change it. I just hope whoever buys it will use it for something that will benefit the town."

Adam stooped down beside her chair, laying his hand on her arm. "Your dad keeps telling me the Lord makes everything work for good. Maybe He's got something planned you don't know about."

She wanted to believe that, but she also knew sometimes the Lord said no, and she was afraid this was one of those times.

Chapter Eight

The rain had moved out. For the last two days they'd been able to work and gotten nearly caught up. The new posts had been installed, a perfect match to the originals. Once they were painted no one would be able to distinguish the old from the new. But they were too far behind for her liking, and there was still a lot to do. What concerned her most was the forecast for this afternoon. More rain was on the way.

The last handrail had been secured when the first drop of moisture touched her cheek. She ignored it. It could be sap from the trees overhead. It wasn't thunder. It was a jet flying over. She frowned and pressed the nail gun against the wood. It couldn't rain. They didn't have time for rain.

The light sprinkles sent her heart into the pit of her stomach. She placed the last nail and forced a glance at the sky. If they hurried, they might be able to get this section of spindles in place before the rain shut them down. Yesterday had been a total loss to the weather. Now half of today would be lost, as well.

Suddenly the sky opened up.

"Adam!" Laura grabbed for a tarp, struggling to cover the spindles to keep them dry.

The wind tore it off. Adam appeared at her side, grabbing her by the shoulders.

"We've got to get out of here. Lightning."

"The tarp. Hurry."

He grabbed the blue plastic and wrestled it over the work table and the now-wet spindles. Laura grabbed the other end and together they managed to tie it down.

"In here."

Adam propelled her toward the interior of the gazebo where it was shielded from the torrential rain by a curtain of thick tarps on all sides. They'd put them up a few days ago so they could keep working in the drizzle.

Laura pounded a fist against one of the thick turned posts. "I can't afford this rain."

"It won't last long."

Laura shook her head. "It's going to last for the next several days. We're already so far behind we'll never finish in time for Founder's Day."

"We've got plenty of time. We'll make it."

"Not if those cypress shingles don't get here soon." She paced back and forth, arms across her chest. "I can't believe this is happening. We should be looking at painting and landscaping by now."

"What happened to the shingles that arrived yesterday?"

Laura pulled off her baseball cap and yanked the clips from her hair. "They were cypress all right, but from 1980, not 1880. I sent them back."

"But you'll find the ones you need, right?"

She nodded. "I did, but they're coming from Savannah. I'm not sure they'll get here in time." She bit her lip to keep from crying. What was wrong with her? She'd been emotional for the past few days. The least little thing choked her up.

"Hey," Adam said softly. "You'll pull this off. I have faith in you."

She wanted to cry. Where did he get off saying sweet things like that to her? "Thanks." She turned and took a seat on the bench that ran around the inside of the gazebo. "Guess we're done for today."

"We'll work harder tomorrow." Adam took a seat beside her. "I'm getting pretty good at installing those little spindles of yours. Me and the jigsaw are one."

She knew he was trying to lighten her mood and she appreciated it, but nothing would help right now. She wanted to be done in time for him to get home. But there was less than a week left and unless something miraculous happened, Adam wouldn't be leaving for Atlanta until his sentence was completed. The wind and thunder swelled. Frustrated, she stood and moved to the tarp, pulling back the edge. The rain had increased, driving down in sideways sheets, whipping the tarps around violently. A blast of cold rain drove her back. "Oh."

Adam pulled her behind him to the center of the gazebo, then hurried to retie the flapping tarp. "What were you trying to do?" he demanded, coming to her side.

She was drenched. Her shirt and light jacket were soaked through. "I thought the rain might be letting up and we could get to the truck."

Thunder roared overhead, causing the gazebo to vibrate. "I think we'll be here awhile."

Great. More time lost. She shivered as the cool air blew against her wet clothes.

"You're going to catch pneumonia." He started to

unbutton his shirt and she took a step back. Before she could move farther, he'd wrapped his shirt across her shoulders.

Its warmth still held his scent. He pulled her against him, one hand wrapped tightly across her shoulders, the other vigorously rubbing her arm to stimulate warmth. She shivered again, but not from the cold. Her hand, resting against the T-shirt that covered his broad chest, moved with the beating of his heart. She told herself to move away. But she was cold and he was warm and strong and she felt oh so safe. She dared a glance at his face. She held her breath and felt him do the same.

The air was charged with electricity. She knew what was going to happen. *Stop this. Stop it now.* But her heart had other ideas. She wanted him to kiss her. She'd wanted him to for a while now.

"Laura."

He said her name reverently and she melted against him. His lips were warm, gentle but eager and she met them the same way. His arms wrapped around her waist, crushing her to his broad chest. She was lost, sinking into the wonder and discovery of it all.

Adam ended the kiss, pulling back only far enough to caress her face with his gaze.

"So sweet." He lowered his head again, then reality struck. What was she doing? She couldn't afford to get involved with someone like Adam. They were too different. He could never stay put and she could never pull up roots and leave.

Fear surged upward into her chest and she pushed Adam away, backing up until she bumped against a post.

Adam stared at her, and the look in his eyes brought

her to tears. Behind the surprise was a pain and sadness so profound she had to look away. A second realization hit her then. This wasn't about Ted or Adam. This was all about her. This was all about her fear of being hurt. More specifically her distrust of God's plans for her life.

"Adam," her voice quivered.

He shook his head, a tight smile on his face. "No need to explain. I understand. I stepped over the line. It'll never happen again. Promise." He turned and moved to the other side of the gazebo and untied the flap.

The rain had eased up. The storm had passed.

"We can make that run to the truck now." Adam kept his back to her.

She pulled his shirt from her shoulders and handed it to him as she passed, careful not to let her hand touch his. Safely in the truck, she tried to ignore the heavy tension that hovered between them as they drove to her parents' house. Adam got out, gave a salute and hurried to the porch. She watched him disappear inside, fighting the need to cry. She should have stopped the kiss. It had only confirmed what she'd suspected. She was in love in Adam Holbrook.

The awful truth was it was one-sided. Oh, he was attracted, she knew that, but there was no future for them. No future for the gazebo, no hope for Keller building and no hope of getting Adam home in time to meet with his father.

Once safely inside her home, she curled up on the sofa and gave in to the tears. This story couldn't have a happy ending because in just a few days, Adam would lose everything and it would be all her fault.

Chapter Nine

Laura stole a quick glance at her passenger. Adam smiled and stretched his body into a more comfortable position. The generous truck cab began to shrink. She was acutely aware of his every move, every breath. Nervousness loosened her tongue. "I'm really hopeful this place will pan out. It's a turn-of-the-century Italianate Victorian just outside town. I need to see if it's worth restoring. Supposedly most of the historic aspects are intact, but I'm not sure about the bones of the place. I want to make a quick check before I hire engineers to inspect it."

"Sounds interesting."

A short time later they pulled into the drive of an old brick mansion. Laura stopped near the carriage house in the back. All concerns about Adam vanished when she saw the old home. Her imagination caught fire with possibilities. It was one of the original homes in Dover and the thought of bringing it back to its former glory excited her.

Laura dug out the key the Realtor had given her and unlocked the weathered side door. They entered through a small vestibule into the sunroom. Three walls of windows rose upward twelve feet, ending in an arched roof made of glass. Laura smiled, her mind filing with vignettes of using the room on a rainy day to read a book, or curling up on a sweet Sunday afternoon with someone she loved. "Isn't it a wonderful old place?" She trailed her hand over the small panes of glass in the windows.

Adam nodded, his attention focused on the woodwork inside the next room. "This is amazing. I've never seen anything like this craftsmanship."

Laura wandered past him deeper into the house. It had fourteen-foot ceilings, one-of-a-kind fireplace surrounds and several stained-glass windows. "Now you can see why I love to work on these old places."

Adam stooped down to examine the tile surround on a fireplace. "What is this stuff?"

Laura came and leaned over him. "Porcelain relief tiles. It was a sign of wealth at the time to have them designed specifically for each room." Adam turned his head and smiled up at her. Her heart skipped a beat and she inhaled abruptly, drawing his woodsy scent deep into her lungs. Her cheeks flushed and her mind replayed their kiss.

Straightening, she turned away, but Adam was right beside her. The air in the old home became oppressive and muggy. Thanks to the hurricane, it was an unusually humid October day in Mississippi. Of course the house would feel stuffy and uncomfortable. It had nothing to do with Adam being so close beside her. So why was her heart pounding and her mind replaying their kiss like some crazy video loop?

She started toward the back of the house to inspect

the kitchen, acutely aware of Adam's every move, every breath. She glanced at him to see if he suspected her discomfort. His green eyes met hers and she knew without a doubt that he was remembering the kiss, as well. She stopped in the middle of the kitchen, intending to comment on its sorry state, when Adam touched her arm. She jumped.

"So what do you think?"

She gulped down the lump in her throat. Was he asking her about that kiss? She'd hoped he'd let it go and forget the entire incident. She looked into his eyes. He stood so close she could see the rise and fall of his broad chest, the day-old stubble on his strong chin. He made her feel so small and feminine. "About what?" she finally managed to ask.

He smiled again. "The house. Can it be saved?"

"Oh. I don't know yet." She turned and hurried through the kitchen and into another room, eager to put distance between them.

Her attraction was getting out of hand. Her pulse raced and her heart pounded in her chest every time she thought about him, but she didn't want him to see how she felt. It would be too humiliating. Her only hope was that when he was gone, she'd get over it and move on with her life. But move on to what?

They wandered through the rooms, but she was unable to make any real assessments. All she could think of was Adam. If he hadn't kissed her, it would have been easier to deal with him. But he had and she couldn't erase it from her mind. Worse still, she found she didn't want to.

She turned to move to the next room and came face-to-face with Adam again. He didn't move. His green eyes caressed her. Her lungs refused to work. Her heart pounded. The air became charged with electricity just like before. He wanted to kiss her again and, Lord forgive her, she wanted that, too.

But the idea terrified her. She found her voice and stepped away from him. "I want to go upstairs. I need to see what condition it's in."

The stale air made Adam even more aware of Laura's scent. The fresh, citrus fragrance that always surrounded her. He exhaled slowly, bracing himself against the feelings her nearness caused. Maybe a little space between him and Laura would be a good thing. "I'll wait down here. You go ahead."

Laura studied him a moment, her violet eyes inquisitive. Did she see his growing attraction on his face? Could she feel the way his heart pounded whenever she was near?

She shrugged. "Suit yourself. I'll be right back."

Adam ran a hand along the back of his neck as he heard Laura tromping up the stairs. He had to do something about these feelings he was having. It wasn't right. Laura was his boss. Her father was his jailer. Falling in love with his daughter amounted to betraying Tom's trust.

He should never have kissed her. He should have tried harder to resist, but she'd looked so small and helpless, her clothes and hair damp from the rain. He'd been overcome with an intense need to comfort her, wrap her in his arms and ward off the cold. But once there, he'd been powerless to deny the question that had plagued him from the moment he'd met her: What would it be like to kiss her?

For a fleeting second, he'd thought she'd returned the kiss, that she'd welcomed it, but the truth had hit him when she pushed him away. She'd never care about someone like him. He didn't belong in her world.

The rejection had been a cold slap in the face, but one he needed. He moved through the old house, staring at the large stained-glass window in the entryway, only partially aware of what he was looking at. He thought about Laura day and night. He couldn't sleep anymore. Was this love? If so, he'd never felt anything like it in his life. None of his relationships had ever produced this need to protect or the driving desire to know everything about her.

Love. What did he know about love? Laura was love personified. A woman like that needed someone who could love her the way she deserved to be loved. He was a cripple in that regard. He closed his eyes. What did he have to offer her?

A loud crash thundered through the stale air.

Upstairs. Laura.

Adam turned and ran for the stairs, taking them three at a time. "Laura!" He heard a low moan and hurried down the hall, searching two rooms before he found her in the back bedroom.

"In here!"

She sounded breathless. He stepped into the room and froze. For the first time in years, Adam Holbrook sincerely prayed. She was half sitting, half lying on the floor. Her right leg disappeared into the floorboards. Her violet eyes were wide with fear. Adam pushed aside his intense fear, unwilling to let her see his own terror. "Laura?" He started across the wood floor.

"Stop." She shook her head. "The floor up here is rotten in spots. You could fall through, too."

He stopped, visually inspecting the floorboards. There was a definite discoloration near Laura, but the wood in the rest of the room was a uniform color and appeared solid. "It's okay. I think the only bad spot is where you are." Slowly he started forward, testing the floor strength with each step. He stooped down beside her, holding her gaze and trying to stay calm. "Where are you hurt?"

Tears glistened in her eyes. "My arm. My leg." She tried to pull it out of the floor but yelped in pain.

"Don't move." Slowly he shifted his position, sitting on the floor and scooting as close as he could without getting too close to the rotten flooring. His stomach clenched when he saw the blood on her arm and the angle at which her leg disappeared into the floor. He forced a smile. "How did you end up in this situation, Boo?" He brushed plaster dust from her hair and glanced upward. A chunk of the ceiling had fallen, the biggest piece missing her by only a few inches.

"I wasn't paying attention. I wanted to see how damaged the window frames were and I didn't notice the rotten floor. When I fell through it must have jarred the ceiling plaster loose and some of it hit my arm."

"Can you move your leg? Can I pull you out of there?"

Slipping his arms under hers, he lifted gently.

"Ow." Tears spilled over from her eyes. "It hurts."

"It's okay. Lie still. I don't want to move you." He reached for the phone in his back pocket only to remember he had no such privilege. "Where's your phone? We need to get someone here to help you."

"My holster."

Adam carefully slipped his fingers along her waist until he located the small pouch that held her phone. He moved gingerly, trying not to cause any movement to the arm that lay limp and bleeding at her side or the leg trapped in the broken floorboards. She whimpered as he pulled it out and he kicked himself for being such a clumsy oaf.

He made the call, then turned his attention back to Laura. She lay half on her side, half on her back. Her hard hat had been knocked off and rolled across the floor. He had to do something to make her more comfortable, but he didn't dare move her for fear of causing more injuries.

"The ambulance should be here in a few minutes."

"I'm not hurt that bad, really." She lifted her injured arm to get a better look. "Oh, great. It's going to be hard to swing a hammer for a while." She lowered her arm, wincing in pain.

"That's why you have me. Try not to move."

"I'm fine. I just feel stupid."

Adam sat on the floor behind her, scooting as close as possible so she could rest her upper body against his chest. "Don't talk. Rest. You don't want to take any chances."

She nodded and closed her eyes. "Sorry."

"For what?"

"I should have taken you back before we drove out here. I just realized that we are probably out of your range. You'll be in trouble."

How typical of her to think of others before herself. "Won't be the first time."

She nodded, then relaxed. "My leg is throbbing."

"Hang on. Help is on the way." Adam reached out and gently brushed a dust-coated tendril of hair from her forehead. Laura opened her eyes and he let himself be drawn into the lovely depths. For a fleeting second he thought he saw behind the pain and the worry, and his heart skipped a beat.

Was it possible that she cared for him a little? Hope filled his soul. He smiled and cradled her face in the palm of his hand. "I shouldn't have let you come up here alone."

"I knew better. I can be a bit bullheaded at times."

"Ya think?"

She laughed, gasping. "My arm."

"Shh. Take it easy." He stroked her head, reveling in the feel of her close against his chest, wishing he could cradle her in his arms, but moving her risked doing more damage. "You know, I thought you looked good with sawdust all over you, but you're even pretty when you're covered with plaster dust." Why had he said that? The smile on his face froze.

Laura held his gaze. "You have terrible taste in women."

"No. For the first time in my life I think I finally got it right." Adam drew his thumb and forefinger down the slope of her face, gently caressing her chin. "You're the most amazing woman I've ever known."

Laura blushed, averting her gaze. "Amazingly stupid. This was an rookie mistake."

"I know about those."

She smiled up at him in understanding and his heart fell into her lap. Whatever the outcome of this little adventure, he knew Laura Durrant would hold a part of him in her small hand forever.

Laura closed her eyes and leaned back against his chest. "Talk to me."

He welcomed the suggestion. Talking was better than dwelling on any of the thoughts rushing through his head at the moment. "Any particular subject?"

"You."

"What about me?"

"Tell me your dreams."

He'd sooner have her ask to cut off a limb, but he'd learned that Laura valued truth and this wasn't the time to embellish or brush her off. "Promise you won't tell anyone? I have a reputation, you know." He tried to keep his tone playful. She nodded.

His stomach knotted. His whole life had been about keeping his feelings hidden, even from himself, yet he was prepared to open his heart to her. "I want a family someday."

She stiffened slightly in his arms, then relaxed. He waited, uncertain whether to go on.

"You do?"

"Surprising, huh? I told you I grew up alone. No child should grow up that way. I'd like to live a normal life, raise a family. Like—" he hesitated "—like your family."

"You want children?"

Adam winced at the question. He knew she was doubtful of his qualifications. He couldn't blame her. "Several, but I don't think it'll ever happen. It's only a dream."

"Why do you say that?"

"I'd make a lousy father. My only role model was my own father. All I know is what doesn't work when it comes to raising kids, not what does."

Laura was silent a long while and Adam knew she was trying to make sense of his pipe dream. It didn't take a genius to see he wasn't cut out for family life.

"Are you sure that would be a big enough adventure for you? Normal life can get boring and monotonous."

Adam wrapped his arms a little tighter around her. Not with her. Life with her would be pure joy. "With the right person, it would be the biggest adventure ever."

Sirens wailed from outside. "The cavalry has arrived." He held her a bit closer as relief washed through him.

"Dover Police."

He'd been expecting the paramedics, but he'd take what he could get. "Up here!"

Officer Barnes entered the room, hand on holster. He eased up when he saw the situation. "What happened?"

Laura frowned. "Isn't it obvious?"

"You're out of your boundary, Holbrook."

He returned the officer's hard stare with one of his own. "I had a good reason."

"The law doesn't recognize reasons."

"I couldn't leave her."

Footsteps sounded on the stairs. The paramedics had arrived.

Laura held up her good arm. "Tell them to be careful. This floor isn't safe. It probably can't hold all of you. If it collapsed under me, it's probably rotten all the way through."

Officer Barnes motioned to the medical team to stay put at the top of the stairs. "Holbrook, you come down with me. We'll go back to the jail. These men can take care of Laura."

"No, I want to make sure she's all right."

Laura touched his arm. "Go. I'm in good hands. I don't want you to get into trouble. Please. Call my dad. He'll help you."

Adam touched her face one more time. He stood and walked to the top of the stairs. One last glance and he followed the officer down as the medics made their way to Laura.

In the squad car, Adam chewed the inside of his mouth anxiously. "Where will they take her?"

"Depends on how badly she's hurt."

"Can you call them and find out?"

"Not now. Let them do their job. I told them to give me a report as soon as possible. I promise, I'll let you know."

"Thanks."

A new concern reared its head as they drove past the town square. "What about the finishing the gazebo?"

Officer Barnes glanced at him. "Since when do you care about that?"

"It has to be done on time. It's important to her, to the town."

Barnes snickered. "Finally figured that out, huh?"

Two hours later, Adam walked from the jail with Tom Durrant at his side. Tom had assured him Laura would be all right, but still his gut clenched with the thought of her suffering. He wouldn't rest until he knew for certain.

"You're sure it's not serious?"

"Adam, she's my baby girl. Believe me, I'm more concerned than you are. Well, almost anyway."

He slid into the passenger seat of Tom's car. "How is she?"

"Nothing serious, but she'll be out of commission

for a while. Minor cuts to her arm, but it's sprained. Same for the leg."

"Thank God." Adam resting his head against the back of the seat. Relief surged through him.

"She was lucky. Bill, the paramedic, said that section of the floor was so bad she could have gone through to the floor below. That would have been a fourteen-foot fall. Good thing she's small and doesn't weigh much."

Adam echoed her father's sentiments. When he thought about what could have happened to her, his blood chilled. He'd been grateful that his own weight hadn't made matters worse.

"Praise God you were there with her, Adam. If she'd been alone…"

"I know." He remembered how small and fragile she'd felt in his arms. He'd wanted to keep her there forever. He'd gladly give up all he had to make that happen.

It hit him like a thunderbolt with a force that left him breathless and shaking. He loved Laura Durrant. He loved her wholly, completely, irrevocably. How had it happened? His heart was so filled with joy. He looked down at his hands in wonder. What a feeling! He'd never experienced anything like it in his life. He turned his face toward the passenger window, unwilling to let Tom see the emotions in his face.

He'd walked the edge of life and death, teetered on the rim of disaster and thumbed his nose in glee as he walked away unscathed. None of that could begin to compare to loving Laura. His heart raced in his chest, making it hard to breathe. Is this what it was like for everyone? Old Mr. Norwood? Did Laura's brother Matt feel like this for Shelby? It was agony. It knotted his gut, left him confused and hurting, but at the same time filled him with an unspeakable happiness. He willed himself to calm down, to retreat into the nice gray existence where he'd spent most of his life. He closed his eyes. *Lord, I don't know what to do with this feeling.*

Mr. Norwood had told him to put one hand in God's and the other in the hand of the woman he loved. That wasn't an option for him. Laura was sunlight and warmth. He was cold and empty. No, that wasn't true any longer. His love for her had chased the cold away and filled the emptiness with love for her.

The outlook for him, however, was bleak. He would do anything for her. Sacrifice all he had, but the one thing she needed most was the one thing he didn't have. He had no idea how to love her.

Laura eased down onto her sofa and turned sideways so she could prop her sprained leg on a pillow. She ached everywhere. Her head throbbed. Wally jumped up on the sofa, jarring her sore leg. She resettled him in her lap, stroking his fur and feeling some of her tension ease.

She wanted to talk to Adam, to thank him for his help. She'd replayed the accident a million times in her head over the past few hours. He'd been so tender, so sweet and thoughtful as they'd waited for the EMTs. Without him there she would have panicked. She might have been stranded there for hours before anyone knew she was missing. She reached up and touched her cheek, remembering his confession about his dreams. His answer, however, quickened her heart. He wanted a family. Had he meant it or had he been saying the things she wanted to hear to make her feel better?

There were depths to him that she'd suspected but

had denied. His kind, tender consideration at the house had further endeared him to her. But she was still afraid to take the last step. She'd seen her brother Matt struggle to love again. He'd finally admitted his fear and allowed himself to love Shelby again. She wasn't as brave or as strong as Matt.

Besides, their relationship was based on a thirty-day sentence. A forced association, not by choice. They each had a goal and those weren't compatible. No matter how she felt, Adam would be leaving soon.

A knock on the door brought a groan from her throat. She'd just gotten comfortable. She scooted around and stood, shooing Wally out of the way. She didn't need to fall over the dog right now.

The silhouette on the other side of the leaded glass door made her think her dad had returned. She opened the door and froze. "Adam, what are you doing here? How did you get here?"

He held her gaze. "I talked your dad into stopping by so I could see for myself you were all right. He's waiting for me. I can't stay long." He came toward her, taking her hands in his and inspecting her closely from the wrap on her arm to the small bandage covering the gash on her neck.

She looked into his eyes and forgot to breathe. The profound concern she saw reflected there stunned her. He cared about her. Truly cared.

"Are you sure you're all right?" His voice was thick with anxiety.

Laura nodded. "Sprained wrist, a couple of stitches in the arm." She glanced down at her leg. "I strained the muscles in my knee and hip. Nothing life-threatening, but uncomfortable."

"Good." His finger stroked the back of her hand, sending tingles along her spine.

"Thank you for staying with me."

"I'm glad I was there."

"Me, too."

She wanted to tell him how much she cared for him, but the words wouldn't come. She searched for something to end the awkward silence. Adam saved the moment.

"I never realized before how dangerous your job could be. Promise me you'll be careful when you go into these old places. You could be seriously hurt."

A shiver coursed through her at the warm concern in his deep voice. It took all her effort to extract her hand from his. "I will."

"No work for a while, huh?"

She shook her head. "But I've got stacks of paperwork and at least a half-dozen plans to go over. As far as the gazebo is concerned, I've asked Shaw to work with you on the gazebo if you want to, weather permitting."

Adam smiled. "Good. I want to keep working. Any word on when this rain will let up?"

She shook her head, painfully aware of what they both had to lose if the rain continued. "I'm sorry."

"Not your fault. You don't control the weather."

"I know, but I was trying to get it all done so you could—"

Adam held up his hand. "I know and I appreciate it, but some things aren't meant to be."

"Don't give up." She reached out and touched his arm. "We can still get the repairs done in time for you to get home for your meeting."

Adam laid his hand on hers. "I'm not giving up. I'm

trying to be realistic. In a few days I may lose everything."

"No." It surprised her much she wanted to make the deadline for his sake. "I'll find a way to get the gazebo done. If the shingles arrive on time we can do a lot of work under the tarps whether it's raining or not."

Adam shook his head. "Your dad told me things happen for a reason and that they always work for good."

"I believe they do, but…"

"Then maybe that's what's happening now." A car horn sounded from outside. "I've got to go." He kissed her forehead, smiling into her eyes.

Laura sucked in a shaky breath. "Okay." He walked out the door, leaving her with a new ache to add to the others.

Chapter Ten

Rain overflowed the gutters, creating a curtain of water along the front of the Durrants' large porch and casting a fine mist several feet inside the railing. Adam ignored the growing dampness on his clothes. "Please, Lord, you calmed the sea, calm this storm so I can complete this job for her sake. For the town's sake."

He rubbed the bridge of his nose, trying to sort through the emotional chaos of this day. His stomach knotted whenever he thought about what could have happened to Laura in that old house if he hadn't been there. He'd thanked the Lord a dozen times for keeping her from serious harm.

The accident had torn open his heart, revealing his love. The emotions at work inside him now were like nothing he'd ever known. They churned with a force that no jump from a cliff, no two-hundred-mile-per-hour rush down a speedway could match. Those had been hollow sensations. Mere kiddie rides in a park. None of those thrills could compare with the love he felt for Laura. But as much as he loved Laura, as much as he'd come to love Dover, he wasn't dumb enough to think he had a future here.

"Adam, everything okay out here?"

He turned at the sound of Tom's voice.

"Something eating at you?"

"No. Yes." Adam ran a hand down the back of his neck.

"Which is it?"

He'd come to value the man's advice and his friendship, and he needed it now more than ever. He took a deep breath, gauging his words. "Have you ever wanted something so badly, but knew you had no hope of ever getting it?"

Tom nodded thoughtfully. "What is it you want?"

Adam crossed his arms over his chest, struggling with the decision to tell him about his feelings or to keep them to himself. The choice was simple. He needed to understand the intensity of what he was feeling. "Laura."

He looked over at Tom, the knowing smile on his face telling Adam his revelation had come as no surprise to her father. "How did you know?"

"I know the look in my little girl's eyes. And there's a certain—" he tilted his head slightly "—energy when you're in the same room together."

Great. Could Laura see his feelings as easily? He'd hoped to keep it from her. "I'm in love with her, but I didn't expect it to feel like this."

"Maybe that's because you've never been truly in love before."

Adam shook his head and sat down on the porch swing. "I've jumped out of helicopters. I've swum with sharks and risked my life more times than I can remember. None of that compares to how I feel about her."

"Love is a powerful emotion." Tom took a seat in one of the wicker chairs.

Powerful? More like overwhelming. The pain of it pressed on his chest like being forty fathoms beneath the sea.

"Does she know how you feel?"

"I don't think so." Adam shrugged. "Maybe. She knows I have feelings for her, but I don't think she knows how much."

"You going to tell her?"

"No."

Tom raised his eyebrows. "What if she feels the same?"

"No, that's impossible."

"With God all things are possible."

"It would never work. We're too different."

"How do you know? Have you talked with her about it?"

"No."

"Why not?"

Wasn't it obvious to Tom of all people? "Because I'm a man under house arrest. And she's my boss."

"I think you've moved beyond that, don't you?"

"I have no future. Nothing to offer."

"Not true. Your future may be uncertain at the moment, but you have a great deal to offer, Adam." Tom rested his forearms on his knees, leaning closer. "I know you think in keeping silent you're sparing her heart, but you're only hurting her more."

"What do I do?"

"Tell her the truth. Admit your feelings and your

concerns and let her decide what she wants to do with that information. Then work it out together. The biggest mistake people make is thinking we know what's best for someone else. It takes two to build and maintain a relationship. Talking. Compromising. Listening to what the other wants and needs. It's worked for me and her mother for over forty years now."

Adam stood and paced. "It's all so messed up. One minute I want to hold her like she's a fragile piece of glass. The next I want to lay down my life to keep her safe. If this is love, I don't want it." He realized who he was talking to and stood and walked to the edge of the porch, putting some distance between them. "Sorry. You're her father. I shouldn't be telling you this stuff."

"I'm the perfect one to tell. I've loved her more and longer than you. And I want her to be happy."

"That's what I want, too, but I'm not sure I'm the one to do that. How do I know it's love and not just some weird fascination that'll fade away?"

Tom rose and came to his side, laying a hand on his shoulder. "When your first and constant desire is for her happiness and not your own, that's love. Then you give it all over to the Lord. The love. The fears. The expectations and doubts. He'll work it all out."

Adam remained on the porch a long while, thinking about Tom's advice. The rain had died down and his hope had started to rise. Tom had put so many things into perspective. He owed the man so much. He'd never be able to repay his kindness, his friendship or his guidance. He felt at peace. His soul was right with God. His body was strong from physical labor and his heart was overflowing with love.

Tom had counseled him to trust the Lord to work

things out between him and Laura. All that he really wanted was for Laura to achieve her goal—the gazebo done for the festival. Nothing else mattered.

Reporting to work the next morning didn't feel right. McKinney had picked him up and driven to the gazebo in half the time Laura took. Without Laura working at his side, he truly felt as if he were serving a sentence. He'd welcomed the chance to take on more responsibility to help her, but now that he was actually faced with the reality, he didn't like the feeling. The gazebo was Laura's pride and joy. To work on it without her seemed disrespectful.

Adam shot the last nail into the last bench seat and straightened. The clouds were casting a dreary pall on the day. It suited his mood. Still, when he looked at the work he'd accomplished so far, he knew a sense of satisfaction. If someone would have told him a few weeks ago that he'd enjoy rebuilding an old gazebo, he'd have called them crazy.

"Not bad. You may have a future in this."

"Thanks." Adam stood, taking the statement from McKinney at face value. They'd barely spoken to each other all day except to exchange information or instruction. "I may need you as a reference soon."

"What?" Shaw frowned.

"Never mind." Adam hadn't made up his mind about the man yet. He couldn't get a solid read on him. He worked quietly, totally focused on his task. He hadn't displayed any desire to talk or joke or even complain. Adam had decided it was a personal grudge against him. One part irritation that he had to help the guy who damaged the gazebo, and one part desire to stand in the gap as protector for Laura.

He had a lot to think about, mainly what he would do when his deadline passed tomorrow and he wasn't in Atlanta. There were other things on his mind, too. "Have you heard from Laura this afternoon?" Today was the first time since arriving in Dover that he missed his cell phone. He wished he could call and check on her, hear her voice.

"Yeah," Shaw replied.

"How's she doing?"

Shaw studied him a moment before answering. "Fine." Shaw dropped his hammer into the loop on his tool belt and set his hands on his hips, pinning him with steely navy blue eyes. "I've worked for a lot of contractors in the South. LC is the best."

"I'm not surprised. She can be scary." Adam chuckled, attempting to lighten what he knew was a looming confrontation.

"She's tough, but she's fair and she's got a heart for people. That's what makes the difference."

"I agree."

"Look, Holbrook, I'm going to put it right out there so there's no misunderstanding. LC is a special lady. She deserves someone just as special."

Adam set his jaw. "You volunteering?" Something dark and ominous passed across the foreman's eyes. He straightened and took a step toward him.

"I work for her. She's a friend. I don't want to see her make a mistake she'll regret for the rest of her life."

"I agree." *Someone better than you.* Shaw McKinney hadn't said the words, but Adam had heard them nonetheless. Someone who could love her the way she deserved to be loved. He had no clue how to do that. He loved her with everything he had, but it could never be enough. She needed someone who understood love, how to give it and how to receive it. He couldn't risk letting her down. She'd already been hurt too much.

He turned his attention back to his work, trying to ignore the knife in his heart. McKinney was right. It was time to be realistic. His sentence was almost up. His future likely gone. He wasn't cut out for family life. All he wanted right now was to give her the thing she wanted most. He'd finish her little gazebo, then be on his way.

"Please, Lord, make the rain stop." Laura allowed the curtain at her kitchen window to drop back into place and reached for her cup of coffee. Another day of on-and-off showers. Thankfully, the forecast for tomorrow and through the weekend was good, so the Founder's Day activities would go on as planned under sunny skies and pleasant temperatures. But it might happen without the historic gazebo.

The old cedar shingles should have been delivered to the job site around noon, but that left only this afternoon and tomorrow morning to get the roof finished. And the cupola still had to be installed. As much as she hated failing in her job to restore the gazebo, she hated failing Adam more. His deadline had come and gone. His world had changed forever. She'd wanted so much for him to make it home. It was important to him and he was important to her. Very important.

Swallowing the lump in her throat, she struggled with her newly discovered feelings. She loved Adam Holbrook. She'd spent the whole night trying to pinpoint the moment she'd lost the fight and fallen in love with him. She'd barely slept. Her head knew full well he was the wrong man to love. He was a rootless adventurer, she was a stay-at-home family kind of girl. But her heart saw a man alone, who yearned for roots and a family. A man who'd reconnected with his faith, who had met a challenge with determination. A man who had learned the inner satisfaction and peace of service to others. A man worthy of love.

Her heart wanted him to stay here. She wanted him to be part of her life in Dover, but she wasn't a fool. She'd tried fitting into Ted's life and was met with disaster. She couldn't ask Adam to try to fit into a world he knew nothing about.

Laura exhaled in frustration and went in search of her keys. She couldn't stay in this house another minute. She had to know how things were going at the gazebo. She had to know how Adam was doing and see for herself he was all right. A few minutes later she pulled her truck to the curb in front of the gazebo and turned off the engine. Her gaze searched out Adam. He was bent over the workbench. His posture spoke of his intense concentration and her heart swelled with pride. And love.

He didn't look up as she came near. She noticed the bundles of shingles, a few of which were already placed on the scaffold. Finally, the end of the project was in sight. Adam turned and stared at her, his gaze cool and indifferent.

"What are you doing here? You're not supposed to be driving yet."

"I'm fine. I wanted to make sure the shingles arrived."

"There're here. Go home."

Laura stared at his stiff jaw, the tense angle of his shoulders. "What about you? I wanted to know how you were."

"I'm working."

"I meant the meeting. Your deadline, I wanted to tell you…"

"It's done. Go home."

Something was wrong. He must be devastated and trying to hide it from her. She reached out and touched his arm. He jerked it away, sending a dark glare in her direction.

"Go home, Laura. I have work to do."

She swallowed her hurt feelings, trying to find her boss facade to duck behind for protection. "You've done more than necessary, Adam." A light rain started to fall and she hurried into the gazebo to keep dry. "It's raining."

Adam started toward the scaffold with the nail gun. "So? Is there a reason why the shingles can't be put on during the rain? Will they melt or something?"

"No, but it's dangerous. The roof will be slippery."

Adam climbed up onto the scaffold. "It has to be done. You can't. That leaves me."

Laura shook her head. "At least wait until the rain stops." He stared down at her, his green eyes dark and angry.

"Don't you think I can do this?"

"Yes, of course, but…"

"Then go home and leave me be."

Tears sprung in her eyes. Her heart burned. She started out of the gazebo, noticing the rain had stopped as suddenly as it had started. Shaw took her arm as she came down the steps, steering her toward the fence. He unhooked it.

"We've got this, boss. Go on. Get out of here."

"I just want to help. This is my responsibility after all."

"We'll be done by noon tomorrow. You have my word."

"He shouldn't be up on that slippery roof. You know how dangerous that is."

Shaw leaned in, his dark blue eyes capturing her full attention. "You heard the man. Go home. Let him do what he has to do."

The fist in Adam's gut had grown larger every minute since Laura had left. He'd watched her drive away, knowing he'd hurt her, and knowing it was for her own good. She'd understand one day. He needed to finish this job on his own. Having the gazebo done in time for the festival was Laura's dream. And he was determined to make it happen.

He was officially cut off. He'd tried to call his father several times this week and had left messages but gotten no response. That bothered him more than the loss of his trust fund. He'd come to understand that he shared equal guilt in the strained relationship with his father. He wanted to go home and try and correct that if possible. Losing Laura, however, was another matter entirely. He placed the nail gun against the old cedar and pulled the trigger. He'd prayed all night, asking for some reason why the Lord had revealed a love for Laura only to deny him the fulfillment of that love.

He placed another shingle and nailed it in place. The gazebo was important to her, to the town. In the past week, signs for the festival had started popping up everywhere. Huge banners on the light posts, signs in windows, flyers. All of which was driving him to complete his task on time.

He'd found himself triple checking his measurements, taking extra care with his work. Somewhere he'd begun to compare the old craftsmanship in the gazebo with the work he was doing alongside of it. Because of Laura's love and dedication, the wood in the repaired section was nearly a perfect match for the old. The old meshing with the new.

It could be a statement about his own life. The old Adam, consumed with self, running after something that would give him a reason to exist. The man he was today was so very different. His first thoughts now were for Laura and what would make her happy. According to Tom, that was love. But theirs was a love with no future. Wasn't it?

Laura curled up in the corner of her sofa, cradling the phone to her ear, while wiping tears from her eyes. "Mom, he lost everything today. I tried so hard to finish early. It's all my fault."

"Nonsense. You did everything you could. I'm sure Adam understands that."

"I don't know. He's changed. Something happened. We were getting close, then today he acted as if he didn't want me anywhere near him."

"He was probably upset, Laura. This must have been a difficult day for him."

"I guess. Or maybe he's just now showing his true colors. He was probably paying attention to me hoping to get out of his sentence early. Then when I couldn't come through for him, he realized there was no reason to play nice."

"Laura, do you really believe that?"

"No." She sagged deeper into her sofa, hugging Wally to her side for comfort. "But he was so distant, so angry today. It scared me. I don't understand."

"He's been like that here, too. Ever since your accident at the house. I assumed he was worried about you, but he's been withdrawing more each day. I asked your dad about it, but he wouldn't tell me anything."

Laura wiped fresh tears from her cheeks. "He'll be leaving in a few days. His sentence is over on Friday."

"And you were hoping he'd stay?"

She nodded. "Stupid, huh? He told me from the beginning that he could never live in a place like Dover."

"Oh, I don't know. I think he's come to like our little town."

"Not enough. He's turned all his energy toward finishing the gazebo. He's working like a madman. Even Shaw made me leave him alone. It scares me."

"He knows how much the gazebo means to you, sweetheart. He's probably wanting to get it done in time. That's all."

Was that it? Was his fierce determination because of the festival or because it was important to her?

"Do you love him?"

Laura froze. She'd only acknowledged her feelings last night. How had her mother guessed? No use in pretending. Her mother could read her like a book. "Yes. Crazy, isn't it? I made a big mistake with a rich guy once before. You'd think I'd learned my lesson."

"Adam isn't Ted, Laura. Anyone can see that. Yes, you made a mistake before, but I don't think loving

Adam would be one. I don't know Adam well, but he strikes me as a man who would find strong emotions very difficult to process. Particularly those of loss and love. Maybe he's afraid he'll fail you."

"I don't care if the gazebo is done or not. The festival will go on regardless."

"I'm not talking about the gazebo. Maybe he's afraid he can't be the man you need him to be."

Was that possible? None of it made sense. There were so many things to sort through and so little time left to do that. Adam would be gone from her life in a matter of days. "What do I do, Mom?"

"Tell him how you feel. You might not get another chance."

Laura thought about her mother's advice as she tried to sleep that night. Should she tell Adam she loved him? What if he rejected her? But on the other hand, what if she was missing her chance at happiness because she was hanging too tightly on to her fear of the past? She'd seen enough with her own eyes to know that Adam was a changed man. She also knew he was scared. Scared of his feelings and his emotions.

Lord, I need some wisdom and clarity. I don't know what to do.

Adam cut the wire binding on the shingles and started the last row. Three hours later, he stood back and scanned the completed roof critically. Officially, his work was done. All that remained was to replace the cupola. The crane would be here in a few hours to lift the large decorative cap into place.

Down below, he could hear Shaw working diligently on all the detailed finish work. He'd made it. The gazebo would be ready in time for the Founder's Day celebration on Saturday. The painters would come first thing in the morning along with the landscapers. By the end of the day tomorrow, everything would be back the way it should be. Laura's goal had been achieved. Dover would carry on with its tradition intact.

He'd kept his promise to Laura and himself that he would complete his job. He'd wanted to prove to her that he could be counted on, that he could accomplish something important besides having a good time.

He turned his back, sensing a weight lift from his shoulders. He'd lost a lot this last month. His inheritance. Laura. But he'd also lost his self-centered attitude. His pride. His sense of entitlement. In its place he'd found his faith and the God he'd forgotten. He'd found compassion and the satisfaction of doing for others. It was time to go home and try once more to set things straight with his dad.

Adam picked up the nail gun and the few remaining cypress shingles on the scaffold. He reached for the rail and froze. A deep sense of dread filled his heart. Once he stepped off the scaffold, his time in Dover would be over. Officially, not until tomorrow morning, but in every way that mattered, it was over now.

He'd never see Laura again.

Adam signed his name and took a deep breath. It was done. He was a free man again. He slipped his wallet into his pocket, the familiar weight bringing a smile to his face. He scooped up the rest of his personal belongings and turned to face Tom Durrant. He'd been kind enough to bring him to the police station this morning to be processed.

Tom had a warm smile on his face. "Well, how does it feel? You can come and go as you please now."

"Great." He lifted his foot slightly. "And the lack of jewelry doesn't hurt either." He started to move, then remembered something important was missing from his stash. "My car keys."

Tom slipped his hand into his pocket and came up with the keys, dangling them in the air. "You looking for these?"

"How did you get them?"

"You'll see." He handed over the keys and placed a hand on Adam's shoulder, steering him to the door. "Be patient."

Adam's curiosity was spinning as they walked out of the police station. But the moment they approached the parking lot, the answer was waiting for him. Parked right in the first slot was his classic Porsche 356, sparkling clean and fully repaired. "My car." He hurried forward, inspecting the vehicle closely. "How did you manage this? I figured I'd have to rent something to get home. I asked about it several times, but no one would tell me anything."

"Well, don't thank me. I had a very small part in this."

Adam turned to face him, the sparkle in the man's eye speaking volumes. "Laura?" His tried to grasp the significance of her action. If she'd gone to all that trouble, then she must have some feelings for him. Something more than friendship and gratitude.

"She wanted you to know how grateful she was for all your help."

He looked around. "Where is she? I thought—"

"She's waiting at her house. She didn't want to see you here, like this."

Adam looked at the keys and then the car. He didn't understand.

Tom inclined his head. "Don't worry. She's anxious to see you. I promise. Adam, I don't know what the future may or may not hold for you and my daughter, but I want you to know that if you two decide to join your lives, I'd be proud to have you as a member of our family. You make my daughter happy and that's the most important thing to a father."

Tom's words of approval meant more than he could ever express. He shook his hand. "Thank you, sir. I'm deeply honored."

"Oh, I nearly forgot." Tom pulled an envelope from his jacket. "I picked this up on the way over here. I thought you might need it for today."

Adam took the envelope, unable to find words to express his appreciation. "Thank you for your help. I couldn't have pulled this off without you."

Tom waved off the gratitude. "Go. Talk to my girl."

The Dover town square was bustling with activity when Adam drove down Main Street a few minutes later. The scaffold had already been dismantled and painters were busy on the newly restored section of the gazebo. A delivery truck from a local garden center was being unloaded. Small tents and displays were going up all over the green for the arts and crafts vendors. Peace and Mill streets were already blocked off. In a few hours all evidence of his accident would be gone.

The light turned red and he stopped at the intersection. The same one where he'd lost control of his car and crashed into the gazebo. He eased off the gas, heading toward Laura's house, the nervous knot in his stomach growing. How would it feel standing in front of her as a free man? Not her saw boy. Not the prisoner in her father's home. But himself, the man who loved her?

But how did she feel? Could she love a man like him? Tom advised him to tell Laura how he felt, to let her decide. Shaw McKinney had reminded him that Laura deserved someone who could love her completely. So who did he listen to?

Chapter Eleven

Laura peeked out the dining room window, then moved to the front door to look at the street in front of her house. Wally barked and sat down in the middle of the hall. He'd been trailing at her heels all morning. Apparently he was tired of trying to keep up. Laura smiled and bent down to pet his head. "Sorry, fella. I just don't know what's taking him so long. He should have been here by now."

Adam was being released this morning. He was no longer a man confined by a sentence and an ankle monitor, and no longer someone she was responsible for. He was just Adam. Things would be different between them now and she couldn't wait to see him.

Her mother had convinced her that his attitude the other day had been from his need to finish the job and prove himself to her. She was hanging on to that hope. She would tell him how she felt and let God work it all out.

A flash of light flickered through the beveled glass door. "He's here." She hurried outside, waiting at the edge of the porch. She wanted to run to him and throw her arms around his neck, but their relationship hadn't progressed that far yet. She watched as he got out of the small car and came up the walk. He looked wonderful, but different. It was more than the dark jeans and the crisp blue cotton shirt he wore. More than the bronze jacket that made his green eyes fiery bright. There was a different tilt to his shoulders and a slow easy gait to his stride. Had freedom restored his confidence or was it something else?

He stopped at the foot of the porch steps. She searched his face for some clue to his emotions, finding herself captured by the warmth and affection in his green eyes. "Good morning."

He glanced toward his car. "You had it fixed."

"Were you surprised?" Her heart raced wildly in her chest.

"Shocked. How did you pull it off?"

"My dad helped. We sent it up to Jackson. There's a guy there who specializes in classic-car restoration."

He came up the steps, stopping in front of her. "Why did you do it?"

He was so close that she could feel his breath when he exhaled. She swayed against the attraction that washed over her. She opened her mouth to speak but her voice failed. She cleared her throat and tried again. "I knew how much it meant to you and I wanted to thank you for all your hard work. I'm only sorry that we couldn't get it done in time for you—"

Adam reached out and took her hand. "Don't. None of that matters." He touched the side of her face gently. "Laura, no one has ever done anything like that for me before."

"You deserved it. You worked hard and got the gazebo done on time. We're all so grateful to you." His eyes darkened to a forest green.

"Is that the only reason you did it? Out of gratitude?"

"No, I knew it would make you happy. And I want you to be happy."

Adam grasped her arms with his hands, drawing her ever closer. "Why?"

She held her breath, her eyes locked with his. She loved him. All she had to do was tell him. "Because… I care for you. A great deal."

Adam smiled. "How much do you care?" He lowered his head and kissed her lips lightly.

She melted into him, drowning in his tenderness.

"And I care about you, too, Laura."

She stepped back, needing to regain her senses. She tugged him toward the house. "Let's go inside. I want to talk."

He stopped abruptly, a teasing grin on his lips. "You going to present me with the repair bill?"

"No, silly." She pulled him along into the kitchen before releasing his hand. "I have coffee and muffins. Have a seat."

"Hey there, Wally." Adam tussled with the dog a moment before taking a seat at the table. She set the plate of muffins on the table along with a hot cup of coffee.

"Did you make these yourself?"

"Of course. My mother taught me and she's a very good cook." Adam smiled, making her heart skip again.

"I know. That's one of the things I'll miss about living there."

She started to ask him what else he would miss, but her courage failed her again. She started to move to the counter again, but Adam took her hand.

"I have something for you. I was going to wait and give it to you tomorrow, but I think this is the perfect time." He pulled a large envelope from his jacket and handed it to her.

Puzzled, she opened the flap and pulled out a legal document. "Oh." She read the paper twice, unable to believe what she was seeing. She looked at Adam for some explanation. "This is the deed to the Keller building."

He smiled. "Look at the bottom line."

Her eyes struggled to focus on the page. "It's in my name." She gasped, one hand covering her mouth in surprise. "How did you do this?"

"I made arrangements to buy it at the auction. I know how much it meant to you and I hated to see you lose it. Your dad helped me work out some of the details. He's a very influential man around here."

"My father?" She lowered the paper. "He's been a busy little fixer, hasn't he? Helping me with your car. Helping you with this." Tears clogged her throat and stung the back of her eyes. "Oh, Adam. I don't know what to say, how to thank you." She moved toward him, arms open. He stood and accepted her hug. She lifted her face to kiss him on the cheek, but he shifted, pulling her against him and capturing her mouth. She melted against him.

He ended the kiss, putting a little distance between them. "Lady, you're dangerous. I think we'd better get back to the muffins. You go sit over there and I'll sit here and we'll keep this nice table between us."

She smiled and nodded, exhaling a shaky breath. "Probably a wise move."

"So, tell me what you wanted to talk about."

"I want you to come to the festival tomorrow." She

chewed her lip, gathering her courage. "You deserve to participate and I want you to see how much having the gazebo done means to everyone."

"Is that the only reason?"

She shook her head, reaching out to gently touch his fingers. "I want to get to know you better. As a…friend, not an assignment."

"I want that, too, Laura."

"So you'll stay? You could even stay for Matt and Shelby's wedding if you'd like. It's next week."

"I'd like to, but I can't." He reached across the table and took her fingers in his. "I'll stay for the festival, but I can't stay any longer. I have to go back to Atlanta and talk to my father."

Her heart clenched. Maybe she'd read him wrong after all. "To see about your trust fund?"

"No. To try and reconcile with him. I've come to realize that I'm as much responsible for our bad relationship as he is. I've always blamed him for certain problems in my life, but I'm equally guilty. I have to try and work things out. Do you understand?"

She did, but she didn't like it. Glancing at the clock, her heart sank. She'd intended to talk to him about so many things and now she was out of time. "I need to leave in a few minutes. I'm driving up to Jackson today to meet with a potential client. Would you like to come along? We could have lunch. Talk."

"It's tempting, but I have some things to do before I leave. I'll pick you up tomorrow morning for the festival." He smiled. "That'll be a nice change. I'm looking forward to seeing you in my little car instead of your big truck."

Laura walked him to the door. He turned and pulled

her into his arms. "Laura... I... Thank you again for caring."

Laura rested her head against his chest, her arms around his waist. *Say it. Tell him now.* "You're welcome." She pulled back and looked up at him. "If you come early, we can have breakfast before we go."

"I'll call you when I get up." He bent and placed a kiss on her forehead.

"See you in the morning." She watched him go, wishing it was tomorrow and wondering why she hadn't told him she loved him.

Laura stepped through the front door of her father's store, turning around to look at Adam. She wanted to see the expression on his face when he saw the town square for the first time. He strode out the door and froze. His eyes widened and his mouth fell open in stunned surprise. He moved to the curb, resting one hand on the iron poles supporting the balcony above the store. She went to his side, glancing back and forth between the scene on the square and the delight on his handsome face. "So? What do you think?"

Adam shook his head and looked at her, his green eyes bright. "This is wild. I had no idea. I expected a few booths and a food vendor or two. But this—" he reached over and pulled her to him "—this is totally unexpected."

Laura caught her breath. She was beginning to like that word. "Unexpected is good, right?"

"Very good."

She took his hand. "Come on. I want you to see everything." The sidewalk beside Durrant's was clogged with clothing racks and tables filled with jewelry and accessories from Jacqueline's Boutique next door, so they walked into the street. It was the only means of moving around the festival.

She'd hoped to have breakfast with Adam this morning, but he'd called last night and said he'd be tied up with some business matters in the morning. Waiting for him to pick her up had been nerve-racking, like waiting for Christmas morning to open her presents. Even the ride in his Porsche had been fun. They'd navigated the back streets and parked behind her dad's store. It was a good home base for the day and offered a respite from the noise and activity.

"Where did all these people come from? I didn't know Dover had this many people."

"Oh, our festival is a really big deal around here. We have hundreds of craft and food vendors from all over the country who are regulars. Some come from as far away as Canada and Mexico." Adam pulled out his phone and took a picture of the area.

Laura took a moment to survey her beloved town. The park around the courthouse was littered with white shade canopies all sheltering various crafts and specialty artists. The broad downtown streets, lined with food vendors in wagons, vans and tents, resembled the midway of a county fair. At the far end of the park stood the gazebo. She couldn't wait to take Adam there.

"This is crazy." Adam smiled down at her.

At the end of the block, Laura pointed down the side street. "The carnival rides are set up down there in an old grocery store parking lot. There's the usual stuff—Octopus, Tilt-a-Whirl, Ferris wheel. If you're looking for a thrill, we could head that direction."

Adam squeezed her hand. "You're thrilling enough."

Her heart melted. "That's also the street where the parade will be."

"A parade? Through all this activity?"

'No. The children's parade. It starts at the old church a couple blocks down and ends right before this intersection. Kenny and Chester will be in it, so we don't want to miss that."

Adam frowned. "Chester? Have I missed a nephew somewhere?"

"No, silly. Chester is his dog. The kids and pets dress alike. It's always fun." Laura continued the tour, strolling along Peace Street and crossing onto Main Street. "The stage is on the far corner. You'll hear all kinds of music throughout the day. Gospel. Rock. Country. The local talent winners will be singing this morning, and tonight we have a famous country group coming in."

"Hey, Mr. Holbrook."

Laura looked around as a man about her father's age approached. She felt Adam brace and gently touched his side.

The man extended his hand, a friendly smile on his face. "My name's Elliot, Ben Elliot. I just wanted to thank you for working so hard to get that gazebo up and ready for this weekend. I live in Sawyers Bend and I know the gazebo belongs to Dover, but we have a special attachment to that little building, too."

Adam cleared his throat and took the man's hand. "Thank you. I appreciate that."

Mr. Elliot nodded, smiled at Laura, then moved off.

"That was a first."

"What do you mean?"

"No one has ever appreciated anything I did."

"I appreciate you." She slipped her arm in his and

started walking again. "Okay, your tour is over. Time to get down to some serious exploration. First we'll shop, then we'll eat. Then shop some more and then eat more." She grinned up at him. "Any objections?"

"I just do what I'm told, boss."

Laura took his hand, entwining her fingers with his and wishing she could keep him at her side always.

Adam leaned against the trunk of the old magnolia tree beside the gazebo. The same one he and Jim had met under. Laura had taken her numerous packages to her father's store, giving Adam the first chance to catch his breath. She'd been like a kid in a candy shop all morning, scurrying from one attraction to another. He'd happily followed along, marveling at her energy and her joy. He'd be perfectly content to bask in the glow of her delight for the rest of his life.

His gaze drifted toward the gazebo. His reason for being here. People wandered in and around the structure. Some had taken the steps into the center, sitting and talking for a while. Others had stopped and taken pictures. Small groups of kids had raced in and around and down the steps again in a game of tag. One couple had slipped inside for a kiss. Hardly a moment had passed when the beloved landmark went unused.

Laura had wanted to make it their first stop this morning, but somehow they'd been redirected to talk to friends or family, then lunch with the Durrants. He'd been convinced to try chicken on a stick and fried Twinkies. His stomach would never be the same.

He glanced back toward Durrant's Hardware. He'd learned a lot about Laura today. She liked handmade jewelry and paintings of gardens. Her taste in scarves leaned toward vibrant colors. She bought any kind of handmade soap, and she had a weakness for funnel cakes. He smiled thinking of her excitement. Laura found something beautiful in everything her eyes touched. From wind chimes to rusty old tools. He couldn't even count the number of times they'd stopped to greet friends and acquaintances, a couple of whom Adam had helped through the Handy Works ministry.

They'd watched the children's parade, cheering for Kenny and his dog, who were dressed like Insect Man. He had no idea who or what that was, but it was the cutest thing he'd ever seen.

This afternoon Laura had promised to take Kenny to the Kids' Zone. From what he could gather, there would be face painting, balloon animals and an inflatable jump house. Cassidy had convinced her aunt to go with her to the Dover princess pageant, claiming she needed to observe for when she was sixteen and could participate.

A month ago Adam would have called all this the worst kind of corny, but now he wanted to soak it all in. The music, the sights, the delectable smells all gave him a sense of belonging. Of home.

"Adam."

He turned, coming face-to-face with Shaw McKinney. He braced. Had he come to warn him away from Laura again? "Shaw."

McKinney smiled and extended his hand. "Good to see you here."

Adam nodded, sensing there was more to come.

"I wanted to let you know I've changed my mind about some things." He slipped his hands into the back pockets of his jeans and inhaled a slow, measured breath. "You did a good job on the gazebo. Better than

I expected. And you worked hard to get it done. That means a lot. Mostly, I wanted to tell you that I was wrong about you and LC. Forget what I said. You're a good man."

Stunned, Adam took a moment to find his voice. "Thanks, but I don't think I understand."

Shaw smiled and punched him lightly on the shoulder. "I saw for myself how much you love her, man. That's all that matters."

"Shaw, sweetie, I got your drink."

A fiery redhead in skinny jeans and a flouncy top sidled up to Shaw and smiled. "Thanks. Tell LC I said hello. You planning on staying in Dover, Adam?"

"I don't know yet."

"Well, if you do, you'd be a welcome addition."

Speechless, Adam watched the couple walk away.

"Was that Shaw?" Laura appeared at his side.

Adam nodded. "He said to say hello. I think that's the first time I've seen him smile. He was always so sour when we worked together."

"Are you kidding? Shaw is as easygoing as they come. And the most eligible bachelor in Dover. I doubt if there's a woman alive who could get him to settle down."

A slow smiled moved his lips. "That's what they used to say about me, too."

Laura blushed and took his hand, glancing at the gazebo. "So what do you think?"

Arm in arm they strolled slowly toward the cherished landmark, an odd mixture of pride and affection swirling in Adam's chest. The gazebo had been completely transformed. All signs of construction had vanished. The once-trampled and muddy ground around the site was now covered with thick, lush sod. Small shrubs and colorful flowers encircled the foundation like a living wreath. A necklace of bunting in green and gold draped around the lattice inserts at the roofline and wrapped around the thick turned posts.

They stopped at the base of the steps. Laura squeezed his arm.

"What do you think?"

"It looks like it's never been touched." He gazed down at her. "You do amazing work."

"You helped. I couldn't have done it without you."

Laura started up the steps, the ones he'd help build. Inside the gazebo, Adam made a slow tour of the structure. He ran a hand along the handrail and over one of the posts, remembering the work he'd put into it. A swell of pride expanded his chest. The accomplishment was a turning point in his life. He understood now the importance of the landmark and what it meant to Dover.

Laura slipped her arm around his waist. "You're a part of us now, Adam. Every time you think of Dover, you'll remember the work you put into this gazebo. You'll carry us with you wherever you go and we'll always have a part of you here with us."

With a fresh coat of paint covering the entire gazebo, he could almost believe nothing had happened. But a great deal had happened. This little building had changed his life. He turned to face Laura, looking deep into her eyes, watching them turn deep purple. Was she remembering the kiss that day in the rain? He started to pull her closer only to remember there were no tarps to shield them today.

He took her hand and started toward the steps. He wished he could capture this moment. Pulling his phone from his pocket, he turned on the camera, flagging down a passerby to take their picture in the gazebo. He pulled Laura to his side, gazing down at her, knowing in his very depths that he belonged at her side. If only he had the courage to tell her how he felt.

Laura gazed out over the courthouse square now bathed in the warmth of streetlights and strings of twinkle lights. The gazebo lights had blinked on, casting a romantic curtain of light down along its sides. From the balcony of her father's store she had a panoramic view of the downtown. Music from the stage across the square floated on the air, underscored by the tinny sound of the carnival rides a few blocks over. The white canopies over the vendors glowed in the waning daylight. She inhaled a deep breath, smiling at the tantalizing aromas of the carnival foods available below.

She smiled when Adam join her, laying his hand over hers on the rail. "This is one of my favorite days of the year. I love the festival."

"I think it's become one of mine, too."

They watched in companionable silence a moment. "We have one more thing to do." She turned and looked at him. "The balloon glow."

"Don't think I've ever been to one."

"What? A world traveler like you?"

"I'm beginning to see my world was missing some key stops. When and where do we view this spectacular sight?"

She pointed toward the southwest side of town. "There's an open field where the balloons are set up. Once it's dark they'll fire up the burners and inflate the balloons. I heard there are going be nearly two dozen this year. It's my favorite part."

Adam slipped an arm around her waist. "I think every part of the festival is your favorite."

Laura giggled. "Guess so."

They caught the tractor-pulled shuttle at the edge of the square and took the bumpy ride to the field. Adam took her hand as they followed the crowds gathering for the event. "I know a good spot to watch from. It's a longer walk, but it'll be worth it." She took a path away from the crowds and up a slight slope. When they reached a rustic wooden fence, she bent down and slipped between the rails. Adam raised an eyebrow. "It's all right. This is part of Uncle Hank's land."

She stopped beneath a live oak, pointing toward the field. "You can see all the balloons from up here."

Adam took her hand in his, pulling her against his side. "I can see all I want to right here."

Now was her chance, the opportunity she'd waited for all day. She'd tell him how she felt, ask him to stay. "Adam, I want to talk to you about something."

"All right. As long as it's nothing bad. I don't want anything to spoil this day. I want to concentrate on you and make each moment count." He held her gaze a moment then glanced off toward the field. "I think your glow is starting."

She turned, finding herself in the circle of his arms, her back resting against his chest.

In the field below, the balloons started to billow and move as the propane burners coughed hot air inside them. The flames from the burners flashed in spurts of gold like fireflies.

First one, then another slowly inflated, their large en-

velopes coming to life. Some were a solid color, some
multicolored stripes, others carried company logos. A
few were in whimsical shapes. A house. An animal.
Even an oddly shaped balloon tree. The field suddenly
exploded in glowing color.

Within minutes the balloons were upright, tethered
to the ground, but their expanded envelopes rising like
glowing mushrooms side by side across the field. "Isn't
it beautiful?"

Adam wrapped his arm tighter around her. "It is, but
not as beautiful as you."

"Tomorrow morning they'll all take to the air and
float over Dover. I love waking up to the sound of the
burners. They drift on the wind so silent and beautiful. I think riding in one might be a small adventure I'd
like to try someday."

"I'll see what I can do."

Laura closed her eyes, imprinting this day in her
memory. A perfect day. A perfect man. Now was the
time to say the words. "Adam..."

A jarring blast of sound broke into the quiet. Adam
pulled his phone from his pocket and turned away. She
heard him mutter under his breath, then groan. "What
is it?" The look on his face scared her. "Adam, what's
wrong?"

"It's my father. He's suffered a heart attack. He's
in critical condition. I have to go, Laura. I need to be
there."

Her disappointment was quickly replace with concern. "Of course you do. We'll head back right now."
She pulled her own phone from her pocket and touched
her travel app. "I'll see if I can get you a flight out of
Jackson to Atlanta tonight. It's the closest airport, but

there aren't many flights. If we can't get a flight out of there, we'll try New Orleans, but it's a two-hour drive from here." Adam took her arm, guiding her through the fence and back down the hill. The shuttle returned them to the square. Back in her father's house, Adam stopped and placed his hands on her arms.

"I wanted to talk to you. I had so much to say, but now…"

She shook her head. "It's all right. We'll talk when you come back. You will come back, won't you?" He hesitated before replying, sending her heart into a deep chill.

"I'll try." He kissed her forehead, then hurried upstairs to pack. Twenty minutes later he was gone, leaving her alone and with a mountain of doubt weighing down her heart.

Chapter Twelve

The antiseptic smell permeated everywhere, even the elevator. Adam doubted he'd ever get used to it. The doors slid open and he stepped out onto the fifth floor of Hillside Hospital, heading toward his father's room. The sight of Orson Gould standing outside filled him with a surge of alarm. He quickened his steps. "Orson, what's happened?"

The slender man, his father's longtime legal counsel and close friend, held up his hand. "He's fine. In fact, it's good news for a change."

Adam released a heartfelt sigh, resting his hands on his hips. In the weeks since he'd come home, his father had suffered another heart attack and major surgery. It would be nice to get some encouraging news for a change.

"I spoke with his physician a few minutes ago, and they believe he'll be able to go home in a few days. I'm going to start making arrangements for his care. Will you be staying on?"

"No. If he's improved that much, there's no reason for me to stay in Atlanta."

Orson stared at him a moment. "Adam, I want you to know, I tried my best to get him to change his mind about the will and the trust fund, but he's stubborn. Once he makes up his mind…"

"I know." He patted the man's shoulder. Orson was his only contact to his father, the only one he could call for help. "I appreciate it."

"Perhaps now that he's had this brush with death, he'll be more amenable to change, at least to restoring your trust fund."

Adam shook his head. "I don't care about the money, Orson. I've found something better."

"Better?"

"I've found peace. And hopefully a home."

Orson nodded. "Ah. You're referring to that matter I helped you with recently in Duncan, Mississippi?"

"Dover. Yes."

"Well, I sincerely hope it works out. I'll talk to you later."

Adam stood outside the room for a moment, praying for another dose of patience and understanding. So far his visits to his father had all started and ended the same way. A less-than-welcome greeting and an order to stay away. He pushed the door open.

His father was sitting in the chair today, a vast improvement. "Hello, Dad. It's good to see you out of that bed. How are you feeling?"

He cursed and glared. "You back again? I don't need you here."

Adam swallowed the knot of hurt and moved to the chair beside his father. "They tell me you're going home soon."

"What's it to you?"

"I'm concerned."

"Concerned about your money. I told you, you're not getting it back."

"I'm not here for the money, Dad. I'm here for you. For us."

"What's that supposed to mean?"

They'd been down this same road before. Adam rubbed the bridge of his nose in frustration. Maybe it was time to lay things on the line. "I came to ask your forgiveness, Dad. I know I haven't been the son you wanted and I'm sorry. I'm hoping you'll forgive me."

Arthur Holbrook jerked his head around. "If this is some of that religious junk you're trying on me, I won't have it."

"No, Dad. I just don't want us to be angry at each other anymore. I'm accepting my part in our strained relationship and I've forgiven you for yours."

"Forgive me. For what?"

"Not being there. Not being a father when I needed it."

"I gave you everything you needed. You threw it all away on fool stunts. Without my money you'll be nothing."

Adam stood. There was no point in continuing. He'd done what he'd come to do. "You're wrong. I've found everything. My faith, a home and someone I want to spend my life with."

"She only wants your money. Once she knows you're penniless she'll leave."

"She already knows and it doesn't make any difference." He walked to the door, all hope of reconciling gone. "I'm going back to her as soon as I can make arrangements. Goodbye, Dad. Take care of yourself."

He had one foot in the corridor when he heard his father call his name.

"You ever coming home again?"

He turned to face his father, surprised to find the stern features had softened a bit and a faint pleading in his dark eyes. A grain of hope, smaller than a mustard seed, sprouted in Adam's heart. "I'd like you to meet her. Her name is Laura and I think you'd like her."

Arthur Holbrook turned his head. "Suit yourself."

It wasn't much, but it was something. Adam strode down the corridor. He'd done all he could. Now it was time to return to Dover and talk to Laura. He just prayed he hadn't stayed away too long.

On Thanksgiving Day, Laura slipped away from the kitchen and sought out the quiet of the formal living room in her parents' home, tucking herself into the corner of the sofa. Normally this was one of her most cherished family holidays. Having her family gathered around, talking, laughing, sharing a turkey dinner filled her heart to overflowing. But this year something, no, *someone,* was missing, and it was hard to enjoy the day not knowing where he was or what he was doing. More important, why hadn't he contacted her since leaving Dover?

Laura fingered her cell phone a moment, then pulled up her contact list. She paused with her finger on the call key. All she had to do was touch it and wait for him to answer. She could say she wanted to know how his father was. It was the truth, but not as much as she wanted to know about him.

The only message she'd received was the photo he'd sent of them taken in the gazebo at the festival. He'd captioned it with the words *Perfect Day*. She'd examined the photo dozens of times, looking for some reassurance in his smile, his eyes. One time she'd thought she saw love in his green eyes. But the next time she didn't see anything but a man having a nice day with a friend.

Closing her eyes, she let her hand fall to her lap, her conflicted emotions immobilizing her once again. She'd tried to call him several times in the last three weeks, but her courage had always failed at the last moment. What was the point, after all? Eventually she'd had to face the truth. Once he'd returned to his life in Atlanta, he'd realized the differences between them were too great.

"Why won't you call him?"

Laura opened her eyes. Her new sister-in-law, Shelby Russell, no, Durrant, was frowning at her. "What good would it do?"

"Maybe none. Maybe a lot. But you won't know until you try."

She shook her head. "It's all my fault. I was asking him to be something he wasn't. I misread everything." She drew her knees up under her so Shelby could join her on the sofa. "What's that old saying? You can take the man out of the city, but you can't take the city out of the man?"

"I don't think that's the way I've heard it, but I get your point." She rested a hand on Laura's. "You miss him, don't you?"

Laura blinked as tears stung her eyes. "Only every time I see that stupid gazebo. I dialed his number once, at your and Matt's reception."

"But you didn't wait for him to answer, did you?"

"No, I chickened out. I thought he cared, but it's been weeks now without a call. All he's sent is one stupid picture."

"What picture?"

Laura pulled it up on her phone and handed it to Shelby.

"Uh, Laura, honey, that is a picture of a man crazy in love."

She took the phone back. "A man in love calls. How lame is that? I believed him when he said, 'I'll call you.' There's only one way to interpret that, Shelby. He's moved on."

Shelby exhaled a grunt of frustration. "Laura, the man bought you a building. I'd say that was a pretty good clue that he loves you."

Laura nodded in agreement. "That was very sweet."

"You really don't know what he's dealing with right now. He's probably tied up at the hospital with his father. You said he was in critical condition."

She drew her legs all the way to her chest and laid her head on her knees. "I know. And I feel awful for focusing on me and not him. I've prayed that his father will be all right and they can find a way to reconcile, but it would help if I knew what was going on."

"I know. But I'd be willing to guess that he's been so tied up with his father he just hasn't had time to call."

"Or it could be that I'm a really lousy judge of men."

"If you mean to say Adam wasn't worth your affection, then yes, you are."

"You didn't know him like I did."

"Maybe not, but your parents and your brother thought well of him and I trust their judgment."

Laura glanced over her shoulder. "Right. Like Dad

showed good judgment when he put the store up for sale?"

"None of you guys wanted it, and he and your mom are ready to retire and enjoy themselves."

"I know. It's just too much to process at once. Matt and you getting married, Dad selling the store, Adam leaving town."

"Call him, Laura. It's Thanksgiving. You have the perfect excuse."

Laura gave her sister-in-law a hug. "Thanks. I'll think about it."

She stared at her phone again, her courage waning. This is what happened when she lacked faith. Her fear of being hurt again had prevented her from telling Adam she loved him. Now he was gone and she wouldn't have the chance to.

She rose and started back toward the kitchen, banishing thoughts of Adam to the far recesses of her mind. Today was all about family. She should focus on that.

Sounds of a football game on the television carried throughout the house. Laughter from the kitchen bounced off the walls, interspersed with the shouts and giggles of her niece and nephew. The noise and commotion that normally comforted her now left her feeling alone and sad.

Pulling a large clip from her backpack, she secured her hair on top of her head, then grabbed her jacket from the hall closet. She had time for a walk before dinner was ready. Fresh air and open space might be what she needed to get herself under control.

Adam stood on the sidewalk outside the Durrant home, gearing up the courage to knock on the door. It was Thanksgiving Day. He hadn't realized it until he'd boarded the plane this morning. Not only was he intruding into Laura's life again, but he was doing it on a major family holiday. He slipped his hands into his jacket pockets and stared at the house again, leaning against the tree trunk at the curb.

He could see them moving around in the dining room at the front of the house. He shouldn't be staring in their windows like a Peeping Tom, but he was compelled to watch them. What he really was longing for was a glimpse of Laura. He wanted to talk to her alone, not with the entire Durrant clan hovering around.

Coward. Truth was, he was nervous about seeing her again. He hadn't called her once since he'd left Dover. Not the way a man trying to win the woman he loved should behave. He'd lost big points there. He knew he'd be welcome in the Durrants' home, but it wasn't their welcome he sought. He'd screwed up and he'd prayed all the way from Atlanta that it wasn't too late, that Laura hadn't forgotten him and moved on.

He should have taken her father's advice. If he would have told Laura how he felt the day he'd given her the deed to the Keller building, they could have worked through the separation together. Instead, he'd chickened out, afraid of not measuring up to the man she idolized—her father. Now he was afraid he might have lost his chance with her forever.

He prayed he'd made the right choice. He'd made a major life decision on faith, trusting that the Lord would actually work this one out. Something he'd never done before.

A noise drew his attention to the front door of the Durrants' two-story colonial. Someone stepped out and hurried down the porch steps and onto the sidewalk along the street. His heart flipped over in his chest a couple of times. Laura. She was a vision in black jeans, heeled boots and a lavender sweater that matched her eyes. He straightened and stepped toward her.

"Adam!"

The sweet, lilting tone of her voice washed over him. She looked soft and beautiful, exactly the way he'd remembered her. Even with her silken hair pulled up into that ridiculous bun on the top of her head. The look in her eyes sent his heart pounding. Was she happy to see him?

"Hi." He wanted to memorize every inch of her. He might not get another chance. The smile on her face gave him hope.

"You came back?" She moved to him, resting her hands on his chest. He took her shoulders in his hands.

"I had to. I missed you."

"I missed you, too."

Suddenly he felt like an awkward, insecure kid. Where did he start? How did he tell her what was in his heart? He saw his own uncertainty reflected in her violet eyes.

"How's your father?"

"Better. It was touch and go for a while, but the doctors think he'll make a full recovery." Nerves and anxiety churned in his stomach. He needed to move before he jumped out of his skin. "Let's walk. We have a lot to talk about." She fell into step beside him as they strolled down the block, slipping her hand through the crook of his arm.

"Did you work things out between you?"

"Let's just say it's a work in progress and that I have hope. I'd like to take you to meet him."

"I'd like that."

"I'm sorry I didn't call. I was tied up at the hospital with my dad around the clock in the beginning. When things finally settled down, so much time had passed I wasn't sure how you'd feel. I sent the picture so you wouldn't forget me."

"I could never forget you. That was a perfect day for me, too."

Adam stopped and pulled Laura around to face him. "A very wise man gave me some advice and I didn't take it. I regret that more than I can say. So I'm taking it now." He inhaled and gazed into her eyes. "Laura, I love you. I want to spend the rest of my life with you."

The smile on her face sent his heart soaring.

"You love me? Oh, Adam, I love you, too. I wanted to tell you that night at the balloon glow, but I was so afraid you didn't feel the same way. You told me you could never survive in a place like Dover."

"I know, but that was before a beautiful lady carpenter stole my heart. I think I fell in love with the you the first time I saw you." He reached up and pulled the clips from her hair.

"And I've loved you from the moment I saw you standing in my brother's old room, wearing that tattered tuxedo and that bandage on your chin."

Adam laughed and pulled her into his arms. "So will you marry me, Laura?"

"Yes!"

She threw her arms around his neck and kissed him, dispelling any and all doubts. Breathless, he pulled back, cradling her face in his hands. "I thought about bringing a ring with me, but I want you to pick out the exact one you want. I'd like that to be the first thing we do together as a couple." He searched her eyes for confirmation.

Laura's eyes filled with tears, her fingers pressed against her lips. Had he already messed up?

"Oh, Adam, how did you know? Did you talk to my dad?"

He shook his head. "No, I never mentioned it."

"You're just like my dad. The first thing he and Mom did when they decided to get married was choose the ring together. I've always thought that was so romantic. The perfect way to start a life together."

She hugged him again. "I told you if I ever found someone as wonderful as my father, I'd marry him." She smiled into his eyes, her small hand on his cheek.

They'd reached the end of the block and started back. "Do you think your parents will be happy?"

"Totally. Mom has been singing your praises since the beginning. You're not going back to Atlanta now, are you? You're staying in Dover?"

"I'm staying." That earned him another hug.

"What will you do? You'll have to find a job. I can put you on as one of my crew or you could run Handy Works."

"Actually, I have something else in mind. In fact, it's already in the works. I was only waiting to see if I still welcome in your life before completing the details."

"What?"

"I happen to know a man who is very interested in buying your dad's store. Keeping it in the family, so to speak." He watched as she processed what he'd said.

"Who? You? Oh, that's the perfect solution!"

Side by side they started up toward her parents' front porch.

"So when do you want to make this official?"

Laura squeezed his arm. "How about Valentine's Day?"

He nodded. Not too far off but plenty of time for her to plan the kind of wedding she would want. "You should be able to have your passport by then."

"Why do I need one?"

"You can't spend a honeymoon in England without one."

"Adam Holbrook, I love you." They stopped at the foot of the porch steps.

Adam started to kiss her again when the front door opened and Angie Durrant appeared.

"Laura? Adam! Oh, how wonderful. Tom! Adam is here."

Tom joined his wife at the door. "Hey, Adam. I thought you might turn up today. What are you two doing out there? Dinner is almost ready. It's Thanksgiving, remember?"

Laura slipped her arm around Adam. "Dad. Mom. There's something we need to tell you."

Her mother waved her off. "We know. Come on inside."

Tom waited for Adam, laying a fatherly arm across his shoulders. "Come on, son. We can't start Thanksgiving unless the whole family is here."

* * * * *

Dear Reader,

I hope you enjoyed Adam and Laura's story and your second trip to Dover, Mississippi. I'm always amazed and delighted when the Lord gives us detours. At the time, they make us upset and irritated because our plans have been disturbed. We've all had them, myself included. But on the other side of the detour, life can hold some surprises and blessings we never imagined. It's during these times we must hold on and trust the Lord to work it all out for good. Adam had a lot to lose when he landed in jail, but what he found during his journey made it all worthwhile.

This story was inspired by a song about a man who had experienced every wild adventure on the planet, but he'd never experienced anything like the emotions he felt when he fell in love. I wanted to take Adam from a man who was looking for adventure in outside things to a man who found love and adventure in caring for others and for someone special. As a result, Adam had blessings heaped upon him that he never could have envisioned. A good lesson for all of us to remember. With the Lord's help, we can all change and become more than we think we are.

I love to hear from readers. You can visit me at LorraineBeatty.blogspot.com.

Lorraine Beatty

WE HOPE YOU
ENJOYED THIS

LOVE
INSPIRED®
BOOK.

If you were **inspired** by this

uplifting, **heartwarming** romance,

be sure to look for all six Love

Inspired® books every month.

Love Inspired®

LIHALO2017R

SPECIAL EXCERPT FROM

Love Inspired®

*Widowed single mom Rebecca Mast returns to her
Amish community hoping to open a quilt shop. She
accepts carpenter Daniel King's offer of assistance—but
she isn't prepared for the bond he forms with her son.
Will getting closer expose her secret—or reveal the love
she has in her heart for her long-ago friend?*

*Read on for a sneak preview of
THE WEDDING QUILT BRIDE
by* **Marta Perry**,
available May 2018 from Love Inspired!

"Do you want to make decisions about the rest of the house today, or just focus on the shop for now?"

"Just the shop today," Rebecca said quickly. "It's more important than getting moved in right away."

"If I know your *mamm* and *daad*, they'd be happy to have you stay with them in the *grossdaadi* house for always, ain't so?"

"That's what they say, but we shouldn't impose on them."

"Impose? Since when is it imposing to have you home again? Your folks have been so happy since they knew you were coming. You're not imposing," Daniel said.

Rebecca stiffened, seeming to put some distance between them. "It's better that I stand on my own feet. I'm not a girl any longer." She looked as if she might want to add that it wasn't his business.

No, it wasn't. And she certain sure wasn't the girl he remembered. Grief alone didn't seem enough to account for the changes in her. Had there been some other problem, something he didn't know about in her time away or in her marriage?

He'd best mind his tongue and keep his thoughts on business, he told himself. He was the last person to know anything about marriage, and that was the way he wanted it. Or if not wanted, he corrected honestly, at least the way it had to be.

"I guess we should get busy measuring for all these things, so I'll know what I'm buying when I go to the mill." Pulling out his steel measure, he focused on the boy. "Mind helping me by holding one end of this, Lige?"

The boy hesitated for a moment, studying him as if looking at the question from all angles. Then he nodded, taking a few steps toward Daniel, who couldn't help feeling a little spurt of triumph.

Daniel held out an end of the tape. "If you'll hold this end right here on the corner, I'll measure the whole wall. Then we can see how many racks we'll be able to put up."

Daniel measured, checking a second time before writing the figures down in his notebook. His gaze slid toward Lige again. It wondered him how the boy came to be so quiet and solemn. He certain sure wasn't like his *mammi* had been when she was young. Could be he was still having trouble adjusting to his *daadi*'s dying, he supposed.

Rebecca was home, but he sensed she had brought some troubles with her. As for him…well, he didn't have answers. He just had a lot of questions.

Don't miss
THE WEDDING QUILT BRIDE by Marta Perry,
available May 2018 wherever
Love Inspired® books and ebooks are sold.

www.LoveInspired.com

Looking for inspiration in tales
of hope, faith and heartfelt romance?

Check out **Love Inspired**® and
Love Inspired® **Suspense** books!

New books available every month!

CONNECT WITH US AT:

Harlequin.com/Community

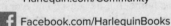 Facebook.com/HarlequinBooks

Twitter.com/HarlequinBooks

Instagram.com/HarlequinBooks

Pinterest.com/HarlequinBooks

ReaderService.com

LIGENRE2018